D0743030

MAGIC SHIFTS

MAGIC
SHIFTS

Ilona Andrews

ACE BOOKS, NEW YORK

An imprint of Penguin Random House LLC
375 Hudson Street, New York, New York 10014

This book is an original publication of Penguin Random House LLC.

Library of Congress Cataloging-in-Publication Data

Andrews, Ilona.
Magic shifts / Ilona Andrews. — First edition.
pages ; cm
ISBN 978-0-425-27067-7 (hardcover)
1. Daniels, Kate (Fictitious character)—Fiction.   2. Shapeshifting—Fiction.
3. Magic—Fiction.   4. Atlanta (Ga.)—Fiction.   I. Title.
PS3601.N5526625M35 2015
813'.6—dc23
2015016065

FIRST EDITION: August 2015

PRINTED IN THE UNITED STATES OF AMERICA

10 9 8 7 6 5 4 3 2 1

Cover illustration by Juliana Kolesova.
Cover design by Jason Gill.
Interior text design by Tiffany Estreicher.

Penguin
Random
House

ACKNOWLEDGMENTS

Telling this story wouldn't have been possible without the editorial input and guidance of Anne Sowards. Thank you so much for your advice and friendship. We would also like to thank Nancy Yost, our agent, for her endless oceans of patience and willingness to deal with a seemingly never-ending stream of phone calls, e-mails, and crises.

As always, we are grateful to all of the people who have worked on making this manuscript into a book. The managing editor, Michelle Kasper, and the assistant production editor, Julia Quinlan. Judith Lagerman, the art director; Juliana Kolesova, the artist responsible for the image on the cover; and Jason Gill, the cover designer.

We would also like to thank our beta readers, who selflessly endure the tortures of proofreading a half-baked manuscript. They are, in no particular order: Ying Dallimore, Laura Hobbs, María Isabel Amoretti de Pagano, Nur-El-Hudaa Jaffar, Kelly Brooke, Beatrix Kaser, Olivia Toune, Nicole Joury, Christian, and especially Shannon Daigle. Thank you to Vibha Patel, Lisa Rigdon, JeNoelle Flom, Liz Semkiu, Olga Zmijewska-Kaczor, and Bambi Parfan for help with medical issues. All errors are ours and ours alone.

Finally, thank you to all of you for sticking with us thus far. We hope you enjoy the book.

≡ CHAPTER ≡

1

I RODE THROUGH the night-drenched streets of Atlanta on a mammoth donkey. The donkey's name was Cuddles. She was ten feet tall, including the ears, and her black-and-white hide suggested she might have held up a Holstein cow in some dark alley and was now wearing her clothes. My own blood-spattered outfit suggested I'd had an interesting night. Most mounts would've been nervous about letting a woman covered with that much blood on their back, but Cuddles didn't seem to mind. Either it didn't bother her or she was a pragmatist who knew where her carrots were coming from.

The city lay in front of me, deserted, quiet, and steeped in magic, unfurling its streets to the starlight like a moonlit flower. Magic ran deep through Atlanta tonight, like a current of some phantom river, slipping into the shadowy places and waking hungry things with needle-long teeth and glowing eyes. Anyone with a drop of common sense hid behind reinforced doors and barred windows after dark. Unfortunately for me, common sense was never among my virtues. As Cuddles quietly clopped her way down the streets, the sounds of her hoofbeats unnaturally loud, the night shadows watched us and I watched them back. *Let's play who can be a better killer. My sword and I love this game.*

None of the monsters took the bait. It might have been because of me, but most likely it was because one of them was moving parallel to my route. They smelled him, and they hid and hoped he would pass them by.

It was almost midnight. I'd had a long day. My back ached, my clothes smelled of fetid blood, and a hot shower sounded heavenly. I had made two apple pies last night, and I was pretty sure that at least one piece would be left for me. I could have it tonight with my tea before I went to bed . . .

An annoying spark of magic ignited in my mind. A vampire. Oh goody.

The spark "buzzed" in my brain like an angry mosquito and moved closer. The Immortus pathogen, the disease responsible for vampirism, killed the minds of its victims, leaving behind an empty shell driven by an all-consuming bloodlust. Left to its own devices, a vampire would hunt and slaughter, and when it ran out of things to kill, it would starve to death. This particular bloodsucker wasn't free to rampage, because its blank mind was held in a telepathic grip by a necromancer. The necromancer, or navigator as they were called, sat in a room far away, directing the vampire with his will as if it were a remote-controlled car. The navigator heard what the vampire heard, saw what the vampire saw, and if the vampire opened its mouth, the navigator's words would come out of it.

Meeting a bloodsucker this far south meant it belonged to the People, an odd hybrid of a corporation and a research facility, whose personnel dedicated themselves to the study of the undead and making money on the side. The People avoided me like the plague. Two months ago they had figured out that the man behind their organization, the nearly immortal wizard with godlike powers and legendary magic, happened to be my father. They had some difficulty with that development. So the vampire wasn't for me.

Still . . . I knew most of the People's patrol routes and this undead was definitely off course. Where the hell was it going?

No. Not my circus, not my undead monkeys.

I felt the vampire make a ninety-degree turn, heading straight for me.

Home, shower, apple pie. Maybe if I said it like a prayer, it would work.

The distance between us shrank. *Home, shower . . .*

An undead leaped off the roof of the nearest two-story house and landed on the road next to me, gaunt, each shallow muscle visible under the thick hide, as if someone had crafted a human anatomy model out of steel wire and poured a paper-thin layer of rubber over it.

Damn it.

The undead unhinged its mouth and Ghastek's dry voice came out. "You're difficult to find, Kate."

Well, well. The new head of the People's Atlanta office had come to see me personally. I'd curtsy but I was too tired to get off my donkey and the sword on my back would get in the way. "I live in the suburbs and come home almost every night. My business phone number is in the book."

The vampire tilted its head, mimicking Ghastek's movements. "You're still riding that monstrosity?"

"Feel free to stomp him," I told Cuddles. "I'll back you up."

Cuddles ignored me and the vampire, defiantly clopping past it. The bloodsucker turned smoothly and fell into step next to me. "Where is your . . . significant other?"

"He's around." He was never too far. "Why, are you worried he'll find out about this romantic rendezvous?"

The vampire froze for a second. "What?"

"You're meeting me in secret on a lonely street in the middle of the night . . ."

Ghastek's voice was so sharp, if it were a knife, I would've been sliced to ribbons. "I find your attempts at humor greatly distressing."

Hee-hee.

"I assure you, this is strictly business."

"Sure it is, sweet cheeks."

The vampire's eyes went wide. In an armored room deep in the bowels of the People's Casino, Ghastek was probably having a heart attack from the outrage.

"What are you doing out in my neck of the woods?"

"Technically, the entire city is your neck of the woods," Ghastek said.

"True."

Two months ago my father had decided to dramatically claim Atlanta as his own domain. I tried to stop him in an equally dramatic fashion. He knew what he was doing, I didn't, and I ended up accidentally claiming the city in his stead. I was still fuzzy on how exactly the claiming worked, but apparently it meant that I had assumed guardianship of the city and the safety of Atlanta was now my responsibility. In theory, the magic of the city was supposed to nourish me and make my job easier, but I had no idea how exactly that worked. So far I didn't feel any different.

"But still, I heard you were promoted. Don't you have flunkies to do your bidding?"

The vampire twisted his face into a hair-raising leer. Ghastek must've grimaced.

"I thought you would be happy," I said. "You wanted to be the head honcho."

"Yes, but now I have to deal with you. *He* spoke to me, personally."

He said "he" with the kind of reverence that could only mean Roland, my father.

"He believes that you may hesitate to kill me because of our shared experiences," Ghastek continued. "Which makes me uniquely qualified to lead the People in your territory."

Showing how freaked out I was about having a territory would severely tarnish my City Guardian cred.

"I'm supposed to cooperate with you. So, in the spirit of cooperation, I'm informing you that our patrols have sighted a large group of ghouls moving toward the city."

Ghouls were bad news. They followed the same general pattern of infection, incubation, and transformation as vampires and shapeshifters, but so far nobody had managed to figure out what actually turned them into ghouls. They were smart, supernaturally fast, and vicious, and they fed on human carrion. Unlike vampires, whom they somewhat resembled, ghouls retained some of their former personality and ability to reason, and they quickly figured out that the best way to get human carrion was to butcher a few people and leave the corpses to rot until they decomposed enough to be consumed. They traveled around in packs of three to five members and attacked isolated small settlements.

"How large is the group?"

"Thirty plus," Ghastek said.

That wasn't a group. That was a damn horde. I had never heard of a ghoul pack that large.

"Which way are they coming?"

"The old Lawrenceville Highway. You have about half an hour before they enter Northlake. Best of luck."

The vampire took off into the night.

A few decades ago, Northlake would have been only a few minutes away. Now a labyrinth of ruins lay between me and that part of the city. Our world suffered from magic waves. They began without warning a few decades ago in a magic-induced apocalypse called the Shift. When magic flooded our world, it took no prisoners. It smothered electricity, dropped planes out of the sky, and toppled tall buildings. It eroded asphalt off the roads and birthed monsters. Then, without warning, the magic would vanish again and all of our gadgets and guns once again worked.

The city had shrunk post-Shift, after the first magic wave caused catastrophic destruction. People sought safety in numbers, and most of the suburbs along the old Lawrenceville Highway stood abandoned. There were some isolated communities in Tucker, but people settling there knew what to expect from the magic-fueled wilderness and it would be difficult for a pack of ghouls to take them down. Why bother, when less than five miles down the road Northlake marked the outer edge of the city? It was a densely populated area, filled with suburban houses and bordered by a few watchtowers along a ten-foot fence topped with razor wire. The guards could handle a few ghouls, but with thirty coming in fast, they would be overrun. The ghouls would scale the fence in seconds, slaughter the tower guards, and turn the place into a bloodbath.

There would be no assistance from the authorities. By the time I found a working phone and convinced the Paranormal Activity Division that a pack of ghouls six times the typical size was moving toward Atlanta, Northlake would be an all-you-can-devour ghoul buffet.

Above me a huge dark shape dashed along the rooftops and leaped, clearing the gap between two buildings. The starlight caught it for a heart-stopping second, illuminating the powerfully muscled torso, four massive legs, and the dark gray mane. The hair on the back of my neck stood up. It was as if the night itself had opened its jaws and spat out a prehistoric creature, something born of human fear and hungry animal growls echoing in the dark. I only saw him for a moment, but the image imprinted itself in my mind as if chiseled in stone. My body instantly recognized that he was predator and I was prey. I'd known him for three years now, and the instinctual response still hit every single time.

The beast landed, turned north, and vanished into the night, heading toward Northlake.

Instead of running away as fast as I could like any sane person would do, I nudged Cuddles, hurrying her until she broke into a gallop. One doesn't let her fiancé fight a horde of ghouls by himself. Some things were just not done.

THE EMPTY EXPANSE of the Lawrenceville Highway spread before me. The road cut through a shallow hill here, and stone walls held back the slope on both sides. I parked myself at the mouth of the hill, just before it melted into a vast, completely flat field. As good a place as any to make a stand.

I stretched my neck slowly, one side, then the other. I'd left Cuddles tethered to a tree half a mile back. Ghouls normally would have no interest in her, but she smelled like me and one of them might try to rip her neck open just out of spite.

The moon rolled out of the clouds, illuminating the fields. The night sky was impossibly high, the stars like diamonds in its icy depth. A cold breeze came, tugging at my clothes and my braid. It was the beginning of March, and the onset of spring was sudden and warm, but at night winter still bared its fangs.

The last time I was this far from the city, I had been the Consort of the Pack, the largest shapeshifter organization in the South. That was behind me now. Thirty ghouls would be rough without backup. Lucky for me, I had the best backup in the city.

When I had claimed Atlanta, the claiming had created a boundary. I felt it fifty feet in front of me, an invisible line of demarcation. I should've gone to inspect the boundary sooner, but I'd been busy trying to separate myself from the Pack and setting up the new house and working my ass off, because eventually our savings would run out . . . But pretending that the claiming hadn't happened had done me no favors.

Something moved in the distance. I focused on it. The movement continued, the horizon rippling slightly. A few breaths and the ripples broke into individual shapes running in an odd loping gait, leaning on their arms like gorillas but never fully shifting into a quadrupedal run.

Wow, that's a lot of ghouls.

Showtime. I reached for the sword on my back and pulled Sarrat out of its sheath. The opaque, almost white blade caught the weak moonlight. Single-edged and razor sharp, the blade was a cross between a straight sword and a traditional saber, with a slight curve that made it excellent for both slashing and thrusting. Sarrat was fast, light, and flexible, and it was about to get a hell of a workout.

The distorted shapes kept coming. Knowing there were thirty ghouls was one thing. Seeing them gallop toward you was completely different. A spark of instinctual fear shot through me, turning the world sharper, and melted into calm awareness.

Thin tendrils of vapor rose from Sarrat's surface in response. I turned the saber, warming up my wrist.

The ghoul horde drew closer. How the hell did I get myself into these things?

I walked toward them, sword in my hand, point down. I had few social skills, but intimidation I did well.

The ghouls saw me. The front ranks slowed, but the back rows were still running at full speed. The mass of ghouls compacted like a wave breaking against a rock and finally screeched to a halt just before the boundary. We stopped, them on one side of the invisible magic divide, me on the other.

They were lean and muscular, with disproportionately powerful arms and long, spadelike hands, each finger tipped by a short curved claw. Bony protrusions, like short knobby horns, thrust through their skin at random spots on their backs and shoulders. The horns were a defensive mechanism. If someone tried to pull a ghoul out of its burrow, the horns would wedge against dirt. A werewolf armed with superhuman strength would have a difficult time plucking a ghoul out of the ground. I'd seen the horns grow as long as four inches, but most of the ones decorating this crowd barely reached half an inch. Their skin was dark gray on the chest, neck, and face, the kind of gray that was most often found on military urban camouflage.

Small splotches of muddy brown dotted their backs and their shoulders. If not for the watery yellow glow of their irises, they would've blended into the road completely.

None of them were lame, starved, or weak. The odds weren't in my favor. I had to think of a strategy and fast.

The ghouls peered at me with oddly slanted eyes, the inner corners dipping much lower than the outer ones.

I waited. The moment you start speaking, you become less scary, and I had no intention of being less scary. The ghouls were sentient, which meant they could feel fear, and I needed every bit of advantage I could scrounge up.

A large ghoul shouldered its way to the front of the pack. Well-fed, with a defined powerful body, he crouched in front of me. If he stood upright, he would be close to seven feet tall. At least two hundred pounds, all of it hard muscle and sharp claws. The brown pattern on his back was almost nonexistent. Instead, long alternating stripes of paler and darker gray slid down his flanks.

The ghoul rocked forward. His face touched the boundary and he pulled back and stared at me. He wasn't sure what he was sensing, but he knew that the boundary and I were somehow connected.

Some ghouls were scavengers. They were harmless and sometimes even gainfully employed. We lived in an unsafe world. Too often bodies couldn't be recovered because they were under debris or the scene was too grisly for the next of kin to identify the remains. Putting the bodies into a mass grave was a recipe for disaster. Human bodies emanated magic even after death, and there was no telling what the next magic wave would do to that mass grave. Most often the remains were cremated, but occasionally the authorities would bring in ghouls to clean the site. It was cheaper and faster.

I'd bet my arm these ghouls weren't licensed scavenge workers, but I had to be absolutely sure.

The ghoul stared at me. I gave him my best psychotic smile.

The ghoul blinked his yellowish eyes, tensed like a dog about to charge, and opened his mouth, stretching his lips in a slow deliberate grin. *That's right, show me your big teeth, pretty boy.*

A row of thick sharp teeth decorated the front of his jaw. Toward the back, the teeth thinned out, becoming more bladelike, with serrated edges. *Got you.*

The ghoul unhinged his jaw. A rough raspy voice came out. "Who are you?"

"Turn around now and you'll live."

He clamped his mouth shut. Apparently this wasn't the answer he'd expected. Kate Daniels, master of surprises. *Don't worry, I'm just getting started.*

"We're a licensed cleanup crew," the leader ghoul said.

"No."

Half a mile behind the ghouls, a dark shape moved through the field, so silent, for a second I thought I was seeing things. My mind refused to accept that a creature that large could be so quiet. *Hi, honey.*

The ghouls didn't notice him. They were conditioned to pay attention to human flesh, and I was standing right in front of them, providing a nice, convenient target.

The leader ghoul turned, displaying a tattoo on his left shoulder.

Columbia, SC

014

Location of license and license number. He thought I was born yesterday.

"We're a peaceful group," the ghoul continued.

"Sure you are. You're just running into the city to borrow a cup of sugar and invite people to your church."

"You're interfering with official municipal business. This is discrimination."

The dark shadow emerged onto the road and started toward us. I'd need to buy him some time to get within striking range.

I looked at the ghoul. "Do you know what is so special about ghouls? You have an unrivaled adaptability. Your bodies change to match their environment faster than ninety-nine percent of anything we've seen in nature."

My favorite monster crept closer on huge paws.

I raised my saber and rested the opaque blade on my shoulder. Faint tendrils of vapor escaped from Sarrat's surface. The sword sensed trouble and was eager for it.

"Let me tell you what I see. Your color has changed from brown to gray, because you no longer have to blend in with the dirt. Your stripes tell me you spend a lot of time moving through the forest. Your horns are short, because you no longer hide in your burrows."

The ghouls shifted closer. Their eyes glowed brighter. They didn't like where this was going.

"Your claws aren't long and straight to help you dig. They are curved and sharp to rend flesh."

The ghouls bared their teeth at me. They were a hair away from violence. I had to keep talking.

"Your pretty teeth have changed, too. They're no longer narrow and serrated. They are thick, strong, and sharp. The kind of teeth you get when you need to hold struggling prey in your mouth. And your fancy tattoo is two years out of date. All ghouls' licenses in Columbia now have the year tattooed under the license number."

The ghouls had gone completely silent, their eyes like dozens of tiny shiny moons all focused on me. Just a few more seconds . . .

"Kill her," another ghoul chimed in. "We have to hurry."

"Kill her. He's waiting," a third voice chimed in.

"Kill her. Kill her."

They seemed awfully desperate. Something weird was going on.

"Who is waiting?" I asked.

"Shut up!" the leading ghoul snarled.

I leaned forward and gave the leader ghoul my hard stare. "You look plump. You've been raiding the countryside and growing fat from gorging yourself on the people you've murdered. I gave you a chance to leave. Now it's too late. Pay attention to this moment. Look at the stars. Breathe in the cold air. This is your last night. These are the last breaths you will take. I will kill every one of you."

The leader ghoul snarled, dropping all pretense. "You and what army?"

I began pulling magic to me. This would hurt. This always hurt. "That's the great thing about werelions. You don't need an army. You just need one."

The ghoul twisted his face. "You're not a werelion, meat."

"I'm not." I nodded behind them. "He is."

The leader ghoul spun around.

Two gold eyes stared at him from the darkness. The enormous lionlike beast opened his mouth and roared. Until I met him, I had never heard an actual lion roar. It sounded like thunder. Deafening, ravenous heart-dropping thunder that severed some vital link between logic and control of your body deep inside your brain. It was a blast of sound so powerful, I had seen hundreds of shapeshifters cringe when they heard it. A wolf howl heard in the middle of the night raised the hair on the back of your neck, but a lion's roar punched through all of your training and reason straight to the secret place hidden deep inside that screamed at you to freeze.

The ghouls stopped, motionless.

I opened my mouth and spat a power word. *"Osanda."* Kneel.

Power words came from a long-forgotten age, so ancient that they commanded raw magic. Few people knew about them and even fewer could use them, because to learn a power word, you had to own it. You made it yours or it killed you. I knew a handful of power words, far more than anyone else I'd met, but using even one came with a heavy price tag. For my father, the power words were a language, one he spoke fluidly and without repercussions. They didn't hurt him, but I always paid a price.

The magic ripped out of me. I braced for the familiar twist of agony. The backlash bit at me, tearing through my insides, but this time something must've blunted its teeth, because it didn't hurt nearly as much as I remembered.

The magic smashed into the petrified ghouls. Their knees and elbows crunched in unison and they crashed to the asphalt. It would buy me at least ten seconds. If the magic wave had been stronger, I would've broken their bones.

I swung my sword. Sarrat met a ghoul's bony neck and sliced through cartilage and thick hide like butter. Before its dead body fell to the ground, I thrust my blade into the chest of the second ghoul and felt Sarrat's tip pierce the tight ball of its heart.

The lion's body roiled, snapping upright. Bones thrust upward; powerful muscle spiraled up the new skeleton. A blink and a new monster lunged forward, a nightmarish mix of man and lion, seven and a half feet tall, with steel-hard muscle sheathed in gray fur and curved, terrible claws. A ghoul leaped at him. He grabbed the creature by its throat and shook it, as if he were snapping a wet towel. A sickening snap echoed through the night and the ghoul went limp.

I carved the third ghoul into two separate pieces and sliced the fourth one's throat.

The ghouls woke up. They swarmed us. The leonine beast swung his claws and disemboweled a ghoul with a precise swipe. Intestines rained onto the road. The bitter stench of ghoul blood mixed with the unmistakable sour reek of a gut wound singed my nostrils.

Claws ripped through my clothes, drawing agonizing scalding-hot lines across my back. *You want to play? Fine.* I needed a workout anyway.

My saber became a razor-sharp wall. It cut, sliced, and pierced, ripping flesh and hissing as the ghoul blood that bathed it boiled from its magic. I moved fast, sidestepping claws and blocking teeth. Another fiery gash stung my back. A ghoul clamped onto my boot and I ripped my leg free and stomped his skull into the pavement. A welcome heat spread through me, turning my muscles flexible and pliant. The world turned crystal clear. Time stretched, helping me. The ghouls lunged, but I was faster. They raked at me with their claws, but my blade found them first. I savored it all, every second of the fight, every drop of blood flying past me, every moment of resistance when Sarrat caught my target on its edge.

This was what I was raised and trained for. For better or worse, I was a killer. This was my calling, and I made no excuses for it.

A ghoul loomed before me. I sliced it down in a classic overhand stroke. It fell. Nobody took its place. I pivoted on my toes, looking for a fight. To the left the werelion tossed a broken body to the ground and turned to me. A single ghoul hugged the ground, caught between us.

"Alive," the werelion snarled.

Way ahead of you. Let's find out who the mysterious "he" is. I started toward the ghoul, sword in hand.

It shivered, looked right, then left, looked at the werelion, then at me. *That's right. You're trapped and not going anywhere.* If it ran, we would chase it down.

The ghoul reared, jerked its clawed hands to its throat, and sliced it open. Blood gushed. The ghoul gurgled and collapsed on the ground. The light went out of its eyes.

Well, that was a hell of a thing.

The lion monster opened his mouth and a human voice came out, his diction perfect. "Hey, baby."

"Hey, honey." I pulled a piece of cloth out of my pocket and carefully wiped down Sarrat's blade.

Curran stepped over to me and put his arm around my shoulders, pulling me close. I leaned against him, feeling the hard muscle of his torso against my side. We surveyed the road strewn with broken bodies.

The adrenaline faded slowly. The colors turned less vivid. One by one the cuts and gashes made themselves known: my back burned, my left hip hurt too, and my left shoulder ached. I'd probably wake up with a spectacular bruise tomorrow.

We'd survived another one. We'd get to go home and keep on living.

"What the hell was all this about?" Curran asked me.

"I have no idea. They don't typically gather into large packs. The biggest marauder pack ever sighted had seven ghouls, and that was considered a fluke. They are solitary and territorial. They only band together for protection, but clearly someone was waiting for them. Do you think Ghastek is connected to this?"

Curran grimaced. "It's not like him. Ghastek only moves when he has something to gain. Having us kill ghouls docsn't help him in any way. He knows what we can do. He had to realize we'd go through them."

Curran was right. Ghastek had to know we'd dispatch the ghouls. He wouldn't have used us to do his dirty work either. For all of his faults, Ghastek was a premier navigator, a Master of the Dead, and he loved his job. If he wanted the ghouls dead, he would've sliced this group to pieces with a couple of vampires, or he would've used this opportunity as a training exercise for his journeymen.

"This isn't making any sense to me," I said, pulling traces of my blood toward me. It slid and rolled in tiny drops, forming a small puddle on the pavement. I pushed it to the side, solidified it, and stomped on it. It shattered under my foot into inert powder. Blood retained its magic even when separated from the body. For as long as I could remember, I had to guard my blood because if it were examined, it would point to my father like an arrow. There was a time where I had to set any trace of my blood on fire, but now it obeyed me. I couldn't decide if it made me a better fighter or just a worse abomination. "They seemed desperate. Driven, almost, as if they had some sort of goal to get to."

"We'll figure it out," Curran told me. "It's almost midnight. I say we go home, get cleaned up, and climb into bed."

"Sounds like a plan."

"Hey, is there any of that apple pie left?" Curran asked.

"I think so."

"Oh good. Let's go home, baby."

Our home. It still hit me like a punch, even after months of us being together—he was right there, waiting for me. If something attacked me, he'd kill it. If I needed help, he would help me. He loved me and I loved him back. I was no longer alone.

We were walking to my donkey when he said, "Sweet cheeks?"

"I couldn't help it. Ghastek's got a stick up his ass the size of a railroad tie. Did you see the look on the vampire's face? He looked constipated."

Curran laughed. We found Cuddles and went home.

2

OUR HOUSE SAT on a short street in one of the newer subdivisions. In a previous life, the subdivision was part of Victoria Estates, an upper-middle-class neighborhood, a quiet place with narrow streets and old towering trees. It was as close to living in the forest as one could get and still stay in the suburbs. Then the magic came, and the trees of Hahn Forest to the south and W. D. Thomson Park revolted. The same strange power of magic that gnawed skyscrapers to mere nubs nourished the trees, and they grew at unnatural speed, invading neighborhoods and swallowing them whole. Victoria Estates fell prey to the encroaching woods without a whimper of resistance. Most people moved.

About four years ago an enterprising developer decided to reclaim the space and cut a new kidney-bean shape out of the forest, building post-Shift houses with thick walls, barred windows, sturdy doors, and generous yards. Our street lay on the inside of the bean, closest to the woods, while two other roads spun out of it to the north and west in widening arches. Ours was a short street, only seven houses on the other side and five on ours, with our home in the middle.

As we turned onto our road, I stretched my neck to see the house. It was a big three-story beast, sitting on roughly five acres, all fenced in, with a stable and a pasture in the back. I loved every brick and board of that house. It belonged to me and Curran. It was our family home. I'd lived in an apartment before. I'd lived in some hellholes. I'd even lived in a fortress, but this was the first house in a long time where I felt completely at home. Every time I left it, I had a terrible suspicion that when I came back, it would disappear, collapse, or be burned to the ground. When I somehow managed to obtain something nice, the Universe usually taunted me with it just long enough for me to care and then smashed it to pieces.

I couldn't see our home yet—the bend of the street was in the way. I resisted making Cuddles clop faster. She had had a tiring night.

Curran reached over and covered my hand with his clawed furry one. "One month left."

Two months ago, on January 1, Curran and I officially stepped down as the Beast Lord and Consort of the Pack. One day we were in charge of a thousand and a half shapeshifters and the next we weren't. Technically we had stepped down a few days prior, but the official date was January 1, for convenience' sake. We had ninety days to formally separate our finances and business interests from the Pack. If anyone decided they wanted to leave the Pack as part of our staff, they had to do it before that time ran out.

Today was March 1. Thirty days and we would be completely free.

Formally, we remained part of the Pack, but we weren't subject to their chain of command. We could no longer participate in governing the Pack in any capacity. For these ninety days, we couldn't even visit the Keep, the huge fortress Curran had built during his reign as the Beast Lord that served as the Pack's HQ, because our presence would undermine the authority of the new alpha couple as they tried to get established. After the separation period was over, we wouldn't be turned away from the Keep, but it was understood we'd limit our time. Just the way I liked it.

Guilt bit at me. The Pack was Curran's life. He'd ruled it since he had hammered it together from isolated shapeshifter packs when he was only fifteen. He was thirty-three now. He'd walked away from seventeen years of his life, because he loved me.

Last December, after my father and I had our little spat over Atlanta, he gave me a choice. Either I stepped down from my position of power in the Pack or he would attack the city. Tens of thousands of lives on one side, being the Consort on the other. I chose to walk away. We weren't ready to fight Roland. People would die because of me, and in the end we would lose.

I couldn't take the guilt, so I left the Pack to buy us time. Curran chose to be with me. The Pack wasn't happy with his decision, but he didn't care.

"Do you miss it?" I asked.

"What, the Keep?"

Funny how he knew right away what I was asking. "Yes. Being the Beast Lord."

"Not really," Curran said. "I like this. Getting the job done and then going home. There is a finality to it. I can look back and say I've accomplished this much today. I like knowing nobody will knock on our door and drag me off to do some stupid shit. No more committees, no more petty rivalries, and no more weddings."

The big maple in front of our house swung into view. It was intact. Maybe the house had survived as well.

"I don't miss the Pack. I do miss making it work," Curran said.

"What do you mean?"

"It's like a complicated machine. All of the clans and alphas and their problems. I miss adjusting it and seeing it work better. But I don't miss the pressure." He grinned, threatening the moon with his scary teeth. "You know what I like about not being the Beast Lord?"

"You mean besides us being able to eat when we want, sleep when we want, and have sex uninterrupted in glorious privacy?"

"Yes, besides that. I like that I can do whatever the hell I want. If I want to go and kill some ghouls, I go and do it. I don't have to sit through a three-hour Pack Council meeting and debate the merits of ghoul killing and its effects on the Pack's welfare and each goddamn individual clan in particular."

I laughed softly. The Pack had seven clans, segregated by the nature of their beasts, and each clan had two alphas. Dealing with alphas had to be one of the circles of hell.

Curran shrugged his muscled shoulders. "Laugh all you want. When I was fifteen and Mahon pushed me to reach for power, I did it because I was young and stupid. I thought it was a crown. I didn't realize it was a ball and chain instead. I'm off my chain now. I like it."

I pretended to shiver. Considering the way he said "I like it," I didn't have to pretend very hard. "Off your chain. So dangerous, Your Majesty."

He glanced at me.

"You might be too scary to let into the house. I don't know if I can risk falling asleep next to you, Unchained One. Who knows what would happen?"

"Who said anything about sleeping?"

I opened my mouth to taunt him and clamped it shut. I couldn't see the house, but I could see the section of the front lawn painted in a yellow electric glow. It was past midnight. Julie, my ward, should've been in bed long ago. There was no reason for the lights to be on.

Curran broke into a run. I urged Cuddles forward.

Cuddles balked. Apparently she didn't feel like running.

"Come on, donkey!" I growled.

She backed up.

Screw it. I jumped off her back and ran to the house. The door handle turned in my hand. I jerked the door open and dashed inside.

A soft electric light bathed our kitchen. Curran stood to the side. Julie sat at the table, wrapped in a blanket, her blond hair a mess. She saw me and yawned. I slowed down just enough not to ram into the kitchen table and burst into the kitchen. A one-armed woman with a mane of dark curly hair sat at the table across from Julie, a cup of coffee in front of her. George. Mahon's daughter and the Pack's clerk of court.

She turned to me, her face haggard. "I need help."

JULIE YAWNED AGAIN. "Bye. I'm going to bed."

"Thank you for staying up with me," George said.

"No problem." Julie gathered her blanket and went up the staircase.

Something thudded.

"I'm okay!" she called out. "I fell up, but I'm okay."

She thumped up the stairs, and then the sound of a door closing announced she had reached her bedroom.

I pulled up a chair and sat. Curran leaned against the wall. He was still in his beast shape. Most shapeshifters could only change form once in a twenty-four-hour span. Shifting twice in a short period of time pretty much guaranteed that they'd pass out for a few hours and wake up ravenous. Curran had higher capacity than most, but we'd had a long night and the change still tired him. He probably wanted to be sharp for this conversation. After Curran's family was slaughtered, Mahon found him and took him in. Curran had grown up with George. Her real name was Georgetta—and she threatened to pull your arms out if you used it—and she was as close to a sister as he had.

"What happened?" Curran asked.

George took a deep breath. Her face was pale, her features sharp, as if her skin were stretched too tight on her face. "Eduardo is missing."

I frowned. Clan Heavy mostly consisted of werebears, but a few of their members turned into other large animals, like boars. Eduardo Ortego was a werebuffalo. He was huge in either shape. In a fight, he didn't battle, he bulldozed his opponents down, and they didn't get up once he rolled over them. I liked Eduardo. He was honest, direct, and brave, and he would put himself between danger and a friend in a heartbeat. He was also unintentionally hilarious, but that was neither here nor there.

"Have you spoken to your dad?" Curran asked.

"Yes." George looked into her cup. "He wasn't unhappy about it."

Why would Mahon be happy that Eduardo had disappeared? The werebuffalo was one of the best fighters Clan Heavy had. When we left for the Black Sea to procure medicine for the Pack, Clan Heavy had three spots on our crew. George volunteered for the first, Mahon took the second, and he chose Eduardo for the third.

"George," Curran said. "Start at the beginning."

"Eduardo and I are together," George said.

"Like together, together?" I thought Eduardo liked Jim's sister.

She nodded.

Knock me over with a feather. I had seen them both in the Keep probably a hundred times since then and I would've never guessed they had a thing. I must've been blind or something.

Now that I thought of it, they did spend a lot of time together on the voyage back . . .

"How long?" Curran asked.

"Since we came back from getting the panacea," George said. "I love him. He loves me. He rented a house for us. We want to get married."

Wow.

"Mahon is a problem?" Curran guessed.

George grimaced. "Ed isn't a bear. Nobody but a Kodiak would do. If not a Kodiak, then at least some sort of a bear. That's why we were so careful. I tried talking to Dad seven weeks ago. It went badly. I asked him what would happen if I got serious with another shapeshifter who wasn't a bear."

She looked into her cup again.

"What did he say?" Curran asked, his voice gentle.

George looked up. Her eyes flashed and for a moment my mind shot back to an enormous bear bursting into a room, roaring. George was a Kodiak like her father. Underestimating her was deadly. I thought she was dejected, but now I finally identified the emotion that sharpened her face. George was pissed off and she was using every ounce of her will to keep from exploding.

She spoke, her voice shaking with rage. "He told me he would disown me."

"That sounds like him," Curran said.

She shot out of the chair and began to pace the kitchen, circling around the island like a caged animal. "He said that I had a duty to the clan. That I had to pass on my genes and make werebear children with a proper werebear man."

"Did you tell him that if he likes werebear men so much, maybe he should marry one?" I said. I would pay money to see Mahon's face when he heard it.

She kept pacing. "Of all the archaic idiotic things . . . His brain must've crusted over. Maybe he's gone senile."

"You know he says shit like this," Curran began.

She spun to him. "Don't you dare tell me he doesn't mean it."

"No, he means it," Curran said. "That man believes in his heart that bears are superior. He means every word when he says it, but he doesn't follow through on it. In the seventeen years I ran the Pack, I had about two dozen complaints about him, always about things he said and never about things he did. He has firm ideas about conduct unbecoming an alpha and a bear. Taking out Eduardo would be out of character for him."

"You weren't there." George kept pacing. "You didn't hear him."

If I gave them a chance, they'd talk about Mahon all night. "What happened after you spoke with your father?"

George shook her head. "You know what this bullshit about passing on genes means? It means that if Eduardo and I had children, my father would think they are deficient. You don't understand, Kate. I'm his daughter!"

"Of course, I don't," I said. "I never had problems with my father."

George opened her mouth and stopped. When it came to Daddy issues, I won to infinity.

"What happened after Mahon and you had a chat?" I asked.

"Eduardo and I talked about it. Eduardo was doing odd jobs for Clan Heavy and also helping me with the legal filings. That would all disappear. Jim needs my dad to maintain his power base. I don't have a shred of doubt that if my dad made a stink, my job with the Pack would evaporate, too."

"Your mom would kill him," Curran said.

"Yes, she would," George said. "But it would be after the fact, and the argument would be that it's already done and Jim couldn't rehire me because it would make him look weak and indecisive. So I began to quietly cash out my investments, and Eduardo rented a house in the city and registered with the Guild."

The Mercenary Guild was the largest for-profit magic cleanup agency in Atlanta. When people encountered some dangerous magic beast or problem, they called the Paranormal Activity Division first, but cops in post-Shift Atlanta were overworked and stretched too thin. In some cases people called the Order of Merciful Aid next, but dealing with the knights meant giving them complete authority. When the cops couldn't come out and the matter was either too minor or too shady for the Order of Merciful Aid, you called the Guild. They did bodyguard details, they did magic hazmat cleanup, they did search and destroy—they weren't picky as long as money was involved. I'd been a member of the Guild for nine years now. It used to be a good place to earn money, but since the death of its founder, the Guild had gone to hell in a handbasket.

"How did he do at the Guild?" I asked.

"He did well," George said. "He said some people gave him trouble, but it wasn't anything he couldn't handle."

Eduardo would do well at the Guild. He fit the type. When people called the Guild, they wanted to be reassured, and a six-foot-four man muscled like an Olympic medalist wrestler provided a lot of reassurance. Some of the regulars would screw with him because they didn't like competition, but the Guild zoned the gigs. Each merc was assigned a territory within the city and if a job fell into that territory, they automatically got it, so while the rest of the mercs could run their mouths and hassle Eduardo, there wasn't much they could do to keep him from earning money.

"I think Dad figured us out," George said. "Last week Patrick came to talk to Eduardo."

I mentally riffled through the roster of Clan Heavy shapeshifters for Patrick. He was Mahon's nephew, a carbon copy of his uncle with a matching attitude and size.

"He told Eduardo that what he was doing was wrong and that if he cared about me, he'd leave me alone and not tear me away from the family."

Curran grimaced.

"Would Patrick do something like that on his own?" I asked him.

Curran shook his head. "No. When Patrick opens his mouth, Mahon speaks. Patrick is an enforcer, not a thinker. That's why Mahon hasn't been grooming him for the alpha spot."

"Eduardo told him he had no idea what he was talking about. Patrick left. On Monday, Eduardo didn't come back to his house. I waited all night."

I grabbed a notepad and a pen from the built-in shelves. "When was the last time you saw or spoke with Eduardo?"

"Monday morning at seven thirty. He asked what I wanted for dinner that night."

Today was Wednesday, just barely, since we were just past midnight. Eduardo had been gone about forty hours.

"He didn't call me at lunch," George said. "He usually does. I thought maybe he got held up. I went to his house Monday evening. He never showed. He didn't call and didn't leave a note. I know there are some bullshit rules about how long a person has to be missing, but I'm telling you, this isn't like him. He doesn't just leave me hanging. Something bad happened."

"Did you talk to the Guild?" I asked.

"I went there this morning and asked about him. Nobody told me anything."

That wasn't surprising. Mercs were cagey.

George's voice trembled with barely contained rage. "When I came out, my car was gone."

Curran leaned forward. His voice was iced over. "They stole your car?"

She nodded.

That was scummy even for the Guild. "They thought she was an easy target," I said. "Young woman, alone, one-armed, doesn't look like a fighter." They didn't realize that she could turn into a thousand-pound bear in a blink.

I got up, walked over to the phone, and dialed the Guild. If Eduardo took a job, the Clerk would know. When someone called the Guild with a problem, the Clerk figured out which zone it fell into and called that merc. If the merc was busy or couldn't handle the job, the Clerk would then call the next person in "the chain" until he found someone to take the job. If he failed to find anybody, he'd pin the gig ticket to a board, which meant anybody could grab it. Some jobs went to select people because they required special qualifications, but the majority of gigs followed this pattern. The gig distribution ran like a well-oiled machine and the Clerk had been there for so long, nobody remembered his name. He was just Clerk with a "the" in front of it, the guy who made sure you had a job and would get paid. If Eduardo had taken a gig on Monday, the Clerk would know when and where.

The phone rang.

"Yeah?" a gruff male voice said.

"This is Daniels. Let me talk to the Clerk."

"He's out."

Odd, the Clerk usually worked the night shift during the first week of the month.

"What about Lori?" Lori was the Clerk's standby.

"She's out."

"When will either of them be in?"

"How the hell should I know?"

Disconnect signal.

What the devil was going on at the Guild?

I turned back to George. "We'll go by there first thing in the morning." Even if the Clerk wasn't there now, he or one of his subs would be there in the morning. "I know this is a hard question, but is there any way Eduardo could've gotten scared off and left?"

George didn't hesitate. "No. He loves me. And if he left, he wouldn't have abandoned Max."

"Max?" I asked.

"His pug," she said. "He's had him for five years. He takes his dog everywhere with him. When I came there on Monday, Max was in the office with just enough water and food to last through the day."

Eduardo had a pug. For some reason, that didn't surprise me.

"What's Jim doing about this?" I asked.

"Nothing," George said. "I reported Eduardo missing to him in private. He told me that he would look into it, and then two hours later he said that Dad was aware Eduardo hadn't checked in."

I glanced at Curran.

"Mahon pulled the clan card," Curran said. "Eduardo's disappearance is a Clan Heavy matter. Unless the shapeshifter is an employee of the Pack overall or the clan requests Jim's assistance, he can't do much. He can tell his people to be on the lookout for Eduardo but won't actively search for him."

"Can't or won't?" I asked.

"Both," Curran said. "An active search would involve questioning members of Clan Heavy, which would infringe on Mahon's authority as an alpha. There are strict guidelines that protect the autonomy of each clan within the Pack, and this would cross the line. George is right. Jim needs Mahon to keep his power base together. He won't do anything to intentionally aggravate him. In a year or two when Jim's well established, it might be different, but for now Jim knows he's walking a tightrope. If he actively searches for Eduardo, Mahon can spin it as Jim insulting him and abusing his position as the Beast Lord. The moment Mahon publicly confronts Jim, it will be seen as a vote of no confidence in Jim's ability to lead, and the rest of the clans will scream that Jim is a dictator who is infringing on their rights. If that happens, Jim can't win. If he doesn't do anything, he'll look weak, and if he challenges Mahon, he'll look like a dictator. It's a bad place to be, and Jim is too smart to go there."

Curran was right about Mahon. It was unlikely that the Bear, as Mahon was known, had made Eduardo disappear. It wouldn't fit with his ethical code. But if Eduardo had managed to disappear on his own, Mahon could take advantage of the situation. He simply wouldn't have to search for him that hard. George had a huge family on her side. She had grown up in Atlanta, and if she vanished, the entirety of Clan Heavy would look for her. But Eduardo was an outsider. He'd arrived in Atlanta roughly three years ago, and as far as I knew, he had no family in the state.

"I don't even know if he's dead or alive." George's composure broke. Tears wet her eyes. Her voice turned into a ragged snarl. "He could be dead in a ditch somewhere and nobody is looking for him. I keep seeing it in my head, him cold and dead somewhere, covered in dirt. I might never see him again. How does this even happen? How can someone you love be there one second and then gone the next?"

Curran pushed away from the wall and put his monster arms around her gently. "It will be okay," he said quietly. "Kate will find him."

I didn't know if I should be happy he had complete confidence in me or mad because he was making a promise I wasn't sure I could keep. I decided on happy, because I could see a mine buried in our path and I had to tell them about it.

George cried soundlessly, worry and anger leaking out from her eyes. She had watched my back during the trip to the Black Sea. She'd fought for the Pack and she'd sacrificed her arm to save a pregnant woman from being murdered. She was the one who was always upbeat, always confident and comfortable in her own skin. She laughed easily and she said what she thought, because she had no trouble defending her opinion. And now she was crying and frantic, and it made me angry, as if something had gone really wrong with the world. Life was unfair, but this was pushing it. I had to fix this.

George stepped away from Curran and rubbed her face with her hand, trying to erase the tears.

"We have a problem," I said. "Once we start pulling on this string, the other end might lead back to Clan Heavy. Even if George officially hires us and Cutting Edge to look for Eduardo, Jim can still block it. It's in our contract. When the Pack authorized seed money for Cutting Edge, they put in a clause that in the event a member of the Pack is implicated in any crime, the investigation has to be cleared by the Beast Lord. Jim has the power of veto."

"Who put that in?" George growled.

I nodded at Curran. "He did."

"It seemed like a good idea at the time," he said.

"So how do we get around this?" I asked.

Curran looked at George. "I am going to ask you a question and I need you to think about it very carefully before you answer. Have you ever heard Eduardo Ortego express an intention to leave the Pack as part of my separation staff?"

Nice. If Eduardo left the Pack with Curran, then Curran would have both the authority and the duty to protect him.

George drew herself to her full height. "Yes."

I had a feeling she had just lied.

"I also intend to leave the Pack with you," she said.

Oh boy.

"Think it over," Curran said. "This means you'll be severing ties with your clan. Your parents won't be thrilled either. If it turns out that your father had nothing to do with Eduardo's disappearance, you might regret it."

"Give me the contract," George said.

Curran didn't move.

"Curran, give me the paper."

He walked over to the shelf, took a binder from the top, and opened it to a blank separation contract. "Once you sign it, you have to completely separate yourself from the Pack within thirty days."

George took the pen and signed her name on the line. "That's not a problem. I can leave tonight."

"No, you can't," I said. "You have to go back."

"Why?"

"Because we can't walk into the Keep and start an investigation," Curran said. "We're blocked by Pack law. You know this. It's a trade-off: we don't attempt to influence people into leaving with us, and Jim can't interfere if they do. We're no longer part of the Pack, but you still are."

"You have to go back, do your job, and listen," I said. "You're well liked and respected. Eduardo was well liked, too. You might hear something. If someone from Clan Heavy did make Eduardo disappear, your being there will be a constant reminder of that. The guilt will eat at them and they might feel bad and come clean, or at least point you in the right direction."

"I can fight," George growled. "Just because I have one arm . . ."

"I know it doesn't slow you down," Curran said. "But I need you inside the Pack. Talk to Patrick. On your worst day you can run circles around him. Compliment him for looking out for you. See what he knows. It might help us find Eduardo."

She thought about it. "Okay."

I pulled the writing pad closer to me. "Now, I need you to tell me about Eduardo. Where he lives, what his family is like, what he likes to do. Tell me everything."

Thirty minutes later we were done.

"I should go home," George said.

"We have more than enough bedrooms," I said. "Why don't you spend the night?"

She shook her head. "No, I want to be home in case he calls. You will find him, Kate?"

George was looking at me with a familiar anxious hope in her eyes. I had seen it before in the faces of people driven to their breaking point. Sometimes you love someone so much that when something bad happens to them, you'll do anything to keep them safe. If I promised to make Eduardo magically appear if George stabbed herself in the heart, she would do it. She was drowning and she was begging me for some straw to grasp.

I opened my mouth to lie and couldn't. The last time I promised to find someone, I found her chewed-up corpse. That was how Julie came to live with me. "I promise you that we will do everything we can. We'll keep looking and we won't stop until we find something or you ask us to walk away."

The relief was plain in her eyes. She hadn't heard a thing I said except "we'll find something." "Thank you."

George left. I headed upstairs while Curran lingered downstairs to check the doors. It was our nightly ritual. He checked the doors downstairs and I checked the windows on the second floor, while Julie checked the third. I climbed to the second floor and stopped. Julie sat on the landing, wrapped in her blanket. She was holding a stuffed owl.

I remembered the look on Julie's face when she told me she'd seen the torn-up body of her mother. It was seared into my memory. After Julie's father died, her mother drank too much and didn't pay as much attention to Julie's existence as she used to, but she loved her daughter deeply and Julie loved her back with the single-minded devotion of a child. A piece of Julie's childhood died that day, and no matter how hard I tried, I could never bring it back. I had wished so badly that I could have found Jessica Olsen alive, but she died before I had even started looking.

Julie didn't talk about it. She never said her mother's name. One day we were walking down the street past a yard sale and Julie stopped without saying a word. She walked over to the box of toys and pulled out a big stuffed owl toy, just a ball of brown velvet with two dorky white eyes, a yellow triangle of a beak, and two flappy wings. She hugged it and I saw a heartbreaking desperation in her eyes. I bought the owl on the spot and she took it home. Later she told me she used to have one like it when she was a toddler. That owl was a secret treasured memory of being happy and being loved, sheltered and protected by two people who adored her, never suspecting that the world would one day smash it all to pieces. It had been a year since we found it and she still hugged it when she went to sleep.

"I gave her the rest of the apple pie," Julie said. "I hope you don't mind. She's a bear and they like sweets. It made her feel better."

"I don't mind," I said.

"You're going to find him, right?"

"I'm going to try."

"I'll help you," Julie said. "Tell me if you need anything."

"I will."

She gathered up her owl and her blanket and stood up. "I like Eduardo and George. They're always nice to me." She hesitated. "I don't want her to feel what it's like."

My heart tried to flip over in my chest. It hurt. "I know."

Julie nodded and went to the third floor.

I would find Eduardo. I would find him because he was my friend, because George had suffered enough and deserved a chance to be happy, and because I knew what it was like to have someone you love ripped away from you.

IT WAS MORNING, the tech was up, and I was in our sunlit kitchen, making a small tower of pancakes. Julie's school didn't start until nine, because traveling through the dark in post-Shift Atlanta was too dangerous for kids, and we made our own hours. In our line of work, we weren't guaranteed a lunch and we weren't always home in time for dinner, so breakfast was our family meal. Shapeshifters had faster metabolisms than normal humans and they consumed a shocking amount of food. Curran was no exception. I had a pound of bacon baking in the oven—cooking it on the stove resulted in burned bacon, a cloud of smoke, and everything around me covered in bacon grease. Two pounds of sausage simmered in another pan, and I was on my tenth pancake.

The sun shone through the windows, drawing long rectangles on the tiled floor, sliding over the light stone of the countertops, and playing on the wood of the cabinets, setting their dark finish aglow with red highlights. The air smelled of cooking bacon. I had opened the window and a gentle breeze floated through the room, too cold but I didn't care.

After breakfast Julie would go to school and we would go to the Mercenary Guild. It was the best place to start looking for Eduardo. According to George, Eduardo's family wasn't in the picture. His parents lived somewhere in Oklahoma, but Eduardo didn't keep in touch. He had no siblings. He was friendly with everyone, but George was his best friend. He spent all of his time with her.

Julie stomped into the kitchen and landed in a chair, tossing her blond hair out of her face. A long smear of dirt crossed her face. More dirt stained her jeans. When I found her on the street years ago, she was starved, almost waifish. She was fifteen now. Good food and constant training were paying off: her arms showed definition, her shoulders had widened, and she held herself with the kind of ready assurance that came from knowing an attack could come at any moment and being confident you can repel it.

"I want a new horse."

I raised an eyebrow at her.

Curran shouldered his way into the kitchen from the back porch. Blond, broad-shouldered, and muscular, he moved like a predator even in his human form. It didn't matter if he wore fur, beat-up jeans, and a simple gray sweatshirt like right now, or nothing at all; his body always possessed a coiled, barely contained strength. A month ago he had gone to our first job together in his other shape and the client had locked himself in the car and refused to come out. Curran turned human, but the client still fired us. Apparently human Curran was still too scary, probably because no matter what kind of clothes he wore, they did nothing to tone down his face. When you looked into Curran's clear gray eyes, you knew that he could explode with violence at a moment's notice and he would be brutal and efficient about it. Except when he looked at me, like now. He stepped close to me and brushed a kiss on my lips. Mmm.

"That's nice," Julie said. "I still want a new horse."

"Request denied," Curran told her.

I flipped my pancake. This ought to be interesting.

"What? Why?"

"Because 'want' is not a need." Curran leaned against the kitchen island. "I saw you in the pasture. You don't want a new horse. You require a new horse. Lay your case out."

"I hate Brutus," Julie said.

I glanced through the window at the pasture, where an enormous black Friesian stalked in circles along the fence. Brutus used to belong to Hugh d'Ambray, my father's Warlord. Killing Hugh was my life's ambition. I'd tried twice now and each time he had dodged death with magic. That's okay. The third time would be the charm.

After our last encounter I ended up with Hugh's Friesian, and Curran, who didn't care for horses, for some reason decided to keep him when we retired from running the shapeshifter Pack. The stallion was impressive and Julie decided to ride him to school. I told her it was a bad idea, but she insisted.

"Take the emotion out of it," Curran said. "You will better persuade the other person if you make them understand the reasons behind your request. You have to demonstrate that in your place they would come to the same conclusion. Once they agree with you, saying no to you becomes much harder because they would be arguing with themselves."

Once a Beast Lord, always a Beast Lord. Old habits died hard, and in his case, they probably never would.

Julie thought about it. "He doesn't obey any of my commands and he keeps trying to throw me off."

"You're not heavy enough," I said. "Hugh weighs over two hundred pounds, closer to two fifty in full armor. You're too light. Hugh isn't gentle with his horses either."

Julie glared at the Friesian. "He's stupid."

"He is. It makes him easier to train for battle." I poured more pancake batter into the pan.

"And mean. Last time I took him to school, he tried to break through the stall to fight with another horse."

"He's a war stallion," Curran said. "He's been taught to view every other horse as a challenge."

Julie's eyes narrowed. "If I keep getting hurt, it will cause both of you emotional distress and you will have to pay for my medical bills. If I lose control of him, he may injure another horse and you would be financially responsible for the damages. And if another child got hurt, you would feel terrible."

Curran nodded. "Valid points. Bring it home."

"I need a normal horse," Julie said. "One I can ride to school and leave in the school stables without any of us worrying about it. A city horse, who would respond well to commands and wouldn't throw me and hurt me."

With the constant dance of magic and technology, horses were the most reliable method of transportation around the city. Julie's school was four miles out and biking there was out of the question. Magic constantly gnawed on roads, and a lot of them were in disrepair. She'd have to carry her bike a third of the way. Not to mention that the amount of books she had to drag to school made it hard to maintain her balance. I'd lifted her backpack a couple of times and it felt like it was stuffed with rocks. On the other hand, if anyone attacked her and she managed to swing it in time, she'd brain them for sure . . .

"Much better," Curran said.

"I'll call Blue Ribbon Stables after breakfast," I said.

Curran raised his head and leaned to glance at the front door. A moment later I heard a vehicle slide into our driveway.

"Who is it?"

"I'm about to find out." Curran rose smoothly and went to the door.

I heard the door swing open. A moment later a tiny Indonesian woman with long dark hair and thick glasses swept into the kitchen and dropped into a chair.

"Dali!" Julie smiled.

Dali waved at her. After we retired, Jim Shrapshire, Curran's best friend, became the Beast Lord. That made Dali the Beast Lady. She now had my job with all the pain and trouble that came with it.

"Consort," I said. "You honor us."

"Fuck you," Dali said. "Fuck your shit. I quit."

I laughed and reached for a potato. Dali, despite being a weretiger, was a vegetarian. Pancakes alone wouldn't hold her over. Julie came over, picked up another knife, and started peeling next to me.

Curran came in. "Did you know there is a dent in your front bumper?"

"I know," Dali said. "I hit some trash cans on the way over here. I was frustrated and needed something to hit."

The neighbors would just love this. "What happened?"

"I had a fight with Jim."

"Why?" Curran asked.

"Desandra."

Figured. Of the seven Pack clans, Clan Wolf was the largest and its new alpha was . . . colorful.

"There is no privacy at the Keep," Dali said.

You don't say.

"I thought of going to my old house or to my mother's house, but Jim would check for me there. So I came here." Dali stared at me. "I liked my house. Living in the Keep sucks."

"I know," I told her.

"Can I stay for breakfast?" she asked.

"Of course."

I had just pulled the bacon out of the oven and flipped the hash browns when another car pulled up. Curran laughed and went to the door.

"He didn't." Dali actually growled. I didn't realize she could.

Jim walked into the kitchen. Some people had special talents. Some were charming. Others were clearly intelligent. Doolittle, the Pack's medmage, could put patients at ease just by saying hello. Jim's special talent was menace. Six feet two inches tall and built like he could punch through solid walls and dodge a bullet at the same time, Jim projected a concentrated promise to kick your ass. It emanated from him like heat from a sidewalk. He never actually threatened you, but when he entered a room full of hard cases, bigger men backed off, because when he looked at them, they heard their bones breaking.

And now I would have to be very careful about our morning conversation. Any mention of Eduardo could set off alarm bells in Jim's head. The last thing we needed was him shutting down our investigation.

"Hail to the Beast Lord!" I waved my spatula for emphasis.

Jim spared me an ugly look and turned to Dali.

"You followed me!" Dali jumped out of her chair, her face furious.

"I didn't. I came here to talk to him"—Jim pointed at Curran with his thumb—"about his money. We just happened to be going to the same place."

"You knew I was here." She squinted at him. "You have your goons following me, don't you?"

"They're not goons. They're our security people. And yes, I have them following you. We're in a dangerous position. We just took over the Pack and I don't want any surprises."

"You're a paranoid control freak."

That was putting it lightly. Before Jim became the Beast Lord, he served as the Pack's chief of security. I thought I had a high level of paranoia, but Jim took it to stratospheric levels.

"My paranoia is keeping us safe." Jim brushed his face. Suddenly he seemed tired. "Dali, I just spent eight hours arguing with the Pack Council. Do you think you could postpone yelling at me until later?"

"No!" She sighed. "Yes. Fine."

I reached into the fridge. We would need more sausage.

NORMAL PEOPLE SPOKE while they ate. They socialized, carried on a polite conversation, and even told jokes, pausing their food consumption while doing all those things. Shapeshifters ate with single-minded focus, as if eating itself were a very important task and they had to concentrate on it completely. Talking while eating beyond the usual "pass that, please" was considered rude.

It took fully half an hour before they finally leaned back from the table. Jim sighed quietly. He looked haggard. It was unusual for him. Dali reached over and quietly stroked his hand. He took her fingers into his and squeezed.

"So what was the fight about?" Julie asked.

"We're trying to pass a security reform," Jim said. "One of the provisions requires Pack members residing at the Keep or at their Clan Houses to sign out before they go into the city. We've had a few issues over the last couple of years with finding everyone when an emergency hits."

"Seems reasonable," I said. Sailors did it on shore leave, soldiers did it when they left a military base, and there was no reason why Pack members couldn't do the same.

"It's his first act as the Beast Lord," Curran said. "The alphas will dig their heels in to see if he will bend."

"We were arguing," Dali said. "And then Desandra said that if the Beast Lord wanted to know where she was at all times, she would be delighted to make it happen."

I laughed. Dali glared at me.

"That's what she does," I said. "When she's uncomfortable, she starts saying uncomfortable things to knock you off your stride."

"I wanted to curse her." Dali jabbed her thumb in Jim's direction. "He wouldn't let me."

Considering that Dali's curses backfired half of the time, that was probably a very good thing.

"We need the Wolf Alpha to pass the reform," Jim said.

"I wasn't going to kill her," Dali told him. "I was just going to seal her mouth shut."

"Knowing Desandra, that would kill her," Curran said.

"I handled it," Jim said. "I told her that if she required someone to watch her at all times, the Pack would accommodate her wishes and assign a nanny to her. Anyway, what have you been doing?"

I'd been thinking about whether Mahon had had a moment of insanity and murdered his future son-in-law. "Hunting ghouls."

"Why?"

I told him about the ghoul horde.

He frowned. "Thirty."

"Yeah."

"That's a hell of a lot of ghouls. Let me talk to my people. We'll see what I can find out. Are you going to see Mitchell?"

"I was thinking about it." The number of people who knew about Mitchell could be counted on the fingers of one hand, and here Jim rattled off his name like it was nothing. Why was I not surprised?

Curran glanced at me. I'd have to explain Mitchell later.

Jim leaned forward, his gaze intent on Curran. "Look, you've had your fun. It's been nine weeks. You can come back now. We'll say it was an extended vacation. A sabbatical."

Curran leaned forward as well, matching Jim's stare. "I'm out."

Jim dropped his fork on the table and sagged in his chair.

"If you hate it so much, step down," Curran said.

Frustration twisted Jim's face. "I can't. They'll screw it up."

Curran laughed.

"That was mean," Dali said.

"It's not funny," Jim growled.

Oh no, it was funny. It was downright hilarious. I grinned at Jim. "I seem to remember a man who brought me a two-inch-thick file just last

September, told me that Clan Nimble and Clan Jackal had declared a vendetta on each other and the details were in the file, and then walked away."

"Oh yeah," Curran's eyes shone with gold. "What was it he said?"

"He said that we'd have to handle it because he had 'real shit to do.'"

"What's your point?" Jim grimaced.

"Payback's a bitch," I told him.

"You can moan all you want," Curran said. "The fact is you wanted the job. You're smarter than I am and you're strong enough to hold the power. You had plans for the Pack and I didn't always agree. Now you've got a chance to do it your way."

Magic rolled over us in a fast invisible tide. Everyone paused for a moment to adjust.

Jim pulled a simple beige file out of his jacket and put it on the table.

"What's in the file?" Curran asked.

"Are you sure you want to know?" Jim asked. "Once we do this, there is no going back."

Curran just looked at him.

Jim opened the folder, took out a stack of papers, and passed them to Curran. Curran read the first page. "What the hell is this?"

"It's like this," Jim said. "You own too much crap. You hold at least a twenty-five percent stake in over twenty-two percent of the Pack's businesses. Only a few of these businesses are established enough to be able to come up with the money to buy you out. A lot of them are new enterprises and each dollar of profit is being put right back into them. If we buy you out now, the way you want us to, the Pack will go bankrupt."

"That's bull," Curran said.

Jim spread his arms. "This is what the accountants are telling me. I understand you might have a cash flow issue, but you wouldn't have one if you were still the Beast Lord."

Curran's face went blank, unreadable like a stone wall. Uh-oh.

"Don't test me."

"I'm not testing you. I'm telling you, this is how it is. The contract you're holding outlines our proposal. Instead of a monetary payout, we offer you a business in trade for fifty percent of your collective stake now, and then, once the other businesses begin to be profitable, you can either continue to own them and collect your share of profits or sell off your stake as you see fit."

"This would make sense," Curran said, "if I had no eyes to read it or no brain to understand it. Did Raphael write this?"

"He might have looked it over," Jim said.

Raphael was the alpha of Clan Bouda. He was too handsome for his own good, mated to my best friend, Andrea Nash, and a complete shark when it came to all things business. If Raphael wrote the contract, it was a good deal for the Pack and a bad deal for us.

We weren't desperate for money, but a large chunk of our ready cash had gone into buying and furnishing this house. I never asked Curran how much money he had, because even though he referred to it as our money, he had earned the bulk of it before he ever met me. But I got the impression that we weren't too far from the bottom of our reserve.

Now that we both had time to devote to Cutting Edge, the business was picking up and it would start putting food on our table within a year. Trouble was, we faced a lot of stiff competition. In the hierarchy of clearing paranormal hazmat, Cutting Edge scraped the bottom of the barrel, with the Guild being our major competition. We had to underbid the mercs, and while the Guild was having serious issues, competing with them was difficult. It didn't help that the Pack had bankrolled Cutting Edge's startup costs and both Curran and I wanted to get that loan taken care of.

"What are you offering?" I asked.

"The Mercenary Guild," Jim said.

"What?" I must've misheard.

"The Mercenary Guild," Jim repeated.

"That's stupid," I told him. "I have the business sense of a walnut and even I know it's stupid."

Ever since its founder died, the Mercenary Guild had been run by an assembly consisting of veteran mercs, admin staff, and the Pack representative. The rule by committee wasn't working. I knew this, because I was that Pack representative. I'd worked for the Guild since I was eighteen. Mercs didn't have a long life expectancy, but I was hard to kill and I had passed the eight-year mark, which made me a veteran. I had street cred, but even with my reputation, my veteran status, and the power of the Pack behind me, I got through to the Guild only half of the time. As long as I was there, keeping the peace, some stuff got done, but when I hadn't been there, from what I'd heard, the infighting got so bad, the Guild was on the brink of bankruptcy. Jim knew all this. He used to be a merc, too, and he had spies all over the city.

"First, the mercs and admins are too busy being at each other's throats," I said. "Second, the Pack doesn't own enough of the Guild to make it worthwhile for us."

"We do," Jim said. "The mercs have been selling off their shares and I've been using the shapeshifter mercs to buy them."

He must have thought I was born yesterday. "They've been selling off their shares because the Guild has hurtled over the cliff and is nose-diving into the ground. Rats abandon a sinking ship, you know that."

Jim dismissed it with a brisk gesture. "That's beside the point. Kate, the Pack now controls thirty-six percent of the Guild. We'll transfer these shares to you, which will make you two the largest single shareholders."

"This is a bad idea," I said.

"We're not taking it," Curran said.

"Bottom line, I'm the Beast Lord," Jim said. "I'm telling you, that's our offer."

"Your offer stinks," I told him.

"Our offer is more than fair."

"You can't compel me to agree," Curran said. "The Pack law is crystal clear: as a retired alpha, I have autonomy."

"No, I can't. But I can control what we offer you and this is what I am offering. You're my friend, but the Pack is my job now. So you want me to go back to these people in whose businesses you invested and tell them that you don't give a crap about their livelihood?" Jim said. "Just trying to be clear."

"I own ten percent of Raphael's reclamation business," Curran growled. "His annual earnings are in the millions."

The light dawned on me. "That's why Raphael wrote the contract. He doesn't want to pay."

"He wrote the contract because I asked him," Jim snarled.

Curran looked at him. An imperceptible shift occurred in the way he held himself. Nothing obvious. A slight hardening of shoulders, a straighter spine, a muted promise in the eyes, but suddenly everyone knew the conversation was over. This was how he used to silence the Pack Council.

"We thank the Pack for their generous offer," Curran said. "The answer is no. Julie needs to get to school and we need to get to work. Thank you for your visit. You're welcome in our home anytime."

Jim rose. "Think about it."

Dali looked at Julie. "Do you need a ride?"

"I'll take it!" Julie jumped off her chair.

Dali drove like a maniac. "Do not kill my kid."

Dali snorted. "I didn't kill her when I taught her how to drive, did I?"

Curran rose and went to the other room. Jim and I traded glances. He reached for the folder.

I miss making it work . . .

"Leave it, please," I said.

THE GUILD OCCUPIED an abandoned hotel on the edge of Buckhead. Once a futuristic-looking tower, it had succumbed to the magic waves like the rest of the business district. High-rises fell in two ways: either they slowly deteriorated until they collapsed in a heap of dust and debris, or they toppled. The Guild's base was a toppler: the tower had broken off about seven stories up as if cut by a blade. The renovations and repairs shaved off another two floors, and now the Guild had five floors, only four of which were functional, the price of living through a slow-motion apocalypse.

We parked in a big open-air parking lot to the right and got out. About two dozen vehicles waited for us. According to George, Eduardo drove a huge black Tahoe that looked like a tank. Not something you'd easily miss. George drove an FJ Cruiser. Neither was in the parking lot.

Curran and I walked down the parking lane. Curran took short quick breaths, sampling the scents. We would need Derek to really follow a trail. Curran's sense of smell was many times better than mine, but he was a predatory cat. He hunted mostly by sight, while Derek, my onetime boy wonder, was a wolf. He could track a moth through pitch darkness by scent alone.

I had called over to Cutting Edge and left a message on the answering machine for Derek asking him to stay put in case we needed him. Curran had saved him when Derek's family went loup, and the young werewolf was completely devoted to him.

"I've been thinking," I said.

"Should I be worried?" Curran asked.

"I would've thought Derek would separate with us. I understand why Barabas didn't—he loves practicing law—but Derek has been working for Cutting Edge since the start."

"It's not really a topic I can bring up," Curran said. "It's a personal decision for each individual involved. There can't be any pressure one way or the other. Jim can't offer them incentives to stay and I can't use their emotional loyalty to pressure them into leaving."

It made sense, I suppose.

We combed the parking lot, predictably didn't find the Tahoe, and headed for the Guild building.

The heavy iron gates stood wide open. Nobody met us in the lobby. I checked the sign-in ledger resting on the metal table. Eduardo had signed in on Monday, February 28. There was no sign-in for Tuesday, March 1.

"He didn't make it to the Guild yesterday," I said.

Curran inhaled the air and grimaced.

"What?"

"It smells like a garbage dump. I get hints of his scent, but they're old. I'd say at least fifty hours or so."

Fifty hours was consistent with our time line. If Eduardo called George at seven thirty on Monday, he probably got down to the Guild an hour or two later.

Curran and I passed through a large wooden door and entered the inner hall. The hotel was built as a hollow tower with an open atrium at its center. Terraced balconies, one for each floor, lined the inner walls, allowing access to individual rooms.

In its other life, the hotel had been beautiful, all light stone, expensive wood, and elevators with transparent walls. It was way before my time, but I'd seen some old pictures that showed the lobby as an oasis of greenery, complete with a koi stream where fat orange-and-white fish drifted gently beneath the lily pads. A trendy coffee shop had occupied one corner, next to it a raised area had been set out for happy-hour patrons, and an upscale restaurant had offered lobster and steak. All of that was gone now. The coffee shop, koi, and greenery had vanished without a trace. The restaurant had evolved into a mess hall, offering cheap but decent food to hungry mercs coming off long jobs, and the raised area that was once the happy-hour hangout housed the Clerk's desk and a big job board behind him.

Usually the board was organized to within an inch of its life. The Clerk would write the open jobs on index cards, mark them with different colors according to priority, and pin them neatly to the corkboard. Today the board was a mess. Random pieces of paper covered it, stuck this way and that, some on top of the others. A couple had coffee stains. One looked a hell of a lot like a used dinner napkin whose owner must've indulged in gravy. What the hell . . . ?

About twenty mercs lounged here and there, some at the tables. I scanned the crowd. Not many veterans. The Guild attracted all sorts of people. Some worked hard and some hung out at the Guild bullshitting or waiting for just the right job to fall into their lap. Most of these guys were of the second variety. A few looked drunk. Most weren't too clean. As we walked through, a woman on the right hocked a loogie and spat on the floor. Charming.

These people hung out at the Guild every day. Some probably slept here. One of them had either stolen a car from a worried woman looking for her boyfriend or knew who had. They would tell me who did it.

The sour stench of rotten food floated in the air. Mud streaks stained the floor. The trash can in the corner was overflowing. The staircase that led up to the three remaining floors had a lovely patina of grime.

"Daniels!"

I turned. A tan dark-haired man in his forties waved at me from a nearby table. Lago Vista. I walked over and took a seat. Curran sat next to me. Lago had been a mercenary all his life one way or another, but he'd joined the Guild about three years ago, when he moved to Atlanta from Lago Vista, Texas. He liked it when people called him Lago. It wasn't really his name, but he never talked about the things he'd left behind, so I didn't ask. He and I had worked together on a couple of jobs. He wasn't as fast as he used to be, but he had a lot of experience and he knew what to do with it. He did his job, he did it well, and he didn't get me or anybody else killed. That made him a decent merc in my book. If you needed a second for a gig, you could do a lot worse than Lago. If you could put up with his come-ons, that is. Lago was an aging jock. He liked one-night stands, and he viewed himself as a smooth operator.

"Haven't seen you around." Lago lifted a coffeepot. "Need some fuel?"

The coffee in the glass carafe was solid black and looked viscous. "Is that last night's batch?"

Lago shrugged.

Last night's batch that had probably baked for about twelve hours. No thanks. "Where is the Clerk?"

"You didn't hear? The Clerk's gone. The cleaning staff, too. All of the admins are gone. You're looking good, Daniels. Looking really good." Lago gave me a long once-over.

"Stop looking at her and you might live longer," Curran said, his voice nice and friendly.

Lago glanced at Curran and held his arms up in the air. "Hey, no offense. Just a compliment."

Curran didn't answer. Lago shifted in his seat, uncomfortable, and turned to me. "Who's the guy?"

"He's my . . ." Fiancé, honey-bunny? "He's mine."

Lago nodded knowingly. "The thing with the Beast Lord didn't turn out, huh? That's okay, I heard that guy is a dick. You don't need that shit."

Curran's face showed no emotion. Lago stuck his hand out. "Lago Vista. Call me Lago."

"Lennart." Curran reached over and shook Lago's hand. I held my breath to see if Lago's fingers would survive. He didn't writhe in pain and no bones crunched. And that was exactly why Curran was such a scary bastard. When he lost control, it was because he made a deliberate choice to do so.

"So what happened to the admins?" Curran asked.

"The Guild Assembly failed to pass the budget. No budget, no paycheck. The cleaning crew was the first to walk off, then the cooking staff. The Clerk hung on for about six weeks, but he left, too."

Holy crap. "Who's taking the calls?"

Lago shrugged. "Whoever feels like answering the phone? It doesn't ring much anymore."

Great.

"Why didn't they pass the budget?" Curran asked.

"Because Bob Carver wanted to raid his pension fund." Lago gulped his coffee and grimaced at the taste.

Bob Carver had been in for about fifteen years, and he was one of the rare breed of mercenary who played well with others. He was part of a four-person crew known as the Four Horsemen and they took the larger, more difficult jobs. Half of the Assembly consisted of admins and the other half of mercs, and Bob Carver was chief personnel officer and the mercs' leader. Before my father decided to take an active interest in my existence, I functioned as the third part of that triangle, representing the Pack's interests. I didn't think I made that much difference, but it must've been just enough to keep the tide of crazy at bay, because in my absence the Guild had clearly gone off the rails.

Curran kept looking at Lago, listening and waiting. Lago gulped more coffee. "It works like this: if you last twenty years in the Guild, you get a pension. You start paying into it from your first job. Not much money, like five percent, but at the end of twenty years it adds up. If you die before your twenty years are up, you're screwed. Whatever you paid into the pension fund stays there. Your family gets the death benefit, but that's it. I don't know what the hell Bob needed the money for, but he wanted to borrow against his contribution."

"That's illegal," Curran said. "And stupid. If everyone raids the pension fund, there will be no pension fund."

Lago winked at me. "I like him. But yeah, you're right. That's basically what Mark said. Mark's our operations manager. Bob really needs the money, I guess, because he got a bunch of mercs on his side and hammered enough votes to stop the budget. He says he won't back down until they give him his money."

Awesome. Just awesome.

I leaned closer. "Lago, do you know Eduardo Ortego? Big guy, dark hair, looks like he can run through walls?"

"I've seen him around."

"Did he have a beef with anyone?"

"Sure. You remember Christian Heyward?"

"Big guy? African American with the bulldog?"

"That's the one."

The Christian Heyward I remembered was a genuinely nice family man, who had a very low tolerance for bullshit. He came in with his American Bulldog, did his gigs, and went home to his wife and kids. "He had a problem with Eduardo?"

"No. He quit the day Eduardo registered, so they gave him Heyward's zone. It's a good zone. Some people got pissed off because of it, but nothing too major. You know how it is: your guy looked like he could handle himself and nobody wanted to get hurt. They bitched behind his back, but that's as far as it got. Nobody wanted their bones broken."

"His girlfriend was here yesterday," Curran said. "Looking for him. Someone took her car."

"That's a shame. Can't help you, man. I wasn't here yesterday. But one of them might." Lago glanced at the gathering. "Most of these assholes are here every day. Good luck getting their attention, though. Half of them are drunk, half of them are hungover, and the other half don't give a shit."

"Thanks." I had no problem with attention getting.

I got up. I needed to do something flashy and loud but not too scary, or the mercs would just take off. I headed for the table closest to the door. If they ran, they'd have to get past us. Curran walked next to me. "So I am a dick?"

"I can't help that you have a reputation."

He grinned. "You want help?"

"No, I got it." His kind of help would likely involve a roar, and the mercs would scatter.

If I started with Eduardo missing, I'd get nowhere. They all probably saw George asking questions about him yesterday. Nobody helped her then and nobody would help me with it now. A missing person was serious business and mercs didn't like attention. They'd clam up. None of them would want to be a witness or to volunteer any information. I had to make it about the missing SUV. That was theft—serious theft, but still only theft—and everyone would understand that we'd handle it without the cops involved.

A dried-up French fry crunched under my foot.

"I can't believe Jim tried to sell us this leaky boat." The next time I saw him, I'd let him know exactly how I felt about it.

"Jim is a Beast Lord," Curran said. "Pack comes first. Friendships come second."

Three feet from the table I jumped and landed on its top. I didn't land softly. I landed with a serious thud.

The mercs turned and looked at me. Recognition registered on some faces.

"You know me," I said. "You know what I can do."

They were looking at me.

"A one-armed woman came here yesterday in a blue FJ Cruiser. Some-one took it. I want to know who."

"Daniels." A woman got up from her table and started toward me. Forty, built like a brick house, and mean eyed. She looked familiar. Her clothes and the bruise on her face said she had had a rough night and was looking for someone she could use to vent her frustration. "I owe you."

I knew her but couldn't remember the name . . . I gave her my hard stare just in case. She kept coming. Shoot. I was out of practice. "Really?"

"Yeah. You took my gig."

Ah. Alice Golansky. The last time I saw her was almost two years ago. Well, wasn't that a blast from the past.

"So let me get this straight. You're mad, because two years ago you were too drunk to do a job and passed out in the Guild's mess hall, and the Clerk sent me out in your place?"

She shrugged her shoulders and raised her fists. Well, well. Someone had some karate training. "I'm going to teach you not to steal jobs."

"You do realize that gig was assigned to me?" Not to mention that the job happened two years ago.

"You think you're so high and mighty. I'm gonna pull you off that table and stomp your face in."

Curran smiled.

Okay. "You thought this through?" I asked.

She looked up at me and punched her palm with her fist. "Oh yeah."

I dropped to my knee and hammered a punch into her jaw. My fist had shot down like a jackhammer. I'd sunk all of the momentum of the drop into it. Knocking someone out was tricky, because it required power, speed, and the element of surprise, but when it worked, it made a statement. Alice's eyes rolled into her head. She went rigid and fell straight back, like a cut tree. Her head bounced off the floor a bit.

The hall was suddenly silent. Ha! Still got it.

"Anybody else got any disputes they'd like to settle?" I asked.

The mercs sat silent.

"I'll ask again." I stood up. "Blue FJ Cruiser. Who has it?"

No answer.

"Maybe you didn't hear her," Curran said. "Or maybe you can't see her well. Let me help."

The table under me moved. Out of the corner of my eye I saw him holding it a foot off the ground with one hand. Okay then.

The mercs froze.

"It was Mac," a large Latino man wearing faded fatigues said from the left. His name was Charlie and he used to be a regular when I worked for the Guild. "Mac and his idiot redneck cousin, what's his name . . . Bubba? Skeeter . . . ?"

"Leroy," Crystal said, tossing back her bleached blond hair. "Mac and Leroy."

The names didn't sound familiar. Curran quietly lowered the table back to Earth.

"Yeah, Leroy," Charlie said. "I saw them getting into it this morning. They were going to do a job in Chamblee on Chamblee Dunwoody Road."

I was pretty sure Chamblee used to be in Heyward's zone.

"The cat lady?" a short skinny guy in a red sweater asked. "The one who called before?"

"Yeah," Charlie said. "She's got something with wings trying to eat her cats on Chamblee Dunwoody Road."

That's right, tell me more.

"Again?" Crystal asked. "Eduardo already went out there on Sunday. He said this lady had a giant tick eating her cats."

"This was no tick," Charlie said. "She said it flew. Ticks don't fly."

"Well, whatever it was," Crystal said, "I know he killed it on Sunday, because he came back here to get paid, and then she called again on Monday and he went out there again. That's the last I saw him."

It was a repeat job. The client called the Guild the first time on Sunday about a tick, and Eduardo went out and took care of it. Then she called again, on Monday, probably because the problem recurred. He went out to that call and disappeared. Then the client called for the third time, today, which meant that either the creature bothering her had a large family or that Eduardo never made it to her job. But he did finish the Sunday job, which meant there would be a record of it.

"Did this lady say Eduardo showed up on Monday?" I asked.

Charlie shook his head. "She was at work, so she didn't know if he showed up. But she was really heated it wasn't taken care of."

"When did Mac and Leroy leave?" I asked.

"Half an hour ago," Charlie said.

We'd just missed them.

"Are they poaching in Eduardo's territory?" I asked.

Crystal spread her arms. "He ain't here to call them out on it, is he?"

"They've got a problem with him?" Curran asked.

Charlie shrugged. "They've got a problem with everyone. Ortego's got good territory. They tried muscling in on him and he beat their asses for them."

"He wasn't worried about it," Crystal said.

"You knew him well, huh?" I asked.

"She talked to him every time he came here," Charlie said.

Crystal shot him a dirty look.

"Don't stare at me." He pointed at us. "They have issues with you. They have no issues with me. Don't drag the rest of us in with your sorry ass."

"I tried to know him well, if you catch my meaning." Crystal made a sour face. "Apparently he's one of those 'got a girlfriend' types. She was over here yesterday. Nothing special. And she's a cripple."

Oh, you sad, pathetic excuse for a human being. My fist itched. I really wanted to punch Crystal in the face.

"So you saw a young one-armed woman desperately looking for her guy. You knew Leroy and Mac took her car and you didn't say anything. None of you assholes told her or offered to give her a ride back home?" I could barely keep a growl out of my voice. "You must've all had important shit to do like sitting here, getting drunk, and spitting on the floor."

Nobody looked me in the eye.

"What are you, the morality police?" an older drunken-looking merc asked.

"Yeah, I am, Chug. Remember that time your leg was broken and Jim and I came to get you out of the hole under a collapsed building?"

"So what?"

"Next time you're in trouble, don't call me."

"I'll survive," he said.

"Don't make promises you can't keep." I jumped off the table and headed for the Clerk's desk. We needed job logs.

"Where are we going?" Curran asked quietly.

"To get the logbook. When a job is completed, it's written into the logbook before the payment is authorized. According to those clowns, Eduardo had already gone to do a job at that address. On Sunday this lady called about a giant tick, and he went out and killed it, and he got paid. The logbook should have a record of it."

The problem he had gone out to fix on Monday was still active, because the client had called the Guild again about it this morning and the car-stealing rednecks took the job. Sometimes that happened—you killed some creature but didn't realize it wasn't alone, so you had to go out the second time and complete the job. We had to talk to the client. Mac and Leroy would've taken the gig ticket with her address with them, so the logs were our best bet.

Something had happened to Eduardo on Monday, during the second job or on the way to it. If he were a normal human, I'd be calling hospitals to see if he was somewhere with an injury, but the standard protocol for hurt shapeshifters dictated that medical personnel notify the Pack immediately. The Pack had its own medmages, led by Doolittle, who had brought me back from the brink of death so many times I had lost count. Eduardo could be hurt, he could be dead, or he could be in jail, arrested for something, but he wasn't in a hospital.

I crouched behind the Clerk's desk and tried the log drawer. Normally it was under lock and key. The drawer door swung open.

The mercs watched us.

"Try to look casual." I pulled the top book out and put it on the desk.

"Why?"

"Because what I'm doing is illegal without a warrant, and we have about twenty witnesses observing our every move."

Curran crossed his arms, making his biceps bulge, leaned against the desk, and fixed our audience with his stare. Everyone spontaneously decided to look anywhere else but at us. Right. Casual, my foot.

"See," he said. "No witnesses."

I flipped the pages. Eduardo was like a brand-new merc. He would do things by the book. Only three log entries on Sunday. Wow. There should have been a dozen or more. On a good day the Guild used to be chaotic with a steady stream of mercs coming and going, and Sunday during a strong magic wave should've been a good day for business.

Second name down. *Mrs. Oswald, 30862 Chamblee Dunwoody Road. Complaint: giant tick eating cats. Status: resolved, Biohazard contacted to remove the remains. Eduardo Ortego.*

One of the two conference doors in the opposite wall opened and Mark Meadows, the Guild's head admin, stepped out. I almost did a double take. Mark had started as the Guild's secretary, but after the death of the Guild's founder, Mark became chief administrative officer. Mark's slogan in life was, "I'm middle management and proud of it." His jaw was always perfectly shaved; his face showed no bruises; his hands had no cuts. His nails were manicured and the light scent of expensive cologne followed him wherever he went. He stood out among the rough-and-tumble mercs like a professor at a prison rodeo. Most mercs despised him, because Mark had no mercy. Profit was his god and no hard-luck story would sway him from following the letter of the Guild's law in pursuit of the bottom line.

That was the old Mr. Meadows.

This Mark had let himself go. His normally impeccable suit was rumpled. His face was red, his expression flustered. His hair looked like he'd clutched at it with his hands but stopped short of actually pulling it out. His face wore a haunted expression. No doubt coming off another session of the Guild Assembly.

Do not see me, do not see me . . .

His eyes lit up. "Daniels!"

Damn it. "I don't have time, Mark," I called.

"But you have time to break the law and invade client privacy by reading the log."

Ugh. "I'm looking for a missing merc."

"Too bad. I'm a member of the Assembly and I call on you to formally appear before the Assembly. You can't refuse."

The hell I can't. I slapped the book closed and slid it into its place. "This is me refusing."

"Well, well, well!" Bob Carver emerged through the open door. He was the same height as Mark, and their hair color was a similar shade of brown, but there the resemblance ended. Mark was in his thirties, ate well, and spent a lot of time at the gym. He was toned. Bob Carver, on the other hand, was lean and hard, whittled by life like a walnut wood carving. In his late forties, he looked like a guy who had been through some rough shit and came out of it tougher.

"Look what the cat dragged in."

He was playing to the audience. Never good.

"Is he talking to me or you?" Curran asked. His voice was deceptively light.

"I don't know," I said. "But I'm sure he'll get around to telling us."

"Hello, Your Highnesses."

Bob pretended to bow with a flourish, eyeing us. Behind him more familiar faces appeared as the mercs inside the room came out to see what the hubbub was about. Veteran Guild members Rigan and Sonia, and the rest of Bob's Four Horsemen: Ivera, a firebug good with bladed weapons; Ken, the mage, tall and phlegmatic with a distant look on his narrow face, as if he were perpetually pondering something beyond human understanding; and Juke. Juke was a few years younger than me, a good deal thinner, and she wanted very hard to be edgy and hard-core. Instead she managed a pissed-off Goth Pixie look: her short hair stuck out from her head in a short asymmetric cut, her arms were thin like chopsticks, and her smoky eyes and purple lipstick made her delicate features even more fragile. She studied Sōjutsu, the art of yari, Japanese spear, and she was pretty good with it.

"So glad you graced us with your presence," Bob said. "Came to slum with us mere mortals?"

Bob and I never had a problem. Juke and I had a problem, because I enjoyed jerking her chain, but Bob and I always leveled. Where was he going with this? I leaned back. "You'd have to clean the place up a bit for it be a slum, Bob."

Bob narrowed his eyes. "I know what you've been doing. I know your Pack conned enough mercs into selling you their shares so you'd control a third of this Guild. I know you're thinking of buying those shares."

Jim would be overjoyed to hear that someone had been talking to the Guild behind his back. That wouldn't increase his paranoia. Not at all.

Bob was building up steam. "So that's it, huh? You thought you'd come here, throw your weight around, and save us. Whip us into shape. I've got news for you." He looked around dramatically. "Nobody's whipping us. There won't be any bowing or scraping."

Curran shrugged. "Okay. Fine by me."

Bob glowered. "I don't give a fuck if you think that's fine or not. I'm telling you how it's going to be."

Bob, you sad, sorry sonovabitch. If I didn't steer this away from Curran, he would redecorate the place with the Four Horsemen's guts.

I grinned. When in doubt, piss them off with humor.

"Something funny, Daniels?" Juke asked me.

"Just enjoying watching your boss here dig the hole deeper." I nodded at Bob. "Keep going, Bob. Don't hold back. Share your feelings with the group. Get it all out."

Mercs at the tables chuckled.

Bob growled. *That's right, concentrate on me . . .*

"You used to be somebody, Lennart."

Damn it. He was asking for his head to be bashed in, and if he said too much more, I would do it myself.

He kept going. "I've got news for you: you're a nobody."

Really? A nobody?

Bob squared his shoulders. "We'll throw you out on your ass . . ."

A deep inhuman sound rolled through the Guild, the sound of a predator's voice, humorless and ice-cold, and I realized it was Curran laughing. I swallowed the sudden lump in my throat.

The Guild Hall went completely silent. *Oh no.*

Curran studied Bob Carver, as if he hadn't really seen him before this moment and now he'd finally noticed Bob existed and decided to dedicate his complete attention to that fact. His eyes sparked with gold, his gaze pinning Bob in place. I knew the weight of that stare. It was like looking straight into the jungle's hungry maw. It knew no mercy and no reason. It only knew that it was hunter and you were prey. Blood rushed to your limbs, your breathing sped up, and your thoughts fractured and melted into your brain until only two options remained: fight or flight. Picking one was torture.

Bob paled. He stepped back, almost in spite of himself, falling into a familiar defensive stance, half-turned toward Curran, his hands raised. All of his bluster faded. Suddenly everyone knew who the baddest monster in the room was and nobody wanted to be his target.

Curran pushed off from the desk, his movement smooth and measured. His eyes were like two shining moons. His voice had a deep undercurrent of a snarl. "So you want to throw me out on my ass?"

Bob swallowed.

"There aren't enough people here, Bob. You need to get reinforcements. Go ahead." He smiled, baring his teeth, a sharp carnivore grin. "I'll wait."

People were slowly reaching for their weapons. The mercs had leaned forward, their weight barely on their chairs. Any loud noise and they'd run.

In the quiet, Curran's voice rolled through the Guild Hall. "When I came here today, I hadn't decided what I was going to do. Thank you. You helped me to reach a decision. You chose to start something here today. When it's over, you will come to me and you will ask me to take charge of you."

I had to give it to Bob Carver. He managed enough willpower to open his mouth. And then his brain must've kicked in, because he clamped it shut.

Curran turned to me. "Kate? Do you have everything you need?"

"Yes."

"Good. Then we're done for now."

We walked out. Nobody said a word.

IT TOOK US fourteen minutes to chant the Jeep into action. Cars with enchanted engines ran during magic waves, but they made enough noise to make even metalhead teenagers beg to turn the volume down. The Jeep's cab had been isolated against noise, but we still had to raise our voices to be heard.

Curran drove out of the parking lot. The streets flashed by. I opened the glove compartment and pulled out a couple of throwing knives. According to the mercs, the cat-eating creature flew. I didn't use guns. I didn't get along that well with tech-related projectile weapons in general. I could manage a decent shot with a bow, but give me a rifle and I'd miss an elephant from three feet away.

Curran's face was calm, the line of his mouth relaxed.

"Are we going to take over the Guild?" I asked.

"Yes, we are. Well, I am. You are invited." He glanced at me. "You should join me. It will be fun."

"After we find Eduardo."

"I wasn't going to drop everything and crush the Four Horsemen," Curran said. "Give me some credit. Eduardo is one of our own. Finding him is all that matters. Besides, if I'd decided to pull Carver's spine out of his body, I would've done it already."

"Can you actually do that?"

Curran frowned. "I don't know. I mean theoretically if you broke the spine above the pelvis, you could, but then there are ribs . . . I'll have to try it sometime."

Okay, then. That was not disturbing. Not at all. "What do you suppose normal people talk about on their car rides?"

"I have no idea. Tell me about Bob Carver."

I sighed. Once Curran focused on a target, getting him to change course was like trying to nudge a moving train to the side.

"Bob is a shark. I read somewhere that sharks have to keep swimming or they drown. I have no idea if that's true, but I can tell you: Bob keeps swimming. I learn things. Every fight is an opportunity. Every time we spar, I learn more. I learned from fighting the ghouls. I learned from watching and fighting Hugh."

A muscle in Curran's face jerked slightly. It was a tiny movement. Had I blinked, I would have missed it. Hugh was still a problem for both of us.

"Bob is like me. People see him and think, 'Oh, he's past his prime. He's good, but he isn't as fast or strong as he used to be.' But Bob is like one of those martial arts instructors who have been honing their bodies for years. When he needs to, he moves fast, because he doesn't think about it. He just does it. I once saw him take down a man who was fifteen years younger, faster, and better trained. A group of seven mercs, including the Four Horsemen, had done a job and this guy didn't like the way it went down. He got it into his head to fight with Bob. His exact words were, 'I'll beat the shit out of you and make you eat it with your face.'"

Curran smiled. "A poet."

"Yeah. Bob warned him that if the guy put his hands on him, it wouldn't end well. The guy said it was fine with him, so they brawled in the Guild Hall. Bob goaded him during the fight. He went for fun cheap shots. A slap on the cheek. A quick kick to the shin. Finally the guy lost his patience and the moment Bob gave him an opening, he went for Bob's throat. Bob almost let him get his hands around his neck and then hit him really fast with the flat of his hand in the Adam's apple. The guy let him go, staggered a bit, and kept going. Thirty seconds and he started getting sluggish. Bob worked him over for another minute and then the guy went down. Five minutes later the Guild paramedic had to cut his neck open. Bob had hit him just right and the blunt-force trauma to the trachea caused inflammation. His windpipe had swollen shut."

"Did he survive?"

"He did. He moved out of the city. Here is the thing: while the paramedic was trying to realign the trachea, Bob went to the mess hall and got himself a hamburger. Bob's not really an asshole, until you put your hands on him or try to screw him over. Then all bets are off. Thank you for not killing him, though."

"I have no plans of killing him. He might be useful, and one should never throw away good manpower."

"If I didn't know better, I'd say in your head you already took over the Guild, restructured it, and found a place for Bob in it."

He smiled at me.

Sometimes he . . . "scared" would be the wrong word . . . alarmed me. The Guild had no idea what was about to hit it.

We turned onto Chamblee Dunwoody Road.

I braced myself with my hand against the dashboard as our Jeep hit a bump in the road. The vehicle jumped, Curran made a sudden right, and the Jeep screeched to a halt. My seat belt jerked me back.

"There it is."

A large two-story house of brown brick rose at the end of a driveway. The house had been built pre-Shift, before magic and technology started their crazy waltz. Modern builders kept their windows small. Less chance of something with teeth, glowing eyes, and an appetite for human meat surprising you in the bedroom after a hard day of work. The windows of this house were large enough for Curran in his beast form to go through. Mrs. Oswald compensated for the windows' size by installing two-inch steel bars over them. Most of the grates were intact, but the bars on a large window above the garage were bent to the sides, as if something had smashed against them with great force.

A beige woman's shoe with a high heel lay on the ground midway up the driveway. A little farther on, a matching beige purse lay on the lawn. Mrs. Oswald must've come out, seen something that alarmed her, and run back inside, dropping her purse and her shoe. Whatever she saw scared her so much, she just left her things sitting there.

I rolled my window down. Curran did the same.

"I don't smell any blood," he said.

No blood was odd. If this was the house, Leroy and Mac should've gotten here by now. They'd left almost an hour before us. The street was empty. Where the hell were those idiots?

"Eduardo's scent is here too, but old and faint. I do smell something odd. Smells like a wolf."

"A wolf?"

He nodded. "With a touch of bittersweet scent to it."

From what the mercs had said, the creature threatening Ms. Oswald's cats had wings. A wolf with wings? Russian mythology included a wolf with wings, and a prominent volhv, a Russian pagan priest, had one as a pet. I really hoped the Russians weren't involved. Dealing with volhves meant dealing with witches, and claiming Atlanta had not endeared me to them in the least.

We sat quietly.

Minutes dragged by.

A high-pitched shriek rang from the sky above. It started on a high note, a forlorn mourning cry, and built on itself, growing harsher and sharper until it shredded the air like a high-velocity crossbow bolt. A dark shape swooped from the sky and rammed the bars. The steel grate shuddered from the impact. For a moment I thought it would fall out of the brickwork, but the bars held.

The creature fell to the ground, landing on all fours. Gray fur covered its lean body, sheathing its flanks and long lupine tail. Its legs terminated in furry, owl-like feet armed with sickle-shaped talons the size of my fingers. Two massive wings spread from its shoulders. The beast turned toward us. An eaglelike head crowned its powerful neck, complete with a dark beak the size of a hatchet.

"Kate?" Curran asked.

"It's a wolf griffin," I murmured. "Lion griffins come from Crete and Greece. This guy is from North Africa. They are mentioned in Berber folklore. Something about a giant bird and a wolf mating."

"Anything I need to know?" Curran asked me. "Does it spit fire?"

I'd run across a wolf griffin only once. "Not that I know of. The one I encountered before didn't, but I can't guarantee this one doesn't."

The wolf griffin ducked its head and fixed us with an unblinking predatory stare. It was at least forty inches at the shoulder.

"Do we take care of it or do we wait?" I wondered.

"We could kill it." Curran focused on the griffin. "That way when those two scumbags show up, we don't have to deal with them and the griffin at the same time. Besides, we need to get into the house to talk to the owner, and that's not happening until this thing is dead."

We both looked at the griffin.

"This is the second cat-hunting creature Mrs. Oswald reported," I thought out loud. "Someone or something is deliberately targeting her cats. If we kill it, there is a good chance that Mrs. Oswald's mysterious nemesis would just send something else."

"It's not our job," Curran said.

"I know, but what if something worse shows up the next time?"

The griffin spread its wings, took a running start, and flew up. We watched it rise with every beat of its wings, until it became a dot among the clouds. We didn't even know if Mac and Leroy would do this job. Maybe they'd decided not to show up.

The griffin swooped down and rammed the bars again. They bent. He hung on for a long moment, his claws scraping at the glass, and dropped down to the driveway.

"The next time he hits, he'll get through," I said. If he managed to get inside, whoever was hiding inside the house would get ripped to pieces. This was no longer about cats.

"We net it," Curran said. "I can wound its wings and we'll wrap it in the net."

"Once we're done with Mac and Leroy, we can let it run home," I finished. Tracking it through the air would be hard, but tracking it on the ground would be a piece of cake. "Right to its owner."

"Sounds good to me." Curran narrowed his eyes, measuring the distance between us and the griffin. "Mind playing bait again, baby?"

"I thought you'd never ask."

Curran and I opened our doors at the same time. I slipped out, held my arms out to make myself bigger, and moved forward. The wolf griffin focused on me. Out of the corner of my eye I could see Curran gliding soundlessly across the pavement.

I took another step. *That's it. Easy does it.*

The griffin spread its wings. Its hackles rose, the fur standing straight up like spikes on a hedgehog.

Easy now.

The griffin bent its neck, turning its wings downward, so the entire width of its gray-and-black dappled feathers faced me. It looked huge. *That's right, pretty boy. Show me all you've got. I'm a threat and I'm coming for you.*

Curran was almost in pouncing range. He could leap from where he was, but the griffin looked agile enough to dodge and then it would be gone. Three more feet and we'd be there.

The roar of an enchanted water engine rolled down the street, coming toward us. Argh. That was the last thing we needed, some idiot neighbor to spook it.

I took another step. The griffin clicked its beak at me, the two honey-colored irises glowing faintly. It was a shame to hurt it, but it couldn't be helped. Curran gathered himself, about to leap.

Easy . . .

A blue FJ Cruiser hurtled toward us, spitting thunder, and screeched to a stop. The doors of the cab popped open. A large man in black pants and a tiger-stripe camo T-shirt jumped out, combat-rolled, struck a pose hefting a cross-bow, and fired two bolts at the griffin.

Curran leaned out of the way, preternaturally fast. The left bolt whistled past his side and planted itself in the garage door. The right bolt bit into the griffin's throat. The beast shrieked in outrage. A second man fired a cross-bow over the hood of the truck. The bolt punched into the griffin's chest. The great wings beat once, in a desperate attempt to launch the body off the ground, and went limp. The griffin sank to the pavement. Honey eyes shone at me for the last time and dimmed.

Did that just happen?

"Yeah, bitch!" the first man roared. "Yeah! Come at me!"

Curran spun around, his face terrible. He sprang at the man, grabbed him, and hurled him across the lawn.

His buddy in urban fatigue pants and a black T-shirt got the hell out from behind the truck, brandishing his crossbow. I moved at him, but my sword was securely hidden in the leather sheath on my back and Curran was bigger and scarier, so Camo Pants ignored me. "Hey! Hey, you let him—"

I kicked him in the gut. It was a low front kick that took him right above the groin. People overextended on these kicks, but the trick was not to kick. The trick was to lift your knee high and stomp. Camo Pants' arms went toward his legs, and he went backward and slammed against the truck.

On the lawn, the loudmouth rolled into a crouch, his crossbow still in his hands. Curran started toward him. The loudmouth fired. Curran leaned out of the way just enough to let the bolt whistle past him and kept coming.

I yanked Camo Pants' weapon out of his hand and threw it aside. He swung at me. I caught his wrist and twisted it, right and up. He went down on his knees and I kneed him in the face. He took a moment to come to terms with it, and I locked his elbow with my left hand and twisted, just in case he developed any interesting ideas.

The loudmouth swung his crossbow like a hammer. Curran caught it, jerked it out of the man's hands, and broke it in half. The pieces of the crossbow went flying. Curran grabbed the man, pinning his arms to his body, and lifted him off his feet. The skin on Curran's face crawled.

"No," I called out.

Curran's human features melted. Bones shifted as his jaws extended, growing thicker, stronger, his skull expanded, and gray fur sheathed his new face. The merc in his grip stared at the new monstrous face. The rest of Curran remained completely human. I never met a shapeshifter who could do a partial transformation the way he did. His control over his body was absolute.

The merc opened his mouth, wide eyes staring into the violent gold in Curran's irises. "Mwa maah maaah . . ."

Curran unhinged his jaws. If he took that man's head into his mouth and bit down, the merc's skull would burst like an egg dropped on concrete.

"No," I repeated.

"He's gonna kill him," Camo Pants wheezed. His eyes were watering. Being kneed in the face will do that.

Curran's fangs emerged from his jaws, becoming longer and longer . . . I never realized how creepy it was to see teeth growing in real time. Here's one for my nightmares.

"Curran, you can't bite his face off."

"Yes, I can," Curran said in a monster voice.

"You shouldn't."

"He stole George's car. And he shot me."

"He missed."

"He missed, because I'm fast and I moved out of the way. If I bite his head off, he won't shoot me again."

"He's gonna kill him!" Camo Pants tried to pull out of my grip and I twisted his arm a little higher.

"If I need your help, I'll ask you for it," I told him. "Curran, please don't bite his head off."

"Why?"

"Because it's illegal. Technically you assaulted him first when you threw him across the lawn."

"I didn't throw him very far."

I rolled my eyes.

"I could've thrown him straight up and let him land on the pavement."

"That would also be illegal."

"You keep bringing this 'illegal' thing up as if it means something to me."

I couldn't tell if he was just scaring them or if he really intended to kill them.

"As a favor to me, please hold off."

"Fine." Curran loosened his grip slightly. "Want to add anything to this discussion?"

The big merc sucked in a hoarse breath. His face shook with the strain of making words come out. ". . . Fuck you!"

Oh, you dimwit.

"Fuck you!"

"Leroy!" Camo Pants barked.

"And fuck your bitch, too!" Leroy declared.

Curran looked at me. "How about now? Can I twist his head off now?"

"Still illegal," I told him.

Curran squeezed Leroy's shoulder. Bones groaned. Leroy clamped his mouth shut.

"Don't!" Camo Pants yelled.

Since Curran was playing with Leroy, this knucklehead had to be Mac. "Don't worry about him. Worry about me. What did you do to Eduardo?"

"I don't know any Eduardo!" Mac wheezed.

I twisted his arm a fraction more. He cried out.

"I know your name is Mac. I know that's your redneck cousin Leroy. I know you're in Eduardo's territory, muscling in on his gig, and I know that you stole the FJ Cruiser from his fiancée. Look at me. Look at my eyes."

Mac looked up at me. His face went white.

My voice was barely above a whisper, but I sank a lot of rage into it. "Eduardo is my friend. His fiancée is my friend. She is his sister." I pointed at Curran. "Tell me everything you know or I'll break your arm right here."

I tapped his shoulder. "Then I'll keep breaking it here and here and here. No amount of medmagic and steel pins will fix it. It'll never work right again and it will always hurt."

Mac stared at me, his eyes glassy. Words came tumbling out. "We don't know what happened to Eduardo. This was his gig, but the lady called this morning and said Eduardo didn't show up yesterday. We took the one-armed chick's car. We were going to do her man's job anyway, and it's a nice car, so we were just going to borrow it."

"Lie better," Curran said, his voice cold. "She came looking for Eduardo last night. You didn't know you would be doing this job until you got a call today."

Mac's voice broke. "What the hell do you want from me, man? Yes, fine, we took the damn car! We took it! Do you know how much a double-engine car costs? It was just sitting right there. We figured if that dickhead didn't come home, he was probably dead anyway. What the hell would his woman do with that car? She's got one arm anyway. We needed a car, so we took it."

And they would do it again. I could hear it in his voice. I'd met his type before. Some people had a moral code. It might not have matched the current laws, but it was still a code. Mac and Leroy's code consisted of one sentence: do whatever helps Mac and Leroy. It didn't matter who got hurt. It didn't matter that a person they stole from would have to do without or could've been injured or killed. If George's half-eaten corpse were discovered this morning because she was murdered while walking home, they wouldn't feel bad about it. They would simply keep going.

If they killed Eduardo, it would have to be a shot to the head with a silver round from far away. There was no way they could've beaten him in a close and personal fight, and they knew it. And if they somehow managed it, they would've taken his car and his equipment and they would be wearing it, because they were too stupid to hide it.

I glanced at Curran. He shook his head slightly. Leroy didn't smell like Eduardo's blood.

"Do you know what the Guild does with mercs who steal equipment from other mercs?" I asked.

Mac shook his head.

"They fine them. Ten grand. Poaching in another merc's zone is another ten grand. That's forty grand between the two of you. Guess what I'm going to do when I go back to the Guild?"

"Nobody knows you," Mac squeezed out.

"You're wrong. Everybody knows me. I have nine years in."

Mac's face went slack.

"So you have a choice, Mac. You can take your idiot cousin and you can leave this city. Or you can go back and face the Guild and work overtime for them for the next five years or so. But we'll be around and I promise you, I'll make your life as hard as I can."

I let go of his arm. Curran casually tossed Leroy on the pavement. Leroy landed on his ass, jumped up, and rushed at Curran. Curran let him get close and backhanded him, almost as an afterthought, the way one would swat a fly. The blow landed on Leroy's ear. The big merc spun, stumbling. Mac caught him.

"Our gear is in the truck," Mac said.

"You can pick it up at the Guild," I told him.

"You're a fucking bitch, you know that?" Mac said.

"I'll have to live with myself."

"This isn't over!" Leroy jabbed his finger at Curran. He probably meant it to look aggressive, but he was swaying on his feet.

"Yes, it is," Curran told him. "Go before I change my mind."

The corpse of the wolf griffin shivered. Flesh bulged in the middle of it, like a bloody red tumor, growing bigger and bigger.

"What the hell?" Curran snarled.

"I don't know." I pulled Sarrat free.

The tumor ruptured.

⇒ CHAPTER ⇐

5

CURRAN AND I backed away. A three-foot-long orange-brown spike shot out of the griffin's corpse, stabbing to the sky. The second spike pierced the corpse from within. The spikes bent, resting on the pavement, each bristling with six-inch-long rigid hair. The corpse shuddered, as if it were being sucked into something from the inside.

The spikes flexed and a huge insectoid head emerged, covered with bristles. Two pairs of dark brown mandibles jutted from it like two crab pincers the size of scimitars. Dark, nearly black serrated teeth lined the inside of each pincer.

Holy crap.

The creature kept coming out of the griffin's corpse: two fat chelicerae supporting the mandibles, a big round blob of a head with a bump in its center crowned with two black baseball-sized eyes, legs, more legs emerging segment by segment, thorax, a long segmented abdomen. The wolf griffin corpse shriveled, deflating, and vanished, pulled into the new creature. The giant insect landed in the driveway. Ten legs, the first pair huge and long, the others smaller, thrust from its ten-foot-long body, held about five feet off the ground. The damn thing was the size of the FJ Cruiser parked behind us.

The giant insect ground its mandible pincers. A grinding screech split the quiet. I winced.

"What the hell is that?" Curran growled, moving to the right.

"I don't know." I walked to the left. It looked like a scorpion and a really hairy spider had somehow mated and their offspring grew to fifty times its normal size. I'd never seen anything like it. Those mandible-pincers looked like they would slice through bone like it was butter. We couldn't let it get into the house. It would rip the whole family apart.

The legs were all chitin. Trying to cut through them with Sarrat would just break the blade. Trying to claw at it wouldn't do any good either. Its fat abdomen was softer, but getting to it would be a bitch.

A deep dry voice rolled through the street, so saturated with magic, it almost reverberated on my skin. *"Die."*

Why me? "We don't do requests. Try Iowa. I hear they're more accommodating." *Hey, Dad, I found a lovely present for this coming Father's Day. Enjoy.*

The insect pointed a leg at me. *"Die."*

Curran's eyes went gold. His clothes tore, falling in shreds to the street, as the massive meld of human and lion spilled out. "Let's see you try that shit on me."

The insect lunged at Curran, shockingly fast. Curran jerked his arms up, catching the insect's front pair of legs in his grip. His feet slid.

Holy crap. His feet *slid*.

I dashed to the side, trying to circle the creature from the left. A leg stabbed at me like a spear. I dodged and it scoured the concrete where I had stood a moment ago, gouging a chunk from it. The other leg swung at me. I saw it coming, but I could do nothing about it. It swept me off my feet. I flew across the grass. My back smashed against something solid, wood snapped with a dry crunch, and I crashed through the fence.

Ow. I rolled to my feet.

Curran stood in the middle of the street, his hands still locked on the insect's front pair of legs. The spider-scorpion was lunging at him again and again, trying to grip him with its pincers. If those mandibles closed on Curran, they'd slice his arms off.

Oh no, you don't.

I charged the spider. The legs stabbed at me. I dodged back and forth. How the hell could it even see me? A leg landed in front of me; I ducked left and saw one of the black eyeballs swivel, following me. It could look back and front at the same time.

I thrust into the opening between two legs. Sarrat sliced into the insect's abdomen and I ripped the blade back, opening a cut. A leg cut at me, scraping against my back and side as I spun to avoid it. Pain lanced me. I jumped back. Clear ichor dripped from the cut, revealing clumps of translucent guts, like clusters of fish bladders. An acrid stench, sharp and fetid, like the odor of rotting fish, washed over me. The insect didn't even notice.

"Kate," Curran ground out. "Hit it with magic."

"I can't." The legs sliced at me like a windmill of blades. "You're holding it. You'll be hit, too. Let go of it."

"If I let go of it, it will tear me apart."

He couldn't throw it either. The insect's center of mass was suspended too high above the ground. Curran didn't have the leverage.

The only word that wouldn't cause him direct harm would freeze the spider-scorpion for four seconds. I wouldn't be able to do enough damage. The moment they both came to, the insect would cut Curran to pieces.

He couldn't hold it forever.

The leg directly above me rose, aiming to pierce my chest from above. I dove under it, right under the abdomen pulsing with contractions, and stabbed straight up. Ichor drenched me. My eyes watered from the stench. I stabbed again and again, ripping the slippery fish-bladder innards. The guts spilled through the gashes, hanging like some gross fruit. I wasn't doing enough damage.

Curran snarled. The abdomen moved up half a foot. The thing was gaining on him.

I thrust my left hand under my T-shirt, where the leg had cut me. My fingers came out bloody. I sat straight up and thrust my wet hand into the cut I'd made. The magic in my blood screamed, eager to be unleashed. I gave it a push. The blood streamed from my wound up my shoulder, up my arm, into the spider-insect, and turned solid. A dozen thin spikes pierced the creature from within.

The spider-scorpion screeched. *Felt that, did you? Have some more.*

The abdomen plunged at me. The insect had reared, trying to crush me. I thrust my arms up, crossing them to block. Suddenly the abdomen disappeared. I rolled right and jumped to my feet.

On the street the spider-scorpion dashed at Curran. The meat chunk of its head that powered the left mandible looked mangled. Curran must've punched it when it reared.

I ran at it.

The spider thrust with its front leg. Curran batted it aside. The second leg stabbed, too fast. The narrow blade of the front segment sliced into Curran's shoulder. He grabbed the leg with his left hand and smashed his right palm against the joint. The front segment broke off.

I lunged between the insect's back legs, jumped, and landed on the spider-scorpion's back. The creature flailed. I stabbed Sarrat as deep as it would go and clung to it.

Curran ripped the chunk of the spider-scorpion's leg out of his body and buried it in the insect's side, right under the broken limb.

I dragged myself up along the abdomen, trying to get to the head and the two black balls of the eyes.

Curran grabbed the broken leg and kept stabbing, hitting the same spot. Ichor flew. The insect screeched like nails on chalkboard and flailed back and forth.

I wouldn't get to the eyes. It would throw me off.

I yanked Sarrat out, grabbed onto the edge of the wound I'd made, and sliced into the creature's thorax, trying to saw its abdomen from its chest.

Curran kept stabbing.

Pierce, pull out, pierce, pull out, pierce . . .

Curran bit into the spider's leg and ripped it out.

Pierce, pull out, pierce . . .

Moments flew by.

My breath was coming out in ragged gasps. *Die, damn you. Die already. Die!*

The spider-scorpion shuddered.

Curran leaped onto its head. Claws flashed and the spider-scorpion went blind. I kept carving. Curran began punching the back of the spider-scorpion's head.

The thorax broke off from the abdomen. The gut swayed and fell, splattering the translucent innards over the pavement in a wet splat. The chitin sheathing the spider-scorpion's head caved in and broke. The front part of the creature careened and fell, taking us with it. I blinked and then I was sitting on the ground face to face with Curran, the wet ichor under us sliding out from the spider-scorpion's crushed carapace.

My whole body ached as if I had run a long race. I was out of breath. Rapidly cooling sweat slicked my hairline. I felt light-headed. I might have pulled out too much blood.

Curran was breathing deep. The wound on his shoulder gaped with red. The edges had begun to pull together, but long brown bristles stuck out of it—the stiff "hairs" that had lined the giant insect's leg.

"Do we have a flamethrower?" Curran asked.

"No."

"We should get a flamethrower."

We looked at each other. The stench was almost unbearable now. I was covered head to toe with spider-scorpion slime and my own blood. Curran leaned over and spat to the side. That's right. He'd bitten the damn thing.

". . . water of the speed and the spirit . . ." a male voice intoned to the right.

I turned.

Across the street Mac and Leroy were trying to chant the FJ Cruiser's water engine into life.

You've got to be kidding me.

The two mercs saw us. My stare and Mac's connected. I forced myself to stand up.

"Oh, no, no, no." Mac jerked his arms up. "Don't get up. We're leaving."

Next to me Curran bared his teeth.

Leroy grabbed a bag out of the car. "This is my shit!"

They took off down the street at a run.

I turned to Curran and pointed at them. I had no words left. He shook his head.

I reached out with my magic, searching for small droplets of my blood. It answered my call. I pushed. The blood flowed out of the spider-scorpion corpse, pooling on the pavement into a small puddle. It turned solid and shattered into powder, all of its magic gone. The wind swiped it off the pavement as if it had never been there.

The front door of the house opened slowly and an African American woman in her forties stepped out. She was wearing a business suit. Behind her two teenage boys craned their necks, trying to see.

The woman walked over to us, carefully picking her way between puddles of slime, and held out a check. The edge of the check danced, trembling. I wiped my hand on my jeans the best I could and took it.

She turned around to her boys. "Get the animals into the crates and take what you need. Tony, call your father and tell him we'll be at Red Roof Inn. He can meet us there."

"If there is anything else . . ." I started.

"There won't be anything else," she said. "We are moving."

MRS. OSWALD WASN'T a cooperative witness. She was mostly concerned with getting her two children, two cats, and a husky into her car and escaping the scene as fast as she could. The only reason we got anything at all was that Curran and I agreed to stand guard over her while she packed and started her SUV. She had no idea who was after her cats. She hadn't fought with any neighbors. She had no conflicts at work, at least nothing that would warrant an attack on her cats. Her husband was out of town on a business trip.

On Sunday, February 27, Mrs. Oswald came home and found a very large tick in her backyard. The tick told her in a creepy voice that it was after her cats. She called the Guild. An hour later Eduardo arrived and killed the tick. Some people from the city—likely the Biohazard division of PAD—came and got the remains that night. The wolf griffin appeared on Monday morning. It was the size of a springer spaniel at first, and it ignored her and her two sons completely. It kept trying to claw its way into the house, but the bars held and the small beast didn't seem like a terrible threat, so she'd called Eduardo again and gone to work. When she came home, the griffin was gone. Considering that the magic wave ended on Monday around nine in the morning, that wasn't surprising. She thought Eduardo came out while she was at work and took care of it or that the wolf griffin flew away.

This morning when Mrs. Oswald was about to leave for work after a magic wave came, a much larger griffin swooped down on her and tried to maul her. She'd run back inside and called the Guild.

Watching it turn into a giant bug was too much for her.

"Can I use your phone to call Biohazard?!" I yelled over the roar of the enchanted water engine.

"Do what you need to do! I have my kids to take care of!"

Mrs. Oswald stepped on the gas and peeled out of the driveway like a bat out of hell. I went inside and checked the phone. Dial tone. Well, something had gone right for once. I dialed the Biohazard number from memory.

"Biohazard," a gruff male voice said into the phone.

"My name's Kate Daniels. I have a giant dead spider-scorpion thing on Chamblee Dunwoody Road. I need you to come and get it."

"Sure," the voice said. "Let me get right on that. You're eighth in line. It will be twenty-four hours."

"It's an RM in a residential neighborhood."

The phone went silent. "How bad?"

"It went from mammal to insect after death. The insect is ten feet long, not counting the legs."

"Sit tight. We'll be there in half an hour."

Experience said it would be more like a couple of hours, but I would take what I could get. I dialed Cutting Edge. Derek answered, his voice raspy. "Cutting Edge."

"Can you meet us here?" I gave him the address.

"I'm leaving now."

"Thanks. Is Ascanio there?"

"Ready and willing," Ascanio said into the phone.

"Call the Dunwoody Police Department for me and please check if there were any complaints against the Oswalds on Chamblee Dunwoody Road." I gave him the address.

"Yes, Consort."

Either it was force of habit or he was jerking my chain. Probably the latter. I hung up and went into the garage. A toolbox sitting by the wall yielded a pair of needle-nose pliers. Perfect.

I found Curran outside. He had turned into a human, had pulled his clothes on despite being covered in slime, and was trying to rinse his mouth out with a hose.

"Did it taste that bad?"

"You have no idea. This goo doesn't wash off with water alone. I tried."

"Let me see your shoulder."

He glanced at me. I lifted the pliers and made pinch motions with them.

"Are we done?" he asked.

"No. We have to wait here until Biohazard shows up."

"Why? It's dead."

I sighed and sat on the stairs in front of the door. "Because it exhibited reanimative metamorphosis. It was dead and instead of staying dead, it turned into something else and came back to life. It also went cross-phylum, from mammal to insect. That means there is a good chance it might come back to life again as something really strange, like a terrestrial octopus shooting lightning from its tentacles."

"Why don't we just set it on fire and scatter the ashes?"

"Because the ashes could still metamorphose into something nasty like leeches or flesh-eating flowers. We killed it. That means we initiated the RM process, so now we have to watch over the corpse until Biohazard shows up and quarantines it."

"And if we don't?" His tone was getting harsher and harsher.

"It's a mandatory ten-year prison sentence."

"So we performed a service by killing this thing and now they are punishing us for it?"

"Yep."

"This is ridiculous. You're bleeding. Don't lie to me, I can smell it. You're hurt. You need a medmage."

"I'm not hurt that badly."

His lips wrinkled, showing his teeth. "How badly do you have to be hurt?"

"There is a right-to-life exemption, which permits us to leave the scene if our injuries are life threatening. We'd have to provide paperwork from a hospital, or a qualified medmage, showing that we had to get treatment or we would've died. My injuries are not life threatening."

"Paperwork is not a problem."

"Yes, but I won't lie."

"How do you know your injuries aren't life threatening? You're covered in the fluid from its guts. How do you know it's not poisonous?"

"If it's poisonous, we'll deal with it when I feel sick."

"Fine. I'll stay here with this thing, and you will drive yourself to the hospital."

"No."

He hit me with an alpha stare.

I opened my eyes as wide as I could. "Why, of course, Your Majesty. What was I thinking? I will go and do this right away, just please don't look at me."

"Kate, get in the car."

"Maybe you should growl dramatically. I don't think I'm intimidated enough."

"I will put you in the car."

"No, you won't. First, it took both of us to kill that thing, and if it reinvents itself again, it will take both of us again. I'm not leaving you alone with it. Second, if you try to physically carry me to the car, I will resist and bleed more. Third, you can possibly stuff me in the car against my will, but you can't make me drive."

He snarled. "Argh! Why don't you ever do anything I ask you to?"

"Because you don't ask. You tell me."

We glared at each other.

"I'm not going to the hospital because of a shallow cut." And possibly a sprained shoulder, a few gashes to my legs, and a bruised right side. "It could be worse. I could've hit a brick wall instead of a nice, fragile old fence . . ."

He held up his hand. "I'm going to get a medkit out of the car."

I didn't even know any medmages besides Doolittle, who worked for the Pack. The woman who used to patch me up before I met Curran had moved away. I'd have to figure this out before long. In our line of work, access to a good medmage was paramount.

His Grumpiness returned with the medkit. I pulled my turtleneck up, trying not to wince, and turned my back to him.

Silence.

"It's not that bad."

His hands brushed my skin, warm and careful. The cold saline solution washed over the cut and I shivered.

"What about this?" Curran's fingers touched the aching spot on my left side.

"That's from the ghouls the other night. I'll chant over it once you're done cleaning. It will heal itself."

Cold wind touched my wet back, making my teeth dance. *Thanks, weather. Screw you, too.*

"The rationale is, since we killed it once, we could probably kill it again. This is a residential neighborhood. We are going to do the right thing and watch over it."

"This is a dumb law," Curran said. "It's easier to just not get involved."

I grinned. "Aha! Now you are catching on. Welcome to human society, Your Majesty."

"Kate. Chant."

Ten minutes later he decided the wound had closed enough to put a bandage over it. I pulled my turtleneck over my back. Unfortunately while it was rolled up, it had time to cool and now it felt like ice on my skin. Being covered in ichor didn't help. Curran sat next to me.

"Shoulder," I told him. He took his shirt off, displaying the world's best chest to the wind. I clamped the first insect hair sticking out of him with my pliers. It was about the size of a thin metal skewer. "Ready?"

"Do it."

I ripped the hair out. It was ten inches long.

He made a short gritty noise. It had to have hurt like hell. I wiped the blood off his shoulder with gauze. "Four more."

"No time like the present."

I managed all four in under a minute. The less he hurt, the better. Curran put his shirt back on and pulled me close. His eyes were dark. Whatever he was thinking wasn't good.

"You okay?" I asked.

"Yeah."

I had a feeling he was thinking that if he were still the Beast Lord, by now he would've had a team of shapeshifters standing guard over the corpse while he drove me to the Keep, where Doolittle would put me back on my feet.

"Being a human isn't that bad, is it?" I asked.

"You remember the Savells? The house across the street from us?"

Heather Savell was a thorn in my side. The area didn't have a homeowners' association, but Heather very much wanted to have one. In her head, she pretended the HOA was real and she was its president. She took those imaginary powers and responsibilities very seriously. "Sure."

"They sprinkled cayenne pepper around the border of their lawn."

I almost ground my teeth. They sprinkled cayenne pepper to keep Curran off the property, like he was a stray dog come sniffing.

"Apparently they don't understand I could step over it."

"I'll talk to them."

He shook his head again. "No. They're scared because they don't know me. I get them. I don't get you. Why are you protecting them?"

"Because they can't always protect themselves."

Curran looked at me, his face hard. "In the Pack, everyone is of a kind. We all belong together. We are united. Everyone contributes, some more, some less. We work toward a common goal of living a safe life."

"So do these people."

Curran grimaced. "If I were beating you in the street, they wouldn't lift a finger to help you."

"If you were beating me in the middle of the Keep, would anyone lift a finger? Or would they all simply decide to look away because alphas are fighting and it's none of their business?"

Curran growled. "Kate . . ."

"You have a prejudice against people who are not shapeshifters." I leaned against him. He put his arm around me. "It's not a baseless prejudice, because when people fear someone, they treat them with suspicion. To a lot of people, shapeshifters are monsters, and you were the king of the monsters. I understand. To the Pack, I was a monster and they treated me accordingly."

"Not all of them."

"No, not all of them. That's exactly my point."

I turned my head and kissed him. His lips were warm and the familiar taste dashed across my tongue.

"You've never lived among non-shapeshifters, Curran. I have. I've seen a man run into a burning building to save a dog. I've seen people sacrifice themselves for strangers. Not all of them are willing to do this, but enough to matter. That's why I help them. Give them a chance. I think they might surprise you."

He sighed and squeezed me closer to him.

"Are you seriously considering taking over the Guild?" I asked him. "It's in shambles."

He grinned at me. It was the happy smile of an amused predator. "I've got this."

"They will never be another Pack. They're too independent. And they don't like authority."

"I don't need another Pack. The Pack has too many rules anyway. I have some ideas for these guys. They just don't know it yet."

"They'll fight you every step of the way."

"I hope so." Curran laughed quietly. "I'd take them on one at a time or in batches. It would be fun."

This unchained thing was making him scary. "That's what I love about you, Your Furriness. Your humility and modesty."

"Don't forget my razor-sharp wit and boyish good looks."

"Boyish?"

"The Guild has something the Pack doesn't," Curran said. "Variety. There are shooters, melee fighters, and magic users. It might be what we will need to . . ." He paused.

"What is it?"

"The wind changed." Curran rose and walked down the sidewalk. I followed him. We passed a lamppost, another . . . Another twenty yards and I would have to turn back. We were getting too far away from the spider-scorpion's corpse.

Curran stopped and crouched. A large pale scrape crossed the sidewalk. He inhaled deeply, wrinkling his face.

"What is it?"

His expression was grim. "Ghouls. Lots of ghouls."

A long ululating shriek of magic-powered sirens rolled through the streets. The cavalry was coming.

6

BIOHAZARD ARRIVED IN style: two black SUVs and an armored semi carrying steel containers instead of a trailer. The SUVs vomited ten people in Biohazard contamination suits and one stocky, dark-haired man in a red hoodie. On the hoodie white letters spelled out WIZARD AT LARGE. Small world.

The wizard at large stabbed his finger at me. "You! The unclean one! Tell me everything."

"Hi, Luther. I thought you worked for the PAD."

He made a sour face. "Too much politics, too little magic. They have issues with my professional strategy. Also, their dental sucks."

"So you got fired?"

"I quit."

"When I quit the Order, you told me I was besmirched."

"That's because you quit in a huff over some silliness like trying to save people's lives. I quit to maximize my earning potential. Don't you know being a hero is a losing bet? The pay is shit and people hate you for it." Luther looked at Curran. "Who is the male specimen?"

Curran offered Luther his hand. "Lennart."

Luther grabbed Curran's hand and smelled it. "Shapeshifter, feline, probably a lion, but not the run-of-the-mill African Simba. You've got an odd scent about you." He glanced at me. "Why do you always hang out with weirdos?"

"It's her special talent," Curran said. "She attracts us like bees to honey."

Luther shook his head and turned to the corpse of the bug. The Biohazard artist was busily trying to sketch it, while the rest of the crew stood around it with acid and flamethrowers. "Tell me about the thing."

I explained Mrs. Oswald's story.

"It spoke?" Luther asked.

"Yes." Normal apparitions weren't sentient. They didn't speak, and if they did, not with that much power. "There was a lot of magic in the voice. You could feel it on your skin."

"I don't like it," Luther said.

I didn't like it either. "Someone has a grudge against cats. I don't know if it was Mrs. Oswald's particular cats or any cats in general. But the cat hater is persistent. First he or she sent a tick. After Eduardo killed it, the Summoner followed it with the griffin, and when the griffin was too small to break through the bars, he or she must've sunk some magic into it to make it bigger. And then it turned into that." I nodded at the corpse. "I don't even know what the hell it is."

"We got a bug guy back at HQ. I'll give you a call when he sorts it out." Luther pondered the corpse. "The cross-phylum metamorphosis bothers me."

It bothered me, too.

The sketch artist waved his sketchbook. "Done."

"Okay, mates," Luther called. "Bag it, tag it, and chain it up."

The crew began rolling out plastic.

"Hey, Luther," I said. "You guys didn't hire any new ghouls, did you?"

Luther spun to me, his eyes focused, like a shark sensing a drop of blood in the water. "You know something. Tell me."

"The Pack scouts found a lot of dead ghouls on a road to the east," Curran said. "We had breakfast with the Beast Lord and he mentioned it."

Luther pondered him. "Sure, I'll buy that. Oh wait, I have a brain. Sorry, completely forgot. The ghouls were found in pieces. Someone ripped them apart with claws and cut them to pieces with a sword. And here the two of you are, one has claws and the other has a sword."

"We're not the only people in the city with swords and claws," Curran said.

Luther squinted at us. "What are you two up to?"

"Right now, nothing," I said.

"I don't believe you."

Derek jogged up the street. He wore a gray hoodie and a pair of old jeans, and he was running in that particular wolf gait that looked unhurried but devoured miles. Nineteen, just under six feet, with dark hair and a muscular athletic body, Derek turned heads. Then people saw his face. A couple of years ago he tried to save a girl. The creatures who owned her caught him and poured molten metal on his face. He recovered, but his face looked different now. His features were rougher, their once-handsome perfection gone. His eyes made it worse. They were dark and hard, the kind of eyes that belonged to someone older, someone who'd been through the grinder of pain and suffering and come out of it damaged but unbroken. He leaned against our Jeep and slouched.

"Fine," I said. "We have a missing shapeshifter and we're trying to find him. We could use some help."

Luther held up his hand. "Stop right there. Shapeshifters are Pack business. Unless they request our help in writing, I can't do anything. I don't even want to hear it."

What a surprise. Hold me before my heart gives out from the pure shock of that surprise. "Wow, so nice of you to care."

"The Beast Lord is an asshole," Luther said. "I've dealt with his representatives before, and let me tell you, I don't want to piss him off."

I really wanted to look at Curran's face, but I would have to turn and it would seem odd. "Tell me about the ghouls, Luther."

"I can neither confirm nor deny."

Seriously? "It's a matter of public record. I can go down to City Hall and spend three hours digging through the Biohazard disclosures or you could just tell me. If I have to waste all that time, I'll be irritated."

Luther leaned back. "Be still my heart. And I suppose I should be terrified of that?"

"No, just pointing out that I don't like to share when I'm irritated. You want to know why a horde of ghouls tried to enter the city. We also want to know why that happened. We will eventually figure this out and then we can take it to you or to your former bosses at PAD."

He sighed. "No, we didn't hire any new ghouls."

"Have you talked to Mitchell?" I asked.

"He doesn't want to talk." Luther grimaced. "Something is going on with him."

"He may talk to me."

"That's true." Luther sighed again. "I tell you what, I'll let you see Mitchell, but if he talks to you, you tell me what he said. I want to know what's happening to him."

"Deal." I'd be an idiot not to take it. "Tonight."

"No, tomorrow night. We fed him last night. He's sleeping it off."

Mitchell didn't like the outside. He hid in his burrow most of the time, and getting him out of it after he ate would be impossible. I had tried before and gotten nowhere. "I'll take tomorrow then."

"Good. We're done here, you are released, shoo, go, scram. Don't do anything I wouldn't do, kids."

I started toward the cars.

"Wait," Luther called.

"Yes?"

He trotted over to me. "Does the city feel different to you?"

"Different how?"

He dragged his hand through his hair. "Something happened in December. Something strange."

Move along, nothing to see here, no city claiming people are on the premises. "Strange things happen all the time here."

"No, this was different. It felt like a storm. A magic storm. It rolled through the city and now it feels different. Does it feel different to you?"

Lie, lie, lie. "No."

Luther searched my face with his gaze. "I'm not crazy."

No, you're not. "That's above my pay grade."

"It's like an itch I can't scratch."

"Maybe you should see a doctor for that," Curran said.

Luther pointed his finger at him. "I don't like you."

"Bye, Luther." I grinned.

He walked away. "I will figure it out! I'm not crazy!"

If he ever figured it out, I would have a lot of explaining to do.

"DOES EVERYBODY THINK I am an asshole?" Curran asked.

"Only people who know you or have met you."

He looked at me for a long second.

"You were a zealous advocate of the Pack's causes," I said. "The Pack's interests are often at odds with human interests. I still love you. Derek still thinks you're the stuff."

Derek was kneeling by the scrape on the pavement and inhaling deeply. "Three ghouls. One male and two females. The scent is about fifty hours old, give or take an hour."

Fifty hours would be just about the time Eduardo would have come to respond to Mrs. Oswald's phone call on Monday about the wolf griffin.

"Interesting timing," I said.

"They came here and left along the same trail," Derek said.

"How long were they here?" Curran asked.

"A few hours." Derek pointed to a narrow spot between the side of the house and a wooden fence. "They hid there, behind the trash cans."

Three ghouls just sitting there waiting while the residents of the house left for work. *Don't mind us, we're just chilling here, behind your trash cans, rubbing our big sharp claws, while your delicious children leave for school.* And that wasn't creepy. No, not at all.

"Why?" I thought out loud. "If they were hiding, there are better places to hide."

"Mm-hm." Curran's face told me he was thinking the same thing. "Bad place to hide but a good place for an ambush."

I glanced back at Mrs. Oswald's house. A couple of houses down, the street ended in a cul-de-sac. Only one way in or out.

"Any other scents?" I asked. "Any human scents? Anyone they attacked?"

Derek shook his head.

Curran looked at me. "Does this seem odd to you?"

"Everything about this seems odd to me. Ghouls are solitary. They live near cemeteries, they hide in burrows, and they travel at dawn or during the night. They don't band into groups and prance about in broad daylight in a residential neighborhood. Unless the owner of that house is a serial killer and he's got his victims buried in his backyard, there is no reason for them to be here."

"There are no bodies in the backyard," Derek said. "I would've smelled decomp."

Sense of humor check, failed.

"The point is, it's highly unlikely that these two odd things"—I pointed at the trash cans with one hand and at the corpse of the spider-scorpion with the other—"aren't connected. I think they were waiting for Eduardo." And I would give a year of my life to know why. "The ghouls we killed in Lawrenceville were answering someone's call. They said someone was waiting for them. They don't meet people for coffee or brunch. I think some being is using them for their own means."

"That would explain their organization and unusual behavior," Derek said.

"Can you track them?" Curran asked.

"Sure." Derek smiled.

"Let's go ask them," Curran said.

"I'll get the car," I said. I would only slow them down on foot.

Fifteen minutes later I chased them in a Jeep. I'd have to send someone back later to pick up George's car.

Lions weren't known for their marathon racing abilities, but Curran was a werelion and by human standards he was a superb runner. He and Derek flew down the street at thirty miles per hour, which for them was probably a refreshing pace.

Ghouls came from the Arabic mythos. One of the earliest known references to them occurred in *One Thousand and One Nights*. The wolf griffins were rumored to have been native to North Africa and were familiar to Berbers. Muslims conquered North Africa around the seventh century BC, so technically there was some tenuous geographical connection between the griffin and the ghouls. And that's where it all stopped making sense. Ghouls didn't answer to any higher authority. They weren't undead, they retained their free will, and all attempts to control them by outside forces usually ended badly. They were cowardly solitary scavengers or predators of opportunity, who dug deep burrows and hid from people and sunlight. I had no idea how the spider-scorpion thing or the cats fit into it.

Maybe whoever was behind the creatures attacking Mrs. Oswald got really annoyed at Eduardo's interference and had the ghouls kidnap or kill him? But that would imply that this whoever could control an army of ghouls. Or maybe knew someone who could and that someone owed him a favor. If you're powerful enough to control ghouls, why would you even care about some cats?

I blew the air out of my mouth. All this wild speculation was just that— speculation. Until we found some evidence, all my outlandish theories were worthless.

Ahead Curran and Derek turned left on Valley View Road. I followed. Small residential houses lined the street, couched in trees and brush. It looked like a relatively quiet neighborhood. No neighborhood was completely safe in post-Shift Atlanta, but this was one of the more stable ones. And as far as I knew, Eduardo had no connection to it besides the random job he'd taken at the Guild.

This mess was getting more and more convoluted. Convoluted wasn't my favorite. I remembered George thrusting herself in front of a blade to protect a pregnant Desandra. My mind helpfully brought up a recollection of Eduardo knocked out cold and covered in his blood. He'd tried to keep a monster from attacking Doolittle and Jim's sister and nearly died. George and Eduardo had suffered enough. They'd earned their happiness. I wanted to put them back together and see them happy. I wanted them to marry and have cute babies.

Where the hell are you, Eduardo? What have you gotten yourself into?

We turned left onto Ashford Dunwoody Road. The remnants of a Walmart came into view on the left. Curran and Derek veered toward it. The three hundred yards between me and the Walmart looked like someone had taken a blender to a warehouse: sharp chunks of concrete littered the ground, bound together by twisted metal rebar and broken wooden beams. Broken glass, dull with dirt, glittered here and there, catching a random ray of the sun. Great. If I followed them, I might as well just jump out and slice my tires now.

Derek slowed and made small circles among the debris. The ghouls must've lingered there.

Curran tensed, his whole body compressing like a tight spring, and leaped onto a six-foot-high concrete boulder. He landed light and straightened, his gaze fixed on the crumbling corpse of the big-box store. His broad shoulders and the line of his back curved slightly. The wind pulled on his sweats, revealing a glimpse of his hard body, muscles ready to launch him at some unseen threat in an instant. That potential power was like a magnet. If I didn't know him and I was driving by, I would've stopped to get a second look, trying to figure out who that scary hot bastard was.

I would go home with him tonight. Go me.

Okay. There was something seriously wrong with me. First, I was staring at him like some sort of love-struck idiot. Second, I was doing it while sitting in the middle of the street with the motor running. If another vehicle came barreling down the road, I'd get to experience the fun and excitement of a head-on collision. I pulled the car to the curb. It was a consequence of the blood loss. Sure. That was it.

Derek did a one-eighty and ran past me down the road. Curran leaped off the boulder and caught up with him. *Here we go again.* I eased off the brake. Meadow Lane Road . . . A ruined parking garage loomed on our left, half-hidden behind pines. Curran and Derek ducked into it. I parked the Jeep and went down the slope after them.

The parking garage stretched before me. I stood for a moment, letting my eyes adjust to the gloom. Bare vines, still reeling from winter, blanketed the right and left sides of the garage, growing denser toward the back, where the ceiling of the structure had caved in. Three cars, pinned in place by the crushing weight of concrete, rusted quietly in the far left corner. Next to them Curran waited. Derek crouched by him. In front of them a fissure split the concrete wall. From here it looked solid black, at least eight feet tall and three feet wide.

Of course. Why wouldn't it be a terrible dark pit? Just once I would like it to be a breezy path through some garden with roses and sunshine.

I jogged to them. Derek pivoted on his feet toward me. "The trail leads in there."

No, it doesn't. "Okay."

Derek ducked into the gap. I looked after him. The concrete ended after about five feet, merging into a tunnel dug in soil, angling down. A cold, dank odor washed over me.

No.

I felt Curran behind me and straightened. My back brushed against his chest. I didn't want to go down into that hole. I would do almost anything else. I just didn't want to go down there.

"Baby?" Curran asked.

"Yes?"

Right now Eduardo could be down there, waiting for help. I stepped into the gap and started moving. I just had to put one foot in front of the other and not think about thousands of pounds of soil and rock that would bury me alive if it collapsed.

"You okay?" he asked quietly.

"I'm great." I could barely see Derek in the darkness moving ahead of me. My imagination painted an avalanche of loose dirt dropping into the tunnel in front of me, burying me, getting sucked into my lungs . . . I tasted adrenaline on my tongue. Tunnels were never on my favorite list of things, but today my body was going into overdrive.

"Your pulse is speeding up."

I just had to pick a shapeshifter. "Apparently dark narrow tunnels leading deep underground don't agree with me."

He wrapped his arms around me. I stopped. My heart was hammering against my ribs. What the hell was wrong with me?

Curran kissed my hair. His voice was a quiet warm whisper in my ear. "This isn't Mishmar."

Memories cascaded through my mind like a bucket of cold water dumped over my head. Being trapped in a tunnel filled with water, clinging to the metal grate, holding Ghastek's head so he wouldn't drown, running through the dark passageways while hundreds of undead chased us . . .

Curran's voice cut through it, calm and reassuring. "We aren't trapped. It's just a hole in the dirt."

I inhaled deeply, leaning on him. Breathing from the bottom of your lungs short-circuited anxiety, and so I breathed slowly, trying to get my exhales to last longer than my inhales, and stood wrapped in him.

My pulse slowed. The odd uncomfortable panic was still there, but it receded far enough that I could keep a lid on it. I squeezed his hand. "I'm good."

He let me go and I pushed my way through, trying to speed up.

The tunnel narrowed. My shoulders brushed the dirt. Great. The anxiety hammered at me. I concentrated on my breathing, slow and deep.

A minute passed. Another.

Just keep moving. Keep moving. It will end.

It will end.

It felt like we'd been underground for eternity. It had to be at least thirty minutes.

It had to end . . .

How far did this damn tunnel go?

A hand rested on the small of my back and slid down.

"Did you just grab my butt?" I whispered.

"What?"

"Curran!"

"Yes?" I could hear controlled laughter in his voice.

Unbelievable. I sped up. "We're tracking ghouls and you're grabbing my butt."

"I always make sure to pay attention to important things."

"Sure you do."

"Besides, if the tunnel collapses, I won't get to do it again."

"You won't get to do it again anyway. I can't even see Derek anymore. He probably heard about your butt-grabbing and decided to give us some space."

"Maybe you just move too slow."

Argh.

"You should try making more noise as you walk, too." Curran suggested. "Maybe the ghouls will mistake you for a small underground elephant and run off."

"When we get out of here, I'll kick you."

"You'll try."

The tunnel turned. A faint light illuminated Derek almost fifty yards ahead of me. He jumped down into the light. I double-timed it. A moment and I grabbed onto the edge of the tunnel's opening. A large open cavern spread before me, its floor about seven feet below, illuminated by daylight streaming in through a hole in its ceiling. The ray of light fell onto a mangled vehicle sitting upright in the middle of the floor, its hood a crushed Coke can of a mess, its back up in the air. Derek was nowhere in sight.

A mangled black vehicle.

A sick feeling pulled at my stomach. I jumped down. The impact of hard ground punched the soles of my feet. The cavern stretched into a large tunnel to the left and to the right, too uniform not to be manmade. It just got better and better.

Curran landed next to me, silent like a ghost. It wasn't fair that a man that large could move that quietly.

"MARTA," I told him.

He frowned at me.

"Metropolitan Atlanta Rapid Transit Authority. We just entered the Red Line."

MARTA began in the 1970s and grew into a network of bus lines and heavy rail stations, some above ground, some under. In its heyday, over four hundred thousand people rode it daily, but the magic waves crushed it. The trains were the first to go. Not that many of them crashed, but magic spawned nightmarish creatures who enjoyed hiding in dark tunnels and grabbing tasty snacks conveniently aggregating on the platforms for them. People refused to go underground. The buses held out for a while, but finally the city threw in the towel. Now MARTA stations stood abandoned, their tunnels turned into lairs by things with sharp teeth.

"How far does it go?" Curran asked.

"I have no idea. They were expanding it when the Shift happened. There are probably miles of rail underground." Tracking ghouls through miles of tunnels would be like hunting a rat in a maze with a dozen exits.

We moved together, quietly walking toward the vehicle. Where the hell had boy wonder gotten off to?

The SUV sat directly under the hole. I looked up. It was just large enough for a vehicle to pass through.

"Is it a Tahoe?"

Curran reached up, grabbed the transmission, and pulled. Metal groaned as the butt of the SUV tipped toward Curran. It's good to be a werelion.

"Yep. It's a Tahoe."

Dread washed over me in a cold clammy wave. It had to be Eduardo's car. The ghouls had killed him, left his body to rot, and pushed the car in here, where nobody would find it.

Curran lowered the SUV and let it fall the last two feet. Long gashes scoured the paint on the sides. Ghoul claws. The tinted windows of the vehicle had cracked but hadn't fallen out. Dust sheathed the cracks. I couldn't see anything. I reached for the driver's-side door. In my head, Eduardo's mangled corpse soaked in his own blood in the driver's seat.

Don't be dead . . . don't be dead . . .

I pulled the door open. It swung with a screech, revealing the cab.

Empty.

Oh phew. Phew.

Curran pulled the other door off. "I smell him. It's his car."

The interior of the Tahoe looked like it had been through a tornado made of knives.

"Does he smell dead?"

"No." He inhaled. "It reeks of ghouls."

"Our ghouls? The ones we killed?"

"No, a different group. These scents are older."

So we had more than one group of ghouls running amok.

Derek walked out of the left tunnel. "The trail stops here."

"What do you mean, stops?" I asked.

"I walked in both directions." Derek leaned against the grimy wall. "The trail comes here and then simply stops. There are no fresh ghoul scent trails in either tunnel."

"They didn't just fly off," I said.

"Could they grow wings?" Curran asked.

"I doubt it." Ghouls with wings, that was all we needed. "If they could grow wings, they would've done it by now. It's a great defensive adaptation and they are cowards."

"Their scent says they got here and then they vanished," Derek said.

I rubbed my face. "That would suggest teleportation."

"D'Ambray teleports," Curran said.

"Yes, but Hugh uses power words and special water that's been messed with by Roland. That teleportation is my father's exclusive trick. Besides, I would know if Hugh were in the city."

"How?" Derek asked.

"I would feel him crossing the border into Atlanta."

Curran leaned toward me. "There is a border?"

"Yes."

"Were you planning on sharing that with the class?" His voice was quiet.

"It didn't come up."

He didn't look happy. When in trouble, change the subject. "The point is, teleportation is a difficult thing that takes a crap ton of magic."

"Is 'crapton' a technical term?" Derek asked.

Smartass. "Yes," I growled. "I examined a scene of teleportation during the Lighthouse Keeper mess. It was done by volhves."

Volhves were Russian druids, and unlike the actual druids, who were struggling to overcome the historical stigma of human sacrifice, volhves didn't give a damn.

"These were really powerful pagan priests, but they had to sacrifice a human being to get enough juice."

"What's your point?" Curran asked.

"Look around you. No signs of a ritual. Just dirt."

The three of us surveyed the cavern.

"I have no idea what we are dealing with," I said. "I really, really don't like it."

"We need Julie," Curran said.

Once magic came on the scene, it was quickly determined that figuring out the nature of magic at any given crime scene was vital. That was why investigators used m-scanners, clunky heavy contraptions that sampled the magic and spat out colored printouts of it: blue for human, purple for vampire, green for shapeshifter, and so on. Julie was the human equivalent of an m-scanner, and she was much more sensitive than the most advanced model.

I pulled the keys out of my pocket. "She should be at home by now."

Curran eyed the hole in the cavern's ceiling. It was fully forty feet up. Derek took the keys, put them in his jeans, and backed up for a running start. Curran locked his hands together and crouched, holding them out like a step. Derek charged him, fast like a blur. His right foot stepped on Curran's fist, Curran straightened, his arms propelling Derek like a spring, and the boy wonder shot up like a bullet. For a second I thought he would fall short, and then his hand caught a broken metal pipe sticking out of the edge of the hole. He pulled himself up and vanished into the daylight.

LONG RIPS SCOURED the Tahoe's front passenger seat, the edges of the fabric frayed, ripped by claws rather than cut. A much smoother cut scarred the dashboard and the far edge of the passenger seat. Dents potholed the dashboard, some with pieces of bone and clumps of dark red tissue stuck to the surface. Several dark smears, thick, the color of reddish tar, stained the inside of the Tahoe, all except for the driver's seat, which meant Eduardo was in it when the fight happened. I sat in the driver's seat—my feet could barely touch the pedals—and swung my hand out. Yep. Eduardo had some sort of a short blade in his hand, probably a machete judging by the cut in the dashboard, and he'd hacked at something with it. Then the blade was ripped out of his hand, and he started bashing his attackers into the dash.

I pulled a small plastic bag out of my pocket on my belt, got a pinch of powder, and sprinkled it on the blood. The dark green powder turned white.

"Ironweed," I explained to Curran. "Ghouls don't like it. Not sure if it hurts them, but it reacts with their blood."

Curran examined the dash. "For being pinned by the seat belt and swarmed, he put up a hell of a fight."

"And that's what puzzles me." I reached over and touched the remains of Eduardo's seat belt. About eight inches of it hung from the top bracket, the end of the section rough and frayed.

"Gnawed through," Curran said.

"Yes. He was wearing the seat belt when they jumped him. You're a ghoul. This guy's hacking at you with a blade and crushing your buddies' skulls left and right, and instead of killing him right here, while he is trapped by his seat belt, you take the time to chew through it and pull him out."

"They wanted Eduardo alive," Curran said.

"But why?"

We searched the rest of the Tahoe. I found Eduardo's backpack with his lunch and his wallet in it with a hundred bucks in cash. The cache of weapons in the back of the Tahoe was intact. Any human predator would've taken the guns and the tactical blades. Whoever took Eduardo had no interest in his weapons or his money, which probably meant our ghoul theory was correct. Not only had the ghouls kidnapped Eduardo, they pushed his car into a hole to hide it. They weren't that devious under normal circumstances. Some sort of malevolent intelligence was controlling the ghouls, and it clearly had a plan. If only we could figure out what that plan was.

I sat on a rock. Curran stretched out next to me. He looked like hell. Some time ago the ichor covering us had begun to smell like rotten fish, and while we crawled around underground, loose dirt had mixed with it to form a cement-like substance on his skin and mine, in my case no doubt tainted by whatever blood seeped through the bandages. My shoulder hurt. My back hurt, too. Neither of us had eaten since morning. Curran had to be starving. Some pair we made.

He noticed me studying him. "Here we are in a filthy hole."

"Yep. Looking like two ghouls who rolled in some rotting corpses."

He flashed a grin at me. "Hey, baby. Want to fool around?"

I laughed at him.

"If I were planning to kidnap Eduardo," Curran said, "and I knew where he was going, the easiest thing would be to station some shapeshifters near his destination so they could ambush him as he arrived. Except that destination happens to be in a residential neighborhood, which meant if my people jumped Eduardo there, they would have to drag him through the streets kicking and screaming."

"Yes. Too risky. Too exposed, and too many potential witnesses," I agreed.

"I would want to grab my victim off the street fast and quiet, so I would scout the possible routes to his destination, find good places to jump him, and put a group of shapeshifters at each route and one final group near the destination itself, just as insurance."

"Makes sense." That was exactly what the ghouls did.

"So what is so special about Eduardo?"

"I don't know." I sighed. "Maybe he's a secret ghoul prince."

I wanted to climb out of the hole and kill something to make Eduardo be okay. Instead I had to sit here, twiddling my thumbs. I reached over to Curran and squeezed his hand.

"Don't worry," he said. "We'll find him. They took him alive, so they want something from him."

"It's not finding him. It's finding him in time."

"He knows help is coming," Curran said. "George loves him. He knows she's searching for him and she'd make the Pack look for him."

"I keep wondering how I missed it," I murmured.

"What?"

"George and Eduardo."

"They were very careful," Curran said. "George loves her father. She didn't want him and Eduardo fighting. Mahon is the Pack's executioner and has more experience, but Eduardo is younger, five hundred pounds heavier in beast form, and he would be very motivated. It wouldn't matter who won. When they were done, one of them would be dead and the other one dying."

"Would he really fight Eduardo?"

"Depends on the circumstances. Martha can pull Mahon back most of the time, but sometimes his brakes malfunction."

"But why? What would that accomplish except makes everyone involved miserable?"

Curran sighed. "Mahon's problem is that he has some very definite ideas about what a man's supposed to be and what a male werebear should be. It sounds great in his head and he gets carried away with it. He isn't shy about sharing his bear wisdom. Then his views collide with reality and they mostly don't survive. At the core Mahon isn't evil. He means well and he wants to be seen as a good person, so when people react badly to the nonsense coming out of his mouth, he gets shocked and has to readjust. For example, the first time Aunt B came to the Pack Council, he took it upon himself to lecture her about how men should be men and women should be women, and Clan alphas should be men with women helping them, not the other way around."

I laughed. "What did she do?"

"She petted his shoulder and said, 'Bless your heart, you must be awful in bed.'"

Ha!

"Then she turned to Martha and told her that if she ever was in need of a man who respected women enough to think they were human beings, she had several available in her clan."

That sounded like Aunt B.

"Mahon turned purple and didn't say another word through the whole Council meeting." Curran grinned. "Never brought it up again. I left him in charge once for about a month, because I had to travel out of our territory, and came back to a full revolt. It wasn't what he did—he actually governed well while I was gone—it was what he said at the Pack Council. He said he was trying to give the other alphas guidance and he was mystified why everyone wanted to tear his throat out. It would be the same with Eduardo. His initial reaction would be to rage and probably goad Eduardo into attacking him, because he loves George and he wants to be a good father, and in his mind the best thing to do, the proper thing to do, is to steer her away from what he sees as a terrible match. He's probably convinced that if George only saw things from his point of view, she would agree with him."

"I'm pretty sure he thinks that about everybody." I'd been on the receiving end of Mahon's wisdom. It made me fantasize about violence.

Curran sighed. "Mahon adores his daughters. If George went to her dad right now and cried and said that she was miserable without Eduardo and she felt awful, Mahon would drop everything and run to look for Eduardo."

I blinked. "Seriously?"

Curran nodded. "But she won't do it and I agree with her. From her point of view, why should she have to manipulate her father? She isn't asking him for a puppy. She's telling him that this is the man she loves, and she expects him to deal with it like a loving parent should. She's his daughter and she's just like him. They've butted heads for as long as I've known them. She always loves him, but sometimes she also hates him. This is one of those times."

It must've been an interesting family to grow up in. "Do you manipulate him?"

"I know what Mahon's version of the Beast Lord should say and do. When I want him to do something, I frame it in that light. With Mahon sometimes it's enough to growl and declare that he will do this because I'm the Beast Lord. He expects occasional dictatorship, because in his head that's what a capable Beast Lord would do. If I tried the same tactic with Jim, he'd tell me he'd come back later after I had my head examined."

"Mahon's Beast Lord is a hard man who makes hard decisions, huh?"

"Mm-hm. And who doesn't have time for foolishness." Curran looked up. "A car."

A moment later I heard it too, the dull roar of water engines. It sputtered and died. Julie's blond head poked through the hole. "Hello."

"Hi," I said.

Julie's head disappeared, replaced by her foot in the loop of a rope. The rope moved down, lowering Julie to the floor of the cavern. She wore her work clothes: old jeans, a black turtleneck, and boots. A tactical tomahawk rested in a loop on her belt. Thirteen inches long, the Kestrel tomahawk weighed eighteen ounces. Its wide bearded blade tapered down to a wicked spike that curved downward, sharpened to a narrow point. It was meant as a tool that occasionally could be thrown at rotten logs for fun. Julie had decided to make it her weapon of choice. None of my explanations about the versatility and lightness of swords made any dent in her.

I sighed. I had plenty of perfectly good swords, balanced and made specifically for her. When she first started carrying the axe, I tried to push her toward the sword and she resisted until I finally asked her why she dragged it with her everywhere. She said, "Because I can make a hole in anything." I decided that was good enough for me.

If the dead could judge the living, Voron, my adoptive father, was probably spinning in his grave over the axe. He'd dedicated his life to teaching me how to use a sword. He viewed it as the perfect weapon. But then Voron was long dead and I had exorcised his ghost out of my memory. He still spoke to me once in a while, but his voice no longer ruled my life.

Julie winced. "Is that Eduardo's car?"

I nodded. Derek slid down the rope.

"Okay." She turned to the half-crushed Tahoe. "Ugly yellowish orange . . . Ghouls. A lot of them."

She circled the car, moving slowly, and looked up, her gaze fixed on a point about six feet above the car. Her eyes widened. She smiled slightly, as if she were looking at something beautiful.

"It's like a flame," she murmured. "Beautiful flame. Not orange or yellow. More like copper."

"Copper?" What the hell registered copper?

"A goldish, silverish kind of copper," she said. "There was an explosion of it right there." She pointed above the Tahoe. "Like rose gold. Very pretty. I've never seen this before."

Blue meant human, silver meant divine, weak yellow meant animal . . . I had never run across goldish-silverish copper before. What the hell was I supposed to do with that? It didn't even sound right. The creature registered a rose gold color . . . I'd get laughed at.

Julie tilted her head. "It's not that variable."

"What do you mean?" Curran asked.

"Magic isn't usually one color," she said.

"The m-scanners print it as one color because they're not really that precise," I said.

"Real magic shifts and changes shades," Julie said. "Ghoul magic looks yellow-orange but it's more like streaks of olive and orange mixing together with some really light brown. Even the vampires have traces of red and blue in their purple." She glanced up. "Whatever that is, it's very uniform. There are very light flecks of gold and silver in it, but most of it is one color."

A uniform magic signature meant whatever made it emitted very concentrated specific magic. "Any blue?"

Julie shook her head.

Blue stood for human magic. Any sort of human derivative, like a ghoul's or a shapeshifter's, showed blue in their magic signature. They could never completely get rid of the traces of their humanity. Whatever this was didn't start out as a human.

I rubbed my face. It didn't give me any new insights. "Whereabout is this copper?"

Julie frowned. "About four feet above the car."

I stepped onto the Tahoe's hood and climbed onto its roof.

"What are you doing?" Curran asked.

"I don't know. I'm just trying to get a sense of things." I stood up.

"Okay, you're in it," Julie said.

I didn't feel anything. I stared up at the sky, waiting for a clue to fall out of the heavens and land on my head. At this point, I'd welcome the hit.

From here I could see the whole cave, the two tunnels, the whole area from which we had come, the dirt floor against which the Tahoe had impacted, the loose soil churned by the ghouls as they scrambled across it. A glint caught my eye to the right. Something shiny reflected the light among the dirt. An identical spark glowed to the left, exactly the same distance. Hmm. I turned slowly. More sparks, buried under the dirt.

I slid off the Tahoe. From here the glint was invisible. I pulled some gauze out of my pocket, knelt in the spot I thought I saw it, and brushed at the dirt. The loose soil slid aside, revealing a narrow ribbon of translucent shiny sand. It looked brittle, but held together as if some great heat had touched the sand and half fused it into glass.

Julie knelt next to me and reached to brush more dirt off.

"Don't touch it." I passed her the gauze. The first rule of staying alive in Atlanta: if you see something weird, stay the hell away from it.

We began brushing the dirt aside, Julie and I from one side, Curran and Derek from the other. In twenty minutes we had it cleared and I climbed the Tahoe again. A perfectly round ribbon of glass sand, about eight inches wide, circled the vehicle, lying on top of the dirt like a thin crust of dirty ice on the surface of a pond after the first frost. Someone, probably the ghouls, had tried to cover it, but there it was.

"Copper?" I asked Julie.

She nodded.

"What does it mean?" Curran asked.

"I think there was a burst of magic up there." I pointed to the area above the car. "It's probably the teleportation footprint. The group of ghouls from the Oswalds' neighborhood came here and were teleported to wherever the rest of the ghouls have gathered. And this glasslike ring is the physical evidence of it." At least it was something. "Teleportation usually requires an anchor, some substance from the place you are teleporting to. Hugh carried water. This glass thing is probably an anchor. I definitely want a sample of it."

Maybe if we got this analyzed, we could figure out what it was and where it came from. And then we would go there and ask the ghouls to give us Eduardo back. Pretty please with sugar on top.

"If it occurred as they teleported, who covered it?" Curran asked.

"Maybe they covered it before they teleported," Julie said.

I jumped down from the Tahoe, pulled a ziplock bag from my pocket, and unsheathed Sarrat. "You might want to give me some space."

They backed away.

I quickly sliced with Sarrat. The thin crust of glass broke into sections. I waited to see if it would sprout needles or deliver some other lovely surprise. It lay in the dirt, looking inert. I used the gauze to pick up a piece, about four inches wide and three inches long, and slid the translucent chunk into the ziplock evidence bag.

Julie squinted at us and wrinkled her nose. "You smell horrible. Did you guys crawl through a Dumpster?"

What would my life be without teenage sass?

"Long story," Curran told her. "Can you see anything else?"

She shook her head. "Lots of ghouls and the copper explosion. That's it."

"We're done here, then," he said.

Eduardo had been missing for well over forty-eight hours. Every minute made finding him less likely, and I had no idea where to look next.

WE SENT DEREK and Julie back to the house, instructing them to swing by the Oswalds' place to pick up George's car, and drove to Eduardo's house. The idea of Julie driving still gave me nightmares, but I had driven at her age, so I had no room to talk.

We drove with the windows down despite the cold wind. We were both too fragrant otherwise. I considered a brief detour to Cutting Edge for a quick shower, but it would be easier to just go and get the home search over with.

Eduardo lived in a nice place in Sandy Springs, a sturdy two-story brick home built post-Shift sitting on a half-acre lot. The walls of the first story looked reinforced, their windows narrow and shielded by steel bars. The second-story windows ran larger, but the steel bars on them were just as well made. No fence. Any shapeshifter gone loup or a loose vampire would scale the tallest fence in the blink of an eye, and razor wire didn't give them much pause either. In post-Shift Atlanta fences didn't keep monsters out. They kept people in for convenient snacking.

Curran unlocked the steel security door and then the solid inner door with the keys George left for us. Hardwood floors. Clean house, airy despite the narrow windows. Neat. Curran inhaled. "I'm getting Eduardo and George, nobody else. I'm going to walk around outside."

I went into the kitchen. Granite countertops, clean and polished. Nice oak cabinets. Happy kitchen towels with bright red apples sewn on them. A big solid table, no frills, and only two chairs. This place must've cost a small fortune to rent. No signs of struggle. No blood. I kept walking. Family room. Bookshelves stood against the left wall, mostly empty. A couple of comfortable shapeshifter-sized couches, each lined with a knitted afghan, offered a soft place to sit. A stack of books lay on the coffee table, the top one half-closed because someone had stuck a pencil into it, probably to hold their place. A teacup, a little bit of tea still in the bottom, waited by the books for its owner. This wasn't some pristine house. This was Eduardo's home, a place where he hoped George would live with him, and I felt odd moving through this space, as if I were invading their privacy without their permission. I could picture George and Eduardo sitting here on the couch, each with their own cup of tea, reading together under the knitted blankets on the oversized couch.

No pictures on the walls. George was right. Eduardo probably didn't keep in contact with his family. In fact, the house was barely furnished. They probably hadn't had a chance to get all the furniture or couldn't afford it.

The living room ended. Another room, a rectangular, relatively narrow space, lay across the hallway. Probably a formal dining room at one point, now it had been turned into an office, with a lone square window, large enough for a person to squeeze through, but too small for anything larger. A desk stood against one wall, supporting a phone and a yellow book. Weapons hung on the walls, mostly tactical blades. Most shapeshifters used their claws. A few, especially those trained specifically for combat, armed themselves with knives. Eduardo didn't grow claws. His arsenal consisted of various short swords. Two massive weapons hung on the wall: a big steel maul with a wooden handle and an equally heavy axe. If I tried to fight with either, it would require two hands and take me ages to swing them. Eduardo could probably swing them about as easily as I swung my sword.

I paused by a pair of Iberian steel falcatas, twenty inches overall, with fourteen-inch blades, single-edged, slightly curved, and convex near the point but concave near the hilt. The swords that surprised the Romans in the Second Punic war.

I had a pair of falcatas from the same smithy—they bore the same small mark on the hilt. These were hand forged from 5160 high-carbon steel and marquenched in a molten salt bath to minimize flaws, distortions, and cracking. There was a great deal of difference between a sword and a swordlike object. I had seen very pretty blades made from stainless steel that looked great until someone actually tried to use them and they snapped in half from stress. Battle-ready swords required fatigue-resistant spring steel like 5160. Pre-Shift, people used it for truck springs. It contained chrome and silicon and was expensive, but 5160 took a hell of a lot of punishment before it broke. Eduardo had good taste.

I moved on to the desk. The corkboard held scraps of paper. Most looked like merc notes, the numbers of clients with small notations by them. *1728 Maple Drive, winged snake in a tree. 345 Calwood, feral dog. Call Guild about Walters, 5 days late on payment.* I plucked the corkboard off the wall. I would go through it tonight. Unlike the fictional detectives who solved crimes in a burst of brilliance, I've slogged my way through investigations and I've learned that being thorough pays off.

A stack of open mail lay on the corner of the desk, pinned in place by a large smooth rock. I moved it aside and flipped through the stack of mail. Bills. All current, no past-due balances. A bank statement. Eduardo had a total of six thousand dollars in savings and two thousand in checking. A page was pinned to the bank statement, detailing a list of expenses, utilities, insurance, and so on, each with a notation by it written in a bold, wide hand. The amounts on some notations were multiplied by two. He was doing the budget for him and George. Underneath in big letters Eduardo had written, *Need more money,* and underlined it twice.

I checked the desk drawer. Paper, pens, sticky notes, a stack of gig tickets . . . I leafed through it. The most recent one was from a week ago. He must've filed them weekly. Some days had three gigs, sometimes six, seven hours apart. He was working himself into the ground. He would take a job, finish it, return to the Guild, and sleep there until another gig came up, and he did it day after day. George couldn't have known. She would've made him stop.

I moved the gig stubs aside. A small wooden box . . . I picked it up and flicked the latch. A ring rested on the cushion of velvet. A big round sapphire set in a framework of triangular petals, resembling a lotus flower studded with tiny diamonds. The metal of the ring was solid black. Fourteen-karat gold plated with black rhodium. It would've been expensive before the Shift; now, with technology suffering, the price was crazy. Shapeshifters didn't like the feel of precious metals. Silver was poison and gold was only slightly better. Rhodium insulated them against gold. Raphael had given a black rhodium ring to Andrea for her birthday, starting a craze. The Pack wouldn't shut up about it for days.

I was looking at more than seven thousand dollars in this tiny box. George was way too practical to ever expect a black rhodium ring. If I asked her, she would tell me stainless steel was just fine. But he'd bought it for her anyway. He wanted her to have the best there was, and if she ever found out how much he worked to get it, she would probably kill him.

The sapphire caught the light from the window, the fire within sparkling, as if a drop of pure seawater had somehow crystallized, retaining all of the color and depth of the ocean inside it. The future of two people sitting here on a velvet pillow. George's words came back to me. *He could be dead in a ditch somewhere . . .* Worry gnawed at me. I packed it away, into the deep place inside me, and snapped the box closed. Eduardo didn't need my emotions. He needed my help.

I reached for the wastebasket. Sometimes the things people threw away said more than the things they chose to keep. A hilt protruded about an inch from the papers inside the basket. The pommel had the unmistakable pale softness of bone. Hmm. Odd.

I pulled the weapon out. A slightly curved dagger in a sheath, about twenty-five and a half inches long overall. The sheath was wood wrapped in black leather. Silver leaf covered the tip of the sheath and about two inches at the top, twisting into a complex ornate pattern with plaited silver wire, gilt filigree, and niello. I counted the braided strands: one, two, five total. The handle had been painstakingly carved to give the bone just enough texture so if the grip became bloodied, it wouldn't slip from your hand. A bright blue-green turquoise stone the size of my thumbnail decorated the grip and an even larger bright-red carnelian graced the pommel, like a drop of opaque blood. Wow.

I wrapped my fingers around the grip. The bone was warm, soft, and slightly rough. Like shaking hands.

The blade came free of the scabbard with a soft whisper. The seventeen-inch double-edged blade shimmered, a ray of sun caught and bound into steel. Silver script, delicate and elegant, ran the length of the grooved blade. I didn't speak Arabic, but I've learned to recognize some verses. It was often used by Muslims against evil spirits. *Hasbiya Allahu la ilaha illa huwa `alayhi tawakkaltu wahuwa rabbu al-`arshi al-`azhim. Allah suffices me; there is no god but He; in Him I place my sole trust; He is the Lord of the mighty Throne.*

A kindjal dagger. Not one of Russian make. The profile was too curved. This was a kindjal with an Arabic spin on it. I balanced the dagger on my finger. Perfect. Full tang, sharp but not brittle-edged, and the kind of weight distribution that let the dagger sink into the body almost on its own. This wasn't a weapon. It was a masterpiece. The kind of blade you treasure and pass on to your children.

So the falcatas were on the wall, but the kindjal got thrown into the wastebasket. Why? If Eduardo didn't like it, why not sell it? He needed the money.

The tiny hairs on the back of my neck rose. My shoulders tensed. Someone was watching me.

I looked up slowly. Outside the window, the sun was beginning to set. Someone stood in the shadow of a tree about fifty yards away, half hidden by a low branch. I could barely make out a dark silhouette by the darker trunk.

Three seconds to the door, five seconds to cover the distance. Too long. If the watcher wasn't completely human, he'd be gone before I'd get out the door.

I leaned forward, focusing on the watcher. My body tensed.

The shadow was still there, by the trunk. Definitely human.

Come out, come out, whoever you are.

The human shape moved.

That's it. Come forward. Come out to play.

The branch slid out of the way.

I reached for my sword.

Curran stepped into the open.

Damn it.

I grabbed a canvas sack from a shelf, slid the dagger, the corkboard, and the bills into it, and marched outside. He was still standing by the tree.

"Quit scaring me."

"Eduardo was being watched." He nodded at the trunk of the tree. A barely perceptible scrape marked the bark about three feet up. I grabbed a thick bottom branch, put my foot against the scrape, and pushed up into the tree, into the spot where the thick trunk split into twin branches. If I crouched, I could still see the window and the desk by it. If the light was on, I could see inside the office.

"It's a layered scent," Curran said. "Human. Male. He came here several times. Last time a couple of days ago."

"A stalker?" I jumped out of the tree.

"Looks that way."

"Did he do anything while here?"

Curran shook his head. "No. He didn't jerk off, didn't spit, and didn't sweat. Occasionally he was in the tree." Curran crouched by the dry leaves and mulch at the roots. "Most people move around while they wait. They shift foot to foot." He pointed at the mulch with his hand.

"Doesn't look disturbed," I said.

He nodded. "The scent is old but dense. He came here often and stayed for some time in one spot without fidgeting. This is a guy who knows how to not be seen. He wasn't indecisive. He wasn't worried about being caught. He just stood and watched. When he was done, he walked to the end of the street. The trail ends there. Likely he had gotten into a car."

Disciplined and patient. Good for him, bad for us.

"Would Eduardo know he was being watched?"

"Hard to say." Curran frowned. "If he were a cat or a wolf, he would've patrolled his territory, so he would notice the scent immediately. Eduardo is a bison. Hell if I know."

"Is it possible he could've missed the scent?"

"This time of year, the wind usually blows southeast. I didn't smell him until I was right up on the tree. Eduardo wouldn't have any reason to come out here, unless he was mowing the yard, which he probably won't do for another couple of months. So yes, it is possible he missed it. But bison have good hearing and an acute sense of smell. So he may have known about it."

"If he had known about it, wouldn't he have ruffled the mulch or something to put his territorial stamp on it?"

"I don't know. I have no idea what bison do besides charging intruders."

"Could we ask somebody?"

Curran stared at me helplessly. "The Pack has one werebison and he's missing."

Ugh. Every clue we found led to a dead end. "You're no help."

"Why am I the expert all of a sudden?"

"Of the two of us, you have more stalking experience."

He leaned back. "Really?"

"Yes. When you let yourself into my apartment before we were dating, did you fidget while you watched me?"

"Will you let it go?" he growled.

"No."

"I didn't fidget. I checked on you to make sure you hadn't gotten yourself killed. I wanted to know that you weren't dying slowly of your wounds, because you have no sense and half of the time you couldn't afford a medmage. I didn't stand there and watch you. I came in, made sure you were okay, and left. It wasn't creepy."

"It was a little creepy."

"It worked, didn't it?"

"Worked how?"

"You're still alive."

"Yes, of course, take all the credit."

We looked at the mulch some more. We were both irritated. Eduardo had been missing for far too long.

"No ghouls?" I asked.

"No ghouls. I walked the entire perimeter of the property. You find out anything?"

"He was making a budget for him and George. He needed money."

Curran stared at the tree, frustration clear on his face.

"Also this." I showed him the dagger.

"Nice," Curran said.

"I found it in the trash can in his office. It was made for a man."

"How do you know?"

"Because this cost a very solid chunk of money. If someone was willing to spend that much on a gift for a woman, it would have gold on it somewhere. In Islam the wearing of gold and silk for men is *haram*, forbidden. Muslim men are supposed to be determined, steadfast, and resolute, dedicated to their faith and the protection of their family. Gold and silk are signs of luxury, which are fine for women but frowned upon for men." I stroked the silver on the scabbard. "This is a dagger made for a male. It has a protective supplication on it, and it's decorated with *feruz*, turquoise, which helps obtain divine help and victory in battle, and *aqiq*, carnelian, which protects against evil and misfortune."

I realized he was staring at me.

"What?"

"How do you even remember all this?"

"It's my job to remember." Blades were the tools of my trade. If it cut a human body, and it cut it well, I knew something about it.

He took the blade from me and smelled it. "It's been soaked in something that kills the scent and then polished with clove oil. Smells like one of your swords."

"This is not Eduardo's usual fare," I said. "He tends to wider blades or heavy weapons. This is a precision self-defense dagger. Ghouls originate in Arabia. Wolf griffins are geographically close. Was Eduardo a Muslim, by any chance?"

"No. We would've seen him pray while on the ship, and he and I talked before and he mentioned he wasn't religious. Maybe he beat up his stalker and took the dagger away. But then why not sell it? Why throw it away?"

"I have no idea. I can take the dagger to a smith tomorrow."

"If it was given to him, I'm wondering about the thinking behind giving a shapeshifter something decorated with silver," Curran said. "Either the dagger was made for someone else originally or the gift giver is clueless."

"Or he might have thought that Eduardo may have to attack something that doesn't like silver." I sighed.

In any investigation there comes a time when you run out of things to do. We had just hit that point. Nothing else could be done until the morning.

"Let's go home," Curran said.

8

I DROVE THROUGH the city, guiding the vehicle around odd obstacles Atlanta threw in our way. Curran relaxed in the passenger seat, his eyes distant.

"What are you thinking about?" I asked.

"Their house," he said. "When I get my hands on his kidnapper, I'll break his neck."

"I keep thinking about Eduardo's stalker," I said. "George said Eduardo had rented the house six weeks ago, about a week after her talk with Mahon. You said the stalker didn't smell like a shapeshifter. Eduardo was racing to make as much money as possible. He spent all his time at the Guild or doing jobs. There wasn't much interaction with the outside world, just the Guild and George."

"The stalker must be connected to the Guild," Curran said. "Someone he worked with or someone he met during a gig."

"Yes. We need to get a complete record of his jobs. Chances are, the stalker guy is somewhere in there."

"How can we get a record?"

"We can't." I leaned back in the seat. "The log only goes back a few days. Knowing the Clerk, he closed the books before he left and filed everything. To get at the complete record, we would have to get Mark to unseal the old logs. He won't do it."

"Why not?"

"Because technically it would be illegal without a warrant, because the Guild could be sued if Eduardo's kidnapping is connected to it, and because he is a Grade A asshole who enjoys using what little power he has. If there is no profit in it for him, he won't even twitch his pinkie. If we had the Clerk, I could talk him into letting me look at the logs, because the Clerk had the ultimate responsibility for them and because the safety of a Guild member is at risk, but the Clerk is gone. Mark won't do us any favors, and Bob and his crew won't either."

I had briefly contemplated breaking into the Guild and stealing the logs, but I wasn't sure where Mark had moved them to, since they weren't in the Clerk's counter safe. And the Guild was never empty. Unless I could turn myself invisible, pulling off this heist while a dozen mercs watched would be very difficult.

"Then I'll get the Clerk back," Curran said.

"You would have to get them to rehire him, and they won't do it. They didn't have enough money to keep him on in the first place and I'm not sure the Guild committee would even want him back. They are all set to raid the pension fund and call it quits."

Curran's eyes grew distant again. "I'll take care of it."

The sun had set by the time I turned onto our street and I saw our house, its windows lit up by the bluish glow of feylanterns inside. The silver in the bars shielding its windows glowed slightly, reacting with magic and moonlight, as if coated in fluorescent paint, matching the glow of the security door.

I had spent the first month after we'd moved in putting up wards all around our five-acre plot, and as I turned into our driveway, the reassuring mild pressure of passing through the defensive spell slid over me, as if the house patted my hair.

My stomach hurt from the lack of food. My shoulder ached with a low gnawing pain. My sides hurt, too. I was tired, starving, and filthy, and I smelled like three-day-old roadkill. The spider ichor had dried to a cement-like substance in my hair. I would've killed for a shower.

Across the street, Heather Savell finished speaking with Mrs. Walton and started toward us. Curran locked his teeth. I had no doubt that, in her head, Heather was preparing a speech on behalf of our neighborhood's nonexistent HOA. She had already kindly pointed out to us that most people hide their trash cans in the garage instead of putting them on the side of the house and that we had a two-foot-wide bald patch in our lawn, where the workers had dug up the ground to get to a burst pipe.

I had very low tolerance for people who tried to tell me what to do. Curran had even less. He'd lived in a cabin in the woods until he was twelve. Then loups killed his family, and he lived on his own for almost a year, starving in the forest, until Mahon found him. Two years later Curran became the Beast Lord. When he spoke, everyone in the Keep went silent. When he entered a room, all eyes were on him. If he wanted something, it was brought to him with apologies that it took longer than thirty seconds. Living among regular people wasn't in his frame of reference, and today had done nothing to put him into a charitable frame of mind. The fact that Heather had sprinkled cayenne pepper on her lawn didn't endear her to him either. Not that he would bite Heather's head off, but I could see him putting it in his mouth and holding it in there for a bit.

"My turn," I told him. "You did the last one."

"Call for backup if you need me." He got out and went inside. I stepped out and lingered by the car. I could do this. I just had to be cordial and not punch her. Piece of cake.

"Hi," Heather said, stretching the word. She walked carefully, as if worried I'd bite her.

"Hi!" *Kate Daniels, a good neighbor. Would you like some cookies?*

"I'm sorry to bother you . . . What is that smell?"

Spider guts. "How can I help you?"

"Umm, the neighbors asked me to bring some issues to your attention."

I bet they did and she bravely soldiered under that burden. "Shoot."

"It's about the mailbox."

I could see the communal mailbox out of the corner of my eye. It seemed intact.

"You see, the mailman saw your husband during one of his walks."

"He's my fiancé," I told her. "We are living in sin."

Heather blinked, momentarily knocked off her stride, but recovered. "Oh, that's nice."

"It's very nice. I highly recommend it."

"As I was saying, he saw your fiancé when he was in his animal shape. How to put it . . . He became alarmed."

That was generally a normal reaction when encountering Curran for the first time.

"We are not sure if they will deliver mail again."

"Did you receive any official notices from the post office?"

"No, but . . ." Heather tried a smile. "We were thinking maybe your fiancé could not do that anymore."

"Do what?" I had a sudden urge to strangle Heather. I was so tired of people acting like Curran was an inhuman spree killer who would murder babies in their sleep.

"Walk around in his animal shape."

No strangling. Strangling would not be neighborly.

"It would also be nice if he limited the range of his walks."

I had had a really long day. My nerves were stretched thin and she was jumping up and down on the last of them.

I inhaled slowly. Two years of sorting shapeshifter politics and their run-ins with humans had to count for something. "According to the Guzman Act, a shapeshifter in the United States is free to wear whatever shape he or she chooses. It's a federal crime to discriminate against shapeshifters based on the form of their body. It's also illegal to make regulations interfering with their ability to freely change shape. I sincerely hope the neighborhood hasn't considered signing such a petition." Because if they did, I would make them eat it. Slowly.

"No, no, of course not."

"I'm sure you weren't suggesting that my fiancé should be limited in which shape he wears on a street in his own neighborhood?"

"No, of course not," she said, backpedaling. "It just that it upsets the dogs . . ."

"Also, he isn't taking a walk. He is patrolling. We live next to a wooded area. I'm sure you've heard coyotes howling. Judging from the 'lost pet' posters taped on lampposts and fences, a number of dogs and cats have disappeared from this neighborhood, but none after January fifteenth. Do you know why that is?"

She didn't answer.

"It's because on January fifteenth we moved into this house. My fiancé is a top-level predator. He has claimed this territory, and all of the other lesser predators know better than to challenge him."

The magic vanished, like a veil jerked aside. The feylanterns went out and the electric porch light came on, illuminating me in all of my bloody nasty glory. Heather sucked in a sharp breath.

"Will there be anything else?" I asked.

"No." Her face turned pale.

"Thank you so much for stopping by. If you get anything from the post office about interrupted delivery, bring it to me. I'll take care of it."

She nodded and took off across the street to her house at a near run.

I walked into our house, locked the security door and the front door behind me, and exhaled. A delicious scent of stew floated to me. My mouth actually watered. So hungry.

I made my way into the kitchen just in time to see Curran, already showered, pull a pot of stew Julie must've made from the coal oven. Grendel, our freakishly large black attack poodle, sprawled on the rug, cleaning a big bone. He wagged his tail at me and went back to stripping shreds of meat. Julie set out the bowls for dinner.

"Did you see the mailman while doing your rounds yesterday?" I asked.

Curran's face turned carefully blank. "Yes, I did."

"Did you do anything to scare him?"

"I was perfectly friendly."

"Mhm." Please continue with your nice story. Nonjudgmental.

"He was putting things into the mailbox. I was passing by and I said, 'Hello, nice night.' And then I smiled. He jumped into his truck and slammed the door."

"Rude!" Julie volunteered.

"I let it pass," Curran said. "We're new to the neighborhood."

The former Beast Lord, a kind and magnanimous neighbor. "So you sneaked up behind him, startled him by speaking, and when he turned around and saw a six-hundred-pound talking lion, you showed him your teeth?"

"I don't think that's what happened," Curran said.

"That's exactly what happened, Your Furriness." I laughed, pulling off my boots.

"George called," Julie said. "Twice."

"Did she say she found out anything?" I asked.

"No, she just wanted to know what was happening. Also, some person called Sienna called and left her number. I put it on the board."

Sienna was the Maiden of the Witch Oracle. Officially the Atlanta witch covens were independent of each other. Unofficially, they all listened to the Witch Oracle, consisting of three members: the Crone, the Mother, and the Maiden. Each of the three had unique powers. Sienna saw into the future. My stomach sank. She never called me. The last few times I spoke to the Oracle, I had been summoned to their lair in what once was Centennial Park.

I went to the phone, checked the number written on the small chalkboard above it, and dialed.

"Hello?" a young woman said on the other end.

"Sienna, this is Kate."

"I am glad you called."

"Does this mean the Oracle decided not to curse me into oblivion?" The witches and I had made a deal: they would help me and I would keep my father from claiming Atlanta. When I claimed the city instead, they didn't take it well.

"I'm not talking to you as a member of the Oracle," Sienna said. "I'm talking to you as a woman whose life you saved. I look into your future, Kate. For obvious reasons."

The witches were worried that I would move against the covens. Me and all of my great power that I had no idea how to access or use.

"In the past I saw your futures. They were many and varied. Lately I've been having the same vision over and over. I see a man standing on a hill. The day is full of sunshine. The sky is bright and blue and the grass under his feet is emerald-green. His face is a smudge and every time I try to concentrate on it, I meet a wall of resistance. He is holding something—I can't see what it is, but I know it's vital—and then he turns and walks away. I think the man is your father. I can't think of anyone else connected to you with enough power to deliberately obscure my vision."

On that we agreed. "Any hint at all at what he might be holding? How big is it?"

"It's . . . a blur. It feels like a weapon, Kate. It frightens me."

Great. "Thank you. Will you tell me if you see anything else?"

"I will consider it."

"Thanks again."

I hung up. Curran glanced at me. Shapeshifter hearing surpassed human, and he would've heard the entire conversation. Whatever my father was cooking up, it would be bad for us. Catastrophically bad. I so didn't need this right now.

The downstairs bathroom door opened and a thin man stepped out. His hair was pure white and his eyes, bright blue, were like the clear sky—not a single thought in sight. Oh no.

Christopher saw me. His eyes sparkled. He smiled as if given a precious gift and uttered one happy, quiet word. "Mistress!"

I SLUMPED AGAINST the wall. Christopher used to be brilliant. He also used to work for my father. We never got the whole story out of him, but something he had done displeased Roland, who punished him and then gave him to Hugh d'Ambray, who put him into a metal cage and was slowly starving him to death when I got him out. Christopher referred to himself as shattered, and that's exactly what he was. His mind floated about, broken into a thousand shards, and you never knew which particular shard was in control. Sometimes he was so smart, it hurt; at others, he was childlike; and then occasionally he did things like climbing to the top of one of the Keep's towers and trying to take flight. He was convinced he used to know how to fly and that he still could, if only he remembered. Usually it took me or Barabas to talk him down.

We had left Christopher behind at the Keep. It was the safest place for him. He knew how to make panacea, a vital medicine the shapeshifters desperately needed to keep from going loup, and the Pack would guard him and see to his every need. He couldn't really be left unsupervised.

I turned to Julie. She shrugged. "He was sitting on our doorstep when Derek dropped me off."

"Mistress," Christopher said happily.

Oh boy. "Hi, Christopher." I made my voice as gentle as I could. "How did you get here?"

"I walked."

Walked. The Keep was almost two hours away by vehicle. How in the world did he even find us?

Christopher kept smiling, his alpine lake eyes blissfully empty.

"Why don't you stay for dinner?" I told him.

IT TOOK ME fifteen minutes and two handfuls of shampoo to get the spider gunk out of my hair. It also gave me time to think. Tomorrow I needed to take the glass to an expert. Unfortunately any private lab analyzing magically amazing sand would have a waiting list, and taking it to the cops would accomplish nothing. Eduardo was a grown man, a shapeshifter, and he had issues with his alpha. From an outsider's perspective, it was entirely possible that he'd simply put some time and distance between him and his problems. They would look for him, but he wouldn't exactly make it on the priority list.

There was one person in the city who might be able to analyze the glass on short notice. Going to see him would make Curran's hair stand on end and it would cost me an arm and a leg. But it had to be done. Time was short.

The kindjal offered another place I could dig. The silver work on the scabbard was elaborate but not exactly unique, but the blade was a dead giveaway. The inscription had been written via the koftgari method, where the smith scratched the blade, hammered fine flat silver wire into it, and then heated it to help the silver stick. Koftgari didn't stand up well to prolonged use and the kindjal didn't look like a refinished antique, so it had to be a recent purchase. There were two smiths in the city who could produce a weapon of that quality, and only one of them used koftgari. The other favored inlay, cutting deep grooves into the blade and filling them with wire. I would go and knock on Nitish's door tomorrow. I had bought weapons from him in the past. He wouldn't like it, but he would talk to me.

I wished I could've spoken to Mitchell tonight, but beggars couldn't be choosers. Mitchell survived because Biohazard hid him from the general public. I could only see him at their convenience. Pissing off Biohazard wasn't in my best interests, no matter how much I wanted to know about the ghouls.

Aside from that, there weren't a lot of paths we could take. A few years ago I would've tried a locating spell, but they've been thoroughly discredited now. The magic behind them misfired most of the time, sending you on a wild-goose chase and wasting time.

I dried off, patting the towel gently over my scrapes, and looked at myself in the mirror. My back had developed a lovely plumlike color. Twisting to look at it in the mirror hurt. Another day, another wound.

I dressed and went downstairs to have dinner.

An hour later dinner was over and I was putting away the dishes Curran had washed. Since Julie had cooked, she was off kitchen duty. She spread her homework out on the table and Christopher sat next to her, leafing through her textbooks.

I dried a plate with a towel. "I'm going to see Saiman tomorrow. I need him to analyze the glass we found. It's going to be expensive."

Curran's eyes turned dark. "Take Derek with you."

"No. I'm going to see Saiman without a babysitter."

"I don't like it."

Christopher quietly got up and walked out of the kitchen.

"Do you trust me?"

The line of Curran's jaw went hard. "I trust you," he said. "I don't trust that degenerate with your safety."

"I know. But Eduardo needs him. Any other lab will take too much time."

"I still don't like it."

"If Saiman tries anything, I'll take him apart."

Curran looked at me. I looked back. I meant what I said. If Saiman got out of line, I would do whatever I had to do to get him back behind it.

"While you're doing that, I'm going to swing by the Guild," Curran said.

"You don't stalk someone you don't know. Eduardo and the man who watched him crossed paths somehow, and while we can't look at the logbooks, I have his scent now. If he's been to the Guild in the past week, I'll recognize it."

"If Eduardo was being stalked, would he talk to anyone in the Pack?" I thought out loud.

"He didn't tell George," Curran said.

That was true. She didn't mention it and it wasn't the kind of thing one would consider irrelevant when your loved one was missing.

Christopher still wasn't back.

"Julie, where did Christopher go?"

She raised her head from her paper. "He said he was going home."

"What?" Home. In the dark. All the way to the Keep.

I tossed the towel onto the island and dashed outside, into the cold. Our front yard was empty. I sprinted to the end of the driveway and spun left, then right. There he was, walking down the neighbors' driveway.

"Christopher!"

He waved at me and headed straight for their door. I ran after him, trying not to slip on the icy pavement. In retrospect, shoes would've been an excellent idea.

I got to Christopher just as he knocked on the neighbors' door.

"Hey," I touched his shoulder. "Where are you going?"

"Home." He smiled. "I like home. It's warm and there are books."

"This isn't—"

The door swung open and Barabas appeared in the rectangle of electric light. He wore sweatpants and a T-shirt that hung from his lean frame. His red hair, spiky as always, stood straight up on his head, making his handsome angular face seem even sharper. He saw me and his eyes got wider.

"Um," Barabas said. "Eh. Good evening, Kate."

"What are you doing here?"

"Eh."

"We live here," Christopher explained to me, and walked into the house.

They'd moved in next door to us. Christopher and Barabas had moved in next door to us and nobody had told me.

Barabas finally recovered his ability to speak. "There is this wonderful invention. It's made of leather and lined with soft fabric, and it goes on your feet to protect them from cold and rough surfaces. It's called shoes. You really should try it."

"You rented a house next to us?"

Barabas wrinkled his nose. "Not exactly. Please come in. Your toes look like they might fall off and Curran would eviscerate me if I let you get frostbite."

I came inside. Their bottom floor was open, just like ours. A big stack of cardboard boxes occupied the left side of the living room.

"You just moved in?" I asked, my voice sweet enough to spread on toast. Moved in and didn't tell me.

"About two weeks ago. Those are all Christopher's books. We are putting shelves in one of the bedrooms and some down there along the wall." Barabas waved at the left side of the room.

Someone knocked on the door.

"Come in!" Barabas called.

The door swung open and Derek stuck his head in. "Hey, do you have any duct tape?"

He saw me, stepped back, and closed the door without a word. Well.

"Coward," Barabas said, loud enough for Derek to hear.

"Where?" I asked.

"The house on the other side of yours."

"And I suppose this house and the one Derek is in just happened to be for sale . . ."

I stopped. Curran didn't rely on luck. He was thorough, and he thought ahead. I recalled our street. On our side, five large houses, including ours, backed to the woods, and I couldn't remember seeing their owners or their cars. He must've bought out the whole street. Oh wow. That explained why we were running low on funds.

"Did you separate from the Pack?" I asked.

"Yes." Barabas invited me to sit on the plush brown sofa.

I sat and tucked my cold feet under me.

"Who else?"

"So far Christopher, Derek, and I. Jezebel was thinking about it, but decided against it."

I nodded. Jezebel was in a relationship with Louis, who was very much a Pack kind of shapeshifter. Louis was a widower. His daughter, whom Jezebel adored, was five, and Louis wanted her to be brought up in the safety of the Pack. After being Julie's babysitter and seeing everything that could happen to a child, Jezebel agreed.

"I get Derek," I said. There was no place for Derek among Jim's people. Derek understood security and he was a good fighter. He had no other skills. I once tried to talk to him about college and he smiled at me and walked away.

The security avenue was closed to Derek. Robert, one of the alpha Rats, had taken over the position of security chief. He had to trust his staff, and he and Derek hadn't worked together enough for that trust to form. Robert would be bringing in his own personnel, and if Derek joined that parade, he would have to start from the bottom up. His only other option was to go back to Clan Wolf, where Desandra would pressure him into a beta position, because he was skilled and respected and because she couldn't afford to have him as a rival. Derek wanted to have nothing to do with clan politics. He was quite clear on that point. It made sense for Derek to separate, but Barabas had thrived as the Pack litigator.

"I don't get you," I said. "You love practicing law."

"Now I will practice it for you and Curran."

He had practically run the legal department in the Pack, and he had walked away from all of it? I didn't know if I had to feel guilty, frustrated, or grateful. "I doubt there will be much work for you here."

"You'd be surprised," Barabas said.

"I thought you were all set to work with Jim."

Barabas shook his head. "I stayed long enough to ease the transition. Jim needs a different lawyer. Trisha is taking over from me. She will do very well for him."

"And Christopher?"

Barabas sighed. "Christopher wouldn't stay in the Keep without you or me. Once he realized that both of us had left, he wandered the hallways crying and then went catatonic."

I ground my teeth. "I told them to call me if there were problems."

"They called me instead," Barabas said. "So I came and got him."

"And Jim just let him go?" After all, Christopher was the one who had brought the recipe for panacea to us.

"He had no choice. Christopher decided to live here with me. I'll take good care of him. Jim always viewed him as a security risk, and if the panacea makers run into any problems, they know where to find him."

Christopher had been doing better. In the past six months he had managed to keep a schedule, dress himself, and maintain personal hygiene. But he still had moments of complete confusion. In the Keep our security staff always kept an eye on him, but here the whole weight of responsibility rested on Barabas.

"He cooks now," Barabas said. "It was very sudden. He walked into the kitchen and just started doing it."

"What did he make?"

"Cream puffs shaped like swans. They were ridiculously delicious."

"Barabas . . ."

"Kate, I like taking care of him. He is no trouble." Barabas raised his head. "Curran is outside."

"Did you hear him?" When he wanted to, Curran moved completely silently, a fact I often regretted because he enjoyed popping up behind me out of thin air and making me jump.

"No. I felt him." Barabas grimaced. "It's hard to describe. It's a kind of awareness, like something large and dangerous passing by you in absolute darkness. You don't hear it, you don't see it, you don't smell it, but you know it's there. It was better at the Keep. He was always at the Keep, so you always felt a small measure of it, and the place was always crowded, which helped some. Now it's more jarring. He isn't there and then suddenly he is there." He blew a long breath out. "This will take some getting used to."

Ha! I wasn't the only one.

Curran knocked on the door.

"It's open," Barabas said.

Curran stepped inside. He was holding the Guild's Manual and Jim's contract in his left hand and a pair of my soft padded boots in his right.

He handed me the boots and smiled.

I smiled back and put the boots on.

Curran held out the Guild's Manual and Jim's contract to Barabas. "The

Guild is suffering from cash flow problems. The mercs want to raid the pension fund, so they forced a shutdown. The admin staff walked off due to nonpayment and they've lost their cleaning crews. I'd like to take it over."

"I'll see what I can do," Barabas said, taking the contract and the Manual. "Do you want to muscle in or be more subtle about it?"

"I want to know my options. I wrote a summary in the front. Look at the last provision in Membership Powers and see if you can find me a way in."

"I'll have something by tomorrow."

I couldn't remember what the hell the last provision in Membership Powers was. I used to know the Manual cover to cover, but it had been a while since I had to pull that knowledge out of my head.

"Don't forget to bill me," Curran said. "Exorbitantly."

Barabas flashed him a quick smile. "I'll be very generous in my billable hours."

We walked home through the cold. "You didn't tell me," I said.

"It wasn't my place to tell."

"I don't understand why they didn't tell me either."

"All of them were part of our inner circle," Curran said. "They knew exactly how much you wanted to be away from the Keep and the Pack. They wanted to give you space."

"Did they think I would throw a tantrum?"

"Baby, you're not the tantrum type. You are the scary-smile-and-stabbing type."

I looked at him.

"Hard-stare type." He grinned. "They knew you wanted privacy. They didn't want you to feel like they chased us down. But it was getting a bit ridiculous, so it's good Christopher gave them a nudge."

I waved at our side of street. "How many of these houses do you own?"

"*We* own, and all of them."

"Do we own anything else?"

"We also own the woods directly behind us."

Those woods extended for quite a while. There used to be a huge golf course and a shopping center behind us, but trees and brush had swallowed it long ago. "How many acres?"

"Five hundred and twelve."

I opened my mouth and nothing came out.

"I thought of calling it the Five Hundred Acre Wood," Curran said.

My mouth finally worked. "How much did you . . . ?"

"Three million."

Oh my God.

"It was a steal. They kept trying to clear it, but the trees there seem to have a really high affinity for magic. Every time they clear something, the woods grow back in weeks, which is perfect for us. Once we allow the woods to develop, the growth will self-regulate."

"Is this why we're out of money?"

"Yes." He smiled at me. "We're not out of money. We just have a firm budget."

I laughed quietly. Somehow it all completely made sense.

"I did tell you about the woods. On three different occasions."

No, he didn't. "I don't remember that."

"Beginning of February, I told you that I was thinking of buying a little extra land with our house."

I had no recollection of that conversation. Also, a little extra land meant another acre. Not a forest five times the one Pooh Bear lived in. "What did I say back?"

"You said, 'You want to talk about this *now*?' And then you said, 'Can't you just bite him in half.'"

Ah, now I remembered. "We were in a half-flooded garage with a deranged lunatic who was shooting lightning at us."

"And then I brought it up again the second weekend after we moved in. We were in our bedroom. You were doing paperwork and I came out of the shower and I said . . ."

That I had a perfect recollection of. "You said, 'Hey, baby, come here often?'"

"Before that."

"I don't remember what you said before that. You made it difficult to concentrate."

"In my defense, you were doing paperwork naked." Curran grinned.

Whatever. "When was the third time?"

"I brought it to you at work and I said, 'Look at this. I'm buying this land.' And you said, 'I feel awkward telling you how to spend your money. If you want to buy extra land, I think you should.'"

Okay, so he had a point.

Curran reached over and squeezed my hand. "What's done is done. The Pack belongs to Jim now and for all of his grandstanding, if I decided to take it back, he would fight me for it. But now we have to take care of our people. The least we can do is to provide them with a place to live, a place to run at night, should they so choose, and the means to earn their living."

The moon chose that moment to break through the clouds, flooding the street with gentle pale light. I always liked the darkness. The world seemed bigger somehow under the endless night sky. An odd calm settled over me.

"I'm worried about Eduardo." I said. "What we have is better than nothing, but all of our leads are slim. We are moving too slowly. The longer he's gone, the smaller the chances of finding him alive. I'm a lousy detective . . ."

Curran's eyebrows rose. "Could've fooled me."

I held up my hand. "I'm a lousy detective, but I'm excellent at annoying people."

"Yes, you are."

Ha-ha. "Normally at this point I would make myself into a pain in the kidnapper's ass. I'd make it personal and become a target, so whoever took him turns himself inside out trying to nuke me. It would give me a way in and it would keep other people from getting hurt."

Curran's eyes shone with a predatory light. "So let's make it personal."

I pointed over my shoulder at the house. "Julie." Before Julie was at the Keep. Now she was here. There was a world of difference between a tower full of killers and a house in the suburbs. It was a very well-protected house, but still.

"Julie will be fine," he said. "We have strong wards and good doors, and our neighbors are very invested in her safety. How do we get under his skin?"

"Ghouls. I don't know if he cares about them, but he uses them."

"So we'll hit his ghouls."

"I'll talk to Ghastek, if you talk to Jim," I said. "Between the vampires and the shapeshifters, someone has to have seen ghouls moving through the city.

We find them and kill them. If we knock out enough of his teeth, eventually he'll get pissed off and come to punch us in the face."

Curran bared his teeth. "I'm going to enjoy this."

"That makes two of us."

At least we had a plan. Even a bad plan was better than none.

The purr of a car engine rolled through the neighborhood. A Pack Jeep pulled up to our driveway. George jumped out.

"Did you find out anything?" Curran asked.

She shook her head. "Did you find him? Did you—"

"We know the ghouls took him," I said. "He was alive when they got him. We don't know why."

Her face was a pale mask, her teeth clenched, her eyes feverish. "Ghouls? What?"

"Come inside," I told her. "We'll explain everything."

CHAPTER
9

CUDDLES CLOPPED DOWN the street at a jerky trot. She galloped like a champ and was comfortable to ride at a walk or a canter, but her trot was rattling teeth in my skull. I slowed her down a couple of times, but she felt like trotting this morning and once she got something into her head, no force on Earth could change her mind. I'd taken her because the magic waves had been coming in short bursts lately, and an enchanted engine took forever to warm up. Also because a couple of weeks ago Buckhead had experienced an invisible hailstorm. You didn't see the hail, but you saw the impact. It didn't cause that much damage—most of Buckhead was in ruins anyway—but it turned the roads into an obstacle course of potholes.

"You're trying to kill me, is that it?" I shifted in the saddle, trying to find a spot where my back didn't hurt.

Cuddles ignored me and kept trotting.

This morning when I woke up, my body let me know just how displeased it was that I wasn't spending the day in bed. I dragged myself up, we made breakfast, and then I went one way and Curran and Julie went the other. Maybe I should have taken a car. I needed to make progress today and Saiman was my best bet.

Saiman made his lair in the posh luxury of a Champion Heights penthouse. The building was impossible to miss. It was just about the only high-rise still left standing in Buckhead. Its owners had sunk an obscene amount of power into its wards, tricking magic into thinking the building was a very large natural rock. During the magic waves parts of it looked like a granite crag, but right now it was a fifteen-floor building, shrouded in morning fog and backlit by the rays of the rising sun like some mystical spire of an evil overlord.

Cuddles snorted.

"I don't like it either," I told her. "But you'll love their stable. It's to die for."

We passed a parking lot filled with slick, expensive vehicles and I steered Cuddles to the stable. Then the stable employee and I had a brief discussion about whether Cuddles actually qualified as a mount. However, I had twenty bucks and was willing to part with it, so I won by default. With Cuddles safely placed into a stall, I climbed the stairs to the front doors, where a security guard leveled an AK-47 at me. I gave him Saiman's pass code and a few moments later the elevator spat me out on the fifteenth floor. They had replaced the hallway carpet since my last visit. The new one was midnight-blue, with ridiculously high pile. If I stepped into it, I'd probably sink in up to my ears. They should've equipped the elevator with a life vest just in case.

I walked to Saiman's door and knocked.

No answer.

He was home. Saiman was a creature of habit. Catching him at night was hit or miss, but no matter how adventurous he had gotten, he would return home in the morning.

I stood by the door and waited. He'd heard my knock. Once was enough. Eventually his curiosity would get the better of him and he would open the door.

A moment passed. Another crawled by.

Saiman and I had a long history. We met during a Guild job. He managed to piss off some volhves and I ended up bodyguarding him for one very long night. Saiman was a polymorph: he could assume any human shape, any gender, any age, and any size within human norm. During the night, he declared that if he assumed the right shape, any person would have sex with him and then he propositioned me. I told him that sex required more than physical attraction. Saiman didn't like being turned down. He gave me a large discount on his services in an effort to keep me around so he could keep trying to prove his point. Then he tried to use me to get back at Curran for some injury to his pride, and my sweet and understanding fiancé broke into Saiman's warehouse, ripped an engine out of one of the luxury cars stored there, and used it to demolish the rest of Saiman's overpriced car fleet. Since then they had somewhat buried the hatchet—lots of money was involved— but there was no telling what sort of reception I would get.

The lock clicked as the deadbolt slid aside. The door swung open, revealing Saiman. He was wearing my father's face.

He'd duplicated it perfectly, from the elegant jaw to the straight nose and the masterful sweep of sable-black eyebrows, but he couldn't reproduce the eyes. Roland's eyes shone with barely suppressed power. Hugh once told me that facing him was like looking into the eyes of the sun. I had done it, and the magic emanating from my father was like an avalanche. It caused me to back down for the first time in a very long time, not because I was afraid I would die but because I was afraid that everyone I loved would die with me. This "Roland" had Saiman's eyes: sardonic, conceited, and resigned to coexisting with idiots who had a fraction of his intellect and weren't worthy to share the air he breathed.

I laughed.

Saiman pondered me, clearly knocked off his stride. He must've planned to intimidate or unsettle me. Unfortunately for him, he couldn't have looked less like my father if he'd been an eighty-year-old woman.

I tried to look at him again, lost it, and laughed louder.

"Come inside," he snapped.

"Yes, Dad." I followed him in, snickering.

Saiman's face acquired a lovely purple tint. "There is nothing humorous about this."

"You're going to have to do something about your new outfit. You keep cracking me up."

Saiman's face crawled. My stomach forgot it was inside me and tried to flee in horror. His bones moved, stretching the skin in a vomit-inducing, grotesque jig as if tennis balls were rolling under his skin. His hair disappeared, absorbed, his build slimmed down, and finally a new man stood in front of me. Bald, of medium build, his face neither ugly, nor handsome. A blank canvas of a face studded with sharp eyes. This was his neutral form, the one he wore most often.

"Much better," I told him, trying to persuade my stomach to keep down breakfast.

Saiman invited me to sit down with a sweep of his hand. His apartment was an ultramodern oasis: curved futuristic lines, steel, glass, black walls, white plush furniture. It was a bit soulless.

I took a seat on the white couch. "For a man steeped in magic, you seem very fond of technology."

"I like its civilizing influence." Saiman sat across from me.

"And the fact that it's getting more and more expensive to obtain has nothing to do with it?"

"That's beside the point, Sharrim."

Sharrim. Of the king. That was what Roland's people called me. Saiman wasn't just a magic expert. He was also an information broker. Secrets were his stock-in-trade and he was trying to rub my nose in mine. That was okay. Two could play this game.

"I think it's perfectly relevant to this discussion, Aesir. Tell me, does Loki ever come to visit his grandson? What does he think of your crib?"

Saiman sat up straighter.

"Let me save you the trouble," I said. "Let's stop pretending that you hadn't figured it out prior to me claiming the city. This is what you do. You saw the words on my skin, and you went with us to the Black Sea and wandered around Hugh d'Ambray's castle. There is no denying that I look like my father. You figured it out and you chose not to do anything about it. You played dumb, because you wanted to know how it would all shake out. Now we know. You have to make a choice, Saiman. Would you rather talk to Sharrim or Kate Daniels? I can be either, but you have my guarantee you will like one much less than the other."

"And if I say Sharrim?" Saiman asked carefully.

I leaned back. "Then we can discuss why you failed to support me in my stand against my father. You have contacts all over the continent. You knew Hugh d'Ambray would be coming. You knew Roland would follow. You did nothing to warn me. Now you are in my city and you have the gall to wear my father's face. Was that a joke or were you trying to make a statement, Saiman?"

I leaned forward and fixed him with my tough stare.

Saiman sat very still.

"I would very much like an explanation."

Saiman opened his mouth. "And if I take Kate?"

I pulled out the plastic bag with the dirty glass in it. "I need this analyzed. I'm looking for a missing shapeshifter. You might remember him: tall, large, turns into a buffalo. His name is Eduardo Ortego and he came with us on our fun Black Sea vacation. I found his vehicle with a ring of this glass around it. The ring was about twelve feet in diameter and half a foot wide. The glass registers copper on an m-scanner. Anything you can tell me. What mythology, what brand of magic, anything. Our usual rate."

Saiman blinked. "That's it?"

"Yep."

He looked at the ziplock bag as if it were a scorpion about to sting him. A feverish calculation was taking place in his head. "And if I say no?"

"Then I will take it somewhere else."

Saiman plaited the fingers of his hands into a single fist and leaned on it, looking off into the distance.

"Take your time." I leaned back on the couch.

"Are you trying to communicate that you have no intention of influencing events within the city?" Saiman asked.

"Not unless I judge them to be in need of my influence."

"It is not an evaluative but a factual question," he said. "There can be only one of two answers: yes or no. Do you intend to rule?"

"No."

Saiman pondered me. "I can't decide if you can't comprehend the precarious nature of your situation or if you choose to deliberately hide from it like an ostrich thrusting its head into the sand."

"You always come up with such flattering metaphors. The last time we had one of our little talks, you compared me to a cactus."

Saiman frowned, wrinkling his forehead. "Kate, it is not just about who you are and the merits of your particular deeds. It's about Nimrod. You are his daughter. You claimed a territory independent of him. Everyone who has an axe to grind against him will come here."

They will be coming after me? You don't say. "Thank you, Captain Recap. Your summary of the things we know was most impressive."

"You will be tested. You will be challenged. You will need a base of support. If you simply walk away from it, the city will turn into a free-for-all as various powers try to tug it away from each other for the privilege of ousting Nimrod's daughter."

"I intend to protect the city. There will be no free-for-all."

Saiman paused and stared at me again. Something I'd said had obviously broken his formidable brain.

"You will protect the city, but you don't intend to rule it."

"Yes."

"What is the point of protecting it? You gain nothing. You put yourself in physical danger for no actual benefit to you. Is it because you want your father's approval?"

"He can take his approval and shove it where the sun doesn't shine for all I care."

"Then why?"

"Because I claimed the city. It's my responsibility to keep it safe."

He didn't say anything.

"I live here," I said. "I like Atlanta. I don't want this to be a terrible place where people are ruled by assholes and afraid. You live here, too. Don't you want this place not to turn into a hellhole?"

The silence stretched.

"Everyone you come in contact with becomes temporarily insane." Saiman slumped on the couch. "Your father, Nimrod, the Builder of Towers, has nearly godlike power. You're a child of a woman who betrayed him and you clearly have no desire to serve him. Your power, your very existence, is a direct challenge to him. Instead of killing you, he's allowing you to operate autonomously, presumably so you can mature into a real threat to him. That savage you decided to take into your bed built a Pack for seventeen years. His very identity was wrapped up in being the Beast Lord, yet he walks away from it all to live with you in the suburbs, even though his retirement was never part of the bargain you struck with your father. And the Pack allows it to happen."

Where did he get his information? "Curran loves me. He walked away because he wants to be with me."

"And your father?"

"He hasn't had a child in a very long time. I'm his firstborn in this age."

Saiman raised his eyebrows. "That tells me nothing."

"He is intrigued by my existence."

Saiman opened his mouth, then closed it. "I won't be part of this insanity." He picked up the ziplock bag and pushed the glass back to me.

"It's the wrong move," I told him.

"Your father will kill you," Saiman said. "Perhaps not today, but certainly soon. If he doesn't kill you in the near future, then whatever power tries to overrun the city next will. When this happens, everyone who ever supported you will become a victim of a purge. You are a leper. Everyone you touch is tainted."

Wow.

"Being your ally is a death warrant. I gain nothing by supporting you. I run the risk of angering you by refusing service, but you left the Pack, so you are no longer in a position to wield it against me, and you won't take any actions to punish me directly, because you are shackled by your own morals."

Okay. At least we knew where we stood. I picked up the ziplock bag and walked out.

I WALKED THROUGH the doors of Kadam Arms at half past nine. The smithy occupied a sturdy building in the southeast part of the city. Seven years ago, when I came here for the first time to buy a blade, it was just Arnav and his son, Nitish, and daughter, Neha. Over the years, the business grew and the smithy grew with it. As I stepped inside today, I saw two journeymen, one showing a blade to a customer, the other restocking a shelf. An apprentice, barely fifteen, ran up to me to ask me what I wanted. I asked for Nitish and five minutes later was shown to the back, where Nitish was quietly examining several blocks of steel.

Nitish glanced at me. He was an average-size man, with thick dark hair, bright dark eyes, and a smile that lit up his whole face. Nitish's family came from Udaipur city, in India, the district that had supplied Mughal rulers with weapons of war since the sixteenth century. Koftgari was in his blood. It was a precise art, especially when it came to lettering. Even the slightest change of a curve in the Arabic inscription or the wrong angle of a stroke in a Celtic rune on the blade could alter its meaning. Nitish was the best in the city.

I unwrapped the kindjal and put it on the table. The smile died. He reached over and quickly threw the cloth over the blade.

"This is one of yours," I said.

Nitish shook his head.

"It is," I told him. "That's your koftgari on the blade. There is only one smithy that does work of this quality and I can tell by the pattern it's not your father's. Who was it for?"

"This is not a good conversation," he said quietly.

"I know the buyer was a man, probably a follower of Islam."

Nitish shook his head.

"My friend is missing. I found it in his office. I know it's not his. He was going to get married."

"I am married. I have children, too," Nitish said.

I pulled the cloth back, revealing the dagger. "I just need a name. It won't get back to you. Somewhere my friend is still alive. He is a good person and his fiancé lost her arm protecting a pregnant woman. They deserve the chance to be happy. I just need one name."

He didn't look at me.

"What if it were Prema who was missing?" I let the name of his wife lie there between us like a heavy rock. I would go straight to hell for doing this to him. "Nitish, I wouldn't have come to you if I had a choice."

Nitish pulled the cloth back over the blade and leaned closer. "Come with me."

I picked up the dagger and followed him through the smithy, past the heat of the forge and the sound of hammers, to a room in the back. He swung open a heavy door, flicked on the lights, and closed the door behind us. Four walls filled with weapons looked back at me.

"I don't know his name," Nitish said quietly. "But I know what he buys." He pointed to a knife on the wall.

Eleven and a half inches long, the single-edged blade started straight at the hilt and then curved ever so slightly to the right, tapering and curving back to the left at the point. The tip of the dagger, triangular and reinforced, was almost needle narrow at the very end. Wicked sharp edge. Strong spine so the blade wouldn't break. Plain hilt, bone wrapped in leather. A pesh kabz. It was seventeenth-century Persia's equivalent to the armor-piercing round. That reinforced tip parted chain mail like it wasn't even there. It would slide in between the ribs, and if you angled it up, it would hit the heart. Crap.

We looked at the blade quietly.

"No watering on the blade," I said softly.

"No. He doesn't usually want Damascus. This is oh-six steel," Nitish said, his voice flat. "A bitch to grind."

The 0-6 was tool steel. It held its edge forever and would outcut the best Damascus every time. It was also untraceable. He'd chosen tool steel because that was what this knife was, a tool. This blade wasn't made to hunt monsters. It was meant to hunt people. It belonged to a man killer.

Nitish stepped forward, took a big, three-inch-wide folder from the table, and leafed through the pages. He paused, showing me the page. Throwing knives. Not the fancy blades, but utilitarian, simple strips of steel, ten inches long, inch and a half wide. Thick enough so the blade wouldn't bend, double edge at the point for the first inch and a half, then single edge. No treatment on the hilt, just plain steel. Contrary to what movies suggested, killing a person by throwing a knife was really difficult. Even if you managed to sink a blade in, it would be unlikely you'd hit anything vital. Most of the time knives were thrown to piss the opponent off so he'd do something stupid, to distract, or just to bleed him and cause some pain. These knives would go into the body like a hot knife into butter and they'd be hell to pull out.

Nitish flipped the page again. Another dagger, straight edge this time. Same plain, workmanlike aesthetic. Same killer blade.

The smith closed the book.

"Any swords?" I asked.

He shook his head.

That meant either the buyer didn't use a sword, which was unlikely considering all the magic crap Atlanta threw at us on regular basis, or he had a favorite blade and he was good enough not to break it.

"Can you describe him?"

"Dark hair. Beard. Large." Nitish raised his hands. "Tall. Wears glasses. Soft voice. Calm. He doesn't look like a man who would buy this." He indicated the blade.

"What does he look like?"

Nitish sighed. "Like a man of peace."

"When is he coming for the pesh kabz?"

"I don't know," Nitish said. "Sometimes he comes the day after I tell him it's done. Sometimes a month. He never calls ahead. He pays up front and then shows up without warning."

"Will you call me after he comes to pick it up?"

"He might not pick it up at all," Nitish said. "A year ago he spoke with my father and had him work on this."

He flipped the book to the last page, where half a page was glued down to form a paper pocket, and pulled a photograph out of it. A round box of blackened steel a little smaller than a soccer ball with a circular lid. At first glance, it looked like a random decorative koftgari pattern had been worked into the dark surface of the steel, but the close-up of the lid made it clear: the pattern wasn't random. Spider-thin Arabic script decorated the steel.

Bismillah ir-Rahman ir-Rahim . . .
In the name of God, most Gracious, most Merciful,
I seek refuge in the Lord of the dawn,
From the evil of that which He has created,
And from the evil of intense darkness, when it comes,
And from the evil of those who cast (evil suggestions) in
    firm resolutions,
And from the evil of the envier when he envies . . .

Surat al-Falaq, one hundred and thirteenth chapter of the Qur'an. The entire box was covered in protective verses.

"He already had the box," Nitish said. "He needed us for the koftgari."

Islam protected its followers against the supernatural. Whatever the stranger was going to put into that box, he counted on divine assistance to keep it in there.

"I looked inside the box," Nitish said. "The inside of it was smooth and looked like bone."

"Ivory?"

"No. Bone. Like the inside of a skull."

Better and better.

"Can I see it?"

"He picked it up two days ago. He didn't even ask about the knife. I don't think he remembered that he had ordered it."

I STARED THROUGH the windshield at a chain barring Cutting Edge's parking lot. The chain secured the parking lot at night. It was almost eleven a.m. It should be lying by one of the posts. Instead here it was, keeping me from driving in.

Derek usually came to Cutting Edge by eight in the morning. Failing that, Curran should have been back from his trip to the Mercenary Guild. He might have gotten held up at the Guild, but it was unlikely. After his response to Bob's tirade, none of the mercs would screw with him. That errand should've taken fifteen minutes. Did he get himself into some sort of trouble at the Guild? My imagination painted the Guild in ruins and my honey-bunny emerging from the wreckage roaring and swinging around the limp bodies of the Four Horsemen.

That would be hilarious.

Okay, this wasn't the most productive line of thinking.

Talking to Saiman had clearly put me into a foul mood. In my head, my dead aunt murmured, *People are fish. They die. You remain.* Saiman was right, in a sense. I was tainted, but not because I was doomed. I was tainted because I had power, the kind of power that corrupted and turned people into warped versions of themselves. I was warped enough as it was.

I parked in front of the building and tried the door. It was predictably locked. I unlocked it and walked inside, into a large main room. The shades were still down. I pulled them up, letting the light illuminate the wide room with four desks. There used to be only two desks, one for me and one for Andrea Nash, but now Andrea was busy running Clan Bouda. She was also pregnant. We tried to have lunch every Friday, and the last time we went, she ate four pounds of barbecued ribs by herself. She wanted to eat the rib bones too, but I talked her out of it. Then she pouted and called me a downer.

Now her desk stood empty, as she had left it. She claimed she would come back to it, but I doubted it. My desk was to the right of hers, Derek's directly behind mine and Curran's behind Andrea's. None of the desks had any notes on them. Great.

I landed in my chair. Saiman was right about one thing: if I fell, the city would fall with me. Being my ally was a death warrant. How the hell was I going to keep them all safe? I couldn't even find Eduardo. Before, I was only responsible for my own safety. Then I became responsible for the safety of my friends, then for the safety of the Pack. Now I had to safeguard the city. My obligations kept escalating and not in a good way.

I didn't want to do it. I didn't want to be responsible for the city.

None of it would have happened if I hadn't claimed Atlanta. But letting my father add it to his growing empire would've been worse. My father understood the concept of democracy and free will. He just felt that they should be exercised within the frame of his own will. My father had been a king, a tyrant, and a conqueror. He was never elected to the office. He would probably laugh at the idea. And if he did somehow decide to hold elections, he would magic the masses into electing him, because he would honestly believe that he was best qualified to rule wisely.

Having a pity party for myself accomplished nothing. It didn't help Eduardo at all. I had to find someone to analyze my glass. The sooner the better. And I had to find a way into the Guild.

I checked the answering machine. Three messages. I pushed the button.

"Hey, you twisted goon," Luther's voice said from the machine. "I had my bug guy check your giant bug. It's a wind scorpion, also known as a camel spider, a solifugid, which makes it an arachnid. The largest species grow about six inches, including legs, and they're not venomous or dangerous to humans. We have a few of these guys in Arizona, but my guy says this one is likely from the Middle East or North Africa. It's not too late to tell me what you know. Call me back, if you have any decency left."

Ghouls, wolf griffins, inscriptions in Arabic, and now wind scorpions. All of this pointed at the same geographical area. Trouble was, I had no idea how it all fit together. I couldn't tell Luther what I knew since I didn't know anything. Maybe if I went outside and gave alms to the poor, some mystic old lady would sell me a magic lamp with a cooperative djinn to answer all my questions.

The machine clicked, rolling over to the next message. "Hi, it's Barabas. Please call me as soon as you get this."

I dialed the number. Just what I needed, another emergency.

The phone rang once and Barabas picked it up. "Hey. I think I found a loophole."

Cancel the freak-out about another emergency.

"Talk to me about the Guild stopgap measure."

Good morning to you, too. "The stopgap is a hiring freeze. The Guild's mercs are contractors, but they still have to formally be hired by the Guild. If the Guild judges that there are too few jobs per merc, the stopgap kicks in until there are more jobs or fewer mercs."

I started drawing a cliff on a piece of paper.

"They're on stopgap right now," Barabas said.

"It doesn't surprise me. The place is falling down around them." I added a bunch of stick figures to the cliff and drew a falling dollar bill under it.

"From my review and the information I received from Jim, it appears that administration staff is central to the Guild being able to turn a profit."

"Yes. The Clerk is the grease that makes the gears go around."

"Correct me if I am wrong. Bob Carver and his Horsemen wanted to access the pension fund. They tied up the Guild's budget, so the admin staff stopped getting their pay. They walked off. Without the Clerk and his staff, there is no effective distribution of jobs. Nobody is taking, assigning, or tracking the jobs, so customers become angry when nobody shows up. The Guild's business dries up, which results in a financial shortage. It's a Catch-22."

"Exactly." I added a stick figure diving after the dollar bill and wrote

Bob above its head. "The Guild needs money to rehire the admins, but they need admins to make the money in the first place."

"We need to break this vicious circle."

"How?"

"There is a provision in the manual that permits each individual merc to contribute money to the Guild and earmark where it goes."

I rubbed my face, but rubbing failed to produce any great insights. "Are you suggesting we give the Guild our money?"

"Yes."

"Barabas, it's a sinking ship already. You want to throw good money after bad?"

"Hear me out."

Famous last words. "Okay."

"We inject cash into the Guild under the condition that it will be spent specifically to rehire the admin crew. The Clerk comes back, the jobs—"

"Gigs." If he insisted on this foolishness, he might as well start using correct terms.

"The gigs are once again properly assigned. Mercs once again make money. It gives us instant goodwill."

"What will happen when that money runs out?"

"We need to make sure that the money lasts until the Guild's finances bounce back. We use the goodwill we earned and our shares to break the budget lock. People don't like chaos. Chaos means they can't earn money. They need strong leadership. We need to develop a reputation as the people you come to when you have a problem you need solving."

"How much money would we need?"

"My budget projections indicate we need at least $142,860 to bankroll admin operations with a skeleton crew for the next four months, which is how long I estimate we'll need before the Guild becomes financially solvent."

I chewed on that number.

"Kate?"

"Give me a second."

"It's a doable number. Curran gave me a $300,000 budget."

Wow.

"Kate?"

Well, he spent millions on the forest, why not the Guild. "Go on."

"The individual contribution is capped at $50,000. Jim doesn't want any Pack members involved, and the stopgap prevents us from enrolling Curran or anyone else. We are stuck. We don't have enough people to donate the necessary money."

"For the record, I think this is a terrible idea."

"I will be sure to note your objection," Barabas said.

"Look in the membership chapter under corporations. I can enroll up to three people as my auxiliary support. The flip side of this coin is that if they screw up, I'll be directly penalized."

"I saw that. That requires you to be a corporate member for at least six months."

"I've been a corporate member for over a year. I converted my membership when Curran gave me Cutting Edge. A very smart Pack lawyer with spiky red hair advised me to do it for tax purposes." Also, the Guild had good dental insurance for its corporate members.

"Pack lawyers give good advice," Barabas said. "Even if they don't always remember it. I'll call you back."

He hung up.

Well. I guess Curran did take care of it.

If we were going to take over the Guild, we'd need the Clerk. I flipped through the phone book. I had no idea where the Clerk was, but I knew where Lori would be. She was his favorite protégé, because, as he had confided to me once late at night, she had more than half a brain. Lori's parents, Karen and Brenda, ran a bakery off Campbellton Road, which was called Sweet Cheeks. I remembered because I had stopped by there to buy a cake pop once, and one of her mothers—I thought it was Brenda, but I wasn't sure—teased me about my sword until Lori came out and told her to stop messing with me.

Ah, here it is. I dialed the number.

"Sweet Cheeks Bakery."

"Can I speak to Lori, please?"

"Hi, Kate, what can I do you for?"

Nice to be recognized. "You wouldn't know where to find the Clerk?"

Lori sighed. "You know how he always talked about running a bar when he retires?"

I didn't, but that didn't matter. "Did he buy a bar?"

"He's got himself a job at the Steel Horse. He says he wants to get a feel for the business."

The Steel Horse was a border bar that sat on the invisible boundary between the Pack and the People's territory within Atlanta. It was a neutral watering hole and I had a lot of pull with its owners. "Hypothetically speaking, if someone offered you your old Guild job back, would you be interested?"

There was a pause before an urgent whisper filled my ear. "Kate, you get me out of here, I'll buy your drinks for a year. If I have to pipe cream on one more carrot cupcake, I'll stab myself."

"Thanks for your help."

I hung up. The Steel Horse wouldn't open for another hour or two.

The answering machine's light blinked at me. That's right. More messages.

I pushed the answering machine's button again.

"This is the attendance department of Seven Star Academy. Your student, Julie Lennart-Daniels, has been marked absent in the following periods . . ."

Julie didn't skip school. I went cold.

"First . . ."

She wasn't sick this morning.

"Second . . ."

Curran would've taken her straight to school.

"And third."

She was absent for the entire morning. Curran and she never made it to school.

"Please provide the necessary documentation within two business—"

The magic wave washed over me. Damn it, just what I needed.

I grabbed the phone and dialed the Seven Star Academy. Work, damn you.

A beep. Another . . .

"Seven Star Academy, this is Emily."

"My name is Kate Daniels. Did Julie ever come to school today?"

"No, ma'am."

"Please call me as soon as she shows up."

I hung up and dialed the house. Ring. Ring. Ring. Ring . . .

What the hell could've happened?

"Leave a message," my own voice said.

"Curran, where the hell are you? I can't find Julie. Julie, if you are there, pick up the phone. You are not in trouble. I just need to know if you are safe."

Silence.

I hung up and dialed Barabas.

"I don't have it yet," he said.

"Did you see Curran leave this morning?"

"Yes."

"Did he have Julie with him?"

"Yes."

"Is he back?"

"No. I was here all morning. I would've heard the car."

"Call me if you see him. Please."

I hung up.

Julie and Curran were gone. Just like Eduardo. It would take an army of ghouls to take Curran down. He would die before he let them have Julie. Where could he have gone with her?

I dialed the Keep, the front guard station.

"You've reached the Pack . . ." Artie said.

"It's me."

"Consort . . . I mean, not Consort. Ex-Consort?"

"Is Curran at the Keep?"

"No. Neither of you can be at the Keep until your ninety-day separation is over—"

I hung up.

Julie used to be a street kid. If she hadn't been kidnapped by ghouls, then she'd skipped school and finding her would be next to impossible. Finding Curran would be easier. Once I found him, he could tell me if he had dropped her off at school. He was going to go to the Guild first. I dialed the Guild's number. I would make one of those assholes tell me if he was there.

A rapid disconnect signal wailed in my ear like a runaway heartbeat. What the hell . . . ? I dialed a number that went directly to Mark's office. The phone clicked once, twice, and screaming punched my ear, the raw high-pitched howl of human terror. "Help! Help me!"

A heavy crash drowned out the voice and a familiar young voice shrieked. "He's coming!"

Julie.

The Guild was less than twenty minutes away by horse. I ran out the door.

10

I WAS A block away from the Guild when a chunk of brickwork the size of a car flew over a building, darkening the sun. I jerked Cuddles to the left. She veered and the brickwork crashed into the pavement with a loud thud, ten feet from where we were just a moment ago. Bricks scattered on the street, bouncing on the pavement. A body fell onto the bricks with a wet splat and lay there limp, like a rag doll. A familiar head lolled, blood pouring from his mouth, dead eyes staring up at the indifferent sky. Leroy. Holy crap.

Cuddles broke into a gallop. We charged down the road, swung around the corner, and shot out onto the short stretch of Phoenix Drive that led to the Guild.

A huge pair of legs blocked my view. Covered with curly dark hair, they rose at least thirty feet before terminating in a flabby wrinkled ass. The feet, at least nine and a half feet long, glowed with orange, like metal just pulled from the forge. Heat scorched me, as if I had flung open the door of a stove with a fire raging inside. I smelled the tar-tinted stench of melting asphalt, the road around the giant softening like the wax of a burning candle.

Cuddles skidded to a stop, shocked. I remembered to close my mouth.

Behind the giant, the Guild's heavy ten-foot-tall doors stood slightly ajar, dented and bent out of shape. He must've kicked or punched them, but the reinforced steel held, so he changed his strategy and went from the top, like a bear trying to dig into a beehive. The doors wouldn't last too much longer—the metal was beginning to glow. Sooner or later the heat from the giant's feet would melt it.

Where were the cops when you needed them? Why wasn't the PAD shooting this man-mountain with everything they had? They lived for this shit.

The colossus turned, showing me his pale back, then his stomach, his skin wrinkled and saggy, as he somehow managed to be thin and flabby at the same time. If he were a normal size, I'd say he was about fifty years old. His head was level with the fifth, half-ruined floor of the Guild. That put him at over sixty-five feet tall.

If Julie was trapped inside the Guild, Curran had to be with her. Why wasn't he out here, fighting? If Curran was inside, the giant should be dead. Was he injured? I'd seen him walk through fire on broken legs.

I had to get inside.

I shoved the cresting fear aside. Calm washed over me. If Julie and Curran were inside, then the fastest way to help them would be to remove the giant. I could panic later.

The heat emanating from his feet was overpowering. No way for a ground strike. No way through that door either. I had to get up to his level, and all of the neighboring buildings were too far to make that jump. Drawing him off would be better. If I could get him to chase me, I could lead him where I wanted him. It was a long shot, but I had to try.

I took a deep breath and screamed at the top of my lungs. "Hey, asshole!"

The giant ignored me.

"I'm talking to you, Wrinkle Ass! Over here, you big hairy dimwit!"

The colossus peered blearily to the left. His face used to be human at some point. Traces of it still remained: human nose, small eyes, balding skull fringed in longish dark hair. But his lips were peeling back, revealing sharp inhuman teeth. His ears were growing, lengthening as I watched, their corners creeping up. The brow ridge curved outward, overshadowing his eyes.

He was still transforming. There was no telling what he would look like at the end of metamorphosis.

"Look at me when I'm talking to you, scumbag!"

The colossus turned away, swinging around and offering me a glimpse of his face again. Something bright shone in his left earlobe, a small brilliant spark. His irises glowed a bright unblinking orange, as if burning from within. No intelligence in the eyes, just a kind of dull, stupid rage.

I tried one last time. "Sixty-five feet tall and your dick is still tiny!"

No reaction. This wasn't working. Either he didn't hear me or he really wanted whatever was inside the Guild.

The giant swung forward. It looked like he was about to bend forward. *Oh no, no, let's not . . . Oh my God.* Some things you could never unsee.

The giant peered through the fourth-floor window, straightened, drew his tree-trunk thick arm backward, and punched the upper floor of the Guild. Bricks flew. His feet glowed brighter. A dark metallic sheen crept up his calves. Tiny bursts of flame dashed up his legs and the acrid stench of burning human hair filled the air. He was turning into metal and judging by those feet, that metal would be red hot. I had seen many odd things, but I had never seen that. The amount of magic that would be required for the metamorphosis and getting the giant summoned in the first place had to be staggering.

Kill it first, sort it out later.

A man leaned out the third-story window and fired two crossbow bolts into the soft tissue under the giant's jaw. The creature roared, slapping at him with sudden speed. He tried to duck back in and lost his balance. The giant palm smashed into the merc. He plunged and fell with a wet sickening sound. The giant raised his massive foot and stomped down.

Sonovabitch.

The iron on his legs climbed another foot. If he turned completely metal, he'd be indestructible. I had to level this playing field and fast.

The only other way into the Guild was through the back door. Normally it was locked and barred from the inside, but it was better than nothing.

I pulled Cuddles to the side and sent her galloping through the street. Buildings flashed by. A left. Another left. People ran past me and on, into the city. I shot out onto the cross street, jumped off Cuddles, and ran around the corner to the back of the building.

A twisted wreck that might have been a large truck at some point blocked the back door, its cab twisted and caved in. A mangled black sedan lay on top of it, and a wooden cart on top of that. He must've grabbed whatever vehicles he could find on the street and piled them against the back door. Smart.

Ten feet above the barricade, a boarded-up window interrupted the wall. It must've been a functional window at one point, because someone had gone through the trouble of installing metal bars over it. The bars were gone now, but the steel brackets and a section of the frame were still attached.

This was a very stupid idea. Climbing up those cars would make me into a sitting duck. If that thing realized what I was doing, I'd have nowhere to go. Not to mention I had no idea what was behind that wood. If it was solid wall, I'd be in trouble. It didn't matter. I had to get into the Guild.

The giant bellowed. Bricks flew above the Guild like a meteor shower. I ducked behind the corner and watched them pelt the ground. The last chunk bounced off the pavement.

I lunged into the open and backed up.

Stupid, stupid, stupid . . .

I sprinted to the cars. Five feet from the truck I jumped and scrambled up the car pile. I stretched, grabbed at the pitted wall, and pulled myself up. The building shuddered. Rock climbing was never my cup of tea. Rock climbing up a shaking wall while a naked giant was having a midlife crisis and pounding on it like a spoiled toddler was at the very bottom of my Would Like To Do list. For my next trick, I might as well set myself on fire . . .

My fingers slipped. I slid down and caught myself on the protruding brick. Easy does it.

The giant roared like a tornado. Poor thing. All stressed-out. *That's okay, wait a few more minutes. I'll cure all your frustrations.*

I pulled myself up to the window, stretched, and grasped the metal frame with my left hand. It held. I hit the wood on the window with my right, testing it. A low sound answered me. Hollow.

I grabbed onto the frame with both hands and brought my knees up. The frame creaked, stressed by my weight, and rocked like a loose tooth. It would probably come out after the first kick. I'd have one shot at this. Maybe two, tops.

I kicked the wood with both legs. The boards creaked but held.

I swung out and hit the window again. The board on the right snapped in two with a loud creak.

A huge hand grasped the side of the building to the right. Crap. He didn't hear me screaming at the top of my lungs, but he'd heard the wood break.

A head came into view: first the cheek, then the chin, then a tire-sized eye. A bright spark winked at me from the giant's earlobe.

I smashed my feet into the boards. The wood snapped, just as the remnants of the frame came out of the wall. I flew through the window and crashed into a table. Papers and cleaning supplies flew around me. Ow.

The light from the broken window vanished, replaced by a hand. Two fingers thrust through the window, hooked the wall, and tore a chunk of it out. I scrambled to my feet. A hand plunged into the room, reaching for me. I drew Sarrat and slashed across the thick fingers. Blood swelled from the cut.

The giant howled and jerked his hand out. I spun around. Metal shelves lined the walls, filled with stacks of paper and cleaning supplies. I was in some sort of storage closet. A small door beckoned in the opposite wall. I grabbed the door handle. Locked. Damn it!

The wall behind me rocked. I glanced over my shoulder and saw a red car coming at me like a battering ram. I lunged to the side, against the wall. The car smashed into the door, crunching with a metallic groan. He was trying to squish me with the car like I was a bug.

The car hammered against the door, clenched in his six-foot-long hand.

I darted left, squeezing between the shelves and his hand, and sliced at the thumb, driving the blade into the flesh. Blood poured. The creature screamed and jerked back, his fingers still locked around the car. I'd severed the extensor tendon. Good luck trying to straighten that hand.

I slashed the hand twice with quick precise cuts. Blood drenched the floor. The giant howled, straining. His fist popped out of the room like a cork out of a bottle. I dashed to the door, leaned back, and hammered a kick just below the lock. The door splintered. I tore my way through it and into the hallway. I was on the second floor, on the inner terrace. Below me the floor of the Guild spread. People huddled by the walls.

The building shook. A chunk of the top floor vanished, snapped off. For a moment sunlight flooded the inside of the tower, and I saw Ken and Juke on the third floor pressed against the wall next to the now-defunct elevator. Ken's lips were moving, his eyes focused. Juke was clutching a bow. Julie and Curran were nowhere in sight.

The daylight faded as the enormous face of the giant appeared in the gap. The giant opened his mouth, showing yellowed teeth. A dull roar tore through the Guild. Oh good. I'd pissed him off.

I sprinted along the terrace to the stairs. A titan-sized hand reached to the bottom from above, fingers spread to grab, like a dragon's mouth, and came up short. The thick fingers raked the air.

Juke shot out of her hiding spot, raised her bow, and fired. The arrow streaked through the air and bit just under the giant's left eyelid. Juke darted back. The giant lashed out, trying to backhand the terrace where she hid.

Ken clapped his hands together. A torrent of yellow steam shot out from between his hands. The giant jerked his hand up to cover his face. The steam hit his palm. Blisters swelled under his skin, rupturing. An earth-shaking bellow rolled through the Guild, so loud it almost knocked me off my feet.

The stairs loomed before me. I sprinted up the staircase. The fourth floor flew by. I rounded the bend in the stairs and saw the sky above me. The giant had taken off a chunk of the fifth floor and now the last flight of stairs protruded above the building, leading nowhere.

I forced myself to slow down and walk up the last few steps. I needed to be close for this to work, and I couldn't afford for him to slap me off that stairway.

The giant roared right in front of me, grasping at the people down below. I pulled the magic to me and spat a power word. *"Aarh!"* Stop.

The magic tore through me like an inferno and smashed into the giant. Instead of gripping him, my power crashed into an invisible wall, ricocheted, and slammed back into me. I tumbled back down the stairs and fell against the wall. Every bone in my body rattled in its socket. I screamed, but the agony dragged me under, robbing me of my voice. I couldn't speak. I couldn't think. I couldn't move. Above me, the giant, a smudged dark shadow, kept digging in the building.

It didn't work. My power word had backfired.

Time stopped. My head swam. A vortex of pain clamped me, dark and merciless. It felt like my very being was being shaved away one thin layer at a time. Razor blades filled my mouth and throat. Dear God, it hurt. It hurt so much. My ears hurt. My hands bled. My chest refused to rise. It felt like I was dying.

I clung to life, but it hurt so much. If I let go, it would stop hurting.

Get up. I had to get up.

My legs had turned to Jell-O. It felt like my bones were broken, and my body was filled with their shards.

The giant straightened and raised his fist. A person struggled in his fingers. Black hair. Don't be Juke . . .

The giant's cavernous maw opened. Yellow teeth bit down.

You sonovabitch.

He tossed the bottom half of the human being aside like a used tissue and reached down again.

No, you don't.

My fury cut through the agony. I gripped it like a lifeline and forced myself to roll up to my hands and knees. I would get up. I had to get up.

Come on, legs. Straighten. An inch. Another inch.

He would not get away with this. I would make him pay. He wouldn't kill anybody else.

The pain snapped inside me. White haze exploded in my brain and I went blind.

I concentrated on breathing. Calm. I needed to stay calm.

The haze burned off in another explosion of pain. I sheathed Sarrat and pulled out two throwing knives. Now I just had to run. Piece of cake.

I charged up the stairs. The pain tore inside me. One step, two, three . . . The last step loomed before me, the giant's back under me as he bent over, stretching to grasp more bodies.

I jumped and plunged down, both knives out. My feet connected with the giant's back. I slid and dug both of my blades into his flesh. Touching his skin was like opening the door to a burning stove.

The giant swung around, trying to knock me off with his hand, but I had landed almost in the dead center of his back, next to the spine. His fingers passed harmlessly below.

I yanked the left blade out, stretched, and sank it in six inches higher. Blood seeped from the wound in a hot flood, drenching my clothes. The giant shrugged his shoulders, muscle rolling under the skin. I jerked the right blade out and jammed it higher than the left. Left, right, left, right. The effort was wrenching my arms out of the sockets. Left, right, left, right . . .

Thick, coarse iron spikes burst from the spine next to me, growing into a crest. His skin was almost too hot to touch. He was still metamorphosing and right now it was helping me. I clutched those spikes and scrambled up.

The big hand reached over the shoulder and slapped the spot a foot above my head. The skin quaked under me. Crap. If I climbed any higher, he would flatten me into a Kate pancake.

A cloud of flies the size of tennis balls erupted from within the Guild, swirling around the giant's head. He waved his arms. The movement sent my legs flying. I gripped the knives and hung on. He stopped turning and slapped at his face. I glanced up. The flies hung in a dense cloud off to one side, then slowly moved to the other. The giant swiped at them and howled.

Someone was helping me.

I climbed up the giant's back, one knife thrust at a time, grabbing a spike when I could. His shoulder loomed. Almost there.

I dug my knife in one last time. The shoulder stretched before me, four feet long and three feet wide. His neck was less than three feet tall. I grabbed a handful of his hair and threw one leg over the shoulder, straddling it. His face was barely human now, his mouth a wide gash, his nose bridge almost flat with two wide nostrils jutting out of nowhere like the nose of a bull. The flies still buzzed around the giant's head. Far below, Ken stood out in the open, chanting, hands out, his face strained.

I pulled Sarrat out. The jugular wouldn't do it. It could take him ten minutes to die. I raised my blade and stabbed it deep into the side of his neck, below the Adam's apple, in the spot before the carotid artery branched into exterior and interior. Blood wet my hands, spurting from the wound in a hot gush. I stabbed deeper, slicing into the artery. I didn't have to sever it. I just had to cause enough damage. A partially severed carotid would bleed him out faster anyway.

Bright blood sprayed out like a geyser, drenching my body and face like a fire hose. Yes!

The giant swayed, off balance. Oh shit. How the hell do I get off this crazy ride?

I slid Sarrat back into the sheath, grabbed the giant's hair with both hands, and held on. The giant rocked back and forth and clamped his hand to his neck, trying to hold back the flood. I clung to his hair. My hands, wet with blood, were slipping. *Go down. Come on, go down.*

With a loud cry, the giant stumbled backward, turning wildly, off balance, then careened forward. The blood kept spraying. I only needed a minute or two. He was dead already. He just didn't know it.

A lurch to the right and I caught a glimpse of the staircase. Someone was running up.

The colossus pitched forward, slumping as if drunk, trying to catch himself on the Guild's building. His head rolled back. The runner leaped, a spear in his hands, and I saw his face. Lago. He landed on the enormous cheek. The spearhead shone, catching the light, and Lago stabbed it straight into the giant's eyeball.

Well, wasn't that nice and dramatic. Way to jump in there at the end. If I weren't holding on for dear life, I'd do a sarcastic slow clap.

The giant bellowed. His whole body trembled. He stumbled around the Guild, trying to catch himself on empty air and failing. His knees gave and he sank down, his face scraping against the ruined top of the Guild. Lago jumped back onto the building. I had no such luxury.

The giant rocked back. If he fell backward, I'd be dead.

The blood was still gushing. He sagged down clumsily and fell to his hands and knees in front of the Guild's ruined doors. About eighteen feet down, all of it strewn with debris from his rampage. I had to take this chance.

I let go and rolled down his bloody back, picking up speed. The back ended and I fell straight down, bending my knees and clamping my head. The impact resonated through my feet. God, that hurt. I rolled, dropped my hands, and saw the giant glaring at me, one eye filled with rage, the other a pale milky blob with the spear sticking out of it. His massive hand blocked the light. I had no place to go. I curled into a ball. The fingers slapped the ground on both sides of me. He missed. He missed!

The hand rose again and I scrambled away, climbing over chunks of bricks and mortar. He tried to follow me, but his left arm gave. The colossus fell clumsily, rolling onto his back. The ground shook.

I backed away, toward the Guild's doors.

His head landed on the pavement. His one good eye rolled back into his skull. He shuddered and lay still. The blood, once a powerful geyser, slowed to a gush.

People burst out of the Guild's doors. I searched the fear-shocked faces, looking for the familiar features and blond hair. Nothing.

A man limped out, behind everyone else.

"Is there anyone else inside?" I called out.

"No. I am all there is."

A woman sprinted from the side, running in the opposite direction to the crowd, her face frantic.

"Mom! Mom! Here!"

Julie. I whipped around in the direction of the voice.

A dark-haired teenage girl dashed out of the crowd. The woman threw her arms around her. A man followed.

Oh my God. That was the voice I heard on the phone. My Julie wasn't in the Guild. This was somebody else's Julie.

The relief rocked me. I sat on a chunk of the building, leaning against it. My arms hurt, my shoulders hurt worse, and the last echoes of the misfiring power words still rolled around inside me, clasping my insides in fiery internal cramps. It hurt to stand. To sit was an unbelievable luxury and so I sat, basking in the wonderful feeling of not resting my weight on my feet.

I pulled gauze out of my pocket and wiped my eyes. The gauze came back drenched in crimson. My power word had backfired. I had had a power word fail before. *Ud*, the word commanding something to die, usually didn't work. To kill something with it, you first had to own your target completely. The first two times I tried it, the pain had been so excruciating that I was convinced I would die. This was worse. *Aarh* was a simple order to stop. It usually froze the target for about four seconds. I'd never had it misfire on me. Was I getting weaker? Was the giant too large? Was he immune to my magic somehow? I had all the questions and none of the answers. Ugh.

The red stream running from the giant's neck finally stopped. He had bled out. It was over.

I closed my eyes and sat very still.

. . .

EVEN IN POST-SHIFT Atlanta, a giant was big news. The PAD was first to arrive, followed by a fleet of ambulances, which were still parked around the Guild. The cops examined the giant, determined he was dead but surrounded him with their tactical vehicles just in case, and interviewed everyone. They took my statement and then told me not to leave the scene. MSDU, the Military Supernatural Defense Unit, came next and promptly got into a jurisdiction war with the PAD, because the PAD wouldn't let them explode the giant's corpse and incinerate the pieces just in case. The MSDU also took my statement and told me not to leave the scene. When the Georgia Bureau of Investigation showed up, I told them up front that I had no intentions of leaving the scene and that I wasn't going to answer any questions unless they produced a police captain who accused me of being a loose cannon and demanded my badge. They left me alone after that.

The news crews arrived next in a rabidly excited flood. With the Internet dead and TV erratic, most of our news came via newspapers, but a couple of TV crews appeared anyway and promptly surrounded Lago. He had been standing there with a charming self-deprecating smile for the last twenty minutes.

"Are you hurt?" one of the reporters asked, a little too loud.

"Nothing serious, but yes, my legs are going to be hurting." Lago winked. "I'm not as young as I used to be. I don't heal as fast, but sometimes even an old dog has to step up to protect his home."

I sat on a chunk of the fallen debris in front of the Guild's doors. My head hurt so much. It felt like someone kept hitting me with a hammer in the back of the head. Every time one of the hits landed, the wave of pain drowned me and my skull threatened to split open, and then for a moment, as the pain receded, an overwhelming relief came until the next blow. I realized that the blows coincided with my heartbeats. Something was wrong with me, with my blood. The magic in it felt like it had been boiling. Every blood vessel in my body had been burned from the inside out. There was nothing I could do. I just had to sit here and wait it out. Once I was done, I would go and see Doolittle. Retired from the Pack or no, he would treat me. Except I was barred from the Keep for the next thirty days. Shit.

The corpse of the giant sprawled about sixty yards in front of me. He had fallen over the far end of the Guild's large parking lot and now lay on his side, his left arm stretching toward Phoenix Drive, his feet pointing toward the Guild. Most of the law enforcement had camped out to my right, in the street. Random spectators gawked at the giant and wandered through the parking lot despite the PAD's valiant attempts to keep them out. A few mercs stood here and there, pondering the damage to their vehicles. Alix Simos, whose souped-up Lexus had ended up directly under the giant's thigh, looked like he had lost a family member.

As I watched, a group of teenage boys ranging in age from twelve to about sixteen approached the giant's body. One of them, a skinny blond kid, was carrying a long branch.

"Hey!" a female cop barked. "Get the hell out of here!"

The skinny kid jabbed the corpse with a branch.

The female cop started toward them with a look of holy wrath on her face. The kids jabbed the giant again and fled, jumping over debris.

Hey, here is the corpse of something big, scary, and magic that used to eat people when it was alive. I think I'll go over and poke it with a stick. That would be awesome. I sighed. Teenagers. Some things even post-Shift Atlanta couldn't change.

A horse-shaped black-and-white creature emerged from the side street, casually clopped her way right past the mercs, police, and soldiers, and nudged me with her nose.

"Hey, you," I said.

Cuddles nudged me again. I reached into her small saddlebag, pulled out a carrot, and offered it to her. Cuddles swiped it off my hand and chewed with a happy crunch. I petted her cheek. The nausea squirmed inside me, refusing to go away.

I tried to think short, simple thoughts. It hurt less. Curran wasn't in the Guild. Julie wasn't in the Guild either. I had no idea where either of them was. I would give the PAD another five minutes and then I'd tell them I was leaving the damn scene whether they liked it or not. If they had a problem with it, I'd sic Barabas on them.

Juke came walking up to me, with Ken next to her. I did a double take. Juke's face was paler than usual, her features sharpened by adrenaline. She looked pissed off. Ken seemed his normal unperturbed self.

"You're not dead," I said. "I thought I saw him bite you in half."

Juke screwed up her face. "It wasn't me. That was Roger."

"Oh." I had only met Roger in passing. Young skinny guy, dark hair.

"How can you stand it?" Juke waved her arms in Lago's direction. "He's pretending to be a fucking hero!"

I shrugged.

"Seriously? That's bullshit!" She stabbed her finger at Lago smiling for the reporters. "You killed it and he's taking all the credit."

"I didn't do it for the credit."

Juke stared at me for a second, cursed, and walked away, into the Guild through the dented doors.

"Thank you for the flies," I told Ken.

Ken paused. He rationed words like they were water and he was in the middle of the Sahara. "You're welcome," he said finally. He glanced at Juke, who stalked off, kicking chunks of brick out of her way. "She's young."

He'd sunk a world of meaning into that word. Juke was impulsive and brave to the point of being rash, and she wanted to prove herself. To her, Lago's being in the spotlight was a great injustice. To me it was a convenient relief. The last thing I wanted was to be mobbed by the reporters. If Lago didn't mention my name at all, I'd be thrilled.

I nodded at the giant. "Do you know how it started?"

Ken leaned on a rock next to me. "A man came to the Guild. He walked in and didn't say anything. He just waited. He didn't look right. Chris asked him what he wanted, and the man said, 'Crush my enemy.' Then he turned and left. Then"—Ken clapped his hands, making a loud pop—"magic. He kicked the front door, but it got stuck. We tried to get out through the back door, but it was jammed shut. You know the rest."

In the parking lot, thin, wiry Alix Simos crouched by the remains of his

Lexus. A few yards away Cruz, six inches taller and about fifty pounds heavier, said something to him. Simos ignored him.

"I thought I saw something shiny in the giant's left ear," I said.

Ken nodded.

"It's not there now. I checked."

"It wasn't there when he fell," Ken said.

"Are you sure?"

He nodded.

We both looked at Lago. *Well, well, looks like our hero got himself a souvenir. You greedy idiot.*

"Bad idea to take it," Ken said.

It was my turn to nod.

The reporters began to walk away. The impromptu press conference must've ended. Lago came striding toward me, his smile bright. "Hey, Kate! Hell of a thing we did today."

"What did you take from the giant, Lago?"

He raised his eyebrows, but his eyes were sly.

"You took something out of his ear."

Lago grinned at me. "I don't know what you're talking about, honey."

Call me "honey" again, see how that works out for you. "That was really stupid. He was naked except for that item, which means it was probably essential to him being a giant. You took an enchanted object of unknown power from a destructive creature who probably used to be human. You have no clue what effect it will have on you."

"You've got one hell of an imagination."

"She's right," Ken said.

"Turn it in," I said. "It's not worth it."

Lago's smile died. "Look, I get it. You're sore that you had to share the credit. But no need to make up lies."

"Lago, I looked into that thing's eyes. They were empty. He started out as a man but ended up as a giant who had the intelligence of a toddler. He couldn't even talk. Is that what you really want?"

He raised his hands to the sides. His voice rose. "You think I got it? Frisk me! Go ahead!"

Cops were looking in our direction. He was too confident. He must not have had it on him. If I searched the hero giant slayer now, I'd have to answer questions and likely be detained. I couldn't afford to be detained and spend hours in a cell or being interviewed. I had to find Curran and Julie.

"I'm trying to save your life," I ground out.

"I always had respect for you, Kate," Lago said, letting his arms drop. "This? This is just pure jealousy. I thought better of you. It's really a shame when veteran mercs turn on each other like that."

Argh.

He turned on his foot and walked away. Behind him the same group of teenagers was making a second pass at stabbing the giant. Both had about the same amount of common sense.

Ken looked after Lago. "I'll need to think."

I arched an eyebrow at him.

"We may have to kill another giant soon," Ken said. "I need to think how."

A familiar Jeep pulled up to the police blockade line and I forgot all about Ken and Lago. The doors swung open.

My heart pounded in my chest.

Curran jumped out, his face hard. He was covered in blood. Julie shot out of the other door, her face, clothes, and axes splattered with red. Behind her Derek and Ascanio got out of the Jeep, both in warrior form. Where the hell had they been?

The tough metal hide of the giant's foot bulged and ruptured, like a boil. A cloud of foul gas drenched us. Creatures spilled out of the corpse. Six feet long, reptilian, covered in thick spiny scales like those of an armadillo lizard, they dashed forward on muscular legs.

I pulled Sarrat out of her sheath.

THE LIZARDS SPILLED out of the corpse in a ragged crescent along the edges of the parking lot like a mottled black-and-brown flood, blocking the way to Curran and the PAD. For a tiny second he and I stared at each other. His skin burst. Gray fur spilled out and then the lizards hid him from my view.

We had reanimative metamorphosis again. It was too rare to not be connected to the wind-scorpion incident. For whatever reason, the cat-hater who'd tormented Mrs. Oswald had decided to take the Guild out once and for all. Maybe it was revenge because we kept killing his pets.

The teenagers froze like frightened rabbits, their escape cut off. The two mercs still in the parking lot reached for their weapons. A lone cop, trapped by the giant's head, slowly drew his tactical blade and backed up, his back against a mangled Chevy truck.

The lizards stared at us, their eyes glowing dark orange. They varied in size: some dark, almost black, and only the size of a boxer dog; others as big as a pony. Fast, agile, and armed with two-inch fangs. The chances of their being herbivores were nil to nonexistent. Reptiles reacted to movement. If we ran, they would chase. There were about twenty yards between them and the teenagers, and another thirty-five between the kids and Ken and me.

There was no way we would make it to the PAD's vehicles. The Guild was our best option.

Next to me Ken raised his hands and began to chant softly, an incessant, low murmur, sinking power into every word.

"Don't run," I called out.

The kids pivoted to me.

"Walk to me. Slowly."

The teenagers started toward me. The two mercs, Alix Simos and Cruz, backed up too, slowly, carefully, watching the sea of beasts swell with more bodies. They were the farthest from the Guild.

The lizards kept coming. One corpse couldn't possibly transform into this horde. It was as if a portal had opened somewhere deep inside the giant's body and vomited them out.

The lizard current split, both streams turning and pooling, as the beasts assessed the battlefield.

The nearest lizard, a big brown creature mottled with black, opened its mouth. A deep voice came out, the word torn by the sharp rows of teeth. "Meat."

Oh boy.

The second lizard spat an identical voice. "Meat."

Animals didn't speak. Either these were really, really advanced mythological creatures, or someone was controlling the entire horde, piloting them the way navigators piloted the undead. Either way, this just went all the way from bad, past worse, straight to *we are all going to die.*

"Meat."

"Meat."

The air shuddered as hundreds of reptilian mouths repeated over and over, "Meat . . . meat . . . meat . . ."

"Don't run!" I called out.

Cruz turned and shoved Alix down, sinking all of the strength of his powerful muscle into it. You sonovabitch. The push took the smaller merc to the ground. Alix caught himself on his hands as if doing a push-up, gripped the pavement, and stayed completely still. Cruz spun and ran for the Guild.

The lizard heads snapped in his direction, drawn to movement like sharks to blood in the water. A small solid-black lizard darted into his way.

A fringe of brilliant vermilion spikes snapped up in a crest along its spine. Cruz swung his machete.

The black lizard opened its mouth, studded with sharp teeth, belched, and spat a jet of foamy slime straight at the merc. Cruz screamed. His skin stretched like molten wax, tore, and slid off him, revealing bare bloody muscle underneath. Cruz crashed down, his voice cut off in midscream. The reptiles dove after him, the spot where his body fell a churning whirlpool of scaled bodies.

"Meat!" the rest of the horde roared. "Meat!"

The teenagers ran. The lizards charged, scrambling after them. Across the parking lot, people screamed as the front wave of the reptiles tore into the first responders.

I sprinted forward, Sarrat out. My head screeched in protest, the headache pounding my skull.

Alix jumped to his feet and charged after the kids.

A tall gangly kid stumbled over a brick and fell. The rest tore past him and past me.

Alix sprinted full force, arms pumping. The nearest pursuing lizard snapped at his feet, its teeth rending empty air less than a foot from Alix's calf.

I lunged in front of the kid on the ground. The first lizard reached me, and I cleaved its head from its neck.

Alix dashed by me, yanked the boy to his feet, and dragged him with him. Too slow. They would need time to make it to the building. If they needed time, I would buy it for them.

The lizards swarmed me. I stabbed and sliced, backing up. The nausea was overwhelming now, the hot, nearly blinding pain in my head threatening to block out everything else.

A din of human screams rose above the Guild's parking lot.

Cut and back up. Cut and back up. I just had to walk myself right out of here and not get torn to shreds by the endless reptile beasts.

The lizards advanced in a ragged semicircle, trying to surround me. Too many . . .

A black shaggy body smashed into the lizards. A jet of corrosive slime shot past me and fell wide, spilling harmlessly on the ground. An enormous black dog clamped his jaws onto the lizard's neck and shook it like a terrier shakes a rat.

Grendel. Curran must've brought him with them.

The lizards froze, shocked.

The massive dog spat the lifeless body and grinned at me, showing huge white fangs. Blue fire rippled on his fangs and danced along his shaggy fur.

"Good boy."

Grendel parked himself on my left side and snarled.

The headache singed my brain again. Vertigo clamped onto me and acid burned my throat. Screw it. I bent over and vomited. Endorphins kicked in and for a brief moment the headache retreated.

The lizards hesitated, their pupil-less eyes glowing with cold hungry fire. So me killing them wasn't scary, but a black shaggy mutt was clearly outside their frame of reference.

"Meat," a lizard mouth roared.

The others caught the cry. "Meat . . . meat . . . meat . . ."

The lizards rushed me as one. I carved and sliced, kicked, thrust, and stabbed. Bodies fell around me. Grendel and I retreated, fighting for each inch. Fangs snapped at me. A lizard caught Grendel's flank in its mouth. He snarled and I buried Sarrat in the lizard's back. Claws raked my legs. I spun and sliced another beast. An arrow sprouted in its throat. Out of the corner of my eye I saw Alix behind me, his bow in his hands. He drew and loosed the arrows in a smooth fast glide that looked as natural as breathing.

"All hands, fall in!" a woman roared across the lot, somewhere behind the lizard horde. "Form a perimeter! Melee to the front! I want a mage here and a mage there. Light them up. Archers, form up on mages. Give me intersecting fields of fire. Act like you've been to a party before."

A foot. Another foot. We kept going. My breathing evened out. My mind cataloged the injuries and ignored them. Grendel bled but he still fought, ripping into reptilian bodies. The horde tightened the ring around us. They were keying on Grendel now, judging him the easier target. They wouldn't get my dog as long as I breathed.

I chanced a glance over my shoulder. Twenty yards to the Guild. They would be a hard twenty yards. I was about to throw up again.

A lizard crashed in front of me, its body broken.

To the right the reptilian bodies flew up and aside, as if bulldozed. Someone strong and very motivated was tearing down the battlefield.

"What the hell is that?" Alix said.

"That's my honey-bunny."

Curran burst into the open, a seven-and-a-half-foot-tall monster clothed in steel muscle and gray fur. Faint stripes crossed his limbs like dark whip marks. Blood dripped from his clawed hands. On the left side, a patch of his skin was missing, muscle exposed and raw.

He grabbed the nearest lizard, twisted it with a loud snap, and tossed it aside. "Hey, baby."

"Hi." I beheaded a lizard. "Where are the kids?"

"With the MSDU." He disemboweled a beast with a quick swipe of his claws. "You're having all this fun without me."

"I'm not doing much. Just having tea and cookies." I cut at another lizard. "Thinking deep thoughts." *I love you.*

"Then I'll join you."

He loved me, too.

We backed away together. The Guild doors loomed behind us.

"Down!" Ken barked.

I grabbed Grendel into a bear hug and dropped. Curran landed next to me, his arm over my back.

A jet of foul yellow steam tore above our heads and slashed into the front row of lizards. They convulsed, their scale hide blistering, and died. I jumped to my feet and ran the last ten yards to the Guild. Grendel dashed between the metal doors, I was next, and Curran was the last. He and I spun around and blocked the narrow gap between the doors. With only twelve feet between the doors, the lizards couldn't come at us more than three at a time. Juke took position next to us, her spear in her hands. Behind her Alix drew his bow.

Curran put his arm around me and I hugged him, gore and fur and all. The feel of his body wrapped around mine was indescribable. There were few moments of true happiness in life. This was one. I hugged him harder, enjoying every moment of touch.

"Get a room!" Juke growled.

We broke apart in time to see her jab the first lizard.

God, my head was about to split open.

"Where were you? What happened?" I carved a chunk out of another lizard's face.

"I just took the kids to fight some ghouls," Curran said.

Oh, so it was fine, then . . . Wait. "You did what?"

He kicked a lizard. It flew into the others like a cannonball. "I called Jim before we left the house to talk about ghouls, and he said they found some in the MARTA tunnels. So I grabbed the kids and did a little hunting."

I would kill him. "Just so I get it right, Jim calls you and says, 'Hey, we found a horde of ghouls in the MARTA tunnels,' and your first thought was, 'Great, I'll take the kids'?"

"They had fun." A careful note crept into his voice. Curran saw the shark fin in the water but wasn't sure where the bite would be coming from.

"You even took the dog."

Grendel chose that moment to try to shove past me. I shoved him back into the Guild and he began running back and forth behind us, growling.

"He had fun, too. Look at him. He's still excited."

Grendel stopped, shook, flinging blood from his fur, and resumed his orbit around us.

"I thought you had a poodle!" Juke said.

"He *is* a poodle."

"That is not a poodle."

"He transforms." In times of crisis Grendel turned into an enormous black hound. Unfortunately, the transformation was governed by his strange canine brain, and sometimes he decided that the proper course of action in battle was to pee and roll in dead things instead.

A black lizard squeezed through the bodies and died before it could open its mouth, Alix's arrow in its throat.

"Okay," Juke said. "Your horse is a donkey, your poodle is a giant wolf breed, and your boyfriend is whatever the hell he is. You have problems."

"Shut up," I told her.

"He got to roll on some ghoul corpses," Curran said. "He had a good time."

That was hardly surprising. Grendel had a warped sense of personal hygiene.

"You're an inconsiderate irresponsible ass."

"Me?" Curran tore a lizard in half.

"You."

Juke grinned.

"You wanted to make it personal. I made it personal. You want to talk about irresponsible?" Curran's eyes sparked with gold. "You saw a giant ripping up a building and you ran *into* the building. And then you climbed onto the giant so you could poke him with your sword. What was the plan to get down off him? Did you learn to fly and didn't tell me?"

"Don't change the subject. I got a call from Seven Star Academy saying Julie didn't make it to school. I couldn't find her. I couldn't find you."

Juke snickered. "Shouldn't have taken the kids with you, huh?"

"Stay out of this," I told her, and pulled Sarrat out of a lizard's body. "You made all these preparations and never once thought what would happen when I couldn't find you or Julie. Would it have killed you to leave a note?"

Juke blinked, suddenly surprised.

"It takes twenty seconds. 'Hi, Kate, taking the kids to fight some ghouls, be back by lunch.'" I waved my arms. "I thought you might be trapped in the Guild with Julie."

"Why the hell would I be in the Guild with Julie?"

"Because you were supposed to go by here this morning and because I thought I heard her on the phone screaming for help."

Curran spared me half a second of his hard stare. "Even if you thought I was in the Guild, what did you think I was doing while the giant was tearing it up? Did you think I was sitting on my hands?"

"I thought you might be injured."

He looked at me. "We've met, you and I?"

I deliberately took a big step back.

"What?" he growled.

"I'm making room for your ego."

"Fine. I should've left a note!"

"You should've."

"Answer me this, did you hesitate at all or did you see the giant, go 'Wheee!' and run toward it?"

"She ran toward it," Juke quipped.

"He was biting people in half."

"I rest my case," Curran said. "A note wouldn't have made any difference."

Note or not, I didn't care. I was just happy he was alive.

The magic wave ended. The lizards fell as one.

The headache exploded in my skull as if someone had poured gasoline on my brain and set it on fire inside my head. Wetness slid from my ears and I realized it was blood.

"Kate?" Curran turned human in a blink.

"My head hurts."

"I can't understand you." His face turned frantic. "What's wrong?"

"My head hurts." I knew I was saying it. I could hear my voice, I just couldn't make out the words.

"Medic!" Curran roared.

The agony in my head drowned out all else. I sank to my knees and slid to the ground. The world went silent except for the pounding of my own pulse.

I OPENED MY eyes and instantly wished I hadn't. The headache had grown sharp blades and stabbed them into my skull through my eyes.

The ceiling didn't look familiar, but the smell in the air was. The exquisite aroma of disinfectant, rubbing alcohol, and that weird "medicine" flavor told me I was in a hospital. Also the IV in my arm and the blood pressure cuff were kind of a giveaway. My hand rested on the sheath of my saber. Someone had put my sword in bed with me.

Why did it hurt so much?

A soft voice tinted with a coastal Georgia accent drifted through my headache, that lowland genteel Southern dialect that refused to die out and swallowed consonants on the ends of words so "better" and "over" came out as "bettuh" and "ovuh." Judging by the intonation in the voice, the doctor was in and not too happy.

What else was new? I had woken up like this to unfamiliar ceilings and upset medmages more times than I could remember. The only question was, which hospital had I ended up in this time?

I tilted my head on the pillow. The good doctor was sitting in a wheelchair talking to another patient or maybe his helper, I couldn't really see. His voice was quiet and soothing, and I couldn't quite make out what he was saying. If I squinted, I could sort of read his lips. *Intracranial hemorrhage.* Something told me I should know what that meant.

He turned. Something stretched in my brain and I recognized his face in a flash of pain. Doolittle. Why didn't I recognize his voice? Wait, if Doolittle was here, that meant we were in the Keep. We couldn't be in the Keep. Our thirty days weren't up. I opened my mouth to call out. No words came out.

Okay, if I couldn't talk, I would sit up.

My back refused to obey. Panic pinched my breath. I felt my body, I felt my legs, my arms, even my fingers and toes. I could feel Sarrat's sheath under my fingertips. I just couldn't get them to move. My muscles were out of sync with my mind.

I was paralyzed.

No. No, no, no. I lived by my sword. I couldn't be paralyzed. I couldn't.

A word surfaced from somewhere within the recesses of my memory. Hemorrhage. Hemorrhage inside the skull was called intracranial. I knew this. I knew it was bad. I just couldn't fight through the headache to what it meant.

A door swung open and a woman stuck her head in. "Doolittle?"

Doolittle turned his chair toward her and the look on his face said he would bite her head off if she were within reach. Serious business.

"Trisha asked if you could spare a minute for some paperwork."

"If Trisha wants to see me, she can come down here." His voice had a snap to it.

The woman withdrew and shut the door.

The other man said something I didn't quite catch in an unfamiliar voice. I blinked, desperately trying to bring him into focus. Curran. What the hell was wrong with me?

"There is nothing I can do," Doolittle answered, his voice stern. "The MRI showed multiple microbleeds. The small vessels inside her brain exploded. They sealed themselves almost immediately, which is why you're not cradling a corpse right now, and her body began to magically heal, but the damage was done. She should be dead. If it were anybody else, they would be dead, but she is too damn stubborn to die. There is nothing I can do right now. Until the magic comes up, my only option is to manage the symptoms. I'm monitoring her blood pressure. I'm administering mannitol to keep the swelling under control and anticonvulsants so she doesn't seize again. And I need to be doing all that and you need to be somewhere else. Did I not give you something to do?"

"What if she stops breathing again?"

"If her internal respiratory drive mechanism is affected, I will put her on a ventilator. Go away."

Curran glanced at me. I blinked and then he was by my bed. "Kate. Baby."

I still didn't recognize his voice.

"Say something."

I opened my mouth. No words came out.

"Curran," Doolittle growled. "Move."

Curran slid to the side, and Doolittle in his chair took Curran's place.

"Can you hear me?" Doolittle asked, pronouncing the words slowly. "Blink once if yes."

I blinked.

"Your MRI shows ruptures in multiple small blood vessels in your brain," Doolittle said, his voice calm.

I was bleeding in my brain, I couldn't move, I had difficulty talking. The symptoms lined up like links in a chain. I opened my mouth. Concentrate. You can do it. One sound at a time.

"S."

I would make the goddamn word come out.

"St . . . stroke."

Next to me Curran dragged his hand over his face.

"Yes," Doolittle said. "You had a stroke. You had several microstrokes simultaneously."

That's me, the overachiever.

Doolittle squinted at me, his face somber. He usually appeared to be in his fifties, but he looked much older today, a tired black man with salt-and-pepper hair and kind eyes.

"How are you feeling?"

I opened my mouth and concentrated on pronouncing a word. My voice was so weak. "P . . ."

They both leaned in, trying to hear me. I fought through the bout of pain, drawing a sharp breath.

"P . . . peachy."

Curran exploded out of the chair, moving out of my view.

"That's good," Doolittle said, his expression somber.

I tried to squeeze my sword. I couldn't do it. My hand rested right on it, because Curran must've put it there. He knew Sarrat would make me feel safe. But now I couldn't even close my fingers around it.

I couldn't hold my sword.

I wanted to go home. I had to go home right now. I needed to be out of this hospital bed.

A man stuck his head into the room. "Ariela is in labor."

Doolittle pushed his chair to the door. "I will be right back. She's confused and sedated. Don't do anything to aggravate her. No stressful topics. Nothing that could potentially upset her. Less information is better at this point. Sam, stay right here and monitor her."

A dark-haired man walked into the room and parked himself at the far wall.

I had to get out of here. Panic took my throat into a clawed hand and squeezed.

Curran blocked the light from the window. I felt his warm hand on mine.

"It will be okay," he said, stroking my fingers. "It will be okay."

I had to tell him that I had to go home.

"What is it?" Curran leaned closer to me.

"I don't think you should encourage her to talk . . ." Sam started.

Curran turned to him. A gold light drowned his irises.

Sam's mouth snapped shut. I heard his teeth click.

"What is it, baby?"

I finally squeezed the word out. "Home."

A muscle in his face jerked. "No, baby. We can't go home. Doolittle will take good care of you. You just have to hold on until the magic starts."

"Home."

"It will be okay."

I had to make him understand.

"She's getting too agitated," Sam said.

"It will be fine," Curran told me. "You're safe. I won't let anyone hurt you."

My eyes felt wet. Curran's face turned pale.

"Home."

"We can't go home right now. We'll go as soon as you're better."

The wetness was running down my cheeks now in hot streaks. "Have to go home."

Curran's face was terrible. Pain twisted his mouth and he forced it down, his face calm again, but I knew. I saw it. If I made him understand, he would take me home.

"Don't cry," he whispered.

"Please," I begged. "Please."

"What's so important about home?"

I opened my mouth. My voice was so weak. He wrapped his arms around me, lifting me to him.

"Want . . . to die at home."

Shock slapped Curran's face.

Doolittle made a screeching noise that sliced against my ears like a knife.

Curran let go of me.

"Get out," Doolittle said, his voice icy.

Curran opened his mouth.

"Get out or I'll have you removed from the Keep."

Curran spun on his foot and stalked out.

Doolittle turned to Sam. "What did I say?"

"I know, but . . ."

"But?"

"He's Curran," Sam said, as if it explained everything.

"I don't care if he is Curran. In your ward, you are god. Go."

Sam fled. Doolittle wheeled the chair to me.

"Home," I told him.

"That's patently ridiculous. Nobody is going home."

Cold rushed through my veins. Too late I saw Doolittle taking a syringe from the IV. Fatigue mugged me, threatening to drag me under.

I struggled to say the words. "Don't want . . . to die . . . here."

"You're just insulting me now. Nobody is dying today, if I can help it." Doolittle said. His voice faded, growing weaker and weaker. "You're safe. Your maniac is just outside the door, watching over you. Rest now. Rest . . ."

I WOKE UP because someone was looking at me. The room was dim. My body felt heavy. I was so tired. All my systems were shutting down one by one. I couldn't tell which symptoms came from the stroke, which from the sedative. I was lost and I couldn't pull myself together.

The soft electric glow of a floor lamp illuminated a teenage girl sitting by my bed. She was pale and blond and, against that light backdrop, her huge brown eyes stood out like two dark pools.

She was important. She was vitally important to me.

Julie.

"Kate," she whispered, her voice shaking. "Kate?"

"Yes?" I managed.

"It's me, Julie. Are you dying?"

I could tell she desperately wanted a different answer. "I love you."

The expression on her face twisted something inside me.

I looked from her to Curran. "I love you so much. Both . . ."

"You can't die." She grabbed my hand. Tears swelled in her eyes. "You're all I have. Kate, please. Please don't die."

My head hurt so much. I didn't like that she was crying. I had to make her better. "It will be okay."

"Kate, don't leave me." Tears rolled down her cheeks. "It's not fair. It's not fair!"

The door swung open.

"Do I need to put a lock on this door?" Doolittle asked.

"Come on." Curran appeared by the bed, took Julie by her shoulders, and gently but firmly pulled her away from my bed.

"Is she dying?" Julie pulled against him.

"She will be okay," he told her.

"What if she won't be? What if she—"

The door closing behind them cut off the rest of her words.

I'd never felt so helpless.

"Home," I told Doolittle.

"Soon," he promised.

Liar. I had to get out of here. I didn't want to end my life in this hospital bed. I had spent too long without magic, and my body was giving out. I felt weaker and weaker. They had to take me home. I wanted to die in our house. "Too long . . ."

"You've only been in here a few hours. It feels longer because you keep waking up despite the sedative."

"Julie."

"Julie will be fine. You don't have to worry about that right now," he said. "Focus on healing. Rest."

I WOKE UP to pain. My brain was slow and confused. My mouth tasted like medicine. I was so tired. I was sinking deeper and deeper into the murky water of pain and exhaustion. I knew the signs. My body was giving out. Why wouldn't they just let me go home . . .

It was night and my room was quiet. Doolittle still sat in his chair, his paperback on his lap, his eyes closed. A hair-thin line of bright orange light marked the edge of the door—someone had failed to close it all the way. Quiet voices floated into the room. I had to strain to make out the words.

"What if she doesn't pull through?"

Julie.

"She will." Curran. His voice was rock steady, quiet, strong, reassuring.

"Ascanio said she might be paralyzed. He said she could get amnesia . . ."

A spark of the old me fought to the surface of the pain for a brief second. Damn it, could that kid not keep his mouth shut for once?

"Don't listen to what that idiot says. Kate wouldn't abandon her family. That's not who she is and that's not what she does."

Which Kate are we talking about? Because the one in this bed didn't have a choice.

"But what if she doesn't?" Julie pressed. Her voice was trembling. "She isn't acting like herself. She's a fighter and she isn't even fighting. Ascanio said he heard her say she wants to go home to die."

If I got better, that bouda was going to regret it.

"Ascanio shouldn't run his mouth," Curran said. "Sometimes when people have head injuries, it changes who they are for a little while. She will be back to normal soon."

And often that change was permanent. I'd killed a man who had turned into a violent sadistic drifter after suffering a fractured skull.

"I know it's scary. But you have to trust Doolittle. She is under heavy sedation. She just isn't herself right now," Curran said. "When the magic comes, Doolittle will heal her."

"What if she never comes home? What would I . . . I won't have anybody . . ."

"You will have me. She will come home, but if she doesn't, I will still be there," Curran said. "We are family. You will always have a place in my house. I won't abandon you. If something happens to me, Andrea and Raphael will step up. Derek will always be there for you. You have people, Julie. You are not alone."

You are not alone . . .

Someone upstairs must've really hated me. I wanted to have people, too. I had wanted to hear those words for so long, and now, just after I'd had a small crumb of happiness, I was about to lose all of it over something so stupid. I had to get better. I had to get better now.

I clenched my teeth.

This wouldn't end me. Not like this. Not right now. I would survive this.

I fought through the pounding in my head, trying to find something, anything, to pull me out of the cold murky depths to the surface. I just had to survive until the magic hit.

I would take anything. Any help, no matter how small.

I refused to sink. I would walk out of here. I would be with Curran again. I would see Julie grow up.

I want to survive.

I fought for it, trying to keep myself up, trying to reach the surface, but I kept sinking.

Something shifted deep inside me, an unidentified muscle clenched tight for too long relaxing in a flood of new ache, and then I felt it, a tiny hint of a current pushing me up. It was weak, oh so weak, but it was there. I wrapped myself in it and for a brief moment my addled brain recognized it for what it was: the city I'd claimed surrendering what little residual magic it had kept during the technology. The land I'd claimed was trying to keep me alive.

It wasn't enough to lift me up. It was barely there, but it stretched to me. I felt the city breathing. It was filled with life. Tiny creatures squirming through the dirt, plants growing in the soil, ivy and kudzu climbing up the ruins, skittish things hiding in their burrows, predators crouching in the dark, people in their homes, all of them sacrificing a tiny crumb of the magic stored within their bodies. It hurt them, it was precious, yet still they gave it to me because I asked.

I stopped sinking.

". . . GO BACK AND tell him that if he thinks he can dictate who I can and can't treat, I quit," Doolittle said. "And I won't be coming back until hell freezes over."

I opened my eyes. The room was still dimly lit. My head still hurt, but I was floating.

A woman stood next to Doolittle, her face obscured. Curran leaned against the other bed like a dark shadow. His arms were crossed on his chest. His eyes were glowing pale gold. Menace rolled off him, and the air in the room turned thick and tense.

"That's not what the Beast Lord says. The law states that a retired alpha can't be in the Keep during the time of separation. Which is why I brought down this paper." The woman held the paper up to Doolittle. "This is an amendment to the Pack law code that gives you the right to treat patients who are not members of the Pack in the Pack's facilities if you determine that their condition requires emergency treatment."

"This is a hospital. I don't need anyone's permission to treat a patient." Doolittle took the paper and read it.

The woman looked at Curran. "Curran."

Curran's face was grim. "Trisha. How did he manage to push that through? The Council wouldn't stand for it."

"They don't know it's for you," Trisha said. "They went into session just before you got here, and Jim brought it up under the Cooperation Act, making a case that if there is an injured shapeshifter within Pack borders, there may not always be enough time to observe all proprieties. He bundled it with an addendum to the border policy, and they passed it without looking closely at it."

"Smart," Curran said.

"It's Jim," Trisha, said as if it explained everything. "Nobody except the personal guard knows you're here. It will get out eventually, but the Council has left the Keep, so we bought you a few more hours. How is she?"

I closed my eyes. I didn't want to be a focal point right now.

"Resting," Curran said.

"Nasrin!" I heard Doolittle roll into the hallway. "I need a second opinion on this paper . . ."

"What will you do if she remains paralyzed?" Trisha asked quietly.

"I'll take care of her," Curran said.

He would. I knew he would. I opened my eyes.

"My aunt is quadriplegic," she murmured. "It is extremely difficult. We could keep her here for you . . ." She caught herself. "Sorry."

Excellent timing. Perhaps she should borrow one of my knives and stab him while she was at it.

Doolittle rolled back, the paper in his hand. "We signed it."

Curran took it from his hand and gave it to Trisha. She took it.

"Did Jim need anything else?" Curran asked, his voice cold.

"No." Trisha realized she was being dismissed. "Good luck."

She turned around and walked out.

Curran looked at the closed door for a long moment.

"It's okay," Doolittle murmured, his voice soothing. "Come on. Let's get you some tea . . ."

Curran shook his head.

"Stay right here," Doolittle said, rolling to the door. "I'll be right back with the tea."

The door closed behind Doolittle. For a moment nothing happened, and then Curran's pose shifted. Tension gripped his spine and his shoulders. He looked like a man backed into a corner, outnumbered and injured, resigned to his fate, but grimly determined to stand his ground. His face was neutral like a mask, but his eyes weren't. They brimmed with pain and fear.

Oh, Curran.

It tried to bend him, and he wasn't used to bending. He didn't know how and he was fighting it, but whatever anxiety churned inside him now was slowly winning. It would drag him down and crush him. All of his power, will, and explosive strength meant nothing and he knew it. He looked like a man at the deathbed of someone he loved.

That someone was me. I put him through this.

I wasn't even that lovable to begin with. I was a selfish ass, but somehow something I did made this man love me, deeply and without reservation. He knew things about me that I would die to keep secret. I trusted him more than I trusted anyone in my life. I mattered to him. He was suffering and I wanted it to stop. I wanted to see him happy. I loved him so much.

I meant to tell him that if he chased Trisha down and brought her back here, I'd punch her in the arm for him. I managed one word. "Bitch."

He pushed off from the bed against which he leaned. All signs of worry vanished from him. He forced a neutral expression onto his face. My Beast Lord.

"Come," I whispered.

He came over to my bed.

"Closer . . ."

He leaned in closer.

It took all of my will. I lifted my hand and punched his jaw. It was the saddest punch on the planet. My fingers barely grazed his stubble and then my arm gave out and fell back on the bed.

Curran blinked.

"You looked sad," I explained.

"Is this you trying to cheer me up?"

"What are you . . . going . . . to do about it?" I asked. "Your Wussiness?"

He touched his index finger to my forehead. His voice was rough. "Tap. You're out, Ass Kicker."

"I leave you alone for five minutes and you're in here punching each other and playing grab-ass," Doolittle said from somewhere in the room. "I expect this from you, Kate, because you have no sense, but you, you should know better. Roughhousing in the hospital. Drink your tea." Doolittle thrust one of the glasses at Curran.

Curran obediently took the glass and drained it.

"The tea was a lie," I told him quietly.

He nodded. "He spikes it with a sedative."

So he knew and drank it anyway. "What kind of a sedative takes down . . . a shapeshifter?"

"I don't know." Curran's face was relaxing. He sat on my bed, moving very carefully. "He won't tell me."

"He needs it," Doolittle said. "He hasn't slept since you got here."

"You get your tea through your IV," Doolittle told me.

"No more tea. It makes me loopy and sad."

"I would be most appreciative if you refrained from telling me how to do my job. If I need some guidance on how to best skewer something twenty times my size and get myself nearly dead in the process, I'll ask you. There is only one medmage in this room, and since I am that medmage, I'll decide what medicine to administer and when. And for your information, it is your head injury that is the culprit, not the sedative."

"Bummer."

I felt oddly light and sleepy.

"Lie with me," I whispered.

Curran stretched out next to me. Our arms were touching. The smell of him drifted over, so familiar and comforting.

Curran's fingers held my hand, his thumb gently stroking my skin. I recalled the way he tasted. The feel of his body on mine. The weight of it. The strength of the arms wrapped around me. His eyes. The way he looked at me . . .

"Stay with me, Kate," he said.

"I will," I promised.

THE MAGIC WAVE jolted me out of my sleep, the crushing headache a familiar agony by now. This one-night stand with my stroke had lasted way too long. The pain was intense but my thoughts were no longer jumbled. The current of the city had pushed me a few inches higher.

I opened my eyes to the morning light and saw Doolittle looking at me. Curran sat on the other bed.

"This is what we've been waiting for." Doolittle rolled his chair close to me. "Oh boy."

"Leave, please," Doolittle said.

Curran rose and took a step to me.

"Remember now," Doolittle warned him. "We have an agreement. I'll hold you to it."

Curran stepped to my bed. His arms closed around me and he squeezed me to him. My bones groaned. His voice was a low growl. "I will wait for you. As long as it takes. Even if you never choose to come back. But it's your choice."

He let me go, turned, and marched out. Okay, then.

Doolittle regarded me with his dark eyes. "Your brain is very delicate. Think of your mind as a forest crisscrossed by many paths along which signals travel to your body. Some are clear, some become overgrown over time, but all have formed naturally. Right now these paths are damaged. I can use magic to restore them."

I sensed a big "but" coming. "But?"

"Think of me as clear-cutting the paths by force instead of allowing the natural development to take place. I will do my absolute best, but my power is limited. The pathways I create won't match the old pathways precisely. I have done this previously on four different occasions. I've restored function and, in one case, memories lost during an amnesia-inducing event; however, one of my patients had a drastic personality change and two others developed severe anxiety and reported episodes of depersonalization, during which they felt unable to control themselves, as if the events they experienced were happening to someone else. They felt disconnected from reality and disconnected from their memories. One of them improved over time. The other left her family and moved out of state. She had four children, a supportive husband, and elderly parents. Nobody has heard from her in over nine years."

"You are a bucket of cheer, Doc."

"There is an alternative," Doolittle said. "You could let the healing take place gradually. There is a possibility that your brain will restore itself."

"How big a possibility?"

"A significant possibility. The only reason you are alive and have regained some minor motor function is that immediately after the trauma that caused the strokes, the blood vessels in your brain sealed themselves. The process of healing had already started before you were ever brought to me. I believe that over time, with my help, you will recover most of what you lost."

"How long would that take?"

"I don't know." Doolittle's leaned forward. "But I've observed it happen."

"How long did it take in the cases you observed?"

"Three years to complete recovery for one patient and fourteen months for the other."

Three years.

"How long if you heal me now?"

"It will be miraculous," Doolittle said. "You will walk out of here when I'm finished and no doubt run straight into another foolish fight."

That was a given.

"I want you to know that you have a choice," Doolittle said. "Curran is . . . Well, there is a reason we all followed him. When he wants something, he can be very persuasive."

"You don't say."

"He will abide by your decision, I promise you that. His feelings, or anyone else's feelings except your own, do not matter here. Only you can dictate the speed of your recovery. We don't fully understand how the mind works, but everything within it is connected. There is no guarantee that after I mitigate the damage, you will experience the same emotions you once felt toward people in your life. Curran will wait for you."

If Doolittle healed me, there was a chance I would no longer want to be me. How hard must it have been for Curran to walk out of this room and take that chance?

"He will take care of you and he won't abandon you if you choose to take your time. Neither will Julie. I will always be here."

There was only one thing I could say to that. "Thank you."

He reached over and gently touched my hand. His stern medmage composure broke. "You shouldn't have left the Keep. Look what happened."

It made me want to cry and I didn't know why. I squeezed his hand. "You really think Curran will wait for me?"

"He gave me his word. Trust me, he isn't going anywhere. He is all yours, so yes, he will wait."

"But will my father?"

Doolittle sighed.

"What will happen when my father finds out I can't hold my sword? Will he wait three years or will he burn the city to the ground because I can't stop him?"

"It shouldn't matter," Doolittle said gently.

"But it does."

"You've made an agreement."

"And I trust that agreement only because I'm here to enforce it. He knows that his power isn't infinite. In a fight to the death I will hurt him and that worries him. I need to be capable of fighting him. I can't protect the city if I am not."

"It isn't the time to worry about the city," Doolittle told me. "This is the time to worry about you."

The silence stretched between us. It wasn't fair. It wasn't fair that after everything we had gone through, claiming the city could cost me everyone I loved. It wasn't fair, but life rarely was. Good people died. Bad people had happy lives. That was why someone had to take a stand, and that someone was me.

"Curran loves me," I said. "Nobody in my past loved me that much. I see it in his eyes. I want him to stay with me. I want Julie to stay with me. I want my family. I want all of you." I would do anything to keep my family. Anything, except betray everything I stood for. "But I am alive because the city saved me. It gave me its magic when I was dying."

"Kate . . ." Doolittle said gently. "The technology has been up the whole time."

"I know. But all of us, everything that is alive, produces and stores magic. We hold on to it even during the strongest tech wave. That's why shapeshifters can still change their form. Last night, when I was dying, every living thing in the boundaries of the land I claimed surrendered a tiny fraction of that magic and offered it to me. And I took it." My voice shook. "I took it to survive."

Doolittle opened his mouth.

"Look into my brain. You will see progress that shouldn't be there. I'm speaking in complete sentences." I leaned forward. "I could've asked for more. I could've taken it all to heal myself. I could've drained all of you dry."

Doolittle's eyes widened as the meaning of my words sank in. I could've unleashed a blight to save myself. He recoiled.

We both knew what happened to living creatures when magic was suddenly ripped away from them. A year ago, the Lighthouse Keepers, a terrorist organization obsessed with banishing magic, unleashed a device that did precisely that at Palmetto, a small town on the outskirts of Atlanta. When we got there, Palmetto had become a mass grave.

Doolittle swallowed. "Roland can't be allowed to claim this land."

"He won't as long as I live. I've assumed the responsibility for it. I'm meant to protect it. We are bound now by something I don't fully understand, but I know that this land didn't sacrifice its magic so I could lie in bed for three years taking my time. Right now there is a creature out there terrorizing the city and sending hordes of ghouls to do its dirty work. It is immune to my magic, which means its powers and mine have something in common. My father could've sent it here. I have to stop it. I can't turn my back on Atlanta. It would mean turning my back on Curran, and Julie, and you. I care too much about all of you. Heal me now."

Doolittle shook his head, rubbing his eyes. "Once I start, I will have to finish. It will take a long time, it won't be pleasant, and you may not recall anything surrounding the moment of your injury. That I cannot heal."

"Thank you."

He sighed. "Everyone has a cross to bear."

"Am I yours?"

He nodded. "I keep trying to decide if it's a punishment or a blessing."

"A bit of both." I smiled. "You might as well bring him back. At least we'll both know what we're in for from the start."

IT FELT LIKE hundreds of spiders crawling through my brain. It made the inside of my nose itch. Occasionally they tugged on something and then nausea gripped me. After I heaved for the first time, Curran brought a big bucket for me. I took it away from him. Having him hold it for me would've been going too far. I still had standards. Nauseated and weak, but what are you going to do?

The control over my body came back slowly. It was like pushing against the current of a very powerful fire hydrant or walking underwater, while heavy blocks fell onto my head from above. Sometimes they slid into place effortlessly and sometimes they landed so hard, it felt like they ripped through my brain. Past events exploded in my head as if my memories had somehow gotten stuck in a replay loop.

Julie crying in a restaurant over crab legs and shrimp.

Andrea dragging me out to lunch.

The flood kept coming, relentless. The flare. Fomorians running across the field.

Mishmar.

Greg's savaged body.

My aunt. *Live long . . . child. Live long enough to see everyone you love die. Suffer . . . like me.*

Curran. *Stay with me, baby.*

I will. I promise I will.

Aunt B dying.

Curran.

Swan Palace.

My father.

. . .

Death. So much death. So many people I'd killed. So many people I cared about who had died. So many corpses in my wake.

You truly are my daughter.

We are great and powerful monsters. Love demands sacrifices. When you love something the way you love your people, Blossom, you must pay for it. Old powers are awakening. Those who have slept, those who were dead, or perhaps not quite dead.

I bent forward under the pressure. Something hot slipped out of my eyes and I realized I was crying.

This is my city. These are my people.

I will hunt you. I will succeed. Maybe not now, but I will never give up.

"Done," Doolittle said, his voice hoarse from the strain.

Curran put his arms around me. It was such a simple gesture, but his touch pulled me out of the tangled chaos of my memories back to now, anchoring me here.

The two of them were looking at me.

"Hey," Curran said quietly.

I swallowed. My head throbbed.

"Did it work?" Curran asked Doolittle.

"I don't know." Doolittle sounded tired.

Curran rose and held up his hand. "Kick my hand."

I pushed off the bed. They said walking was just controlled rhythmic falling. My falling turned out to be uncontrolled. I landed on my ass.

Curran didn't move.

I got up to my feet. My body felt like a numb limb coming back to life.

I snapped a crescent kick. I'd whipped it with my hip and it was so fast, it blurred. My foot slapped his hand. He took a step back. His eyes narrowed.

"Tap," I told him.

"It worked," Doolittle said.

≈ CHAPTER ≈

13

"WHAT'S THE LAST thing you remember?" Doolittle asked me.

"My power word backfired for some reason. I think the back-lash of magic caused my stroke. I tried to freeze the giant and failed. The recoil from it hit me and it felt like my head exploded." I felt oddly flat. As if there were no emotion at all in me.

"It did," Doolittle said.

Curran was watching me carefully.

"It was the worst headache of my life. I thought I was dying." I tried to scrounge up more memories. "I was killing the giant. Lago jumped on it, but I had already cut the vein in the giant's neck. We fell. Nothing after that." My voice sounded flat too, as if it were someone else talking.

"You killed the giant. Law enforcement showed up. His corpse started spitting lizards," Curran said.

"How big? What color?"

It took him about ten minutes to bring me up to speed. It was Friday, March 4, three o'clock in the afternoon. I had lost Thursday and a good chunk of Friday, although I could've sworn I'd been in the hospital bed a lot longer. The twenty-four-hour delay might have cost Eduardo his life.

"No news on Eduardo?"

"No," Curran said.

"Where were you? I thought you and Julie were trapped in the Guild."

"I went to kill some ghouls," Curran said.

"You should've left a note."

"I should've left a note," he said. His jawline was tight.

I pushed off the bed and walked to the bathroom. My legs obeyed me. The last remnants of the headache lingered, but they too began to melt. I brushed my teeth and splashed cold water on my face, feeling numb and somehow disconnected, as if I wasn't truly in my body but was standing nearby, watching some strange woman washing her face.

"You need to be alert," Doolittle's voice floated to me. "There is no way to determine how much function she has recovered. She may become disoriented. There might be sharp personality fluctuations. Normally I would expect her to panic, but we both know . . ."

"She will probably stab someone instead," Curran finished.

I wiped my face with a towel and looked at myself in the mirror. Slowly, very slowly, a hint of recognition stirred in me. *Hi. My name is Kate Daniels. Nice to meet you. I can still kick people in the head. I am still me. I have people I love who love me back. I have a job to do.*

I felt better. My body had been resting in the hospital bed for hours. Very slowly, bit by bit, it began to feel like me again. I felt fresh as if I had gotten up on Monday morning after a very relaxing weekend.

I stepped out of the bathroom.

Doolittle rolled to the door.

"Where are you going?" I asked.

"I'm going to lie down," he said. "Because I am old and tired, and I have exceeded my monthly dose of excitement. Kate, no strenuous activity. No fighting, no sex, and no power words. Especially not against any giants. If you repeat that experience, it will kill you. Your brain is still healing. Don't do anything that could raise your blood pressure. Come and see me in a week. I don't know why I prattle on because I'm sure you will ignore me."

I came over and hugged him.

"There now." Doolittle shook his head.

"Thank you for everything."

"You listen to me." Doolittle fixed me with his stare. "I do not want to bury you. I don't want to see you in a coffin. At some point, no matter how stubborn you are, you need to stop treating your body as if it were a sword that you can resharpen every time it breaks."

"If it breaks, sharpening alone won't fix it."

Doolittle made an annoyed grunt. "Kate! Take care of yourself. If you don't care about an old man like me, do it for the sake of your future husband and your daughter."

"No power words against the giants," I promised.

He left. I closed the door behind me and turned.

Curran stood by the bed, his arms crossed on his chest. I walked over to him.

"Are you back or are you not?" he asked quietly.

"Somewhat."

"Kate."

The way he said my name made me want to reach out and touch him.

"I need to know where we are." His gray eyes had grown dark, not angry but resigned. "Are we okay? Are we complete strangers, are we on a first date, or are we going home together tonight?"

I stepped closer to him and kissed him. For a moment he didn't respond, and then he opened his mouth and pulled me to him, gripping me. I licked his tongue, letting his taste wash over me. Anticipation flooded me. This felt right. He was mine. My Curran. I'd almost lost him, but I'd fought for him and here he was, loving me. I slid my hands up his chest and around his neck. We stood locked, intertwined, almost one, tasting the same taste, breathing the same breath, and in this moment I felt whole.

I felt on fire.

He thrust his tongue into my mouth, pressing it against mine, his body so hard and strong against me, his skin hot, his hands roaming my back, sliding lower along the curve, and cupping my butt. He kissed me, hard and ravenous, drinking me in. Every stroke of his tongue against mine made me crazier and crazier. I slid my hands into his short hair, pressing into him. I wanted it to last forever, to stay like this, wrapped up in him, whole, loved, and wanted. I needed more.

People rose from my memories: my adoptive father, Greg, my biological father . . . *Get lost, all of you. He is mine. I want him, I picked him, and he is mine. I don't have to justify it to you or anyone else. If you don't like it, piss off.*

We broke apart. His eyes were full of golden sparks. Whatever restraints held him back, I had just torn into pieces. His gaze should've melted the clothes right off my body, and I had no idea why they were still there. I raised my chin and he dipped his head to my neck. His teeth nipped the skin there, sending delicious shivers down my spine.

"Love me," I whispered. "Love me and we'll be okay."

His hands roamed my body, caressing, stoking the need in me with every brush of his hard fingers. He inhaled my scent. I ground against him and felt the long hard length of him behind the fabric of his jeans. *Yes. Please.*

Someone knocked on the door.

"What?" Curran said, his voice even.

I kissed the sensitive spot under his jaw, tasting his skin and the faint scratch of stubble. It drove him nuts. I remembered that, too.

His eyes went completely gold.

"You wanted an update on the Guild," Derek said through the door.

God damn it.

"They're having a meeting in an hour. Also, Trisha says we have half an hour to clear the Keep before it causes issues. They are having trouble containing the fact that we're here.

"Curran?" Derek called.

"We got it." With a low growl, Curran let go of me, looking as if it physically hurt him to step away.

"He has the worst timing," I said. "Always."

"It's his superpower." Curran grimaced. "We have to stop anyway. I don't want you to regret this later. And I don't want your head to explode."

"Really? You're so good that my head would explode?"

It took him a moment. His expression changed from intense to speculative. "It's a possibility. I'm not a doctor, but Doolittle says it could happen."

"That's a lot of expectation to live up to."

"I exceed expectations."

So modest, too.

"Do you want to go home?" he asked.

"No. I want to go to the Guild and then I want to find Eduardo." And kick his kidnapper's ass out of this city.

He pulled a bag from under my bed. "Your gear. I had Derek stop by the house."

I eased the bag open and saw my belt, my throwing knives, my old beat-up jeans, and a bag with the strange dirty glass we had found by Eduardo's car. "I love you."

He squeezed me to him, kissed my forehead, and breathed in the scent of my hair. The relief was so plain in the way he touched me.

"It's okay," I told him.

"I know." His voice was quiet. "I will always be there. I will walk across the whole planet if I have to."

I closed my eyes and whispered, "I'll meet you halfway."

A couple of minutes later we emerged into the waiting room. Derek was slouching against a wall. Julie sat next to Ascanio. The same Ascanio who'd told her I might end up paralyzed or with amnesia and that I wanted to go home to die.

Julie saw me and jumped to her feet. Ascanio grabbed her hand, trying to hold her back.

Amnesia, huh. Well, let's see how it plays out.

"I don't know who you are," I told him. "But don't touch my kid."

Surprise slapped his face. He let go and Julie hugged me. I hugged her back.

"Are you okay?" Julie asked.

"I'm okay." I told her. "I'm not going anywhere. I'm not leaving you. You got it?"

"I got it." She nodded. We'd talk about it more later when we weren't in front of other people. Some things were better discussed in private.

Curran was moving and I walked next to him. We had to get the hell out of the Keep as soon as we could.

Derek and Julie fell in behind us. Ascanio chased me. "Kate! It's me."

"'Me' is a terrible name," I told him. "You should aim for at least three letters."

"Ascanio! You have to remember me."

I shook my head. "Nope."

"It's not fair!" he declared.

"Yes, make it all about you," Julie told him.

Ascanio stopped. "I will make you remember me!" he called.

The four of us kept going.

"You do remember him?" Julie whispered.

"Of course, I remember him."

She snickered.

"Where is Barabas?" Curran asked.

"He said he would be at the Guild in case we decided to attend their meeting," Derek said. "He packed us a care package. It's in my car."

"Good," Curran said.

"We'll need to stop by the Steel Horse to pick up the Clerk," I added. Walking into the Guild with the Clerk would be like sucker-punching Bob right in the gut.

"Did you get a look at the giant?" I asked Julie.

"Yes."

"What color was the magic of the corpse?"

"Bronze," she said. "Just like the Tahoe."

That's what I thought. "Let's talk more in the car."

We opened the big doors. Six people barred our way. I recognized two. The Beast Lord's personal guard.

Curran didn't even slow down.

"Um . . ." one of the men said.

"Move," Curran said.

They moved. We headed down the hallway. A petite woman turned the corner and rushed toward us, adjusting her large glasses. Dali. Hey, I recognized her. Score one for me.

"Wait." Dali blocked our path. "Kate, you're walking?"

"Yes." *And kicking.*

"Can you tell me what's going on? I know that whatever you're doing is connected to the Pack, but Jim is ducking me."

"We're handling it," Curran told her.

"I'm not asking you." Dali turned to me. "What's going on?"

In the old days I would've walked down the hallway and made sure nobody could hear us so I wouldn't cause an incident, but I was no longer the Consort and I didn't give a shit. "Eduardo is missing and Mahon won't look for him because he doesn't think Eduardo would make a proper son-in-law. George asked Jim to help, but he doesn't want to overstep his authority."

Dali blinked and turned to the personal guard. "Rodney. Go and get Eduardo's file for me."

"I can't." The big shapeshifter arranged his face into an apologetic expression. "Jim won't like—"

Dali leaned forward, her stare direct and heavy. "I don't care what Jim likes. Do it."

Rodney hesitated.

"What are you waiting for?" Dali asked. Her voice made it clear she wasn't interested in an answer.

"He's waiting for an 'or,'" I told her.

"What?"

"Usually there is an 'or' attached to this kind of threat. Do it or something bad happens."

"He doesn't get an 'or.'" A faint green sheen rolled over Dali's irises. "There is no 'or.' Do it. Because I said so."

Rodney ducked his head. "Yes, Alpha."

We watched him retreat down the hallway.

"You're getting good at this," I told her.

She shrugged. "I figured it out. Most people will do just about anything you tell them to do, if you act with authority, give them no choice, and accept the responsibility for their actions. That's kind of scary, isn't it?"

GETTING THE CLERK out of the Steel Horse proved to be ridiculously easy. Curran and I walked in there and sat at the bar. The Clerk was drying shot glasses with a towel. He was a trim middle-aged man with light brown hair. He would've been a good bartender. He liked to listen to people.

"Kate. Long time no see." The Clerk eyed us. "What will it be?"

"You like being a bartender?" I asked.

"It has its moments," he said. "It's a complicated business. Have to keep track of suppliers. Have to deal with customers." He didn't sound especially enthusiastic.

"What did you make at the Mercenary Guild?" Curran asked.

"Forty grand."

"I'll pay you sixty if you come back."

The Clerk pulled the towel off his shoulder and called to the back. "Hey, Cash? I quit."

As we walked out of the bar, the Clerk smiled. "I would've done it for less."

"I don't want you to do it for less," Curran said. "You need to be paid what you're worth. If you get the Guild running, we'll talk about a raise."

The Clerk smiled wider. "I'll hold you to it."

Now he was following our Jeep in his truck. One small victory at a time.

Curran drove. The magic was in full swing and the engine roared, but the soundproofing in the cabin dampened the noise enough so, even though we had to raise our voices, we could carry on a conversation.

"Here is what we know," I said. "The ghouls originate in ancient Arabia. So do the wolf griffins and the wind scorpions. Before the griffin, the Oswalds were attacked by a giant tick, but ticks are universal. They're on every continent, except probably Antarctica, and I wouldn't rule that out completely either. So it could have been a tick from Arabia."

"What about the lizards?" Julie asked.

"I can't remember what they looked like, because of the head trauma, but it's possible they are azdaha."

"What are azdaha?" Derek asked.

"Azdaha. Persian dragons. The old Iranian mythos is full of dragon slayers."

This line of reasoning was pointing me to a very troubling conclusion and I was trying to do my best to hold up denial as a shield.

"There is a pattern," Curran said. "Everything is connected by the place of origin."

"Yes. Also, reanimative metamorphosis is rare. To have two occurrences of it so close together is very rare. I would bet my right arm that whoever is behind the wolf griffin and ghouls is also behind the giant and the azdaha."

"We need to get Julie to your friend the wizard," Curran said.

"You mean Luther?"

He nodded. "You said they quarantine the bodies. Would he keep the wind scorpion on ice?"

Knowing Luther? Yes, he would keep it on ice and screw with it until someone higher up lost their patience, took it away from him, and set it on fire. I knew what Curran was thinking. If the wind scorpion also emitted bronze-colored magic, we would have confirmation that everything we'd encountered so far was connected.

"Luther promised me access to Mitchell." I glanced at Julie over my shoulder. "Would you like to go to the PAD morgue with me to look at weird remains and then visit the PAD's pet ghoul?"

Julie wrinkled her nose. "I could do that or spend the evening writing an essay for Contemporary English on an extremely boring book about people living in a pre-Shift small town, which has absolutely no bearing on my life and helps me not at all. I don't know, both options are so enticing . . ."

"I think this new school made your sass even worse," I said.

"You made me worse," Julie said. "I'm your punishment."

I shook my head. "Anyway, everything we've run across while trying to find Eduardo comes from Arabian mythology, which means it comes from the same geographical region as my magic. Same as my father's magic."

"You think Roland is behind this?" Curran asked.

"I don't know. I do know that the giant was immune to my power words. My magic bounced off it and there was hell to pay. I can't risk using a power word against this creature again or my head will explode."

"We just lost one of our biggest guns," Derek summed up.

"Not necessarily," Curran said.

"I can't attack it with power words directly, but I can attack the environment around it. My magic doesn't work only against the creature itself. I used a power word on ghouls who were clearly answering this creature's call, and it worked as intended."

"Why?" Derek asked.

"Because there are some very key differences between the ghouls, the griffin, and the giant," I said. "Let's assume that some being, some Summoner, is behind all of this. He has some sort of agenda, but he is limited because he can only accomplish his goals during magic, so he somehow finds a way to control the ghouls and uses them to do his bidding. My power words work against them because while they are under the Summoner's control, they still retain their own magic."

"That makes sense," Derek said.

"Good. Now, a griffin is a summoning, something the Summoner pulled out of thin air. It's an expression of his magic, so my power words may or may not work on it. I don't think the giant is a summoning, because he was clearly wearing an object of power. It was shiny. I saw it in his ear. I think it might have been a piece of jewelry of some sort."

"How do you know it was an object of power?" Julie asked. "Maybe it was just some random earring."

"Because the giant was naked except for it and it was clearly too small for him. That object most likely turned him into a giant, and he probably started out as a person, not a summoning. For that kind of transformation to take place, the Summoner would have to imbue the human body with his power completely."

"I get it," Julie said. "The Summoner possessed the person and turned him into a giant, which makes the giant an avatar. It's almost as if the Summoner himself became the giant."

"Exactly. My power words work on the creatures he controls, they might work on the creatures he summons, but they sure as hell don't work on him directly."

"No power words," Curran said.

"I agree," Julie said.

"I have no plans to use power words unless I absolutely have no choice." I made a mental note to ask Luther if the object of power had been recovered. It felt like I was missing something, some vital piece, but when I reached for it, I found nothing.

"I don't understand why he attacked the Guild." Derek grimaced. "What was the point?"

"Revenge," Curran said. "Look at it from his point of view. First, he decides he has something against cats and starts attacking the Oswald family. He summons a tick. Eduardo, a merc, comes and kills it. Then Kate and I kill some of his ghouls. Then he summons a wolf griffin, and two mercs from the Guild kill it. He turns the griffin into a wind scorpion, and Kate and I, who had just come from the Guild, kill it. Then you, Ascanio, Julie, and I go into the MARTA tunnels and kill more of his ghouls. If I were him, I'd be pissed off and come over to the Guild to make the mercs pay and to make sure they stopped screwing with me."

"The problem with our theory is that Eduardo doesn't fit," I said.

"Why not?" Derek asked.

"They didn't kill him," Curran said. "If Eduardo just happened to be targeted because he was a merc, than why not just kill him? Why go through the trouble of kidnapping him? What's so special about Eduardo?"

"We won't know until we pull his other jobs from the Guild," I said. And to do that we needed two things: for the Clerk to help us, and for the rest of the Guild to look the other way. Everything hinged on the Guild, one way or the other.

Curran turned onto Phoenix Drive. The top floor of the Guild was in ruins, its roofline ragged and broken, but all of the debris from the parking lot was gone. The wrecked cars and chunks of the building had vanished. An inch of silvery powder covered the street.

"The MSDU did a shake and bake," I said.

Curran glanced at me.

"They torched the contaminated ground and salted it."

Salt was a universal detergent for all things magic. When you didn't know what sort of magic you were dealing with, you had two options. You could set the contaminated object on fire or you could bury it in salt. MSDU usually opted for both, which was known as a shake and bake. They had excellent flamethrowers and there had to be truckloads of salt on the street. If anything magical survived that, I would be surprised.

"Okay, put your game faces on," I told the kids.

We parked on the side. I grabbed the bag Barabas had given Derek for our show-and-tell at the Guild. Curran got out of the car and swung his cloak on. The cloak was Barabas's idea. Big, black, and edged with black feathers, it was gathered on Curran's right shoulder. The Pack had made it for him after he ripped off the Raven god's head during the flare. He never wore it. Barabas had sent it in via Derek with my change of clothes and a note for Curran that said,

Wear it, please. It forced you to focus on his face, and you didn't want to look at that face or to see the power in his eyes. Curran the Godkiller.

The Clerk caught up with us, his expression stretching as he surveyed the damage. "Jesus. I came to see it yesterday but couldn't get close. The authorities had the place cordoned off."

"We'll put it back together," I told him. "Like new."

"Better," Curran said.

We walked to the Guild. The salt crunched under our feet.

The long-suffering metal doors of the Guild were open about a foot. Some halfhearted attempt had been made to push them together. It must've taken several people, because the edges of the doors left scrape marks on the salted pavement.

"You should do the dramatic door-opening thing," I told Curran.

"Would you like to see me do the dramatic door-opening thing?"

"Yes, I would. Very much."

A quick smile bent his lips. We picked up speed. We were almost marching now. A merc stuck his head out of the gap, saw us, and disappeared.

We reached the doors. Curran didn't even slow down. He raised his arms. His hands hit the doors. He pushed and they swung open with a metal groan, scraping the floor.

Curran kept walking. My scary, scary bastard.

We walked into the Guild Hall. The floor had been stripped bare. Most of the roof was gone and open sky rose high above us. This would take so much work. Work and money.

Mercs sat and stood by the walls. I saw Barabas standing to the left. Our stares connected and he smiled.

In the middle of the floor stood Mark; Bob Carver; Ivera, who was the only other member of the Four Horsemen in the Assembly; Rigan, a big blond bear of a man who looked like he accidentally got left behind by some Viking raiders; and Sonia, a graceful African American woman muscled like a fencer. Oh good. The Guild Assembly was all here.

Everybody looked at us. Mark spared us a glance and turned back to the crowd. His suit sat askew on his frame. His tie hung loose around his neck. He looked feverish.

"For years, I ran this hellhole. I babysat your idiot founder," Mark said. Faces turned grim. Insulting Solomon Red's memory wasn't a good move.

"*I* bargained with suppliers. *I* got you the big-ticket contracts. *I* handled the VIP clients. The Malinov contract? *I* got that for you. The Horowitz job? *I* arranged that. Not Solomon Red. Not the Clerk. *I* did that."

Oh goody. We'd caught him in the middle of his "I'm a special snowflake" speech.

"That's bullshit," Rigan said. "I was on the Horowitz job. They wouldn't even talk to us until Solomon convinced them we were good."

Mark spun to him. His eyes narrowed. "You know what, Rigan?" He took a deep breath.

Wait for it . . . Wait for it . . .

"Fuck you!"

There it is.

"Fuck all of you."

He was going to walk. I could feel it. Bob knew it too, because he wasn't talking. Unlike three-quarters of the people present, Bob also knew that running the Guild without Mark would be almost impossible.

"I'm done defending myself. I'm done justifying myself. This place is finished. Finished!" Mark grinned. "Well, I'm not going down with this sinking ship. I got myself a job. I am done."

"What the hell are we supposed to do?" one of the mercs called out.

"I don't give a goddamn crap what the rest of you shit-sniffing animals are going to do. I am out. I just wanted to let you all know how much I hate each and every single one of you. Rot in hell for all I care."

Mark turned to leave.

"Wait," Bob called. "What about your shares?"

Mark spun around. "You want my shares, Bob?" He giggled. "Is that it? My worthless shares that you and your Neanderthals drove from two hundred and seven dollars per share to fifty-six cents? You're not getting them, Bob. I already sold them. And I got above market value, too. Enjoy the rest of your lives in this busted-ass ruin."

Mark bowed with a flourish, turned, and took off.

Silence reigned.

"Who bought his shares?" Sonia asked.

"I did," Barabas said.

Everyone looked at Barabas. Bob Carver had the expression of a man who was feverishly calculating his odds.

"I'm invoking the Donations and Charitable Contributions provision," I said. "The last entry under Membership Powers in the Manual."

Everyone looked at me.

I raised my bag. "I am donating twenty thousand dollars to the Guild to be used only to fund the Clerk's salary and the salary for an assistant of his choice for the next two months, if the Guild is willing to reinstate him."

"You can't do that," Bob sputtered. "You can't just buy your way in."

"Yes, she can," Rigan said. "Hell, yes, she completely can."

Bob turned to him. "We had a deal."

"Your deal didn't mention her donating money. What the devil do you think this is, the Order?" Rigan turned to the crowd. "Raise your hand if you work here for free."

Nobody moved.

"Who here wants to get paid?"

A forest of hands went up. It's nice when they do your work for you.

"Three of my last paychecks were short," Sonia said. "Three! I'm sick of it."

Bob turned to Ivera. She shrugged.

"Why are we still talking about this?" Rigan asked. "I move to reinstate the Clerk. All in favor?"

He thrust his hand up. Sonia joined him. Ivera raised her hand. Bob hesitated, but his hand went up. Voting against the Clerk in front of the whole Guild would slam the lid on the coffin of his leadership.

"Majority," Rigan announced. "You're reinstated, Clerk."

Someone in the back clapped. The crowd caught it, and the hall erupted with stomps, applause, and whistles.

The Clerk made a little bow.

"Alright, alright," Bob yelled. 'We have bigger problems. Like no damn roof."

"Under the corporation provision, I request to enroll three people as my auxiliaries," I said.

"This can wait." Bob glared at me.

"No, it can't," I told him.

"Last time I checked, Daniels . . ." Bob started.

"She killed the giant," a woman called out. "She cut his neck. Lago took the credit, but I saw her do it."

Lago took the credit? Sounded like something he would do. And I didn't remember a bit of it. Must've happened between the giant falling and the lizards Curran told me about.

"What does that have to do with anything?" Bob yelled.

"If it weren't for her, the Guild wouldn't be standing," the woman answered. "Let her do her thing."

"Where were you, Bob?" another merc called out.

"I was on the job," Bob barked.

"Let her talk." Alix Simos stepped forward. That was unexpected. I barely knew him.

"Who are you enrolling?" Sonia asked me.

"Him, him, and him." I pointed to Curran, Derek, and Barabas.

"No," Bob said. "Don't you see? She's using it to avoid the stopgap."

Barabas opened his mouth. I shook my head. It would be better if I said it.

"Bob, it's not up to you. I've been registered as a corporate member for over a year. I can enroll my auxiliaries any time."

"She's right," the Clerk said.

"You'll be liable if they screw up," Bob said.

"Fine, you're enrolled," Sonia said. "The Clerk will do the paperwork." Bob spread his arms.

"What?" Sonia gave him a look. "I want to see where this is going. The three of you are in."

I stepped back. Barabas stepped forward. "Cutting Edge invokes the Donations and Charitable Contributions provision. In accordance with financial limits, Cutting Edge donates $150,000 to the Guild, $50,000 per auxiliary member, to be earmarked as follows: $18,000 for the repair of the roof, $10,000 for the repair of the interior, $12,000 to settle the outstanding balances on utility bills . . ."

He kept going. How had he even managed to figure out all of this in less than forty-eight hours? With each item Bob's expression darkened a little more.

"... and finally the remaining $16,000 to restock the supply of ammunition for the weapons room. In the interests of making sure the money is distributed as assigned, Cutting Edge designates me as the treasurer for these funds."

"All in favor of grabbing this money before they change their mind and appointing that guy to handle all the admin crap with it?" Rigan asked.

"Don't you see?" Bob pointed at Curran, who loomed next to Barabas in his dark cloak. "It's him. He's bankrolling it."

"I don't give a flying snake who is bankrolling it," Sonia told him. "It's money, Bob! Money in hand!"

Bob ground his teeth. "We all fought for this spot. We earned it. You can't just let an outsider come in and take it over. He's buying his way in."

"Would you care to explain how exactly I am an outsider?" I asked. "That's mean of you, Bob. My feelings are all injured."

The crowd snickered.

Rigan turned to Bob. "He isn't asking for anything."

Bob opened his mouth and clamped it shut.

Yep, you've just been outmaneuvered. Curran didn't ask for any position in the Guild except for that of an ordinary merc.

Curran smiled.

"The man is giving us magic money with no strings attached," Rigan said. "He hasn't asked for any special power. He isn't bargaining with us. He's just offering us money. Do you have money, Bob? If you want to give us 150K, I'll use yours instead. Hell, I'll use anybody's money to get gigs coming into the Guild again."

"Let's vote," Sonia said, and raised her hand.

Rigan put his hand up. Ivera hesitated.

"Ivera, shit, piss, or get off the pot," Rigan said.

Mercs, people of genteel disposition and refined manners.

Ivera raised her hand. Bob shot her an injured look.

"We need the money," Ivera said quietly.

"Done." Rigan rubbed his hands together. "We just passed the budget for the next two months."

Bob spat on the floor and walked out. Ivera followed him. Wrong move. He'd just given Curran the run of the field, and Curran wouldn't waste the opportunity.

Curran pondered Bob's spit. "We need to clean this place up. Grab a shovel or a broom, and let's go."

"I'm not a janitor," Paula, one of the mercs, called out.

Curran turned to her. "Funny, I'm not a janitor either. Although that depends on who you ask. Sometimes I end up cleaning up other people's messes. But we've all been there. That's what being a merc is, right?"

"You wouldn't know," Paula said.

Curran glanced at her. "I take it you come to us from a privileged background."

Paula drew back. "That's none of your business."

"I don't come from money," Curran said. His voice rolled, filling the space. "Everything I have I made with my own two hands, and I have to work hard every day for it."

"Even Daniels?" another merc asked.

That got some giggles. Curran cracked a smile. It was a bright, infectious smile. "Especially Daniels. I work to keep her daily. Otherwise she wouldn't put up with me."

More laughs.

"I thought I was going to be rich at one point, but when I left my people, instead of paying me, they gave me shares in this Guild."

"You got suckered," someone called out.

"That's what they thought, too," Curran said. "Turns out I suckered them. I think this place is a cash cow."

People laughed.

"You need to have your head examined," Paula volunteered.

He ignored her. "I'm not here to make speeches or to run anything. I've been there and done that. I have a family now and I'm here for only one reason. I'm here to make money."

He had said the magic words. They were listening now.

"When I hire someone, I look at the tools of his trade and his place of work. If I am hiring an electrician, I want her shop to be clean and organized and her tools to be in good repair. If I am hiring a killer, I want to know he has respect for his job and his weapon. Look around you. There is garbage on the floor. Dirt. Old food. The place doesn't smell too good and looks worse."

The mercs looked about, as if seeing the Guild for the first time.

"If I walked through that door right now and saw this, I wouldn't hire us. We look weak. We look sloppy." Curran shook his head. "Judging by this place, you could never tell that this is a guild of skilled tradesmen. Because that's what you are. You put your life on the line every day to make a buck and to help people. Not every Joe Blow can do this job. This is just as much a guild as an electricians' or masons' guild, except that when a member of this guild screws up, instead of the power going out or the building looking crooked, people die."

They were hanging on his every word now.

"You deserve better than to come to work in garbage. Once the gigs start coming in, we'll hire janitors and we'll pay them well, because we'll have the money to spare. But for someone to hire us, he has to make it through the front door without gagging. Besides, that's my kid over there." He nodded at Julie. "I don't want her to think that I work in a dump. So I'm going to get off my ass and clean this place up. If you are too well bred to take pride in this place or if you are too scared of dirt, I don't mind. Go sit out of the way with the rest of the special snowflakes."

FIFTEEN MINUTES LATER I stood next to the Clerk as he pulled the list of Eduardo's jobs. I was feeling light-headed. My left side itched all over. But if these were the worst side effects I got, I would be thrilled.

The Guild had turned into a bustling hive. Trash was being swept, debris was being shoveled into wheelbarrows and, across the floor, Curran single-handedly picked up huge chunks of brickwork that had fallen off the walls and carried them outside.

"Here is everything." The Clerk handed me a handwritten list.

I scanned it. Routine, routine, routine . . . Nothing even remotely pointing to Arabian mythology. Nothing in that particular subdivision. This looked like a dead end . . . Eduardo had worked a lot in these few weeks. Did he ever sleep?

Wait.

I pointed to an entry on the fifth of February. "It says here he declined a gig."

Clerk checked the list. "I remember that. He took a job in the morning, came back two hours later, and dropped it."

Dropping a gig wasn't unheard of, but once you committed to a gig, you had to do it, so the Guild allowed only three dropped gigs per year. This was a blue gig too, which meant double rate. "What happened?"

"It was a bodyguard detail, VIP client. Rose was with him on it. I did the interview with her afterward for the liability and evaluation, and she said that everything was fine until Eduardo saw a neighbor come home. Hold on . . . I don't remember this that well." Clerk flipped through another book. "There. 'A man in his early fifties, six foot tall, large frame, dark hair, dark eyes, short beard, olive complexion, glasses . . .'"

I'd bet my arm this was Nitish's customer.

"'. . . riding a breathtaking black Arabian horse.'"

"Arabian?" That by itself didn't mean anything.

"Yes. Rose knows her horses. She went on for about five minutes about how good that horse was. Let's see, Rose 'made a comment to Eduardo, "There goes a million-dollar horse." Eduardo looked at the man as he was dismounting. The man recognized Eduardo and called him by name. Eduardo didn't answer, went inside the house, got his gear, and left. The man watched him leave but didn't interfere.' The end."

Hello, Eduardo's stalker.

The Clerk looked up. "He came straight here, dropped the gig, and took another one. I told him it was a bad habit to get into and he said it was personal."

"Can I have the address of the neighbor?"

"No, but here is the address of the gig." Clerk wrote it down on a piece of paper. "Just this once."

"I promise."

"Was he a friend of yours?" Clerk asked.

I didn't like the sound of that "was." "He still is."

"I hope you find him."

"So do I."

I needed Derek. It would be dark soon and I had to talk to Mitchell, because he was still my best bet to figure out if something was influencing the ghouls in the Atlanta area. I couldn't miss that date.

I glanced up and saw Ascanio picking his way across the floor. A middle-aged African American man in a suit walked next to him.

Ascanio saw me and made a course correction.

"What are you doing here?" I asked.

"This is Mr. Oswald," Ascanio said. "He came by the office, so I thought it would be better if you talked to him yourself."

Mr. Oswald. The woman whose family we saved from the wind scorpion had the last name of Oswald.

I held out my hand. "Mr. Oswald?"

"Thank you for saving my wife and my kids," he said.

Normally I would offer to take him to one of the side rooms, but right now everything was filthy, so we might as well stand. "No problem, sir. Sorry about the accommodations. We had some trouble the last magic wave. How is your family doing?"

"They're doing well," he said. "We've hired movers and put the house on the market. We don't want to take any chances."

"That's understandable." Keep him talking . . .

"Pamela mentioned that you asked if anybody had a problem with us or our cats."

Please tell me that someone had a problem with you and that you know his name and address. Please, Universe, do me this one favor.

"A couple of weeks ago I was doing some yard work after that storm we had. I was in the front yard and this man came up to me and started ranting about how our cats get on his car."

"Have you ever seen him before?"

Mr. Oswald shook his head. Of course not. That would be too easy.

"I told him that he must have me confused with someone else, because Sherlock and Watson are inside cats. It makes no sense, if you ask me. A cat is a predator. He must go out and hunt to be fulfilled, but the kids are scared that something will eat them, so we keep them inside."

"What did the man say?"

"He became very agitated." Mr. Oswald frowned. "He raised his voice, waved his arms around, and proceeded to what I can only describe as ranting. I thought he might be intoxicated. Eventually he got to the part where he told me that everything was fine until 'you people' moved into the neighborhood with 'your spoiled brats.' At that point I told him to get off my property."

"Did he?"

"He told me that now his hands were tied and walked off."

I pulled my small notebook out. "What did he look like?"

"Late fifties, dark hair, balding, average build."

"White, Hispanic . . . ?"

"White. He wore a suit and tie. Glasses."

Too generic. "Anything else? Anything you can remember?" I asked. "Tattoos, scars, anything out of the ordinary?"

"He wore an earring." Mr. Oswald thought about it and nodded. "Yes, I remember. He wore an earring in his left ear, one of those dangling earrings with a very large glass gem in it. I thought it was strange because it didn't fit him at all."

"How do you know it was glass?"

"It was bright red and the size of an almond in a shell, almost an inch long. I thought it looked ridiculous."

Alarms went off in my head.

"Can you draw the earring?" I passed the notebook to him.

He sketched a quick shape and passed it back to me. It looked like a cluster of large grape berries fused together and covered by a metal cork with the gem in its center.

"It was obviously a very bad imitation," he said. "The gold looked too pale, like one of those metallic paints, and the earring was old and dented."

Crap. Old was bad. A simple design was also bad.

"Was the gem faceted?" I asked.

"No, it was smooth. What is it called?" He grimaced.

"Cabochon cut," Ascanio said.

"Yes."

And we just went from bad to worse. "Thank you so much, Mr. Oswald. You were of great help."

"Of course. Sorry we didn't tell you sooner, but I never mentioned it to Pamela. She was already worried about the neighborhood."

"Why was she worried about the neighborhood?"

"We had some odd things happen. It started with the cars. We've got a neighbor down in the cul-de-sac. He's what you might call a bike enthusiast. Every damn Sunday if the tech is up, right when we're trying to sleep in, he starts riding his bike up and down the street. Two weeks ago I saw him crying on the curb. Someone had crushed his bike and all of his cars. I saw what was left—it looked like someone stepped on them."

You don't say. "When was this?"

"Last Monday. But the worst thing was last Thursday. We decorated for Shift Day. There are a lot of kids on our street."

Shift Day was a new holiday, born from the terror of the first magic wave years ago. On the anniversary of it, people put out decorations: streamers made with ribbons, crosses, crescents, the Star of David. They lit blue lights and little kids went up and down the street knocking on doors and handing out little charms in exchange for cookies and candy. It was a way to celebrate life on the anniversary of the day when one-twelfth of the Earth's population died.

"We had all the decorations out, the ribbons, the wire monsters, everything. The whole subdivision was decorated. Then overnight everything disappeared." Mr. Oswald cleared his throat. "All of it gone in the entire neighborhood, like it was never there. I talked to Arnie across the street and he says he was coming home late that night. He drove past the decorations, pulled into the garage, and then remembered to go grab the mail, so he walked back out. We are serious about the decorations at our house. We'd wrapped our tree in ribbons. It took the kids a good hour. Arnie might have been a minute in the garage, but when he came out, everything was gone on the entire street. What kind of magic can make it all vanish in a couple of minutes?"

The kind of magic that turned a normal middle-aged man into a sixty-five-foot giant. Last Thursday was February 24. Eduardo disappeared on Monday, February 28. "Mr. Oswald, could you think back for me. When did you talk to the man about your cats?"

"A few days ago," he said.

"Was it before or after that Thursday?"

He frowned. "It had to be before. I left on Friday, so it must've been . . . It was Wednesday. I remember it was Wednesday, because I took the trash to the curb."

"And you don't know who might be behind this?" I asked.

"No idea. But I hope you find the bastard. Well, I better get going."

"Of course. Thank you so much for your help."

He went out.

"Why is it important if the gem was faceted?" Ascanio asked.

"Because people didn't start cutting gems until the fourteenth century. Before that they didn't have the tools, so they shaped them into cabochons. That man saw an ancient earring with an inch-long ruby in it."

I turned to Ascanio. "Do you work for me?"

"Yes. You promoted me from unpaid to paid intern."

"Whose idea was it to make you an intern in the first place?"

"Yours. Andrea thought it was too dangerous," he said helpfully.

"That's because Andrea has a better head on her shoulders than I do." There was a reason why she was my best friend. "I need you to call the Chamblee and Dunwoody Police Departments and ask them if there were any complaints against the Oswalds specifically or anything in their neighborhood." Given that the Oswalds' house was right on the border, there was no telling to which department the complaints might have been placed.

Ascanio got a weird look on his face. "You already told me to do that. They had no complaints."

"Did you call or go there in person?"

"I called."

Since he was an intern, I had to train him. "A loud motorcycle, a bunch of bright decorations, and cats who sit on people's cars. What do they have in common?"

"A cranky neighbor who shakes his cane and yells at people to get off his lawn."

There was hope for him yet. "Cranky neighbors complain and they usually complain to the authorities, and often in writing." And sometimes, when their complaints are ignored, they make deals with arcane powers. Unfortunately, there was always a price to pay. "Can you be charming, Ascanio?"

Ascanio unleashed a smile. He didn't just grin, he launched a smile like a missile from a catapult. It would likely have the same catastrophic impact on anything female, ages fifteen to thirty. Perfect.

"I need you to go to the Dunwoody Police Department and be charming. Ask around. Someone has to remember this man calling in. If you don't find anything, go to the health department, then to animal control. Do you have a car?"

"Yes." He nodded.

"Go and do this for me. Don't come back until you dig something up. I need a name."

"Okay. And then will you remember me?"

"I don't know. I have amnesia, paralysis, and a death wish, and they don't go away just like that."

He opened his mouth and froze. "Okay. I'm an ass. She wanted to know what could happen, so I told her. But I shouldn't have."

Good call. "Bring me a name. Then I'll give remembering a shot."

He took off and I went to collect Julie. We needed to find Luther and ask him some questions.

14

THE BIOHAZARD DIVISION occupied a large solid building made with big blocks of the local gray granite. A large black sign in front announced its official name: The Center for Magical Containment and Disease Prevention. I parked in the front in a visitor spot. It was just me and Julie. I had asked Derek to go to the suspect stalker's address and watch his house, doing whatever he had to do not to be seen, and Curran was still at the Guild.

The day had burned down to a cold evening, the sky an icy purple in the west as the sun rolled toward the horizon. The magic was strong tonight.

Curran had offered to come with me, but I insisted. He needed to stay and get his hands dirty, because the mercs would respect that, and I needed to see a man about a ghoul. He offered again and I told him no, and not just because Mitchell wouldn't crawl out of his burrow if he smelled Curran coming.

Curran was impossible to ignore. He wasn't quite hovering around me, but he was very forcibly there in case I was about to collapse. Right now he was the equivalent of having a squad of trained killers at your beck and call, ready to defend you at the slightest provocation. My stroke had put him on edge. I could feel him surfing that narrow line between maintaining his composure and losing all semblance of rational thought. He had lost his parents and his siblings to loups, and he had never recovered. The fear that something would happen to me constantly gnawed at him, and sitting on his hands for two days waiting to see if I'd die while the kids were freaking out had driven him nuts.

He was wound so tight, the energy rolled off him. If someone accidentally bumped into me, he'd rip them to pieces. What he wanted most was to stuff me into an armored room lined with padded pillows and stand guard over it until all the insanity that drove him boiled down to the simple realization that we were both going to be alright. He would never say it and he would definitely never try it, but the urge was there. I saw it in his eyes.

Maybe it was because he was extra wound up, or maybe it was the way we always were, but I felt completely secure when he was near. I felt safe. He was like a one-man army.

Right now I didn't want to have the luxury of feeling safe. I needed to feel fear, the good electrifying kind of fear that kept me sharp when my life was on the line. I needed to know I could function, that I was still fast and could still kill, and that I could handle Atlanta on my own. That I was still me.

"I know you're worried. I need to do this. Either I go or I might as well pack it up and retire," I had told him. "I'll be careful."

"You should wait," he had said.

"How long?"

The answer had been clear in his eyes: forever. I had to go, because I wouldn't always have the luxury of having him with me and we both needed to deal with that.

"Promise me that if you run across another giant, you won't go after it until I get there," Curran had said.

"I promise." A giant was an anomaly. Running across another one was highly unlikely.

"I mean it, Kate. You can't take another stroke."

And neither could he. "I give you my word."

Now we were in front of the Biohazard Division. I hoped my arms and legs would work as well as they did before all this mess happened.

"How do they get 'Biohazard' out of CMCDP?" Julie asked.

"The Center started as a division of the Atlanta Police Department. Before the Shift, whenever there was a murder or some violent altercation, people would call crime scene cleanup crews. They cleaned up blood, body decomp, animal feces, that sort of thing. Biohazard." I got out of the car and started toward the building. Julie caught up with me.

"At that time, magic was new, but it quickly became clear that its little presents had to be studied and contained. Nobody quite knew how to do that, and the APD ended up creating its own Biohazard Division. They gave it a familiar name, probably because it made them feel better and everybody knew what it stood for. Over the years, Biohazard expanded, until finally the governor separated it and brought it under state authority by an executive order." I stopped by the wall and pointed at a dark shiny spot in the granite. "Do you know what this is?"

Julie squinted at it. "No."

"Dark tourmaline. This building is made with Stone Mountain granite, which has natural tourmaline inclusions. Why?"

Julie wrinkled her forehead. "Tourmaline is frequently used in purifying. It can generate a weak electrical current when rubbed or heated by the sun, and it is a good magic conductor, which makes their wards stronger."

"What else?"

She looked at me. "Uhh . . ."

"Scrying," I told her. "It's used as a scrying stone. It helps them with their research. Come on."

We walked to the big doors. A ward squeezed me, cutting off my breath for a moment, and then the pressure vanished. We were through.

I nodded at the guard at the fortified reception desk. "Kate Daniels. I am here to see Luther."

"Go in," the woman told me. "Second floor, big door on the right."

We went up the stone stairs. People walked past us, talking in quiet voices, sometimes relaxed, sometimes intense. We made it to the second floor and turned right. A deserted hallway stretched in front of us, lit by the blue glow of feylanterns.

"Kate," Julie asked, her voice small.

"Mm-hm?"

"You do remember me, don't you? You don't have amnesia?"

Oh, Julie. I turned on my foot and hugged her. She leaned against me, limp.

"Do you remember when I took you to Pelican Point? You ate shrimp and cried."

She sniffled.

"And when we bought the owl?" I said. "The woman wanted thirty bucks for it, and then, when we got home, I had to fight with you to wash it?"

"Yes," she said.

"Even if I had amnesia, I would still remember that I love you."

She hugged me once, squeezing me tight, and let go. We walked down the hall as if nothing had happened, right up to the big metal door blocking our way. I knocked and swung it open.

Luther stood by the laboratory table, holding a clear plastic container filled with dried herbs. He wore pale scrubs that had been bleached too many times and his face was sour. On the table, splayed out and butterflied like a chicken for the grilling, sprawled the corpse of a scaled lizardlike beast. Luther bent over it and sprinkled the herbs onto the exposed tissue. Ugh.

"Really, Luther, if I knew you were that hungry, I would've picked up some takeout."

At the sound of my voice, he turned. "You!"

"Me."

"What is this?" He looked at Julie. "Mini-you?"

"Julie—Luther. Be careful with him, he's sharp. Luther—Julie. She's my adopted daughter."

"Showing her the ropes?" Luther squinted at Julie. "What is that magic you've got there? A sensate? You've been sitting on a sensate all this time and you didn't share? Not cool, Daniels. Not cool at all."

"I'll share if you do."

Luther spread his arms. "All things that are Mine are Yours, and Yours are Mine."

"John seventeen, the Prayer for Disciples," Julie said. "But not the King James version."

That's right. The King James version would've had "thines" in it.

"New American Standard," Luther said. "I'm a patriot and proud of it."

"Is that the lizard that came out of the giant?" I asked before they decided to dazzle each other with their brilliance.

"It is, and I had to fight the military and the GBI for it. I just sprinkled mugwort on it."

Nice. Whatever faults Luther had, stupid wasn't one of them. I walked over and looked at the carcass.

"Why mugwort?" Julie asked. "I thought it was for warding off evil?"

"Because it is associated with Goddess Nu Wa," Luther said.

"There is a reason why Nu Wa was depicted in ancient Chinese art as having the head of a human and the body of a serpent," I told her.

Luther checked the clock "Three, two . . . one."

The exposed muscle turned bright emerald green.

"A draconoid," I said. Out of the frying pan and into the fire.

Luther stared at the ceiling and made a frustrated growl.

"Why is that bad?" Julie asked.

"There have been four documented sightings of a real dragon," Luther said. "They are the UFOs of our age. We don't know a lot about them . . . no, scratch that, we have a wealth of myths so we know a lot about what they might be, but we have almost no empirical evidence to justify any of the bullshit. We do know that they are beings of immense magic power. Three of the sightings have been during a flare."

"A draconoid is a catch-all name for the proto-dragons," I explained. "A proto-dragon is almost like a primitive dragon, not quite a dragon but definitely not just a lizard or a serpent. They pack a serious magic punch. If the Summoner can produce hundreds of these, what else can he summon?"

"But I thought you fought a dragon a long time ago?" Julie said.

"No, I fought an undead dragon, a pile of bones with a very faint memory of what it used to be. If the Summoner calls out a dragon, we'll be in deep trouble."

"It wouldn't even have to be a dragon," Luther said. "If he summons a drake, we're in deep sewage. There are no protocols for fighting dragons. We have no idea what to expect. We would be fighting blind. This city isn't ready for a dragon."

I looked at Julie. "Color?"

"Same," she said. "Bronze."

That's what I thought.

"Bronze?" Luther blinked. "What the hell registers bronze? Daniels, what are you not telling me?"

Denial only goes so far. I took a deep breath. "I think we have a djinn."

. . .

LUTHER SANK INTO a chair. "How sure are you?"

"Sure enough to say it out loud."

He dragged his hand across his face. "You know, if anyone else had told me, I would've smiled and nodded and after he left, I'd make calls to his emergency contacts and suggest they hospitalize him ASAP."

"I know."

"A djinn is problematic because it's a higher being?" Julie asked.

I nodded. True gods couldn't manifest except during the flares, times of uninterrupted magic. At other times, so-called gods were just constructions of the Summoner's will or a creature inhabiting an avatar or an effigy. Their powers in these forms were severely limited. Most of the creatures we encountered post-Shift either started as human and transformed into their new shapes or had powers that were not significantly greater than that of an average human. Even so, these creatures clung to magic. Fomorian demons attacked during a flare, and rakshasas had made excursions into our reality through a portal, running to it any time the magic dropped.

The djinn and the dragons were on another level entirely.

"How did you arrive at a djinn?" Luther asked.

"It's a long story."

He got up off the chair and pulled a lever. A thick metal hood descended on the table, hiding the lizard's body. Luther threaded a thick chain through the rungs in the hood and the table, wrapping it several times around the hood, secured it with a padlock, and disappeared into the side room. A moment later, he emerged with three mugs and a carafe of coffee.

I started with the encounter with the ghouls and laid it all out, glossing over details like Ghastek pointing me toward the ghouls in the first place, protecting the city, and having microscopic strokes. It didn't take him long to connect the dots. We had a disgruntled neighbor who somehow got himself involved with a magical heavyweight from Arabian mythology. He made three wishes and then in turn the magic power possessed his body, turning him into a giant. The giant punished the Guild for interfering. All of this was consistent with a djinn. They granted wishes, they came from the Arabian mythos, and they held a grudge. It was a solid theory, but it was solid in the same way Swiss cheese was solid. We still didn't know what the djinn wanted, why he was gathering ghouls, or why he'd kidnapped Eduardo.

When I finished, Luther exhaled.

"Unlimited power at this guy's fingertips, and he wishes for his neighbor's bike to be crushed, steals the kids' decorations, and summons a monster to eat all of the cats."

"Thank the Universe for small favors." It could've gone much worse.

"That kind of show of power requires a higher being, so you are right. As freaky weird as it is, we might have a djinn. Why now? Why here?"

I had been asking myself that same question. If a djinn existed, he would be as much of a threat to Roland as he was to me. My magic was my father's magic. Was this some sort of extra-special test? Did my loving father send me this lovely present to see if I could deal with it? Was it his way to undermine me without becoming involved? Was it completely unrelated? There was really no way to tell.

"If it's a djinn, what kind?" Luther frowned. "Is it a marid, an ifrit, a shaytan?"

"It's not a jann," I thought out loud. "They don't pack enough power. It could be a marid, but if the literature is to be believed, their power is elemental in nature."

"But marids are described as giants," Luther pointed out.

"True. I have something for you." I reached into my backpack and pulled out my bag of dirty glass. "We found a ring of this around Eduardo's car. I think it's melted sand that was used as a teleportation anchor. We need to know where it's from."

Luther grabbed the bag and held it up so the light of the feylantern shone through it. He squinted. "What is that squirmy shiny thing inside the glass?"

The only thing inside that glass was dirt. I had looked at it through a magnifying glass. I sighed. "Luther, we don't all have magic vision. We can't see what you see."

He pulled the ziplock bag open and passed his hand over the glass. "Ooo. This is something."

"What is it?" Julie asked.

"I don't know yet, but it's not nothing."

Mages. Clear as mud.

"You think there's a three-wish cycle?" Luther asked. "He grants three wishes, then possesses the body? Why?"

"I don't know. Can I talk to Mitchell?" I asked.

"You can try. I tried last night. I even brought very delicious carrion with me, but he wouldn't come out of his burrow."

"I'll give it a shot."

"Okay," Luther said. "I'll get the tranquilizer gun in case the magic fails."

"Is this dangerous?" Julie asked.

"Yes," I told her. "I'll need you to stay with Luther. You can see everything from the balcony."

"But—"

"If you come with me, Mitchell might not come out."

Her face fell. "Fine."

Luther came out of the back room carrying an oversized rifle. "Shall we?"

We followed him out of the examination room, down the hallway, to a door leading to the outside. Luther pulled a key chain out of his pocket, flipped through the keys with one hand until he found the right one, and unlocked the door. We stepped out onto a private concrete balcony running along the side of the building for about fifty feet. In front of us a large lot stretched, secured by a twenty-foot stone wall topped with coils of razor wire. The wire had some silver in it and the light of the rising moon coated it in a bluish glow. Trees dotted the lot, some normal, some odd and twisted. On the left, black tar-like goo oozed from one of the trunks. On the right, a group of bushes with small red leaves sprouted two-foot-long bright orange thorns. Tiny blue spheres floated in the grass, moving in different directions. Magic pooled and coursed through it, twisting between the trees and leaking from the leaves and spiraling into the ground. Even the ground itself was changed. Sharp outcroppings of translucent citrine-colored crystal cut through the surface like the fins of mythical sea serpents swimming under water. Here and there small veins of pale white rock stretched to form knobby protrusions about a foot high and buttressed to the ground by thin roots.

"What is this?" Julie asked.

"The dumping ground. This is where we put things we want to study," Luther said.

"This is where they put things when they have no idea what they are or what to do with them," I told her. "Luther, don't bullshit my kid."

Luther rolled his eyes. "Yes. What she said."

"What if they get out?" Julie asked.

He pointed up. Julie leaned out. I knew what he was pointing at, but I glanced over all the same. Massive catapults and guns lined the roof of the building, pointing at the dumping ground. Anything that tried to leave would be pounded to a bloody pulp.

I stripped off my jacket and pulled off my boots.

"So why do you keep a ghoul in there?" Julie asked.

"Because he used to be one of us," Luther said. "Mitchell was a brilliant guy. He studied ghoulism and we all thought he would crack it. Turned out he was a point zero zero zero two percenter."

"Oh." Julie nodded. "That makes sense."

Mitchell and I went way back. I knew him when he was still human. He was one of those health nuts who did things like running punishing marathons and then got upset if he wasn't one of the first ten to cross the finish line. When his transformation hit and he disappeared, Biohazard hired me to find him and bring him back quietly, because they felt responsible for him. Every time a new case of ghoulism became public, people freaked out, which was why the PAD eliminated all new ghouls with extreme prejudice. Nobody at Biohazard wanted Mitchell to be hunted down and shot.

Only two people out of every ten thousand, 0.0002 percent, were susceptible to ghoulism, and evidence showed that they were probably related to each other. Statistically, a citizen of Atlanta had a higher probability of being mauled by a shapeshifter, but every new case of ghoulism invariably caused a panic, because for those two out of ten thousand there was no cure. Shapeshifters were still human. They lived in houses, held jobs, had kids, and led semi-normal lives. But ghouls hid in cemeteries and gorged themselves on corpses.

When I started looking for him, all that marathon running made no difference. Mitchell had done the exact same thing that most human and supernatural fugitives usually did—he ran a little ways and squatted down in the first hidey-hole he found, which just happened to be the South River Sewer tunnel. I found him and brought him in before the PAD managed to get hold of him.

I pulled off my turtleneck. "Mitchell likes it in the dumping ground. He feels safe, he is fed well and on schedule, and nobody bothers him. It's probably the best place for him right now. He wouldn't do well out in the wild on his own."

My sword followed, then my belt, and my pants. A cold wind hit me. Argh.

"Damn, Daniels." Luther shook his head.

I glanced down. Huge purple bruises covered my legs. I couldn't remember how I got them. "Occupational hazard."

Normally after being treated by Doolittle, everything would've been healed. He considered it a point of professional pride. My memory served up an image of Doolittle rolling out of the room. *I'm tired* . . . Healing my brain had drained him dry. He didn't heal my bruises because he had nothing left.

I was an ungrateful asshole who took him for granted. Once this was over, I would have to take him out to lunch and tell him how much I appreciated his help.

I shivered. I was down to my sports bra, underwear, and socks.

"You're not going out there like that," Julie said.

"These are the rules," I told her. "Mitchell gets scared easily. He likes to be reassured that I am not carrying any weapons."

"That's why Mitchell talks to her. Crazy, right?" Luther set the rifle down and turned a heavy crank on the side of the balcony. A foot-wide metal ramp slid from under the balcony, crossed the line of the fence, and stretched down, halting about five feet above the ground. "I won't go in there naked, and I am a qualified mage. It's not just what we put in there, it's all of the things that spawn in there by themselves . . ."

"Not helping," I growled.

Luther glanced at Julie and shut up.

I swung my legs over the concrete rail of the balcony and stepped onto the ramp. The cold metal burned my feet. Another gust of wind chilled me, and I felt it all the way down to the bone. How do I get myself into these things?

"Remember, try to keep him in plain view," Luther said. "I can't bind him if I can't see him."

I started down the ramp. Walking on slippery ice-cold metal thirty feet above hard ground, while a cold wind was trying to scour the skin off my body. If I fell, I'd end up right in the razor wire. Wheeee.

God, that wind was cold.

And how did you spend your Friday night, Ms. Daniels? Out on the town, having a lovely dinner and a dance like a normal person. Yeah, right. When I finally caught up with whoever was behind this mess, I would vent all of my frustration at once. I'd been beaten, cut, clawed, and thrown around like a rag doll; my magic had backfired and exploded in my brain; and I'd lost pieces of my memories. Memories I treasured and required to protect those I loved. I'd nearly lost my family. I had a hell of a lot of frustration built up. A bloody overabundance of it.

"Your second mom is a nice person," Luther said quietly behind me. "There aren't many people who care about whether they're scaring a ghoul."

I expected Julie to tell him I wasn't her mom. She didn't say anything.

I reached the end of the ramp. It terminated right over a rocky outcropping. Perfect. Just perfect. I crouched, sat, and slid down gently. My feet hit the hard stone. My teeth chattered. I wanted to hug myself, but there were things watching me from the darkness. Looking like a victim encouraged predators. I squared my shoulders and picked my way across the rocky ground.

Something shivered in the tall black-leafed bushes to the left. A pair of silvery elongated eyes ignited. The hair on the back of my neck rose. Adrenaline coursed through me, the instinctual fear hot and sharp.

I stared at the eyes. "Piss off."

The eyes narrowed to slits. The bushes rustled as their owner retreated. *That's right. Keep going.*

I skirted a pool of slimy orange goo and came into a small clearing, exactly thirty feet wide. I knew the size because Luther had it mowed once every few weeks. It took five people to do it. One drove an armored lawn mower and the other four guarded the driver.

A large white rock jutted out of the center of the clearing. Next to it a hole gaped in the ground, so dark it looked like it was filled with liquid blackness.

I chose a spot about ten feet from the rock, picked up a stone the size of a grapefruit, crouched, and knocked on a rocky outcropping.

Knock. Knock.

Nothing.

Mitchell required patience. I knocked again, hitting the rock against the stone in a steady measured rhythm. My back was to the brush. I presented an awesome target, crouched and nearly naked.

Knock . . . knock . . . knock . . . *Come on, Mitchell. Come talk to me.*

Knock . . . knock . . .

Something stirred within the darkness of the ghoul burrow.

I put the rock down and waited.

A long spadelike hand armed with straight, narrow claws emerged, followed by a thin arm, a grotesque head, and then shoulders. A moment and Mitchell squeezed himself out of the burrow and crouched in the open. Moonlight slid over his dirt-colored skin mottled with patches of gray and deeper brown, and set his eyes aglow with eerie silver. His horns, the curved spikelike protrusions on his back and shoulders, were almost six inches long, a full three inches longer than the last time I saw him. Something had terrified Mitchell and his body had responded. A long chain wrapped around his left ankle and a rough band of thick scar tissue encircled his leg right above it. He had clawed at his own flesh trying to get the chain off. If Luther had put him on a chain, he and I would have words once I was done.

Mitchell didn't move. Neither did I. We crouched, barely three feet between us. Some picture we must've made, a naked ghoul and a nearly naked human shivering in the cold, sitting nose to nose.

Mitchell turned his head and looked at the moon, his eyes glowing.

"Tell me about the chain," I said.

"I found it." His voice was rough, as if he were grinding gravel with his teeth. "The thing chained to it was dead, so I took the chain."

So he had put himself on the chain? "Why?"

"Do you not hear it? The call?" Mitchell looked at the moon again. "He's calling. It's like a weight. It grinds on you, it pushes and pushes, and it hurts." He looked back at me, his face contorted. "It hurts." He touched his forehead. "In here." His clawed hands slid lower to his neck. "And here." Lower still to his chest. "Here. And here. In the stomach. It squeezes me. It hurts."

Sudden rage flooded me. Mitchell had suffered enough. He had lost his humanity and his family. He was a scared, quiet creature who had never hurt anyone. All he wanted to do was to live in his burrow and be safe. And now some supernatural asshole was torturing him.

"Who is calling you?"

"I don't know. But I feel it. I can see him in my mind. I don't want to go." Mitchell looked at the chain. "I don't want to go. I will die if I go, but the pain is getting stronger. One day I will gnaw through my leg and go."

"Can you tell me where the call is coming from?"

"Why?" Mitchell's voice dripped with despair.

"So I can go there and make him stop."

"You can't. You're not strong enough. Not strong enough for his magic."

"I can and I will. I've never failed you before. I won't now."

Mitchell didn't answer.

"Let me help you," I whispered. "Let me make it stop hurting."

Mitchell's face trembled. His whole body shuddered. As I watched, the patina of spots on his skin shifted, turning darker. His horns grew another quarter inch. Holy crap. That was crazy even for a ghoul. He was scared out of his mind.

"He will know," Mitchell whispered. "He will know if I tell."

"How?"

"He's sent others to get me, but I burrowed deep and they got scared before they could dig to me. They watch me."

Damn it. "When was this?"

"The day I fed."

So on Tuesday. "How did they get through the fence?"

Mitchell leaned even closer and whispered. "They dug a hole. They are waiting in there even now, watching us."

They dug a tunnel. Of course. Once we finished here, Luther and I would have to find it. "If you tell me, I promise I will kill them and then I'll find him and kill him, too."

Mitchell's skin turned almost black. "No. He has others. Some like me and some like I was meant to be. He has others. He has a man in a cage."

Eduardo. This was my only chance.

"You will die and then he will send others for me."

"I have never lied to you." I scratched the back of my left arm with my nails. A tiny drop of blood swelled. "I will stop him."

I stretched my arm to him. His nostrils flared. He focused on the blood, his eyes glowing.

"Taste it," I whispered.

Slowly, Mitchell rested one clawed hand on the ground, leaned forward, and dipped his head. A thick tongue slid from between his teeth and scraped the trace of blood off my skin. Light burst in his mouth, a beautiful fire, as if he had swallowed a tiny yellow star. The veins in his neck ignited with fiery radiance. It dashed down his blood vessels to his heart, through his body, to his limbs.

Mitchell surged upright, glowing, his body larger, stronger, more muscular. Fire swirled around him, caressing his form but never touching. His face snapped into a long muzzle that might have belonged to a dragon or a demonic dog. Horns of fire spiraled out of his head. His eyes flared with bright orange, as if an inferno burned inside him. A foreign intelligence regarded me with cool detachment.

Mitchell cried out. I felt the magic explode inside him and dove to the ground. A blast of heat tore through the clearing, snapping branches. Mitchell shuddered and collapsed back into his old form.

It was so fast, I thought I'd imagined it. Maybe I did . . .

"Holy shit!" Luther barked.

Nope, I didn't.

Mitchell raised his head. His eyes were still on fire.

"Take it!" he whispered.

The fiery eyes burned into my mind. Magic stretched between us, woven with power and heat. It touched my mind and exploded into fire in my head. Images swirled. *A cavern . . . No, the inside of a half-collapsed building. The floors had fallen down and only the outer walls remained. Pale beams of moonlight shining down through the holes in the roof. A human-sized cage suspended from the ceiling. A man in the cage, thin, his clothes torn and bloody. Eduardo. Ghouls. Dozens of ghouls below, blanketing the floor with their bodies . . .*

A surge of light and fire, as if someone had slit reality open and cosmic flames spilled out.

A face within the fire. Rough, heavy-jawed, muscled face, with bright black tattoos marking the cheeks and the brow. So humanlike, yet so alien . . . Long pointed ears bearing golden hoops, one after another. A collar of gold inset with bright green jewels. A mane of straight black hair, each hair shaft glowing with a golden core like an ember barely covered with soot. Wings rising . . .

Eyes of fire, filled with arrogance and insanity.

A voice rocked through my mind. "You're weak. You will die. The betrayer will die. Your city will kneel before me."

"This city doesn't kneel, asshole. I'm coming for you. Start praying."

The vision tore apart and reality took me back into its cold embrace. I blinked and saw Mitchell's feet as he dove into the burrow.

"Wait . . ."

I felt someone's gaze on my back. The stare stabbed me right between the shoulder blades. I held still, crouched, one knee to the ground.

A second crawled by, painfully slow.

Make your move. Let's see how well you dance.

Something exploded out of the bushes. I pivoted and saw a ghoul in midleap, curved claws raised.

There was no place to go.

I rolled onto my back, matching its momentum, and kicked with both feet. My heels smashed into the ghoul's belly, driving it forward over my head. It landed hard, its back slapping the ground. I flipped and lunged at the ghoul just as it managed to turn on its stomach. My knees came down on its back, hard. The ghoul tried to rise and I grasped the sides of its head, shoved it down toward its spine, locking the vertebrae, and twisted. Its neck broke with a dry crunch like a twig.

The ghoul gurgled, shaking. In a moment it would regenerate the neck.

"Clear shot!" Luther screamed. "Give me a clear shot!"

I grabbed the rock I used to call Mitchell and smashed it into the ghoul's skull. Tiny drops of blood flew. I pummeled its head with the rock as fast and hard as my arm would move. The skull cracked like an eggshell, the bone fragments caved in, and I crushed the soft brain underneath with my rock.

The ghoul went limp. I jumped to my feet. Silver eyes glared at me from the darkness. One, two, three . . . Too many.

I sprinted to the fence, flying across the rocky ground. Behind me the undergrowth rustled. The sound of claws and labored breathing chased me.

On the balcony Luther thrust his hands straight up, his arms vibrating with tension, turned his palms out, his fingers rigid, and forced his arms down, straining, as if he were swimming. An eerie green glow swirled around him, a glowing nimbus. Julie grabbed the crank of the metal bridge.

Luther jerked his left hand up, fingers curved like claws. Dark roots burst out of the ground in an explosion of dirt clumps and surged upward, sprouting foot-long green thorns. The ghoul to the left of me screeched. Out of the corner of my eye I saw it flailing in a clump of the vines. Luther thrust his other hand in the air. Another ghoul screamed.

I was almost to the ramp. Ten feet and I would be there.

A ghoul dodged the roots, sprinting forward on all fours, and lunged at me from the side. I grabbed its right forearm with my left hand, pulling the arm straight and jerking him down and forward, and slid my right arm over the back of its neck and all the way under its armpit. My forearm pressed on the back of its neck and I dropped down to one knee, bringing all of the force of my body onto my elbow, ripping the soft tissue and crushing the vertebrae. The whole thing took half a second. I released the convulsing ghoul and ran to the ramp.

Three feet from it I jumped. My fingers caught the cold metal, and I pulled myself up and dashed across the bridge. Julie spun the crank, retracting it as I ran. I leaped over the last five feet, landing next to her, and turned around. Seven ghouls howled in impotent fury by the fence, their eyes glowing, their teeth bared.

The smallest of them turned to run. Roots shot out of the ground, forming a crescent barrier about thirty yards in diameter. The ghouls whirled, realizing they were trapped.

Luther smiled. "Oh no, my pretties. This is my domain and you've trespassed. There is a price to pay for that."

Luther took a deep breath, his arms rising as if he were about to take flight. Magic shuddered in front of him, like elastic rope wound too tight. The muscles of his back flexed and he snapped his arms to the side and down, palms up.

The ground under the ghouls moved as if the Earth had suddenly became liquid. They sank down, feverishly trying to free their limbs, but the soil held them fast. A green bubble formed in the center of the clearing, grew to the size of a basketball, and exploded. Bright emerald dust shot out, glowing. Spores, I realized. Millions of spores. The green spores washed over the ghouls. Their movements grew less frantic, then slow, slower still, until they were struggling in slow motion as if their very flesh had gradually petrified. The spores sprouted. A dense carpet of moss in a dozen varieties grew, sheathing the ghoul bodies like a velvet blanket. Delicate pink stalks formed over the barely recognizable bodies. Tiny white flowers opened at the ends of the stalks, releasing tiny dots glowing with gold. The air smelled sweet, like a forest just after a morning rain.

Luther inhaled and smiled.

"Very pretty," Julie said.

"Well, we don't just sit on our butts filling out paperwork," Luther said. "We work for our living."

I pulled my pants on. My feet were beat to hell from running on rocky ground. My middle left toe was probably broken.

"I thought you promised Curran nothing violent." Julie handed me my turtleneck.

"No, I promised him I wouldn't fight a giant."

"So you obey the letter of the law and not the spirit," she said.

"Yes." My teeth finally stopped chattering. I loved my turtleneck. I loved my jacket. I loved my boots. Mmm, wonderful warm boots.

"How come when I do that, you chew me out?"

"Because you don't do it well enough to get away with it."

Julie blinked. "What kind of move was that, at the end?"

"It's from Escrima, a Filipino martial art. I'll show you when we get a minute, but you will have to practice, because it has to be done really fast for it to work."

"Did you get anything from Mitchell?" Luther asked.

"Yes. It's an ifrit, a very powerful one. Coal-black and red in color and very fond of fire." If it had been a marid, folklore said it would've been blue, and we had to go by folklore until real life disproved it. "He has a hell of a lot of power, and for some reason he's keeping Eduardo in a cage."

I had seen a bowl of water in Eduardo's cage, but no food. His shoulders had been sticking out of his T-shirt and his face was gaunt, so he was likely starving. An average human could survive roughly twenty days without food. A shapeshifter had to consume two to three times as many calories as a human of the same size. Their regeneration slowed down the starvation somewhat but not enough. If we didn't get Eduardo out of that cage in the next three days or so, we wouldn't need to bother looking.

A piercing shriek tore through the silence. It came from inside the building.

L UTHER JERKED THE door open and sprinted down the hall. Julie and I chased him.

"What the hell is that?" I yelled over the shrieks.

"My alarm! Someone just broke into my lab."

We rounded the corner and almost collided with four other people, one in a suit, two in scrubs, and one in a biological containment suit without helmet or gloves. Each was charged with enough magic to level a small building. Luther shoved past them and thrust the door of his lab open. The metal hood was raised, the body of the draconoid out in the open. A deep puncture wound gaped in its side.

"Damn it!" Luther dragged his hand through his hair. "He stabbed my specimen!"

Someone had gotten into the building, bypassing all of the security measures, and broken into Luther's lab. If the press found out that Biohazard, the repository of all things strange and dangerous, had had a security breach, there would be no end of heads rolling.

"This way!" a woman screamed. "He's going out the front door!"

The mages spun and gave chase. The guy in the biocontainment suit shoved the nearest window open. Flames burst over his fists. He punched the air. A fireball broke free of his hand, streaked down to the street, and exploded.

Oh boy.

Everybody except for the firebug ran for the staircase. I decided to run too, just so I wouldn't be left out.

We collectively burst out the front door. The street lay empty. Nothing but five-foot-wide scorch marks.

"Where did he go?" Luther yelled.

Nobody answered.

"Where is Fluffy?" a woman asked.

"Jana took her on a job," a man answered.

"Oh, come on! What good is a tracking dog if she's never here to track?" Luther threw his hands up.

A fireball tore over our heads and splashed flames onto the street.

"Garcia, will you stop setting things on fire?" Luther roared.

"Sorry!" the man from the window called. "It was an accident."

I put my hand over my face. Next to me, Julie pressed her lips together and was making small meowing noises trying not to laugh.

The door of Biohazard flew open and Patrice Lane, the head of the Infectious Diseases department, emerged with a gaggle of her techs behind her.

"Alright, where is he? I'm charged with *Staphylococcus*. Give me two seconds, and he'll be covered in boils. He'll tell us everything."

"He got away," a dark-haired woman explained.

"What?" Patrice blinked.

Julie bent in half and began snorting.

"Stop that," Luther told her.

A man walked out of the shadows. He wore jeans and a brown jacket with a hood that right now rested on his back. Of medium height, he had light brown, slightly curly hair and a pleasant, friendly face with hooded blue eyes, a big nose, and the stubbly beginning of a mustache and beard. There was something vaguely familiar about his eyes.

He came over to me. "Consort. It's such an honor to meet again. Oops. Shouldn't have called you that." He had a light Irish accent.

"She might not remember you," Julie said. "She—"

"Jardin," I said. The last time we had met he was in his wererat form and

I almost stabbed him. He worked for Robert, Alpha of Clan Rat and the Pack's current security chief.

"Ah," Jardin said. "You remember. I am so flattered."

"Who is he?" Luther demanded. "Who are you?"

"It's not him," the dark-haired woman said. "The other guy was older and taller and wore black."

"He's a member of the Pack," I told him.

"Oh. Wait!" Luther's eyes lit up. "Can you track?"

"Yes." Jardin nodded.

"Great. A man ran out of here. Do you have his scent?"

"Sure," Jardin said. "I saw him and I can smell him, but you see, you won't catch him."

"What?" the man in a suit demanded. "Why?"

"He had a horse."

"A horse?" Luther waved his arms. "We have several advanced vehicles. We can beat a horse. With all of us chanting, we can start it in under three minutes."

Ha. If more than one person chanted, the cars started faster. Why hadn't I ever tried this? I filed that tidbit away for further study.

"It was a very fast horse," Jardin said.

"How fast?" the dark-haired woman asked.

The wererat smiled. "It had wings."

The street turned completely silent.

"Beautiful black wings," Jardin said.

So. We had an ifrit holding Eduardo at some undisclosed location and our only lead had flown away on a winged horse.

Everybody spoke at once. The mages waved their arms.

Luther's voice cut through it. "I'll call the Order."

Really? I raised my eyebrow.

"Sorry, Daniels," Luther said. "It's protocol. We need the heavy artillery now."

I stepped away and smiled at Jardin. "Black horse?"

"Yes." He nodded.

"An Arabian?"

"I'm sorry, I wouldn't know."

I bet it looked like a million-dollar horse.

"Was there something you wanted?"

He reached into his jacket. "My alpha brought this to the attention of the Beast Lord, but Jim doesn't feel this is the right time. My alpha has a different opinion. He feels this is a threat to the Pack and to the city. He said you should know about it."

He handed me a stack of Polaroids. The first one showed a big gray block formed from the remnants of different buildings. A person stood next to it. The block had to be at least thirty feet tall. My heart jerked in my chest. I had seen this before. That was how my father had made Mishmar.

I flipped through the rest of the Polaroids. Another block. Another. A small wooden model standing on a folding table in the middle of a field. My father standing next to a man holding a blueprint. He was still wearing his "wise father" persona, an older man with the features of Zeus or perhaps Moses toward the second half of his life, wise, beautiful, possessing other-worldly power, his dark brown eyes ageless . . . My father's profile blurred. He turned toward me in the photograph and winked. Cute.

Julie clamped her hand over her mouth. Jardin turned pale.

Sonovabitch. He was building another tower. He would not take this land.

"Where was this taken?"

Jardin recovered enough to speak. "Near Lawrenceville."

Just outside my territory. *Oh no, you don't. Over my dead body.* Better yet, over his.

"Thank you," I told Jardin. "Tell Robert I will handle this."

I turned and marched toward our car. Approaching my father directly could be seen as an act of war, and trying to contact him by magic means was just asking for trouble. In the magic arena he was miles ahead of me, and opening any kind of connection through magic was unwise. I had no idea how to get hold of him, but I knew someone who did.

"Are we going home?" Julie asked, speed-walking next to me.

"No." My voice had a lot of steel in it. "We're going to the Casino. I'm going to have a chat with my father."

. . .

"How DID HE do that with the photograph?" Julie asked. "How? The tech was up when the picture was taken."

"I don't know." I would've loved to know what Sienna's vision meant as well, but so far I had no sage insights. It bothered me.

We were walking through the parking lot of the Casino, where the People, my father's pet cult/undead petting zoo, made its headquarters in Atlanta. The Casino, a replica of the Taj Mahal, perched in the center of a huge lot where the Georgia Dome had once offered seventy-some thousand seats to sports fans. The Dome was long gone, fallen casualty to the magic waves, and now the Casino dominated the area. During the day, the tint of its pure white marble changed depending on the color of the sky, but at night, painted by the glow of a powerful feylantern, the intricate marble lattice work appeared completely otherworldly and weightless, as if the entire massive building had been spun out of moonlight by some magic spiders. Long rectangular fountains, decorated with statues of Hindu gods caught in mid-move above the tinted water, stretched toward its doors, and as we walked between them toward the Casino, the tiny red lights of vampire minds glowed in my mind. They crawled along the textured parapets, they moved inside the Casino, and below the building, where the stables lay, the ground was completely red, like the tide of some bloody sea. I would've loved nothing more than to reach out and crush them one by one, until the sea of red lights vanished and only peaceful darkness remained.

"How does this not freak you out?" Julie demanded.

"I can't afford to be freaked out. Neither can you."

"Well, I . . ." Julie stopped, her eyes wide open.

I turned to her.

She stared at the Casino, looking down, where the stables would be. "Are those . . . ?"

This wasn't her sensate magic at work. We were too far away and separated from the stables by tons of rock and soil.

"Vampires," I told her.

A while ago she had almost died and I had purified her blood with mine to save her. It was my father's blood ritual, but it was the only way. It bound her to me in the same way Hugh was bound to my father, and like Hugh she could never defy a direct order from me, something I had tried my best to keep secret. Unless my memory failed me, so far I had avoided it, simply because Julie usually did what I asked without my having to order her, and in those rare times when I had to issue a command, Julie was willing to obey. One day the time would come when she would want to do the exact opposite of what I said and would find out that I had robbed her of her free will. I dreaded that day, but I would deal with it when the time came. Right now I had to deal with a whole different side effect. It seemed that my blood was changing Julie.

"They have so many," Julie whispered.

"Yes." I stood next to her. "They keep it quiet. If people knew how many vampires are under the Casino, nobody would ever come to gamble."

Her gaze swept the Casino.

"Can you feel each one?" I asked.

"Yes."

"Do you think you could reach out and grab one?"

She narrowed her eyes. "It feels like I could."

"Good. Once we find Eduardo, we can practice. Now follow me and keep your power to yourself."

We walked up to the door of the Casino. Two guards studiously ignored us. We passed into the lobby. The sound hit me first: the mechanical whirring of the slots, redesigned to work during magic; the din of human voices; the excited shouts of someone winning that sounded almost like a bird in pain; the clanging of metal tokens; all of it blending together into a disorienting, hysterical cacophony. I saw the main floor: dozens of machines, lit up by feylanterns and crowded with users, and, past them, green card tables and roulette wheels, the faces of the poker players devoid of any human emotion. Servers glided through it all, and here and there a journeyman in black-and-purple Casino colors watched over the patrons.

One of the journeymen, an average-sized man in his midtwenties with a pinched face, stepped in my way. "Excuse me, we will need some ID."

I frowned at him. "My ID?"

"Hers." He pointed at Julie. "Minors are not permitted on the Casino floor."

"Tell Ghastek that Kate is here to see him. He'll make an exception for me."

The journeyman's face took on a pompous expression. "I'm sorry, he isn't accepting visitors right now."

"He will accept me."

"No, I don't think so. I work directly under him and I'm quite sure he won't be seeing you today." He pointed at the door with his hand. "Please. I would rather not call security."

I sighed. "Fine. I guess I'll tell him myself."

I reached out with my magic and grabbed the sea of red lights underneath us. The entire vampire stable sat still. Holding two hundred vampires was really difficult and my brain really, really didn't like it.

The journeyman in front of me noticed nothing. "Perhaps I wasn't clear," he said, speaking with exaggerated slowness. "Sometimes I go too fast."

"That's because of your blinding intellect, isn't it?" Julie asked.

I tried really hard not to laugh. Here's hoping someone noticed that all of their undead were facing in the same direction and not moving, because I could feel my magic ripping at the seams.

The journeyman's face turned red. "Look, you, there are two kinds of people who belong here: those with talent like me who work here and those who come here to have a good time and spend money. You don't work here and"—he gave my jeans and beat-up boots a long once-over—"you don't look like you have any money."

Rowena emerged from the back. Her bright red hair crowned her head in a heavy complex braid. She was five feet, two inches tall and her figure, adorned by a kelly-green shimmering gown, was impossibly perfect: tiny waist, generous breasts, perfect butt, nice legs. Her face was shockingly beautiful. She didn't just turn heads, she kept them turned, and given that she was the Casino's PR person, this was quite handy. She was also the third strongest Master of the Dead in the city and made a formidable enemy. Normally her entrance was an event, but right now it was rather comical. Rowena was running as fast as her narrow gown and six-inch-high green pumps would allow, which wasn't very fast. Behind her two journeymen, a man and a woman both in their midtwenties and wearing business suits rather than uniforms, were trying to find a delicate balance between hurrying and overtaking her. The late-year apprentices, close to graduating.

I let go of the vampires.

Rowena saw me and put an extra effort into her speed-walking.

"You don't belong here," the journeyman continued. "We don't tolerate panhandlers."

"You're in so much trouble," Julie told him.

Rowena caught up with us. True to form, she was smiling, but her eyes were terrible. The journeyman saw her. "Master, I can handle—"

She hit him on the back of the head. He flinched.

"Bow," she squeezed through the smile.

"What?"

"Bow, you idiot."

The journeyman bowed, his face surprised.

Rowena smiled at me. "Sharrim. Our deepest apologies for the misunderstanding. He is new and we didn't expect you."

Sharrim. Of the king. I hated being called Consort while Curran was the Beast Lord, but I would take it over Sharrim any day. "No worries."

The journeyman was still bowed. Judging by his face, he had no clue what was happening.

"This way, please."

Julie and I followed Rowena. Behind us the journeyman straightened. "Who was that?"

"Never mind," the female journeyman told him. "This is your sick pass. You need to go home."

"What?"

"You're very sick," the male journeyman ground out. "You need to go home and lie down. You were home all evening, and if Ghastek asks, you have no idea who was working the floor instead of you. Go."

We turned the corner and descended the staircase. A dry revolting stench washed over me, the odor of undeath. A vampire hung from the ceiling directly above us, fastened to it with its long claws. Skeletally thin, gray, and hairless, it shed foul magic. Gagging would've totally ruined the moment, so

I did my best to ignore it. We moved down, and the undead followed us, its eyes glowing dull red.

Rowena kept her expression carefully neutral. Her mother and mine were distantly related, which she had probably figured out by now. She owed a favor to the witches, and the witches in turn had bound her to help me, because at the time they were trying to make me stronger since the Covens didn't fancy being enslaved by Roland. Nobody except the Witch Oracle and the two of us knew about this arrangement. Whatever emotions churned inside Rowena, she was keeping them under lock and key.

We descended deeper and deeper, into the bowels of the Casino, passed through a steel door and into a concrete hallway, and kept walking into a maze of tunnels designed to confuse the unpiloted vampires in case the locks on their cages somehow failed. The tunnels finally ended and we emerged into a vast round room filled with vampire cells, two to a row, stretching toward the center of the chamber. The stench was overpowering. Next to me Julie inhaled sharply.

"No need to worry," Rowena said. "They're secured."

Julie glanced at me. I put a hand on her shoulder, trying to reassure her. Too many undead. Their magic was overloading her senses.

"I see Ghastek didn't want Nataraja's office?" The People's former head used an opulent office in the dome of the Casino, complete with a golden throne and priceless works of art on the walls.

"We stripped it and converted it into a club for children, so they would be entertained while we separate their parents from their money," Rowena said. "We are aiming to be a family-friendly destination."

I almost choked on that.

We turned left and walked up a staircase to a balcony of opaque glass overlooking the enormous room. Rowena knocked and held the door open for us. I had been in Ghastek's office before. It hadn't changed much—same shelves supporting books and assorted odd objects lining the walls, same late-sixteenth-century witch shackles hanging in a place of honor on the wall, same crescent-shaped reed sofa, and of course, a vampire perched in the corner, like a vigilant hairless cat.

Ghastek stood by the floor-to-ceiling window, sipping coffee from a white mug that read, *Graveyard Shift: We do it in the dark*. From this side, the glass of the window was crystal clear, offering an excellent view of the undead stables, and Ghastek surveyed it like he owned it, because he pretty much did. He wore a tailored pair of sleek navy pants and a woven gray sweater with a hint of blue. Both looked elegant and deceptively simple, which probably meant they were hideously expensive. A small black velvet triangle interrupted the texture of the weave just below the flat-knit collar. The triangle alone probably cost him an extra three hundred dollars.

The clothes fit him with some slack. He needed to eat more.

For some reason, the thought of Ghastek and food made me uneasy. I puzzled over it until the answer floated up oh so slowly: we'd starved together in Mishmar. That was it.

"So you liked the mug?" I asked. I had sent it to him for Christmas.

Ghastek pivoted toward me. Rowena sat on the sofa.

"Thank you for the lovely gift," Ghastek said, managing to put exactly zero emotion into those six words. "What can I do for you?"

"I need you to call my father."

GHASTEK STARED AT me. Rowena blinked.

"What do you mean, call your father?"

"Dial his number, use the phone, and ring him up."

Ghastek struggled with it for a few seconds. "One does not simply *ring* Roland."

Oh boy. I supposed I would get a lecture on the dangers of wandering into Mordor next. "Okay, how do you normally contact him?"

"We don't," Rowena said.

"If something that we view as crucial arises," Ghastek said, "we file a petition."

The phone rang. Ghastek picked it up. "I said hold my calls."

His eyes widened. Very carefully he set his mug down and held the phone out. "It's for you."

I took it.

"*Blossom,*" my father's voice said in my ear. His magic washed over me, as if someone had split the atmosphere and the universe in all its glory rained down on me. The sheer monumental power of it took my breath away. He must've been working on something—probably on that damn tower—because the last time I spoke to him, he took the time to tone it down and the impact of his words wasn't quite so cosmic.

I pressed the speaker button and put the phone down. I wanted both hands free in case something jumped out of it and tried to rip out my throat.

"*My night is brighter,*" my father said.

Rowena froze, completely still like a statue. Julie pulled a piece of chalk out of her pocket, drew a protective circle on the floor, and sat in it. At the other end of the room, Ghastek clenched his teeth, probably trying to mitigate the effect of Roland's voice. Yeah, good luck with that.

"*How have you been?*" my father asked.

Say something diplomatic . . . something . . . "If you build a tower in Lawrenceville, I will smash it, set it on fire, and salt the ground it stood on."

Ghastek put his hands over his eyes and pressed them into his face. I couldn't tell if it was from frustration or terror.

"*We should have this conversation in person. I know, why don't we go out to dinner?*"

What? "No."

"*When I first awakened, a few years before the Shift, I used to frequent this low-key chain of restaurants, with a wide variety on the menu. I can't quite recall the name but it had a fruit and an insect.*"

Ghastek mouthed something at me. I shook my head. I was distracted enough already trying to keep my magic shields up. Talking to him during tech was a lot easier. "I consider the tower to be a declaration of war. You are preventing me from expanding my domain. That specifically violates our agreement."

Ghastek grabbed a piece of paper off his desk and drew furiously.

"*I would love to see you.*"

Ghastek held up his drawing. It was a butt with a bee flying over it. What?

"*I haven't spoken to you in over one hundred days.*"

"That's wasn't an oversight on my part."

I must've made a face, because Ghastek scribbled on the paper and held it up. He had drawn a leaf on the butt. *Well, yes, that explains everything. Thank you, Mr. Helpful.* I waved him off. Rowena got up, tiptoed over to Ghastek, and took the paper away from him.

"I'm free tomorrow at five," he said. *"Bring the family."*

Rowena held up the paper. On it in large letters was written *APPLEBEE'S*.

Oh. "I'm not having dinner with you at Applebee's."

"Tomorrow at five. Thank you for inviting me into your domain. I am so glad we could do this. It will give me a chance to stop by our local office as well. I look forward to catching up."

The disconnect signal beeped at me.

God damn it.

I reached over and carefully pushed the off button.

Julie exhaled and stepped out of the circle.

"Did that help?" I asked.

"I don't know," she said and looked at Ghastek. "I'm sorry I drew on your floor."

He dismissed it with a wave of his hand. "It's fine."

Rowena raised her eyebrows at him. "Did you forget how to write?" she asked softly.

Ghastek just looked at her. I understood perfectly. Being in the presence of Roland's magic demanded your attention. You concentrated on blocking it until it short-circuited your normal thoughts. It was like trying to carry on an intelligent debate while being sucked into a maelstrom. You had to tread water to stay afloat and it took every iota of concentration you had.

I had come here intending to declare a possible war and instead ended up planning a dinner date with my father at Applebee's. There was only one Applebee's that had survived the Shift in Atlanta. The chain had started in Decatur, Georgia, in the 1980s, and a single restaurant bearing the name still stood there, claiming to be the first and original Applebee's.

I would have to go to dinner. Stopping by the local office was a threat. I wasn't sure if Ghastek and Rowena knew it, but I understood his message crystal clear. It was up to me how this surprise inspection would go and how many heads would roll because of it.

For a man who hadn't been sure I existed for most of my life, my father got my number very fast.

Ghastek leaned back and crossed his arms. "I had a promising career. I had achieved recognition and some infinitesimal measure of security. And then you came along."

Aha. He and the dozens of hostages working in this building could cry me a river. "Who taught you to draw, Ghastek? That doesn't even remotely look like an apple. It looks like a butt."

"More like a peach," Rowena said.

"I have an inspection in less than twenty-four hours," Ghastek said, his voice dry. "If we have quite finished critiquing my ability to draw fruit, I have things to do."

I leaned back. "Are you worried about it?"

He looked insulted. "No. We can be inspected at any point, and we would stand up to scrutiny."

"If you are anxious, I can make sure he eats something deliciously sweet before he comes over here. Like a generous helping of tres leches cake or a chocolate sundae."

Ghastek stared at me. "Get out."

I rose and made a show of sniffling. "Come on, Julie. Clearly we are not wanted here."

"I will show you out," Rowena said.

I went to the door, turned, and looked at Ghastek. My father had my number, but I was his daughter and I had made a career out of studying him.

"You keep thinking of him as a god. He is a man. He loves life and he pays attention to every moment. Each second is filled with endless wonder for him. He notices the texture of the couch under his fingertips and the color of the tea in his cup. This is how he stays alive, because if he ever grows bored and disillusioned with the world, he will become a shadow of his former self and die, just like my aunt. Treat him as a man. If you want to make a good impression, don't do a big official welcome. Meet him yourself and make sure to afford him the small, everyday courtesies."

I walked out.

.   .   .

"CAN I SPEAK to you in private?" Rowena asked under her breath as we walked into the lobby. "Outside?"

"Sure." I had a pretty good idea how that conversation was going to go. *Why didn't you tell me you are my nearly immortal boss's daughter? It didn't come up. Where do we go from here?* Ugh.

But she was bound to me by the oath she had sworn to the witches. I turned to Julie. "Go ahead of me and start the car, please."

Julie gave Rowena a sideways glance filled with enough teenage scorn to instantly incinerate a small army and sped up ahead of us.

"That child is just like you," Rowena said, her voice making it obvious it wasn't a compliment.

"Thank you."

We were almost to the door when a journeywoman with short dark hair nearly sprinted to us across the floor.

"Trouble," I told Rowena.

She turned. The journeywoman ran up to her.

"Not now," Rowena said.

The journeywoman gulped some air and whispered, "Frederick exposed himself to two young women in front of the ladies' bathroom."

Rowena's eyes went wide. She turned on her heel toward me. "One minute."

"Take your time. I'll wait for you by the fountain."

I walked out of the Casino's doors. After the stench of the undead, the night air tasted refreshing, like a gulp of cold water in the heat of a summer day. I'd had enough of the People's hospitality for one night. Maybe if I splashed some water from those pretty fountains on my face, it would wash the stench off.

A man stepped in my way. "Kate!"

How did I know him . . . I had seen him before. He stepped forward and the light shone on his face. Lago Vista. Except this Lago seemed to have lost at least two decades. The Lago I recalled had seen forty-five. In my head, his hair was thinning, his muscle drooped a bit off his frame, and lines had begun to crop up on his face. This Lago was in his prime. He stood straight, his shoulders were broad, his chest filled out his leather, and as he sauntered toward me, his gait betrayed no trace of a limp. His hair was thick, his eyes bright, and his smirk had gone from self-deprecating to smug.

All my warning sirens went off at the same time.

"Hey." Lago winked at me. "Didn't know you gambled."

"I don't. Strictly business." There was something important I needed to remember about Lago. Something vital. It was making my head hurt, but when I reached for those memories, there was nothing there.

"I just wanted to tell you that you and I are cool. I don't hold grudges."

"What the hell are you talking about?"

Lago grinned. "That's the right kind of attitude. Water under the bridge." He waved his arm as if tossing an invisible baseball. "Whoosh, gone and forgotten."

Okay. An important chunk of my memory was definitely missing.

"So where is your guy?"

"At home."

"Oooh. Out on the town by yourself." He nodded. "I like it. Come on, I'll treat you to a couple of spins on the roulette wheel."

"Can you afford to gamble, Lago?"

He reached into his jacket. It looked brand-new. New pants, too. New boots. Lago pulled out a wad of cash held together with a rubber band and held it up between his index and middle finger. "I'm flush."

I could almost remember it. I could feel the tail end of a memory squirming somewhere just outside my reach. "You got a rich uncle I don't know about?"

"Nahh. I'm a self-made man. So what do you say, Kate? Let me show you a good time. Your guy doesn't have to know."

Lago had some serious balls.

"Sorry," I told him. "I'm meeting someone here in a couple of minutes and then I'm going home."

Lago pondered it. "You know, you're right. Why go in there? Too many people. Let's go for a drive instead. I always thought you were hot, Kate. Mmm, legs."

And we had gone straight into creepy territory. I really didn't want to break his arms. "No."

"No?"

"Move on, Lago."

He smiled at me. "Well, shoot. I guess I'll have to do it the other way. I want this one."

Magic clamped me, trying to pull me forward. Overwhelming, catastrophic power squeezed me. An alien intelligence brushed against me. Every hair on the back of my neck rose. I dropped my shields and pushed back. My legs shook from the strain. I couldn't cry out. I had no voice. It was taking everything I had to not move.

Lago made a come-here motion with his hand. "Car, car, car. Quickly now."

A sleek silver convertible slid from the shadows, completely silent.

Lago swung the door open. "In you go."

The magic squeezed, grinding me. It was streaming from Lago, but it wasn't his magic. He was merely a shell, an anchor for something ancient and powerful with a familiar flavor. We'd just had a chat in Biohazard's dumping ground.

So here you are, precious. Didn't wait long.

The power pressed on me, demanding compliance. Strong. So strong. I clenched my teeth and pushed back. The ifrit's magic recoiled slightly, shocked at the resistance.

That's right, punk. Try me. I'm coming for you.

The power clamped me, harder and harder. I concentrated on lifting my hand. Lago must've gotten hold of whatever shiny thing the giant wore in his ear. *Oh, you stupid fool. Never bargain with beings you don't understand.*

"I said, I want this one," Lago said. "What's the matter with you?"

The power squeezed, trying to pull me off my feet.

I'm going to kill you. I'm coming for you and I will kill you.

My hand crept up, ever so slowly, as if I were swimming through cooling tar. It felt like my muscles tore and snapped off my bones one by one. The presence behind the spell threw all of its weight against me. My magic and its magic ground and clashed like two swords locked against each other.

My hand was almost to Sarrat's hilt. *Another inch and I am so there. Sorry, Lago. Take out the anchor and the ship will drift away.*

"Kate?" Rowena walked up to us.

Lago stroked his chin. "Oh my God. No offense, Kate. Forget that one, let's take this one instead."

Rowena's face went slack. The magic vanished. I flew backward twenty-five feet and landed on my ass on the pavement. It took me half a second to roll to my feet. The car was already speeding away into the night, Rowena in the passenger seat, her eyes blank.

I sprinted after the convertible.

A vampire barreled into me, knocking me off my feet. We rolled and it landed on top of me, red eyes burning. The massive mouth unhinged an inch from my face, the twin fangs like sickles in the moonlight.

"Do not move!" A navigator barked in my ear. "Identify yourself."

I punched the bloodsucker in the head. "You moron. He's kidnapping your Master of the Dead. Get the hell off me. Get Ghastek! Tell him an old power took Rowena. Move, damn you!"

For a moment the vampire froze.

The gates of the white minarets above me opened wide and vampires rained onto the pavement.

FIFTEEN-YEAR-OLDS MAKE TERRIBLE drivers. They speed, they pay no attention to the rules of the road, and they think they're immortal. There are times when you absolutely have to have a fifteen-year-old behind the wheel. Chasing a convertible driven by the kidnapper of a necromancer down Atlanta's deserted streets in the middle of the night was one of those times.

"He's too fast," Julie growled.

We hit a bump. The Jeep went airborne and landed with a creak. I ran my tongue along my teeth to make sure they were all still there.

Above us, vampires dashed along the buildings.

Something landed on the roof with a thud. I rolled down the passenger window and a vampire stuck his head in, hanging upside down.

"I'm not amused," Ghastek said through the vampire's mouth.

"Well, pardon me. You can get your refund back at the ticket booth."

"Just once, could you visit my place of business without causing a major incident?"

"I didn't cause an incident."

"No, you're right. I misspoke. You talked to a man who then kidnapped a Master of the Dead, requiring us to make a massive show of force, which will no doubt result in financial losses and negative publicity less than twenty-four hours before your father inspects our facilities. 'Incident' would be too mild a word. If this is a diversion, it won't work. More than a third of our force remains at the Casino under capable leadership. They are able to repel any attack."

"It's not a diversion," I squeezed through clenched teeth. "It's an ifrit who wants to take over the city." Also, he'd only brought less than a quarter of his total vampire force.

The vampire's face became completely still as Ghastek mulled it over.

"Hold on." Julie took the corner at a breakneck speed. The vehicle careened. I grabbed the handle above the window. We flew on two wheels for a stomach-pinching second and landed back on the road.

"A djinn," Ghastek said finally.

"Yes. It's an old power, probably tied to an item. The man in the car is a merc. I believe he got a hold of the item, made himself younger, wished for a magic car filled with money, and for a woman, and now it will be time to pay the piper."

"The djinn will take over the human host," Ghastek said. "So the giant who destroyed the Guild was of djinn origin and, since this man's three-wish cycle just ran out, we can probably expect another giant."

Whatever faults Ghastek had, stupidity wasn't one of them.

"What do I need to know?" he asked.

"It's an ifrit, so it loves fire. The last giant was almost seventy feet tall. He was still transforming when I cut him down: metal legs, high heat. Low intelligence, no speech, lots of rage, and fun reanimative metamorphosis once he's down. His corpse transformed into draconoids."

"Lovely," Ghastek said. "Do the human host's abilities affect the giant's performance?"

And why hadn't I asked myself that question? "I have no idea. Lago is a good, well-trained merc. I guess we'll find out."

The vampire's head disappeared and I heard Ghastek's voice. "Team Leader One and Two, merge to bandit. Team Three and Four, maintain. Team Leader One, tap, if no response, stop and dismantle. Watch for heat damage."

The vampires picked up speed, converging on the vehicle. Six vampires on the right dropped onto Lago's convertible. They were in midfall when the top of the car snapped closed. Metal plates formed on the vehicle, overlaying each other like scales. Five vampires landed on the scales, nimble like cats. The sixth slid off and fell, rolling.

"You must be faster than that, Evgenia," Ghastek said.

The bloodsuckers ripped into the vehicle, clawing at the armor. The lines of the car flowed, reshaping themselves as the armor grew thicker, covering the wheels. Two of the vampires managed to pry open the top panel. It went flying and a new armor plate snapped into its place.

"I don't get it." Julie swerved. "So the djinn takes over the body after three wishes?"

If the ifrit didn't kill us, her driving would for sure.

"That's the theory." And because the djinn wanted to take over a host for reasons unknown, he would've actively pushed his victim to make the wishes. For a weaker-willed person, the compulsion to wish for something would've been impossible to resist and the more wishes they made, the greater their break with reality would become. Under normal circumstances, Lago wouldn't have tried to kidnap me. He was a self-proclaimed Casanova, not a rapist. And the Oswalds' neighbor probably wouldn't have let a deadly monster loose in a residential neighborhood. We had to stop this now, before anyone else got hurt.

"But Lago already had his three wishes. Why is the car making armor?" Julie asked.

"Because the ifrit needs time for the transformation. If we kill Lago now, we stop it, so he's protecting him."

Julie stepped on it. The Jeep squeezed another small burst of speed out of its engine. We were ten feet behind Lago.

"But why is he making giants?"

"If we knew that, we would have this problem solved."

The armored scales sprouted spikes. The bloodsuckers dodged in unison. One of the undead squirmed, impaled, pulled himself off the spike, and kept clawing at the armor.

"Team Leader Two, stop and dismantle."

We were barreling down the road when Lago turned again. Great. We had zigzagged through the three-square-mile block of the city and now we were almost exactly where we had started . . . Hmm. If we kept going straight, we'd run right into the Mole Hole. The Mole Hole, once the site of Molen Enterprises, was a 140-yard-wide crater lined with a foot of glass. It formed when one of the richest Atlanta families tried to hatch a phoenix. All kinds of fun activities took place at the Mole Hole, from roller derby to street hockey tournaments, but right now it would be deserted.

"The car is glowing," Julie reported.

The metal scales shielding the car had gained a soft bright glow on the left side. Lago was transforming and if we didn't hurry, Rowena would be cooked alive.

I knocked on the roof. No answer.

I unbuckled my seat belt.

"Are you going to jump onto his car?" Julie asked. "I can get closer."

"What are you, out of your mind? No, I'm not jumping on his car. That only works in movies." I stuck my head out of the window. "Ghastek!"

The bloodsucker swiveled its head toward me.

"Hold on to the car," I told him, dropped back into my seat, and buckled up. Lago might have a magic convertible, but I had a kid who'd learned to drive from Dali. "He has a sharp right coming up. He will slow down for it. Julie, do you remember how to do a PIT maneuver?"

Julie grinned. "Can I? Can I, please?"

I braced myself. "Hit him."

Lago's car slowed for the turn. Julie stepped on it. For a moment our Jeep overtook the former convertible, pulling up alongside it on the left. The two cars connected gently and Julie threw the wheel to the right. The impact shook the Jeep. The convertible spun and slid off the road, skidding across the pavement into the Mole Hole.

Welcome to the twenty-first century, asshole.

The Jeep kept going, veering dangerously close to the building. We missed a lamppost by three inches and Julie brought us to a stop.

She hit the wheel with both hands and sang in a high-pitched voice, "Cru-u-u-u-shed it."

"Great job." I jumped out of the car, sword in hand, and ran to the rim of the Mole Hole. The convertible lay on its side. Two vampires clawed at the passenger door.

"Secure Ms. Daniels," Ghastek ordered behind me.

Four vampires landed in front of me.

"What the hell?"

"This is a People matter," Ghastek said, his voice crisp. "I will consider any violence on your part a declaration of war."

"Like hell!"

"I mean it. You have a very important dinner tomorrow. I'm not taking any chances."

Argh. Punching Ghastek's bloodsucker would accomplish nothing because Ghastek wouldn't feel a thing. I still wanted to do it. I wanted to cut its head off. My hand itched.

"Kate!" Julie's voice rang out. "You can't fight a giant. You promised."

Damn it. I slid Sarrat back in its sheath. "I'm going to remember this," I ground out.

"I shudder at the thought," Ghastek said, his voice dry. "Excuse me."

The bloodsucker dashed forward and took a huge leap. It landed between the two vampires clawing at the door and stabbed down with its hand. The door popped open. Ghastek's vampire dove inside and emerged with Rowena's limp body. It spun and handed her off to a different bloodsucker, who sprinted away from the car.

The convertible exploded.

A cloud of smoke billowed, spiraling up. Something solid moved inside it. Something massive and filled to the brim with magic. The smoke whipped into a column, spinning like a tornado, and a towering giant spilled forth. Hard muscle sheathed his seventy-foot-tall frame. His eyes glowed with red, his ears were pointed, and a mane of straight black hair fell down his back, but his face was still recognizable. He looked like Lago.

The giant clenched his fists, his enormous arms bent at the elbows, and he roared at the sky. A blast of heat rolled at us. Something shiny sparked at Lago's throat. I squinted. An earring. He had pierced the skin below his clavicle with it, probably to conceal it. The earring must've required blood contact. *Lago, you fool. You stupid, stupid fool.* Now he would die. There was no way to save him. Such a waste.

"You promised," Julie said next to me in a small voice.

"Settle down. I'm not going to fight him."

Ghastek's voice rolled through the Mole Hole. "All teams, take him down."

. . .

I CROSSED MY arms. "It's been fifteen minutes."

"Sixteen," one of my vampire babysitters said in a female voice. "Ma'am."

That didn't exactly make things better.

The question of whether the host's body affected the giant's power had been answered. Lago had survived nine years as a merc. He was damn fast. The vampires sliced at him, but he caught them, broke them, and tossed them aside. They regenerated, and he broke them again.

Glossy metal scales had begun to form on his legs, slowly climbing their way up. They were midway up his thighs now.

Something fell off the giant and lay in a heap. It looked like a human-sized pale maggot. I squinted at it. It was a vampire. Normally gaunt, it had swollen to ridiculous proportions, as if someone somehow had gotten the Michelin man from the old commercials and turned him into an undead monstrosity. As if the vampires weren't already revolting enough.

The vampire next to me opened its mouth. "Strike Leader, we have a one-twenty-eight in progress. Permission to retrieve?"

"Permission granted."

The vampire sprinted across the glass crater toward the undead maggot thing.

"What's wrong with it?" Julie asked.

"Too much blood," one of the navigators said through another blood-sucker. "It's an almost never-seen phenomenon, but it's been observed in a controlled study in a lab environment. It takes an average of forty-eight liters of blood consumed in a continuous stream, or the blood of roughly 1.28 Holstein cows, to induce this state in a vampire."

The giant had too much blood and he was regenerating. They couldn't drain him fast enough. I couldn't use a power word on him, but I could do something.

The vampire that left us picked up the bloated undead, slung it over its back, raced back across the glass, and dumped the abomination beside us. The vampire's eyes had turned dull.

"Ew." Julie shuddered. "Ew."

"Ew" didn't even begin to cover it. Its skin looked ready to rupture. "Why is nobody piloting it?"

"It won't be able to move for another hour," the male navigator explained.

"Please relay a message to Ghastek for me," I said. "Your way isn't working. Let me help."

The vampire dutifully repeated the words.

"He says, 'The situation is under control.'"

"Tell him, no, it's not. You can't contain it now. What happens when the metamorphosis is complete?"

"He says, 'Your concern is duly noted.'"

Argh. "Asshole."

The undead opened his mouth and paused as the navigator caught himself. "Should I . . . ?"

"No," another navigator told him. "You shouldn't."

A caravan of black SUVs clogged the street leading to the Casino. The SUVs pulled up in a semicircle around the Mole Hole and disgorged Ghastek and a flock of journeymen. I recognized two Masters of the Dead: Toakase Kakau, a dark-eyed woman of Tongan descent, and Ryan Kelly, a large Caucasian man who looked the corporate shark in every way, except for a very long purple mohawk.

The journeymen and the Masters of the Dead thinned out, forming a loose ring around the Mole Hole. A journeywoman next to Ghastek raised a large horn to her lips and blew a sharp note.

Vampires dashed into the crater. A journeyman could pilot one; a Master of the Dead could control two or in Ghastek's case three. There were about twenty people around the Mole Hole and probably thirty vampires below. Each was marked with a bright smear of fluorescent paint in a dozen colors, some with a cross, some with a ring. Something really weird was going on.

The vampires swarmed Lago, climbing up his legs to his chest and stomach. He roared, throwing them around. They landed on the ground, some on their feet, some in a broken heap. The scales were up to his waist now. His feet began to glow. The glass under him would melt before long.

Ghastek raised his hand. The horn screamed in response.

In my mind, the dull red smears of magic that were the thirty vampires in the Mole Hole turned bright red.

Dear God. They had turned the vampires loose.

An unpiloted vampire went into an instant rage. It would slaughter until nothing with a pulse remained. If the PAD found out, nobody would be arrested. They would shoot everyone here out of principle. This was insane. Now I understood the paint—they'd marked the bloodsuckers so they could quickly grab them again without getting confused.

The undead tore into the giant. He roared, frantically trying to knock them off. Flesh flew as they ripped, clawed, and burrowed into his body. The vampires piled on, maddened by bloodlust.

A minute passed. The giant was still standing.

Another . . .

Two vampires dropped down, their bodies engorged with blood. Lago stomped on them.

"Steady," Ghastek said.

The giant careened, rolling his shoulders in, as if trying to gather himself into a ball. The vampires nearly covered him now.

Magic exploded like a clap of thunder. With a deafening howl, Lago jerked upright, his arms straight out. The vampires fell off, knocked aside by an enormous force.

"Acquire!" Ghastek snapped.

The horn screeched again, frantic. The navigators grabbed the minds of their vampires.

Smokeless orange flames sheathed Lago's feet. He turned, roaring, his face no longer bearing any trace of humanity. The metal scales were up to his collarbone now and those at his waist and below glowed orange. The glass under his feet softened, melting. The giant turned in our direction, casting a long look at the city, and raised his foot . . .

Oh no, you don't.

I drew Sarrat, sliced my left arm, and stabbed the bloody blade into the body of the bloated vampire. My blood dashed down the blade, its magic spreading through the undead blood, like a spark charging down a detonation cord. In half a second, all of the blood was mine. I yanked the blood out of the undead's body. It hovered before me in a massive round sphere. I thrust my bleeding hand into it, flattening the liquid into a solid disk, two feet across, spun, and hurled it with all my strength and with my magic.

It flew, expanding as it whistled through the air, its edge turning razor sharp, and cleaved the giant's neck. The impact shattered the now five-foot-wide disk into dust. The giant's head flopped to the side, his neck three-quarters severed, his mouth contorting silently, his red eyes looking in different directions. Blood gushed out, washing over the torso, and hissed, evaporating as it met the hot scales covering his skin.

There. No power words.

The Mole Hole turned completely quiet and in the silence, the sound of hoofbeats rolled through the night. A huge gray horse galloped toward us, bearing a rider in a gray cloak. He carried a lance tipped with a glowing green spark.

The giant dropped to his hands and knees, his neck jerking, trying to flip the heavy head back into its proper place. The wound on his neck tried to seal itself.

The horse leaped onto the giant, pounding its way through the flames up his spine, to his head. The rider clamped the lance to his body and rammed it into the bloody stump of the giant's skull. The horse reared, silhouetted against the orange flames. The rider's cloak flared, his hood falling. Nick Feldman, a knight of the Order.

Oh hell. We were so screwed.

The massive horse jumped, clearing the gap between the giant and the side of the Mole Hole.

The giant's head exploded. Brain and blood flew, splattering the vampires in front of me and drenching me in gore.

Fan-freaking-tastic. That's just the cherry on top of the sundae of this day. Curran would kill me.

Nick's voice boomed through the clearing. "The Order thanks you for your assistance. Kindly disperse."

Ghastek stepped forward, clearly untroubled by the size of the horse. Two vampires moved in unison to sit on both sides of him like loyal dogs.

I braced myself.

"This is a People matter," Ghastek said, his voice ice cold.

"The People have no jurisdiction here," Nick said. "This investigation belongs to the Order."

"A crime has been committed against a member of the People and we responded to it decisively and with overwhelming force. The People find the Order's presence and response insufficient to properly secure the body."

Translation: there is only one of you and a lot of us.

"I am the law," Nick said. "Impede me and you will suffer the consequences."

"Last time I checked, the Order was not a law enforcement agency," Ghastek said, his voice dangerously mild.

"You're only one man," someone called out.

Ghastek took a moment to glance toward the speaker. Heads would roll when they got back to the Casino.

Aw, hell. I really hated the Order.

"Three," I said.

Everyone looked at me. Julie pulled out her axes.

"He is three. Biohazard brought the Order in on the previous giant appearance. Therefore, this occurrence is a continuation of an ongoing investigation, authorized by a formal petition from a state law enforcement agency. He is the law. I will uphold the law."

Ghastek paused. Some sort of calculation was feverishly taking place in his mind. He couldn't back down. There were no good choices. If he let the body get away, he would have to explain to Roland how a djinn kidnapped Rowena and how he had wasted several vampires and a bunch of resources trying to kill it but had nothing to show for it. If he claimed the body, he would have to explain to Roland why he'd attacked a knight of the Order, broken about half a dozen laws, and generated a quickly rising mountain of legal bills.

He would go for the body. The value of a corpse possessed and transformed by the djinn would mean more to Roland than the legal problems.

I flicked my sword, warming up my wrist. This was about to get bloody. Ghastek raised his hand. The undead leaned forward as one.

"Stay next to me," I told Julie.

Sirens howled, growing closer and closer. A fleet of Biohazard and PAD vehicles turned the corner, filling up the street. Ghastek stared at them for a long moment. "Get the legal department."

I looked up at Nick. "It's an earring. About the size of a plum. He wore it like a piercing on his chest."

He gave no indication he heard me. *You're welcome.*

"The ifrit is moving from host to host in an attempt to acquire a more powerful host. You need to secure the earring."

Nick rode off without saying a word.

"Fuck."

"Did you expect gratitude?" Toakasa asked.

"No. I expect him to contain the magic so we don't have another giant." I'd have to find Luther. He would at least listen to reason.

A woman ran up to me and thrust a piece of paper into my hand. I glanced at it. A bill for eighty-two thousand dollars. "What the hell is this?"

"The cost of the destroyed vampire," the journeywoman chirped. "Have a nice day."

I REFUSED TO leave until the earring had been found. It took four hours for Biohazard to sift through the gory carcass, quarantining each section of the corpse they had removed. I sat on the edge of the Mole Hole and watched them do it. Julie fell asleep in the car. For a while the People's lawyers and Biohazard's lawyers squabbled over who would get the earring when it was finally found, but eventually they too grew quiet and just watched.

Biohazard techs gingerly placed it into a box carved from a cube of salt, which was then placed into a plastic box lined with volcanic rock. Volcanic rock had been exposed to such high temperatures that magically it was found to be inert and impervious to all types of fire magic.

The techs sealed the box and then Nick promptly confiscated it.

"You can't do that!" If Luther got any more worked up, he would suffer apoplexy right here. He was wearing a biohazard containment suit, and he'd taken his helmet off to talk. "It needs to be examined and studied."

"Examined how?" Nick asked. "Are you planning on having tea with it and asking it about its family? We know it's a djinn. We must contain it. That's all that matters."

Luther turned to his lawyers, who by now had lost all semblance of professionalism and lounged on blankets next to the People's lawyers, who were sharing their coffee. "Can he do this?"

"Yep," a Hispanic female lawyer said, pushing her glasses up her nose.

"How?"

"You gave him that power when you signed the petition," a thin, dark-skinned, male lawyer told him. "I told you not to sign it."

Nick placed the box in his saddlebag.

"The corpses exhibited reactive metamorphosis in every single case," I told him loud enough for Luther to hear. "Except this one. That means the djinn wants you to have that box. He wants a more capable host and we don't know what his endgame is. Nick, do not put it into the Vault where every knight can have access to it."

Nick ignored me. Right. I guess we knew where we stood. I had a feeling my parentage and the fact that he somehow shared his last name with my deceased guardian had a great deal to do with it, but now wasn't the time or the place to discuss any of it.

"Whatever you think of me, you know I wouldn't lie to you about it. Do not put that box on a shelf in the Vault where anybody can get to it."

Nothing. Big blank wall. God, this night sucked so much.

Luther waved his arms at the lawyers. "Can't you contest it or something? He's about to ride off with it."

"You're screwed," one of the People's male lawyers told him. "The Order petition is ironclad."

"What he said," the female lawyer with glasses said. "So does this mean we're done here?"

"You're done when you get me that body," Ghastek snapped.

The lawyers collectively groaned.

Nick rode off into the night.

"If a djinn possesses a knight of the Order, we're screwed," I told Luther. "Look what he did with a merc."

Luther pondered the body below for a long moment, punched the air, kicked it a few times, and threw his helmet on the ground.

Sometimes being a law-abiding citizen really sucked. I went to the Jeep to wake Julie up. I'd had my fill of Atlanta for one night.

"WE ARE NOT going to tell him about the giant," I told Julie. The sun was rising and the morning promised to be lovely. I had given Curran my word that I would not attack a giant, and I'd broken it. I didn't want to fight with him now. I didn't want to fight with him, period, but especially now. A week ago I would've said our relationship was rock solid. A lot had happened in a week and we were both really stressed-out. Today I wasn't sure how far I could push him. I just didn't know. I was too tired to handle it right now.

Also I needed sleep. And food. I would kill for food. And a shower. And sleep. I had to stop thinking in circles. I had briefly considered going to Cutting Edge to shower, but Curran would've smelled the blood on me anyway. It would take a very long soak before I managed to get it all out of my hair and off my skin, and I just wanted to go home.

I would have to tell Curran about it eventually, because we had agreed not to lie to each other and because the ifrit was a vindictive sonovabitch. I had insulted him and nuked his giant again. Well, technically Nick had, but I had played a large part in it. That meant he would likely send us a lovely surprise when he regained his magic. Too bad there was no way to tell how long that would be.

Julie opened her eyes so wide, you'd think a purple flying elephant had landed in front of us. "Are you asking me to lie?"

So when it suited her purposes, Julie had no problem bending the truth, but when I suggested it, there was shock and outrage. How exactly did that work? "No, I'm telling you not to volunteer information."

"What if he asks me?"

"Tell him to ask me."

"Are you and Curran going to get a divorce?" Julie asked, her voice small.

"We can't get a divorce. We're not married."

"Oh God, I'll be one of those kids."

"One of what kids?"

"With weekend parents."

"Julie, damn it, we are not getting a divorce . . . Why the hell are six cars parked in our driveway?"

We both stared at the completely full driveway, occupied by four Pack Jeeps; Pooki, which was Dali's Plymouth Prowler; and a sleek-looking silver Ferrari, which was Raphael's favorite ride.

"Something happened," Julie said.

I parked fifty yards away, just in case, and hightailed it to the door. The door handle turned in my hand. Unlocked. I walked in, Julie at my heels.

"I want to know why nobody told me she almost died!" Andrea said.

I followed her voice and stepped into the kitchen. She sat at the table, eating handfuls of trail mix. Raphael sat next to her, stroking her back.

"I'm her best friend. I had a right to know!"

"You had a right to know?" George waved her arm. "I'm directly involved in this and nobody told me."

"We all had a right to know," Robert said, one hand over the phone receiver's mouthpiece. His husband, Thomas, stood next to him, drinking coffee out of a mug with a kitten on it. Both alphas of Clan Rat were in attendance.

"She claimed the city. It's a matter of Pack security," Robert said, then put a hand over his free ear and went back to his phone call.

"It's a matter of Kate and Curran," Dali said.

Jim dragged his hand over his face. "You weren't told because you would bicker about it all day and by the time you were done deciding, she would've been dead."

"Oh please," Desandra said. "It's not like we're children."

"Could've fooled me," Dali told her.

The blond alpha of Clan Wolf winked at her.

Curran stood near the stove, behind everyone. Our gazes met. Relief showed in his eyes and then I saw the precise moment he realized I was covered in gore. A gold fire sheathed his irises.

"It was my decision," Jim said. "Deal with it."

"What is that smell?" Andrea turned. Suddenly everything went quiet.

"The scouts report there was a giant incident near the Casino," Robert said, hanging up.

"What kind of a giant incident?" Desandra asked.

Curran's face was terrible.

"An incident with a giant in it," Robert clarified, and saw me.

Curran moved.

One moment I was standing and then I was in the hallway, my feet in the empty air. He'd clamped his hands on my shoulders and lifted me to his face. His voice was glacial. "One thing. I asked you to do one thing."

He was really pissed off. I would've preferred it if he'd roared.

"I'm sorry."

Something thudded against the front door.

"You gave me your word and you broke it."

"Yes. I'm sorry. I had no choice. I was trying to save Rowena."

He opened his mouth.

"Reckless, stupid, wrong, broke your trust, I'm sorry," I told him. "Don't be mad at me."

The door thudded again. Curran dropped me down and jerked it open. "WHAT?"

A thirty-foot-tall bull with enormous metal horns glared back at us with eyes the size of teacups. Flames sheathed its huge legs, flaring around its hooves. The bull opened its maw and vomited fire.

Curran spun me around, clamping me to his chest, his back to the flames.

The fire smashed into the invisible shield of the house ward and splashed back, falling harmlessly to the ground. Curran thrust me aside. His human body tore and a seven-and-a-half-foot monster spilled out and charged the bull.

The eight shapeshifters in my kitchen went furry as one and sprinted through the hallway past me, followed by Grendel barking his head off.

"Alive!" I called after them. "We need to ask him some . . ."

The bull ducked his head, ready to gore Curran. Curran grabbed the bull's left horn and punched the enormous bovine in the face. The bull's head snapped to the side, but Curran jerked it back and hammered another hard punch into its skull.

Never mind.

Curran punched it again and again, his fist like a jackhammer, smashing into the bone. The bull attempted to back up, jerking its head, trying to free its horn, but Curran held on and kept punching. Blood flew from the side of the bull's head. The monster pushed forward, trying to bulldoze Curran off his feet. Curran locked both hands on the bull's horns and thrust his clawed feet into the ground. Muscles bulged under his gray fur, the faint dark stripes standing out like whip marks.

Curran's feet slid and stopped. They struggled, face to face, the bull's maddened fiery eyes staring into Curran's ice-cold gray. The shapeshifters waited in a ragged semicircle.

The bull strained, but Curran held it.

Holy shit.

The bull opened its mouth and bellowed. Curran roared back, the sound of pure fury. Tiny hairs rose on the back of my neck.

Fire flared, sheathing the bull's sides. Curran vaulted onto its back, one hand still on the horn. His enormous leonine jaws gaped open and Curran bit into the side of the bull's throat. The monster screamed and the shapeshifters ripped into the bovine monster, oblivious to the flames.

"This is good," a wererat in a warrior form said next to me in Robert's voice. "He was very stressed-out. Excuse me."

He pushed past me and joined the slaughter. I slumped against the door frame and watched.

"WILL YOU STOP eating it," I growled.

"No," Andrea said. She was sitting on the ground and chewing on some unidentifiable chunk of bull flesh.

"It's a piece of meat from something a djinn summoned."

"You don't know that."

"Who else would send a bull made of fire to my house after I helped kill a djinn-possessed giant? Stop eating. It might have been a person," I told her.

"I don't care."

"Andrea! You don't know what this will do to the baby!"

"It will make it nice and strong." Andrea bit into the piece of meat, shredding it with her sharp bouda teeth.

"It's evidence."

"You have all that evidence over there." She waved at the rest of the bull corpse, spread in about a hundred pieces across our lawn. Curran had torn it to pieces with his bare hands. "I've been starving all day and eating that bird-food trail mix. I'm pregnant, hormonal, and tired, and I am damn hungry. I'm going to sit here and eat my meat."

"She's right," Desandra told me, biting into a chunk. "It's really decent. Tastes like grass-fed Angus to me. So kind of your fiancé to tenderize it."

That was it. I was done. I just didn't even care anymore.

I marched my way up the driveway to the house. An enormous white tiger sprawled in my driveway, flicking her tail at a small flock of butterflies that bounced on bright wings around her brilliant white fur. I circled Dali and the butterflies and went inside. Curran sat on a couch in the living room. He was back in his human skin. The couch was covered in blood. That was fine. I was having second thoughts about the color anyway.

I sat next to him. Watching him rip the bull apart wasn't just frightening. It was one of those things I would never forget. It was imprinted in my brain. Curran's control was absolute, so when he opened the door and the feral lethal monster shot out and reveled in unrestrained destruction, it made your blood run cold. He'd had less outlet than usual since we moved out of the Keep. There people recognized what he was. If he wanted something, he had only to pick up the phone and people would run to do his bidding. Here, he was trying his best to be a good considerate neighbor. To be a normal human, not in the true sense of the word, but in the meaning other suburban families would accept and find nonthreatening. I hadn't fully understood how hard it was for him until now.

It was over. People saw it. They stopped and stared, and there was no going back. And I couldn't be happier about it.

"Julie asked me if we are getting a divorce," I told him.

No response.

"I told her that we couldn't get one since we aren't married."

Silence.

"I understand now," I told him. "You left the Pack for me and threw it all away, because you thought we would have a happy peaceful life together. You've been so good and assumed this calm, nice role of a man who lives in the suburbs with his family and instead this messed-up crap keeps happening. I—"

He put his arm around me and pulled me closer to him.

I shut up.

We sat together on the couch.

"I didn't touch the giant. I didn't use any power words. I only threw some undead blood at it. I just got splattered with gore." I almost said *I promise* but held my tongue.

"I will kill anything that tries to hurt you," he said, his voice quiet.

"I know. I will kill anything that tries to hurt you," I told him.

Curran looked at me. "I just can't figure out what to do when you hurt yourself. Who am I mad at?"

I opened my mouth. Nothing smart came to mind. "If anyone can figure it out, it would be you. You're the only one who'll put up with me."

He didn't answer.

"I have some bad news." Might as well drop all of the shoes at the same time.

"Tell me."

"The Order claimed the earring that houses the ifrit. They won't let anyone examine it. Eduardo is being held in some abandoned building. He is starving and we have no way to know which building he's in. I saw him in a vision. He doesn't have long."

"Anything else?" Curran asked, his voice even.

"Yes. My father is building a tower near Lawrenceville. He wants to have dinner tonight. At Applebee's."

The arm holding me shook. I glanced at him. Curran was laughing.

"I love you," I told him. "I don't give a crap what anybody thinks or says.

You don't have to be anyone or anything but you, Curran. Don't do this for me, because I just want you."

"You realize all of the neighbors are going to move, right?"

"Screw them. Good riddance. I couldn't care less if we fit in with them or don't. I never wanted the 'good' neighborhood or to be seen as 'normal.' I just wanted to live in a house with you and Julie. You can be yourself. You let me be myself, so it's only fair. Stop trying so hard to fit in. I love you because you don't."

He kissed my hair.

"Anything exciting happen while I was gone?" I asked.

"Remember how we sent George to have a subtle conversation with Patrick?"

Oh no. "I'm afraid to ask . . ."

"He tried to lecture her on her duty to the Clan and she told him to shut up. He told her he would take her in hand for her dad."

I squeezed my eyes shut for a few seconds. "Is he alive?"

"Oh yes. She didn't kill him. Both of his legs are broken, but he is alive."

"Was that an official challenge?"

"No, they are classifying it as a family dispute, since George decided to separate and isn't in the clan chain of command anymore."

Raphael walked into the room. He was wearing worn-out jeans and a leather jacket, and if you sent him and the leading male model down the street, he would turn more heads. There was just something about Raphael that broadcasted sex, loud and clear, and I had yet to meet a woman who didn't respond to it. Of course, they usually did their best to hide that response because Andrea was a crack shot.

Raphael crouched by Curran and said, "Hey. I just figured out how we all could make a lot of money."

"Go on," Curran said.

"I'm going to buy out your neighbors and offer their houses to Pack members who live in the city. Any Pack family would give up their life's savings to live next to the former Beast Lord, and something tells me your neighbors will be extremely eager to sell."

Curran laughed again.

"We'll make a small fortune," Raphael said. "All you have to do is go out once in a while in your warrior form and roar. Especially when it's dark. They'll line up to sell so fast, we'll have to give out numbers."

I laughed.

"I'm completely serious." Raphael was grinning. "You could use the extra cash."

"You should get your wife to stop eating unidentified meat," I told him. Curran stroked my back.

Desandra thrust her head into the room. "You better hurry. Mahon is here."

MAHON STOOD ON the lawn. Large, burly, with a curly beard, he looked like he needed a chain-mail hauberk, a mace, and a castle to defend. His beast form made his human body look weak and puny, which was why Mahon served as the Pack's Executioner. His glower made hardened fighters run for cover. His daughter couldn't have cared less. She stood defiant in the middle of the lawn, holding a blanket around herself with her one hand. Usually transforming from a human to a beast and then back to a human would've put her down for a nap, but the tilt of her chin told me she was very motivated to stay awake. George was pissed off. They both looked ready to explode. I braced myself.

Across the street a crowd of neighbors had gathered at Heather Savell's house. Awesome. Nothing better at a shapeshifter family brawl than conveniently placed innocent bystanders.

". . . Separation is ridiculous. You've had your fun," Mahon said, his voice deep. "This foolishness stops now. Come home."

"No." If George had freezing powers, that one word would've turned her dad into an icicle.

"You are not leaving the Pack."

"Yes, I am."

Mahon exhaled rage. "For what?" His voice boomed. "For some boy?"

George bared her teeth. "He isn't a boy. He is a man. My man. The one I chose."

"Yes, just like you chose Aidan before, and what's-his-face, Nathan. This will pass. Don't throw your life away."

"Staying with you would be throwing my life away. You want me to marry a werebear and be a good little brood mare."

Oh boy.

"I want you to stay with your family!" Mahon roared.

"Do not raise your voice at me!" George roared back.

"We raised you, we clothed you, we fed you, we educated you, and this is how you repay us?"

"You did all the things that parents are legally obligated to do. Congratulations, Dad. You weren't a neglectful parent. Thank you. It doesn't give you the right to shackle me for the rest of my life. You're not entitled to it. This is my life and I will live it."

"She isn't leaving your family," Thomas said. "She's leaving the Pack."

"The hell she is." Mahon seemed to get bigger somehow, his face darker. He pointed at Curran. "Is this it? Is he your example? You want to throw it all away because some . . . human couldn't stand living in the Keep? She nagged at him and nagged at him until he gave in and now look at him. Years wasted! Years! And we are all worse off for it. He thinks with his dick, but you, you were always smarter than that."

It's funny how loud horrified silence can be.

Curran laughed.

Mahon stared at him, incredulous.

Across the street Heather was gaping at me. I smiled and waved at her.

"What about this is funny?" Mahon roared. "You were supposed to be the Beast Lord. You were supposed to start a legacy!"

"I'm happy," Curran told him. "Don't you want me to be happy?"

"It's not about being happy! It's about duty and obligations and doing something with your life!"

"What about your obligations?" Curran asked, his voice mild. "What was your duty to my mate when I was comatose?"

Mahon opened his mouth.

"Did you protect her?" Curran asked. "Did you help her? Did you do anything to support this future legacy?"

"She was not a proper mate. She will never be a proper mate. She is a human!"

Well, of course.

"You don't get to decide that." Curran said. "It isn't your place. I chose her. I led the Pack for seventeen years and it failed me when I needed it most. You failed me."

Mahon recoiled.

"My obligation to the Pack is over," Curran said. "You failed to uphold your end of the bargain."

"Speaking of duty," George put in. "What the hell were you thinking, sending a fifteen-year-old against Andorf? He was a berserk bear with years of experience and Curran could barely shave. Why didn't you go, Dad?"

"Be quiet," Mahon snapped. "You were barely twelve. You have no idea what was involved. I sent him because we needed a leader. Because the packs wouldn't follow me!"

I went and sat by Andrea. I'd had a long day and I was tired of standing.

"So your convenience and lofty ideals justified sending a child to the slaughter and then unloading the burden of being in charge of people's lives on him?" George raised her eyebrows. "So you could stand behind the throne and have fun playing kingmaker? You should ask yourself, Dad, why all your children want to escape. Maybe we're not the problem."

"This is it!" Mahon roared. "This ends now. You're coming with me, if I have to carry you. You're not separating from the Pack. I will put you under lock and—"

"Enough." Jim's voice cut through Mahon's roar like a knife.

"—key, I'll—"

"I said, enough!" Jim snarled. "No member of the Pack will interfere with separation. No member of the Pack will be restrained against her will because her father is on a power trip. Mind your conduct, Alpha."

If I slow-clapped, Mahon's head would probably explode.

"You need to rethink that," Mahon told him.

"You will not break the law you yourself helped put in place. The law applies to everyone." Jim glared at Mahon. "You will obey it. If you find yourself unable to follow the law, step down and Clan Heavy will find an alpha who can."

"You—" Mahon began.

"I am the Beast Lord," Jim said.

"Not for long," Mahon snarled.

"Is that a challenge?" Jim bared his teeth. Dali rose from her spot in the driveway and stalked over, paw over massive paw, like a silent majestic shadow, and stood beside her mate, her blue eyes staring at Mahon with unyielding intensity.

Mahon glanced at Curran.

Curran shook his head.

"You would side with them against me?" Mahon looked shocked.

"You're wrong," Curran told him. "The law is the law whether you like it or not. Either you're an alpha and you uphold the law, or you are not."

"It's always like that with you," George said. "You've been after Curran for years to find a mate, and when he found one, you didn't approve of her, so you decided that none of the things you were supposed to do as his father applied. You've been asking me for years when I planned to settle down, and when I did, you didn't like him either. Now he's disappeared and it's your responsibility as an alpha to look for him, but you don't like it, so you chose not to do it. All your talk of duty and obligations means nothing. You think you know better than any of us. You don't. Look at what you're doing, Dad. You're challenging the Beast Lord you swore allegiance to because you don't like the man your daughter loves. Because it hurt some weird little place in your pride. This is how you serve and lead your clan. Don't you have any integrity at all?"

A burning rock the size of a basketball streaked across the sky and landed in the street in front of our house. I lunged in front of Andrea, trying to shield her. The explosion shook the ground.

"What are you doing?" Andrea hauled me back. "I'm a shapeshifter. I regenerate!"

"You're pregnant."

"Oh, shut up."

A brilliant golden flame ten feet high and five feet wide ignited in the middle of the street. Inside it, Eduardo writhed in his cage. The ifrit was punishing Eduardo because we'd killed the bull.

A voice rolled through the street, a voice charged with inhuman power that prickled against my skin like static. It raised every hair on the back of my arms. "All who are guilty will die. Witness the betrayer spawn. See his suffering."

George ran. I jumped to my feet and chased her. Jim made a grab for her, but he wasn't fast enough. George dashed into the street, right into the fire. It broke apart into a thousand sparks and transformed into a thirty-foot-long, glowing snake.

George screamed at the top of her lungs. It was a scream of rage and pain, rolled into one horrible, soul-crushing sound. She screamed as if something inside her had torn and nothing could put it back together.

The snake lunged at her. George grabbed it by its neck, heaved it upright, and slammed the body against the pavement. The snake hissed, the massive coils trying to wind around George and crush her. The werebear planted one foot on the snake. The muscles on her arm flexed and she tore the reptile in two. The light went out of the snake's eyes, but George didn't stop. She mauled and ripped the creature again and again, venting her grief on its body.

We watched her rage, tears welling in her eyes, until she finally let it go, and then Curran and I led her back into the house off the street.

18

I OPENED MY eyes. I lay in our bed, on my side. Something felt odd. I puzzled over it and realized Curran wasn't with me.

The blackout curtains had turned our bedroom into a quiet, dark place. I had no idea what time it was. After George had calmed down, Lyc-V finally took its toll and she crashed in one of our spare bedrooms. I tried my best to describe the building I'd seen in the vision to Raphael. He owned a reclamation company that took useful things out of crumbling skyscrapers, and he had files on just about every major ruin in the city. He wrote everything down, but I could tell nothing clicked with him. My description had been too generic. He said he would look through his files and Dali said that she would send a survey team out to the buildings Raphael identified. Curran told me that when he had dropped Derek off at the address the Clerk had given us for the gig Eduardo had turned down, he had recognized the scent permeating the area. It belonged to the man who'd stalked Eduardo. We still didn't know who he was or why he was obsessing. It was nice that two and two fit together, but so far they still equaled twelve, which didn't help us.

The djinn spoke English this time and it wasn't just a single word. He was growing in power. Nobody liked that news.

Finally everyone left. I dragged myself upstairs, took a long shower, and collapsed on the bed. I had woken up when Curran came in and went into the bathroom to wash the blood off. He never came out of the bathroom. I would've sensed him moving. Exhausted or not, my instincts still worked.

I slipped out of the bed, walked across the slick wooden floor to the bathroom, and nudged the door with my fingertips. He was sitting in our enormous cast-iron bathtub, leaning back, his eyes closed. The tub was his favorite place aside from our bed. Huge, custom-made to accommodate him even in his lion-form with more than enough room to spare, the tub was heated with electricity during tech and with a magic volcanic rock at other times. Usually his face was relaxed when he soaked, but right now it looked tight. He was almost frowning, his thick eyebrows furrowed, the line of his square jaw hard.

There was something I'd been wanting to do, ever since I woke up in the hospital bed and saw him stalking through my room, worried and angry, all coiled strength and hard will.

I slipped off my T-shirt. My panties followed and I walked naked to the tub. Tubs always got me into trouble. I touched my fingers to the water. It was near scalding.

Worth it.

I stepped into the water. It came midway to my thigh.

His eyes stayed closed.

I bent my knees and sank in on top of him, straddling him. My thighs brushed against his long lean legs.

Curran's eyes snapped open, a feral, piercing gray. I pressed my lips against his and licked his bottom lip with the tip of my tongue.

Come back to me. Come out of whatever dark place you're in and feel me instead.

He opened his mouth and kissed me back, his fingers tightening on my back. I felt him harden under me. His tongue slid into my mouth, the kiss deepened, and I moved on top of him, my body hot and pliant. He made a low growling noise in his throat, harsh and male, filled with raw need, and I felt him leave whatever he was thinking behind. He was mine now. There was no worry, no dread, no tomorrow. There was only us and now.

He broke the kiss and nipped my neck, inhaling my scent, and I arched my spine, rubbing against him, wanting to feel him inside me, wanting more. His hands locked on my butt and he pulled me closer, rough and hard, in a single possessive movement. His mouth closed on my breast, his tongue pressing against my nipple, and I nearly melted.

"So fucking beautiful," he whispered, his voice ragged.

He kissed me again, his body rock hard and rigid under me. I slid my hands up his carved chest. His skin was as scalding as the water. I dragged my hands up his muscular shoulders and ran my fingers through his short damp hair, trying not to lose all control. His hand slid lower, down my back, across my butt, across my leg, brushing the sensitive skin of my inner thigh. He touched me. I jerked and broke away from his lips, as his hand covered me. His fingers slipped inside me, his thumb brushing the most sensitive spot, dragging a moan from me. *More. More, please.*

His skilled fingers dipped in and out, teasing, stroking, and my body gave in to his rhythm. Whatever control I had vanished. I rode his hand. He watched me, his gray eyes filled with intense need, and it made me hotter. My breasts ached. A low steady pressure pooled in the bottom of my stomach, threatening to break.

"Come for me," he told me, his voice commanding. "Come for me, baby."

My body clenched around his fingers, waves of pleasure drowning me. I slumped back, limp and boneless, but he caught me. "Not yet."

His fingers kept going, stroking me. My breath was coming out in ragged gasps. My world shrank to the movement of his fingers.

"Again," he told me.

No, there couldn't possibly be an again . . .

I climaxed again, shuddering, held in place by his hands as the orgasm rocked me. I felt heavy and exhausted, floating in my private hot bliss, the vapor rising from the water swirling around me. This was what happiness felt like.

He thrust inside me, the thick length of him stretching me. My body clenched around him, still rippling with the echoes of a climax, and he groaned.

"Your turn," I breathed.

"Not yet."

I leaned on the wall with one hand to steady myself and rode him, matching his movement, squeezing him. He gritted his teeth. I could feel him pulling back, trying to disconnect and slow himself down. Oh no, he wasn't going to last, because I wanted him to come. I wanted him to float in the bliss with me and I had no plans to play fair. I slid my right hand down into the water and my fingers closed around the base of his shaft with him still inside me. He gasped. I pumped him, sliding up and down.

"Kate . . ." he growled.

"I love it," I whispered, pumping him again. "I love when you do this to me. I love when you're inside me."

He snarled and flipped me over. I landed on my knees, catching the edge of the tub with my hands. He buried one hand in my hair and thrust into me from behind, plunging deep, building to a fast hard rhythm. Whatever little semblance of control was gone now and he pounded into me. I lost myself to it, each powerful thrust pushing me closer and closer to the edge, until I finally hurtled over it. He shuddered inside me and we sank into the water together.

THE WATER WAS too hot, but I had no strength to get out. I felt exhausted and drunk, so I just lay there, my head on his chest. He was sliding his fingertips up and down my arm. His eyes were closed, his face relaxed. A slight beginning of a smile curved his lips.

"Let's not go anywhere," I told him.

"The magic is up," he said quietly.

"And?"

"If we don't show up for dinner, your father will manifest in this bathroom."

"Maybe you can scare him away with full frontal," I said.

He laughed.

"What were you thinking about before I came in here?" I asked.

"I was thinking that I never got to know my father," he said. "All I recall of him are childhood memories. I have no idea what kind of man he was or what he stood for. Mahon became my father, but his approval always felt conditional. Still, he's all I got. You had Voron."

"Who was royally fucked up," I said. "Now I have Roland. That kind of says it all right there. My only living blood relative is a megalomaniac with cosmic power and an unshakable belief that he knows best." And saying it out loud just hammered it home. Ugh. "We just don't have the best luck with fathers. But you knew all that."

"It occurred to me that one day I will be a father," he said. "And I have no idea how the hell I'm going to do that."

"You're already a father. Sort of."

"Julie was already a good kid when you found her. Most of the hard work was done. I am talking about raising a little human from the first breath. I don't even know what the hell I would do with a baby."

"I think you will make an excellent father. I'd worry more about what kind of mother I would make."

We would screw up our children. It was inevitable. Julie had taught me that you never get the child you want or expect. You get the child you get and you try your best to make sure they turn out to be a decent human being. That was all that mattered.

An image of pregnant Andrea sitting on our lawn and eating the remnants of a bull flashed across my mind. "If I get pregnant and we kill something magic, don't let me eat it."

He grinned.

"If Aunt B were alive, there's no way Andrea could get away with it."

But Aunt B was dead. She would never see Raphael and Andrea's baby. Hugh d'Ambray's Iron Dogs had killed her, but Hugh was a tool and my father used him like a battering ram when he wanted to break down a door. Roland bore the ultimate responsibility for it.

"I found out what it means to claim the land," I said.

"Tell me."

I did. "It wasn't a hallucination, Curran. I improved when I shouldn't have."

He made a noise, half a growl, half a frustrated grunt. "That means he wields magic even during tech. He won't hesitate to shield himself."

"Yes. Attacking him during technology while he is in his territory means risking the lives of everyone in it. He will drain them dry to keep himself alive. He will deeply regret it and be conflicted about it later, but he will do it. His will to live trumps everything else."

"We'll get him," Curran said.

"I know." I just had no idea how. How do you kill someone with that much power?

"We're going to be smart about this. We're going to watch him, test him, and when we know we can win, we'll crush him."

And that was why he was a scary bastard. "Curran . . ."

He kissed my hair. "Yes?"

"I can't get Sienna's vision out of my head. I've been trying not to think about it, but it keeps popping up."

"It's a possible future," he said. "Not the definite future."

"I know. I just wish I knew what it meant. I usually see him on a grassy hill in my dreams, too. Only when I see it, there is always a tower being built." My father was an active participant in those dreams. I wouldn't be surprised if I saw what he wanted me to see.

"Before Jim and Robert left, I asked them when the construction on the tower had started," Curran said.

"And?"

"The day we killed the wind scorpion."

"What are you getting at?"

"There was nothing there until the scorpion died. That evening he put the first block down and he wasn't at all subtle about it. Why build a tower now, in plain view? He has no power base here. He isn't ready to defend the tower, unless he camps out in it."

Curran had a valid point. Roland spent most of his time in his little budding empire in the Midwest. His version of the new world order was rather fragile; he had to be there to keep an eye on it. Why would he drop everything and come over to build a tower here? He had to know I would lose it when I found out.

Ah. That explained it.

"It's a diversion."

Curran nodded. "For some reason, he's worried about the djinn. Every time we made progress, he escalated the construction until you could no longer ignore it. He is fucking with your head."

"But why? I thought the djinn might have been some sort of screwed-up test he shoved our way, but if it's a test, why not just let us deal with it?"

"Your magic doesn't work on the djinn directly. Does his?"

"I don't know. The natural resistance would still be there, because my magic is Roland's magic and I bounced hard off the ifrit's host. But Roland has a lot more juice than I do and he's been at it for thousands of years longer. He might be able to overpower the ifrit, but it's possible it would cost him a lot of magic. We're not talking about just any djinn. He's an ifrit, which is supposedly second only to the marids in the raw magical power department. According to the myths, the ifrits have a society much like we do. They exist in clans, and they have their own aristocracy based on power. I think our guy was high up in the food chain, because he was wearing gold and emeralds. I also got a glimpse into his mind. It's a mess. He's completely bonkers, but the amount of power he has is staggering. You should've felt it—it was like a damn volcano."

Curran leaned back. "So if it's not a test and the ifrit can present a challenge to Roland's power, why not help us deal with it? He wins if we take the ifrit down."

"I have no idea."

"The intel from Robert shows that the timeline matches up perfectly—every time we took a step closer to the djinn, Roland made his construction even more obvious. It's like he doesn't want us to interact with the djinn at all. He doesn't want us to kill it."

"I'm not even sure we can, Curran. The ifrit's power is growing. The first two times he summoned something, he seemed to be only fulfilling wishes, so he could then take over the host. This time he summoned a giant bull and then dropped a meteor and a snake on us. We don't even know if he's taken control of a new host yet. This is just him venting his hurt feelings because of the giant. I can't let him keep doing this. He is a threat to more than Eduardo or us. He is a threat to anything in his vicinity."

Curran grimaced. "Did you hear what he said?"

"About betrayer spawn? Yeah, what the hell was that all about?"

"I don't know, exactly," Curran said. "But Dali did some checking. Eduardo's Pack admission paperwork is on file. In the Place of Birth section, he listed Atlanta, Georgia. She had people make some calls to Oklahoma. The werebison herd isn't talking to the Pack officially. They're circling their wagons around Eduardo's parents."

"Why?"

"Nobody knows. But unofficially Dali's people were able to find out that Eduardo's mother became a member of the herd six years after Eduardo was born. His father is a werebison and is high up in the herd's chain of command, and he doesn't want any of this."

"If Eduardo's parents somehow betrayed the ifrit, it's possible he's punishing Eduardo. Wouldn't they want to help?"

"Dali got a feeling that Eduardo's mother hadn't even been told. Whoever her people spoke to said they saw her at a birthday party yesterday and she was laughing and having fun. By all accounts she really loves her son. If she knew he was missing, she would likely be here."

"Did they pull the marriage license?"

"Eduardo was seven when they married."

That could mean absolutely nothing. Plenty of people waited to get married. Or it could mean that the man married to Eduardo's mother was his stepfather.

"You think her husband is protecting her?"

Curran nodded. "We're not going to get any help from them."

"Then we'll have to work with what we've got."

Maybe I could ask Roland about it. Wouldn't that be a hoot? *Hey, I know we're mortal enemies, but can you help me with this thing?* I sank deeper into the water. I didn't want to go.

"Did you ever want to kill Mahon?" And why did I just ask him that? Argh.

"No. There was a time I would've done anything for his approval."

It didn't surprise me. After he watched his family being slaughtered, Curran lived on his own in the woods, hunted by the same loups who had eaten the bodies of his parents and his sister. Then Mahon led a party of shapeshifters into the woods. Mahon was older now, and I was strong, but I would hesitate to fight him. To a starved twelve-year-old, he would've seemed larger than life.

"As I got older, I realized he was manipulating me to get what he wanted." Curran said. "I remember the first time it clicked. I was eighteen. He wanted me to pass a law and I wanted to go play with my new girl."

"What girl?"

"You don't know her. She was blond and had huge boobs." He frowned. "Something with a K. Kayla . . . Kelly . . . Something." He grinned. "Jealous, baby?"

I stretched against him, my voice slow and lazy. "Is Kelly in this tub? No? Then I have nothing to be jealous about."

"Mahon nagged me, so I told her to wait and sat there for two hours reviewing this long-ass law about the percentages the Pack received from the profits of their businesses."

"Sounds riveting."

"Oh, it was. When I was done, Mahon told me my dad would be proud of me. It occurred to me that my dad was an isolationist. He wouldn't have given a shit about the Pack or if the masons should pay twelve percent while the teachers paid seven. It was this empty encouragement Mahon offered to me when I did something he liked, because he knew I missed my father and I wanted to make him proud. I sat there after he left and tried to think of all the occasions he'd used it. He'd used it quite a bit."

His face hardened. *Hello, Beast Lord.*

"I knew I had to cut the leash then, because I wouldn't be anyone's pet ruler."

No, being someone's pet didn't suit him. No more than being Sharrim suited me.

My life had always been a vector pointed to the same goal: kill Roland or die trying. That vector didn't survive collision with reality. Roland's power was too great and I didn't have the spine to die trying to murder him while watching everyone I loved burn in the same funeral pyre. The exact thing Voron had warned me about had come to pass. I had fallen in love. I had accepted responsibility for a child. I had friends, and I wasn't capable of condemning them to death for a cause that wasn't truly my own. I survived.

Looking back at it, it was the right choice. The only choice, really. But Voron's conditioning didn't just wear off. He raised me so I could kill Roland or die. Either way Roland would be hurt, and it was good enough for Voron. The nagging sense of failure was still there, and I felt enough guilt and shame to fill a small lake. The guilt fed my anger, and every time I thought of Roland, my sword hand itched. I knew I wasn't ready for the confrontation, but somehow I deluded myself into thinking I could win the same way I usually won—by brute force and my skill with the sword.

It was time to grow up. I had a responsibility to the land I claimed and everyone alive within its borders. I had a responsibility to Curran and Julie, to my friends, and to myself. I deserved to have a life at some point. Running at my enemies with sword drawn and pounding them with power words with all of the delicate subtlety of a hammer no longer worked. We were playing in the big leagues now. The stroke was a painful lesson, but it helped bring home the point: I had to fight smarter.

"We can't let on that we figured out the tower is a diversion," I said. "I'm going to focus on that and maybe we can learn something about the ifrit. He thinks both of us just pummel things with our fists anyway. He won't suspect any sophisticated subterfuge."

Curran smiled. "Would you like me to snarl at the appropriate moments and promise to bash heads to pieces?"

"Would you mind?"

"Well, it might be a stretch for me, since I never do anything like that." I chuckled.

"But if I am properly motivated, I can give it my best shot."

Oh boy. "Do you have any specific motivation in mind?"

He leaned toward me, tiny gold sparks playing in his eyes. "Yes, I do."

A muffled knock sounded through the door of the bedroom. Curran rose, wrapped a towel around his hips (which shouldn't have been hot but was), and opened the bathroom door. "Yes?"

"We need to leave in twenty minutes," Julie called through the bedroom door.

"You're not coming," I told her.

"I'm all dressed and I've put my makeup on."

"No," I growled.

"What if this is a clever ploy and while you're at dinner Hugh d'Ambray comes and kidnaps me?"

Oh, for the love of . . .

"You won't be able to get it out of your head now," Julie called. "You'll worry about it all night."

Curran laughed.

I sank deeper into the water.

Why me? Why?

"Also, Ascanio is downstairs," Julie said. "He says that he was charming and the cranky neighbor's name is Justin Thomas Rogers. Ascanio has the address. Mr. Rogers's daughter reported him missing yesterday. He got this picture. I'm sliding it under the door now."

Curran walked into the bathroom and held a photograph to me. A middle-aged man looked back at me, balding, thin but somewhat flabby. The giant that had rampaged through the Guild had worn his face. There it was, the confirmation we'd been looking for.

"Can I tell him that you remember him now?" Julie asked. "He invited me to his pity party, and I really want to leave."

CHAPTER

19

I WALKED INTO Applebee's wearing my work clothes: loose dark pants, boots, a gray sweater, and a simple black jacket. Sarrat's weight rested comfortably between my shoulders. Curran walked next to me. He wanted to wear sweatpants, because "they tear easier." I asked him if he wanted me to get him some male stripper jeans so he could avoid looking like a Russian gangster from pre-Shift movies, after which he got all offended and put on a pair of regular jeans instead.

Julie brought her Kestrel axes. She also wore her big black steel-toed boots, the burgundy-colored sweater I'd knitted for her, and a short pleated skirt with no stockings despite the cold. Some things had no logical explanation. You just had to roll with it.

The hostess looked at the three of us and pointed to the sign above her head. "We have a strict no-weapons policy."

"What if my fists are lethal weapons?" Julie asked.

A manager emerged from the back room, saw us, and nearly sprinted down the hallway.

"You may keep your fists," the hostess said. "But—"

The manager nearly slid to a halt in front of us. "This way. Your table is waiting."

The hostess opened her mouth and snapped it shut.

He led us to the back of the restaurant to a table by a window. The table was designed to seat six. My father sat by himself, wrapped in a plain brown cloak. The cloak had seen better days and the deep hood that hid his face was frayed. He was trying his best to be inconspicuous, his magic folded and wrapped around him. His "god in beggar clothing" act was impressive, but I saw through it anyway.

As we approached, he pushed the hood back and my father's face greeted me. Hugh once described it as "if the sun had risen." Saying Roland was handsome would be a gross understatement, like calling a hurricane a gentle breeze. My father was beautiful, his face perfectly proportioned, with bronze skin, a square jaw traced by a short graying beard, a full mouth, a powerful nose, high cheekbones, and large dark eyes under dense eyebrows. The moment you saw those eyes, you forgot everything else.

There was a passage in the Bible in the book of Job that said it wasn't age that guaranteed wisdom, but it was the spirit in a person, the breath of the Almighty, that gave sage men understanding. When you looked into my father's eyes, his spirit looked back at you. They shone with power, as if the magic itself filled him, ageless but very much alive. He was a man who walked the Earth before the Bible had ever been written, and his wisdom was as towering and timeless as the Sarawat Mountains. It didn't keep him from making very human blunders or being immune to small petty things like revenge, punishment, or murdering my mother because he thought I was too dangerous to be born.

Yep, that last one did it.

Behind me Julie stumbled but caught herself. Curran appeared completely unconcerned. Former Beast Lord—not impressed.

Curran approached the table and pulled out two chairs. I sat in one, and Julie sat in the other, on the side. If things went sour, I could shove her into the booth next to us with my left hand in half a second.

Curran sat next to me. His face was relaxed, his expression unreadable. The manager hovered next to us, a look of complete devotion on his face.

"Iced tea," I said.

"Coke," Julie said.

"Iced tea," Curran said.

"Iced tea for me as well. That will be all," my father said.

The manager took off.

"Is there any way you could refrain from magicking our waiter?" I asked.

"I abhor poor service," he said and smiled. "I took the liberty of order- ing potato skins and onion rings. I'm so glad we could do this."

It was time to play my part. "The tower, Father. I want it gone."

"It's not a tower. Merely a tall building."

I pulled the Polaroid from the inside of my jacket and put it on the table. "This is a model of a tower."

"We consider it a threat," Curran said. "If you want a war, you will get one."

"I'm building a residence," Roland said.

"Why?"

"So I can be closer to you, of course. I've come to dislike hotels over the years and I want to have a comfortable place to stay while I visit you."

"I don't want you to visit me."

"Parents don't always do what their children want them to do," Roland said. "Sometimes they show up unannounced and nag you about your eat- ing habits. And I am about to do just that. Have the two of you set a date for your wedding?"

"Don't change the subject," I growled.

"Blossom, I purchased the land. You can't really prevent me from build- ing anything I want on it. But if it causes you distress, I will be willing to stipulate it won't be more than two floors in height."

Yes, and each floor would be a hundred feet in height. "No more than fifty-five feet in height for the entire building."

Roland smiled. "Very well."

A waiter arrived, a stocky dark-haired man in his late twenties, bearing a wide platter with drinks, potato skins, crunchy fried onion rings, mozza- rella sticks, and pretzels with beer sauce, and he began setting them on the table. Apparently my father had ordered the entire starter menu.

"Now that I've conceded that point, the wedding. When are you going to stop living in sin?"

"This is rich, coming from you. I'm sorry, how many wives did you have?"

"Recently, only one."

"Yes, and you murdered her."

The waiter valiantly clutched onto his stack of small appetizer plates.

Roland sighed. "Let's not talk about that again."

"She was my mother."

The waiter nearly dropped the onions.

"Yes, and I loved her deeply."

The waiter set the last plate on the table and paused. "May I take your order?"

"French fries with cheese," Julie said.

"I don't care," I said.

"Bring me some meat," Curran said.

My father turned to the waiter. "The child's order stands, with the addition of a Shirley Temple. My daughter prefers Baja tacos, shrimp sautéed not fried, hold the onion and bring her a blackberry iced tea with extra lemon. My future son-in-law enjoys lamb, medium rare, no pepper, baked potato with butter and salt, no sour cream, and a Newcastle Werewolf, although he will settle for a Brown Ale or a Blue Moon. I'll take a bourbon steak and a glass of red."

The waiter almost saluted before taking off.

My father had us watched. Not just followed, but observed thoroughly enough to know I picked cooked onions out of my food.

"Now if we could all stop pretending to be lesser versions of ourselves, I believe this conversation will flow much easier." Roland dipped his pretzel into beer sauce.

"Okay. How many spies do you have in our territory?"

"Enough." Roland smiled. "I can't help it. It's the lot of a parent. Even when our children don't want us in their lives, we can't help but watch from afar and stand ready to protect and render aid."

Watch from afar . . . Interesting.

"You didn't answer my question about your wedding."

I leaned back. "Why does it matter to you?"

"Consider me old-fashioned," he said. "People talk. People ask when or if there will be a formal union."

"Who are these people?"

"D'Ambray," Curran said.

"How is the Preceptor?" I asked.

"I haven't seen him." My father shrugged. "He is taking a sort of a sabbatical. A journey to find himself."

"Was that his idea or yours?" Curran asked.

"A bit of both."

The waiter appeared with our drinks, cleared the empty plates, and vanished.

Hugh had been exiled as a punishment for his failure. "And while he's on this sabbatical, you have complete deniability. You can't be held responsible for whatever crazy crap he pulls off while he's in exile. How convenient."

"It is rather convenient, isn't it?" Roland smiled.

Argh.

"Your continuous insistence on keeping your options open is causing a stir," Roland said. "Don't get me wrong, the elaborate plotting is highly amusing, but this Judeo-Christian age does come with some stricter conventions. It's evident in the language. 'Living in sin,' 'make an honest woman,' 'shacking up'—the implication of that last one, of course, being that you are too poor to get married and so must live in a shack. It isn't a matter of money, by the way, is it?"

"Stop," I growled.

"I understand you've been burning through your reserves," Roland said.

Oh no. He didn't.

Curran took a swallow of his beer. "Your spies have been falling short. We didn't burn through our money. We shifted our cash reserve into real estate holdings. Currency falls and becomes devalued, but land will always retain its value. They don't make any more of it. However, if you find yourself short on cash, let us know. We can liquidate some of our holdings on short notice."

Ha! Shots fired.

"I'll be sure to keep it in mind. I don't mean to nag. I simply want to walk you down the aisle, Kate."

Be civil, be civil, be civil . . . "No." *There. Good.*

"What if there is a child?" Roland asked.

"So?" Where was he going with this?

"You don't want your children to be bastards, Kate. It never turns out well."

I put my head on the table. It was that or physical violence.

The food arrived. I picked up one of my Baja tacos and ate it out of desperation. I needed fuel to continue this conversation.

"How's school?" Roland asked Julie.

All of my senses went into high alert.

"Fine," she said. "Thank you. I just got an A on my essay on Daniel."

"Did you use the Apocrypha?" Roland asked, his voice mild.

"Of course," Julie said.

The Apocrypha, a collection of ancient writings that had been edited out of the modern Bible for various reasons, had a whole chapter on Daniel. The ancient Daniel kicked a lot of ass, unlike his modern version that stressed humility and passive resistance. It was entirely possible that I was reading too much into this conversation, but the way they spoke suggested that this wasn't their first discussion. Julie had some explaining to do. And my father had to stop inserting himself into my life, or he would regret it.

"Your grandmother is in poor health," Roland said to me.

Who, what? Where? "My grandmother is dead." And her magic, trapped between life and death, fueled the madhouse of Mishmar, my father's prison.

"Your other grandmother," he said.

I froze.

"Your mother's mother is still alive," he said. "Barely. She is eighty-nine years old. I visit her sometimes and she is rapidly declining."

"Does she know what happened to her daughter?"

Roland shook his head. "She knows she died."

He kept finding ways to avoid saying my mother's name.

"She does know about you. She doesn't have much time. If you wish to know more about your mother, I can arrange for transportation so you can speak before this chance is lost forever."

My world turned upside down. I didn't remember my mother. Not a hint of her face, not a whisper of her voice, not even her scent. He was dangling bait in front of me and I wasn't sure if I hated him more for using her memory or myself for considering snapping it up.

"Where is she?" I asked.

"Seattle," Roland said.

There it was. He wanted to get me out of the city and away from the ifrit. He'd picked a hell of a lure. Sure, he would arrange transportation there. He said nothing about arranging it for the trip back.

"You can be there in three days," he said.

In three days Eduardo would be dead. I was sure of it.

Curran glanced at me and I saw a warning in his eyes. *Yes. I know. He is trying to distract me and get me out of town.* For some reason, my father really didn't want me dealing with the djinn, and that was precisely why I had to stay.

"I'm sorry, but I have to pass." The words hurt coming out. "I have things I need to do here."

"Kate, you won't get another chance."

"I'm not going to trouble an old woman who has never seen me in her final days. My place is here. I have something to do and I can't leave until I see it through."

"Very well," Roland said. Not a hint of disappointment. *Very nice, Dad.*

I wanted to jab him with my fork. He'd used my mother's memory to manipulate me. He would regret it.

"Besides, you knew Kalina best."

I watched him closely and the corners of his eyes trembled when I said her name. *How does your own bitter medicine taste, Father? Have another spoon on me.* "Why don't you tell me about her? You were there till the end. You saw the light go out of her eyes."

Roland took a swallow of his wine.

"If you wish to know how your mother died, I will tell you, Blossom. Ask me."

Walk away. Walk away, because that way lie dragons.

Screw the dragons. I needed to know. "Tell me how my mother died, Father."

He waited.

We were stabbing each other and pretending that it didn't hurt.

I wanted to squeeze the word out through my teeth, but I wouldn't give him the satisfaction. It took all of my will to make it sound casual. "Please."

"There is a small café in the south end of Wolf Trap," he said. "That's where I first saw your mother."

Wolf Trap, Virginia, northwest of Arlington, was a new town, built from the ground up by the Order. That was where the Knights of the Merciful Aid made their headquarters. My mother had worked with the Order for a while. And my father had visited it, walking its streets in the plain view of dozens of knights, knowing they would fall over themselves trying to kill him if they only knew who he was.

"She sat at a table by herself reading a book and drinking coffee from a chipped white cup."

His voice weaved a spell, filled with longing, love, and grief. I wanted to believe it was false, but it felt so genuine. So real.

"The sun shone through the window and her hair glowed like the finest gold. I sat at her table and I asked her why she didn't ask for another cup. She said that there was a unique beauty to the imperfection. No other cup would ever be chipped in quite the same way. It reminded her to pay attention, for every moment could offer an experience that would leave her forever changed. When she decided she was tired of running, I found her there again, in that café, sitting at the exact same table. I took the other chair and told her that I loved her. I told her that she didn't have to run, and that if she wanted the moon from the sky, I would reach out, pluck it from heaven, and give it to her. She told me that you were a beautiful child. That you were a part of her and a part of me and you were perfect. She took my hand, kissed my fingers, and said, 'I love you. Don't look for her.' Then she stabbed me."

The pain in his eyes pierced me, still alive and vibrant after almost thirty years.

"Your mother knew that your existence challenged my power. She had betrayed me for your sake. It wasn't a private event. She had subverted my Warlord and turned her back on our union. The core of my power, those closest to me, knew about it and expected action. My pride and my reign demanded it. A betrayal that cut that deep required public punishment. Voron was merely a pawn. You were a babe and bore no responsibility for what had occurred. That left only your mother. When she drove a knife into my eye, I knew she sacrificed her life so you would live. If she was dead, the public demand for revenge would be satisfied. And so I honored her wish and killed the woman I loved for a child I had helped bring into the world."

He'd loved her still, after all those years. He must've loved her more than anything, and he was both an instrument and a cause of her death. If he hadn't loved her, he wouldn't have agreed to my conception. He wouldn't have imbued me with his power and then he wouldn't have had to try to destroy what he'd created out of love. I had told him that our family were monsters and he had corrected me. He said we were great and powerful monsters. But none of our power mattered. We were still cursed.

"Your mother loved you before you were ever born. Nothing, not even me with all of my power, could diminish it. I wanted her more than I ever wanted anything in all of my years. To think that all that I am was undone by the simplest and most basic of things—a mother's love for her child."

He reached out to me and touched my hand. Too late I realized I had dropped my shields and my magic had filled the room, plain for anyone with a gift to see it.

"Your magic is beautiful, my daughter," the Builder of Towers said, his eyes luminescent with power. "You should show it more often, for you are perfect."

BY THE TIME we were almost done with our plates, Julie announced that she was cold. Curran offered to take her to the car to get a sweatshirt. They got up at the same time and walked out. A moment later our waiter appeared and placed a small plate with a slice of chocolate cake on it in front of me.

I looked at Roland. He shook his head. "Not me."

"The gentleman ordered it on the way out," the waiter said, then put a coffee in front of Roland and departed.

Chocolate was really expensive. I sliced a tiny sliver of the cake with my fork and tasted it. It melted on my tongue. I had to eat this very slowly so it would last.

"Do you think he really loves you?" my father asked.

"He does." And I had to change the subject before he started on the second round of the wedding conversation. "Father, why is our magic bouncing from humans possessed by an ifrit? Is it because of the geographical proximity?" Oh yes, that was smooth. Not.

"What did you try to use?" he asked.

"A power word."

"I remember trying that. Worst pain of my childhood. Let me teach you. There is so much you don't know, Blossom. Let me help you make sense of it. At the very least, let me keep you from making rudimentary mistakes."

"You tried it." I sliced another bite of the cake.

"I was eight."

Oh.

"And I did it because I was specifically told not to." Roland drank his coffee. "I wanted to know what would happen."

That sounded very much like something I would do.

"You are partially correct, the resistance is due to the geographical proximity and a miscalculation on the part of your great-great-great-great . . ." He frowned. "No, that's right. Great-great-great-great-grandfather. The ifrit were threatening his borders, and he decided that a child of mixed blood would be a great idea, so he married a half-human, half-ifrit woman. She was his fortieth wife. I remember because it was a nice round number. He begat a child, a daughter, and as expected, she had partial immunity to the ifrit magic and was fierce on the battlefield. She was far down in the line of succession, so he hadn't worried about her, and by the time he decided to worry about it, it was too late. Bararu, the Shining One, the Star of the Valley, had cut her way through his progeny to his heart and took his throne. She was your great-great-great-grandmother."

"She killed her brothers and sisters and her father?"

"Well, in all fairness, he did execute the man she wanted to marry."

"Why?"

"He was trying to check her power. She was becoming too popular with the army."

I rested my chin on my fist. "That's a heartwarming story, Dad."

"You called me Dad." Roland smiled.

"I wouldn't read too much into it. Were any of our family members ever famous for doing something nonviolent?"

"Your great-great-grandfather cured the Plague of the Godless. It was a very virulent strain of influenza and it threatened to wipe out the human population on the entire continent."

"That's good to know."

"Of course, he felt obligated to do it, because your great-great-granduncle had unleashed it in the first place."

I just stared at him.

"History provides us with vital lessons," Roland said. "For example, I have no plans to murder Curran."

He couldn't murder Curran, not as long as our agreement held. "Why, you're afraid I might take your throne?"

"No, I don't want the heartbreak of having to kill you, Blossom."

Mm-hm. "Heartbreak."

"You don't trust me," he said.

"No."

He smiled, and I realized that was what parental pride looked like. He was proud because I had enough brains to anticipate that he could entrap me. I wished he'd come with some sort of secret manual, so I would know how to deal with him.

"So how shall we move forward?" he asked.

"You could teach me here and now. I need to know about the ifrits."

He paused for the briefest of moments. It took half a blink, but I was watching him very carefully. For some reason he really didn't want to tell me about the ifrit.

"Very well. We might as well make good use of the time my future son-in-law is so kindly providing to us. Answer one of my questions and I will answer one of yours."

Nothing was ever simple. "Okay."

"When Hugh came to kill Voron, he found no sign of a child living in the house. You had gone into the woods, but where were your belongings?"

So Hugh and Roland had a long chat before the Preceptor was exiled. "Hugh didn't look well enough. Voron knew a clairvoyant." Her name was Anna, she was the ex-wife of my dead guardian, and she no longer returned my calls. "I think he must've been told to expect something bad to happen when he sent me out of the house, because whenever I went into the woods, I packed my duffel bag and buried it under the pines on a hill behind the house."

"But there had to be other signs of your existence," Roland said. "A child's life doesn't simply fit into one bag."

"Mine did. A week's worth of underwear and socks, two pairs of jeans, five T-shirts, a sweater, and two pairs of boots. My knives, my belt, and sword fit in there as well. Toothbrush, hairbrush, a favorite book, and that was it." I could pack it all into my bag in ten minutes and it was as if I had never existed.

Roland looked at me, his expression odd.

"You may ask a follow-up question," I told him.

"Toys, makeup, jewelry, dresses, cute shoes, a kitten, perhaps a puppy?"

I laughed at him.

"Not even a pet." Deep regret reflected in my father's eyes. He was actually bothered by this.

"Pets teach children empathy. Voron was trying to turn me into a psychopath. Besides, we would often take off without warning. We couldn't be tied down."

"A child's life should be filled with joy. It pains me to know you lived like that."

"If it had been up to you, I wouldn't have lived at all."

Roland exhaled.

"My turn."

"As agreed. You may ask one question. Think carefully. Most of the battle to get the right answer depends on asking the right question."

There was so much I needed to ask. One question didn't even begin to cover it. I had to ask the most important one.

"If an ifrit is trapped in an ancient earring, what would he hope to achieve by granting three wishes to the owner of the earring, turning said owner into a giant and rampaging through Atlanta, and then repeating this process?"

"How do you know it's an ifrit?"

"I saw him in a vision."

"Did he wear jewelry?"

"Yes. Gold with large green stones."

"Emerald or peridot. So we have a sultan, then."

Don't ask a question. He only said one question and there had to be a price for failing to follow the rules. "One would think that an ifrit sultan would wear a ruby, because it's the color of fire. Humans living in the Arabian Peninsula prize emerald above all stones because it's green and Arabia is mostly arid. But djinn are not human."

Roland leaned forward, a sly look in his eyes. "One would think that. Then one would brush up on her geology and learn that the purest peridot is found in *harraat*, the lava fields in the west of Saudi Arabia. When the volcanoes in the west erupted, they brought peridots with them from the depths of the magma chambers. The djinn treasure these stones because they were bathed in the fiery lifeblood of the planet. Only the highest ranks of the ifrits wear them."

A waiter came to refill his coffee.

"God created men from clay and djinn from smokeless fire," Roland said, once the waiter left. "Even people not versed in the Qur'an know this line. Have you ever wondered about the meaning behind it?"

"People are made of clay. We are tied to the Earth and soil; our magic is its magic. Also clay soil is almost impossible to enchant."

"But you can enchant a clay pot."

I thought about it. "But to make a clay pot, you have to first add water, which holds enchantment, and then treat it with fire."

"Precisely."

"So djinn have a lot more magic than we do."

"Not only do they have a lot more magic, they *are* magic. They require a large amount of it just to survive. A djinn absorbs the magic from its environment, storing it like a battery. Now let's take your ifrit, for instance. He is confined to an earring, imprisoned, likely driven mad by the thousands of years of confinement. He wants freedom but he lacks the magic to break free and to exist in our volatile world."

"The only way he can manifest is by possessing a human host," I said. "I gathered as much."

"The granting of the three wishes is an ancient ritual. In reality, it simply makes the possession that much easier; to express a wish, you must first open your mind to the djinn and then accept his magic. You have to believe that he can grant any wish. Instead of a hostile takeover, the process becomes a seduction. With each wish, your body becomes more and more receptive until finally your mind submits to the djinn completely. Some djinn can take over a human in a single wish, but most of the time it takes three. As soon as the ifrit possesses a body, the reserve of that human's magic belongs to him."

"That still doesn't explain why he turns them into giants."

"Two reasons. First, from what I have been told, he turns them into giants and then attempts to transform them into heated metal. In my time the most powerful of the ifrits transformed into armored giants before the battle. This state also permitted them to absorb a large amount of magic from the environment."

"So every time he makes a giant, he grows stronger." I managed to make that into a statement rather than a question, but this one came too close for comfort.

"He does."

It was like jumping on a trampoline. The first bounce was low, the second higher, the third higher still. First the djinn took over someone with only a little bit of magic, which gave him enough power to take over Lago, who had more magic, which in turn would give him enough juice to possess someone with yet a bigger magical reserve. Such as a knight of the Order. I really hoped not. "You mentioned two reasons."

"Djinn are vindictive by nature, and of all of them, the ifrits are the most likely to hold a grudge. They are creatures of enormous pride. Wrong them once, and they will hunt you across an endless desert just to watch you die. Once you strike out against one, he will be your enemy for life. If you frustrate his efforts in any way, you will find that out."

"I did." He sent a bull made of fire to my house.

"So I hear. What would you want in his place?"

"Revenge against those who imprisoned me. But they are long dead."

"Blood never dies, Kate. It grows like a tree through generations. The ifrits can feel their own, especially those related to their particular clan. Look for someone he hates. He is likely gathering magic to become powerful enough to unleash his rage upon the descendants of his captors. Because he is a noble, he will call lesser djinn to him to do his bidding. He will identify his victims, and he will torture and maim them and do whatever he can to extract maximum suffering. The ifrits are not fond of granting a quick death."

Eduardo, the betrayer's spawn. He must've been a descendant of the ifrit's captors. Now the ifrit was torturing him.

"Once he finishes his revenge, he will turn against the lesser targets. He will seek to rule because that's what he did in life."

And we would be his targets. We had to end this chain of power-ups before it went any further.

"You've allowed me one question. I will allow you one as well," he said.

"Why is he using the ghouls?"

"Because he is used to ruling. He likely thinks that he requires an army to do his bidding, and they, by their very nature, are easy for him to dominate for him. Your cake is getting warm," Roland pointed out.

The fountain of knowledge had run dry. I had more questions. I wanted to ask about ghouls and about defeating the ifrit, but my time was up. One question was all he would answer, so I settled down to eat the rest of my cake.

THE EVENING WAS dying slowly, the sun bleeding its lifeblood onto the horizon when Curran pulled into our driveway. We had taken a short detour. The answer my father gave me at dinner made me rethink our stalker, so we stopped by the address the Clerk had given me. Derek had emerged from the shadows as we had pulled up and reported that he hadn't seen anyone. We picked him up, I left a short note by the door, held in place by a rock, and we went home.

The magic had ebbed. Technology once again took the planet in its grip. At least we'd get a short break from the ifrit.

There were so many things I had wanted to ask my father. I wanted to know about the ghouls. I wanted him to tell me why he had broken Christopher's mind. I wanted to know more about my mother. But this was a slippery slope.

There was one person I could ask about all of this. Trouble was, he wasn't always reliable.

I stepped out of the Jeep.

"You okay?" Curran asked me.

"Yeah. I'm going to go talk to Christopher for a little bit. Do you think the note will work?"

"It can't hurt."

I walked to Barabas's house. Here's hoping Christopher was lucid.

Barabas let me in and went back to the Guild Manual. I found Christopher on the floor of the downstairs living room, sitting on a rug, surrounded by open books. His face lit up when he saw me, his eyes clear.

"Mistress."

"Hi, Christopher." I sat on the carpet outside his book fort.

"I'm glad you didn't die." He smiled.

"I'm glad I didn't, too. I've come for advice."

"My mind is shattered," he said. "But I will try."

"What do you know about ghouls?"

"Ghouls are the fallen djinn," he said.

"Fallen like demons are the fallen angels?"

He leaned back, shifting his weight. "The djinn are creatures of magic. They require it to survive. The more magic, the more . . ." He struggled for a word.

"Powerful? Larger?"

"Evolved. When they lose their magic, they become ghouls. They are fallen."

Christopher held his hand out, parallel to the floor. "Ghoul." He raised his hand up as far as he could. "Marid."

I nodded. A marid would have much more magic than a ghoul.

Christopher struggled with it for a few seconds and brought his hands together into a ball. "One S. Two S. Two P. Three S."

And I lost him. "I don't follow."

Christopher frowned. "One S." His hands moved wider. "Two S. Two P."

"He is talking about the electron configuration of an atom." Barabas came over with a piece of paper and a pen, sat next to me, and drew a circle on the paper. "This is the nucleus of an atom, protons and neutrons bunched together into a mass. It has a positive charge."

He drew a circle around it and put a dot on it like a planet around a star. "The electrons have a negative charge. They have set orbitals." He drew another circle, wider, and then another. "These orbitals are identified by scientific notations. This lowest one is 1s. This one is 2s. This bigger one is 2p. The farther away the orbital, the more electrons it can fit. The first can fit two, the second can fit eight, and so on."

"Okay." This was way above my pay grade, but if I could learn cuneiform, I could learn about electron orbits. "What does it have to do with djinn?"

"I'm not sure." Barabas looked at Christopher.

"The electron jumps." Christopher said. "It's excited."

"Ah. The electron can exist in two states: the ground, or lowest energy state, and the excited state. To make it really simple, the electron naturally wants to stay at the lowest orbit. However, if the electron absorbs some energy, it might 'jump' to the next orbit. I'm bungling this badly, but it's been a long time since college chemistry. For example, if you have a neon atom, it has a configuration of $1s^2 2s^2 2p^6$, if I remember correctly. If we give it some energy, by shining a light on it for example, one of these electrons might 'jump' to a higher orbit such as 3s or 3p or sometimes even 5s. Then the electron emits the energy in a form of light and 'falls' back to the ground state."

"Djinn," Christopher said helpfully.

"So let me get this straight. A ghoul is the ground state of the djinn. The lowest magical form. Then, if the ghoul somehow gets some magical energy, it will evolve to a higher-order djinn, just like an excited electron jumping to the farther orbit?"

"Yes." Christopher smiled. "It will be what its true nature meant it to be."

"But then it will revert back into a ghoul when the magic runs out?" I asked. "It will fall again?"

"No." Christopher shook his head. "Higher-orbit djinn make more magic."

"Does this make sense to you?" Barabas asked.

"Sort of. We don't really know why ghouls are ghouls. But we do know from folklore that they were relatively rare in ancient times, when magic was strong. The other types of djinn were mentioned more frequently. Yet now we have an abundance of ghouls but no djinn. We also know that some djinn tended to interbreed with humans. If we suppose that a very small percentage of the human population carries the djinn genes somewhere deep inside. They have the djinn blood but very little magic. It follows that with the influx of a magic wave, they would transform into ghouls. Their magic is too weak for them to be anything else. That's probably why we haven't figured out what causes ghoulism. There is probably some sort of catalyst that initiates the change, but it's not a disease. It's a genetic predisposition."

Christopher smiled at me.

"It would explain why they devour corpses," Barabas said. "Human remains, especially after a supernatural event, have a lot of residual magic."

"They're probably instinctively driven to it to try to get enough magic to transform."

Barabas nodded. "But, if I understand correctly, if a ghoul somehow got enough magic to evolve into its true form, he wouldn't 'fall back' the way an electron does?"

"No, because once it's transformed, it will gain the ability to absorb more magic from its environment and will be able to survive. It's getting them past that threshold that is the problem." So far this was lining up with everything my father had told me about djinn. "Christopher, could my blood give a ghoul enough energy to evolve?"

Christopher pondered it, got up, and began looking through the boxes. A minute crawled by, then another. He pulled an old book out, flipped through it, and placed it in front of me. Hmm. Alchemical symbols. Looked like standard Renaissance nonsense . . . I flipped the page. A circle, within the circle the symbol for ether, a triangle pointing down imposed on the triangle pointing up. A creature writhed in the center, caught in flames. Above it blood poured from a cup held by a disembodied hand. Let's see, *viridis flammae*, green flames. Blah-blah-blah . . . Spirit of box, salt of vitriol . . .

Barabas was looking over my shoulder. "Can you understand any of this?"

"Yes, it's basic alchemy. They used methanol and boric acid to make trimethyl borate and set it on fire. It burns bright green." A plan tried to cobble itself together in my head. I could actually do this if all else failed.

"So you don't know about electrons but you understand medieval chemistry?"

"Electrons don't help me survive." I smiled at Christopher. "Thank you, Christopher. You were great."

He hugged me. It was such a simple wordless gesture and so not like him.

Christopher didn't like to be touched. He'd spent too much time in Hugh's cage starving slowly in his own filth. Any physical contact had to be initiated very carefully, but here he was hugging me, so I held still and smiled at him. For a few moments we sat on the floor next to each other with Christopher gently hugging my shoulders.

Someone knocked on the door. Barabas opened it. Julie stood in the doorway. Her face said she was clearly put upon and no adult could ever understand the full extent of her suffering.

"Mahon came to talk to George, but she won't let him in her bedroom, so they are talking through the door," she recited in a monotone voice. "Could you please come home because Luther and some knight of the Order are here to see you and Curran can't talk to them because he has to stand in the hallway and make sure Mahon and George don't break the door down and kill each other."

Why me?

I WALKED INTO my house to see the knight and the wizard sitting in my kitchen, drinking coffee. If you added in Julie's thieving skills and my sword, we almost had an adventuring party.

"It's too bad we're missing a cleric," I said.

They both looked at me like I had grown a second head.

Never mind. "What can I do for you, gentlemen?"

"The earring is gone and I can't account for one of my people," Nick said.

I sat in the chair and rubbed my face. Julie positioned herself on the couch with a notebook and several books.

"Go ahead and get it off your chest," Luther said. "It will make things easier."

"I told you not to leave it where people had access to it."

"I didn't. I put it into the Vault, into the wall containment unit, until an expert from Wolf's Head could examine it."

The Vault served as the Order's repository of all things dangerous and magical, but too valuable to set on fire.

"Is the expert missing?"

Nick didn't say anything. Great.

"What's done is done. Let's not point fingers," Luther said.

"This is a waste of time," Nick said.

"Why don't you like me?" I asked.

Nick leaned back. His hair was cropped very short and his features looked like they were carved from granite. "I could fill the room with it, starting with who you are and what you did."

He had to be referring to the claiming of the city.

"I had no choice."

"No, there is always a choice."

Luther was giving us odd looks. "Should I give you two some time?"

"No," I told him. "I get it. You have a problem with me. What are you going to do about it?"

"I haven't decided. I'm contemplating killing you."

"Knight-protector," Luther said.

Nick got promoted. He had been a crusader before. He was like a scalpel: when you had a nasty boil, you sent in a crusader to lance it. He got the job done, cleaned up the mess, and moved on. The last time I saw him, he was deep undercover pretending to serve Hugh d'Ambray. He'd spent years infiltrating Hugh's Iron Dogs, and the former head of the Order, Ted Moynohan, blew his cover just before he died. All of the things Nick had endured were useless. The experience had changed him. The man I had met years ago was deranged but human. The man in front of me now looked like he'd petrified from the outside in. And now he had Ted's job. Who the hell thought it would be a good idea to put Nick in charge of Atlanta's chapter of the Order?

And now he threatened me in my own home, where Julie could hear.

"Contemplate it all you want," I said. "When you're done thinking it over, go and get every knight in your chapter. Bring them here and then, maybe, if all of you bigoted fanatics work together, I'll think about taking your threat seriously. Until then, shut the hell up, because if you threaten me in front of my kid again, I will finish what Hugh started."

Something slid under Nick's skin, like two golf balls rolling down his arms.

"Okay," Luther said. "I can see there is a lot of tension and some unresolved issues. However, none of this is helping us with the ifrit. He has escalated in power and now he has a hold of a knight of the Order. I hate to be a downer, but the city may not survive the next magic wave, so why don't we all put away our angry faces and try to act like reasonable adults."

The intensity died down in Nick's eyes. Whether he liked it or not, he had a duty to Atlanta and so did I.

"You should apologize to the child," Luther said quietly.

"Sorry," Nick called out.

"That's okay," Julie said without lifting her head. "I'm used to it. Just let me know if you're going to fight, so I can go into another room. I have a paper due tomorrow."

Luther turned to me. "See? He apologized. What do you have?"

"You first," I said.

He reached into his bag and placed a photograph on the table. In it a balding man in his midfifties smiled at the camera.

"Justin Thomas Rogers." I couldn't resist rubbing Nick's nose in it.

Nick scowled. I'd have to thank Ascanio later.

"He was an auctioneer. His exact title is Certified Estate Specialist. When a stranger dies in the city, Atlanta hires one of three firms to liquidate the estate. Rogers and Associates was one of them. The last sale he made was on Saturday, February nineteenth. He didn't show up to work on Monday."

"What was the last estate he sold?" I asked.

"Two families, which checked out, and a state case," Nick said. "An unidentified man walked into traffic in Unnamed Square a week ago. He had a note on his body that suggested he arrived by boat into Savannah. The boat is now gone. The papers said it came from New York, but the New York ports have no documentation of it."

"Smugglers."

Nick nodded.

"If we assume that the earring passed from that man to Rogers, that means he had it in his possession for over a week," I said. "He must've been remarkably strong-willed, because the djinn subverted Lago in forty-eight hours."

"Rogers was a conscientious, principled man," Nick said. "He did a lot of charitable work. He was a harder nut to crack than a merc."

"The two of you are forgetting Samantha Binek," Luther said. "The knight who is missing. The djinn broke through the Order conditioning in less than a day. He is getting stronger with each host."

"Tell me about Binek," I said.

Nick grimaced. "Thirteen years in, knight-archivarius. She wasn't one of mine. She came down from Wolf's Head specifically to determine if the earring can be moved to the HQ vault. She had a sterling reputation. She went into the Vault to examine it. A knight-defender escorted her. Three hours later Maxine went to check on them. Binek had activated one of the artifacts in the vault, incapacitated the knight, and taken off."

"What did she use?" I asked.

"An iron mask. He spent two hours thinking he was trapped in a slave ship. He'd ripped half of his nails out trying to break through the walls."

Knights-archivarius were specifically trained to handle dangerous magic objects. This woman would've had all of the training, she would've evaluated hundreds of artifacts over the years, and she would've taken every precaution. This wasn't good. We had to get to the djinn before she made her wishes and transformed. The amount of destruction he could unleash with her body would be catastrophic.

"My turn," Luther said. "I analyzed your glass sample. It's sand that has been cooked by very high heat. The sand contains concrete dust, so it was likely part of a building, and magically charged algae. It doesn't look like algae got into the concrete and sand naturally. It appears the algae has been deliberately mixed into it."

"Algae?"

He nodded.

That was what those in our business called a clue or potentially a gift from above. How many buildings in Atlanta could have magic algae in them? I was betting not that many. I got up and dialed Raphael's number.

"Yes?" he said.

"It's me. I need help."

"I'm here," he said.

I put him on speaker. "Is there any reason why debris from an old building might contain magical algae?"

"Lazarus Builders," Raphael said. "About two years after the Shift, when they started seeing the first evidence of magic-induced erosion, a builder firm came out with a surefire way to proof the buildings against the magic waves."

When it came to magic, there was no such thing as surefire anything.

"They found that a particular type of algae had the potential to absorb a lot of magical energy, so they mixed it into their concrete. Initial tests suggested it would be magic-resistant. It worked great for about five years, and then the first flare hit."

Flares were like magic tsunamis—several days of uninterrupted, ridiculously strong magic. It was the time when gods could manifest.

"Turned out the algae was like a water balloon. It would absorb some magic, but when the flare overloaded it, it popped. Everything they built with Lazarus concrete fell either during the flare or within a month after it. It was one of the bigger scandals in Atlanta real estate."

"How many buildings are we talking about?"

"That's the bad news. They licensed the recipe. They even mixed it into stucco and claimed it would magic-proof residential construction. Lazarus was the darling of the business community back then, because everyone panicked and rushed to have new magic-proof corporate headquarters built. Basically anything built between the Shift and the first flare will have that crap in it. It's so common, I don't even have a separate file on it."

Fate sucker-punched me in the face and then laughed.

"I can go through all of my files and pull every somewhat large building out by date, but it will take a while. A couple of days. Do you want my guys to do that?"

"No." Eduardo didn't have a couple of days and neither did the city. "Thank you, Raphael."

"You're welcome. Any time, Kate. I mean it."

"Dead end," Luther said. "Lovely."

"There is something else we can try . . ."

Someone knocked on my front door. I got up and opened it. A tall man stood in the doorway, carrying a backpack on his left shoulder. He looked older, close to sixty. He wore dark trousers, loose enough to not restrict his movement, tucked into tall boots, a sweater, and a gray cloak over it, a common outfit for someone on the streets of Atlanta. His shoulders were still broad and his posture straight. He must've been very strong once, but age had stolen some of his bulk. I could tell by the way he stood that he carried at least one knife under the cloak and he was ready to use it at a moment's notice.

Lines marked his olive skin, but his dark eyes behind round glasses were smart and sharp. Gray sprinkled his once-dark hair and a short precise beard hugged his jaw. He reminded me of a human version of my father.

Julie leaned from her couch. "Mr. Amir-Moez? What are you doing here?"

"Hello, Julie." His voice was quiet and calm.

I glanced at her. "Do you know this man?"

"This is Mr. Bahir Amir-Moez," Julie said. "He teaches ancient history and Islamic studies at my school."

Mr. Amir-Moez turned to me. "I found your note. I accept your help."

Finally something had gone right. "Honey!" I yelled.

"Yes?" Curran called down.

"Can you tell George that Eduardo's father is here?"

THE SEVEN OF us sat around the kitchen table. George was glaring daggers at Bahir. Mahon, a big looming shadow, occupied the chair next to his daughter. They agreed to table their discussion until we sorted things out. Bahir, as he asked to be called, took the chair next to me.

"How did you know?" he asked me.

"We put it together," I told him. "We found out that Eduardo was born in Atlanta and that his mother married her current husband when Eduardo was seven years old. The ifrit referred to him as betrayer's spawn, which suggested that Eduardo's ancestors served the ifrit in some capacity and he might be part ifrit himself. We also knew that Eduardo reacted violently when he saw you and walked off a job, despite badly needing the money. When asked why, he said his reasons were personal. We found the dagger you gave him, which seemed inconsistent with Eduardo's stance on religion. Then this evening I had dinner with my father."

Nick burst into a coughing fit. I gave him a moment to come to terms with it.

"He said that parents can't help themselves and, given a chance, they will watch over their children."

"It does seem rather obvious when laid out like that," Bahir said.

He reached into his backpack, pulled out a metal box, and set it on the table. Pale silver lines of koftgari stood out, the script tiny, as if written with an enchanted pen on the blackened steel. The Ayat al-Kursi—the Verse of the Throne, Surah al-Fatiha, the last two verses from Surat al-Baqara, the first verse of Surah al-Imran, a large portion of Surat al-Jinn . . .

"How long did it take the smiths?" I asked.

"A year," Bahir answered.

"You knew the ifrit was coming?" Luther asked.

He nodded. "It started on the day Eduardo was born. At first there were dreams. Violent disturbing dreams. Rima and I had been married for three years, we had an infant son, and I didn't want to jeopardize them, so I sought treatment. I went to a psychiatrist. I got a prescription for medication, which I took on schedule. The dreams persisted. At first they made no sense; then gradually the meaning began to emerge. Something was coming. Something was hunting me. The visions were full of death.

"I had made a conscious choice to reject the visions. We'd discovered that Rima was a shapeshifter and she had a difficult time dealing with it. She was a werebison, an uncommon breed, and to her knowledge, she had never been attacked by a shapeshifter. Neither of her parents were shapeshifters, and it caused a great deal of tension between her mother and father. Her father asked her to undergo a paternity test. She was so deeply hurt by it. She saw it for what it was—a rejection of all the years her father had been a part of her life. To her it didn't matter if she was or wasn't his biological child. She cut off all ties with her family. She needed me, so I spent another year trying to convince myself that I was simply disturbed. My parents were dead. I had nobody to ask for guidance."

Bahir sighed. "One night I was coming home from work. It was dark. A nervous woman came up to me asking for directions. She drew a knife sheathed in fire and stabbed me with it. I didn't die. The blade passed through me and when she withdrew it, there was no wound. I was whole. I almost choked her to death out of sheer fear, but reason prevailed and I let her go. She told me that I was an ifrit, part of the ancient line stretching back from the time lost in history, when some ifrit, sensing the waning of magic, sought to mix their bloodline with humans in an effort to preserve it. The ifrits can sense those of the same clan. She said there were others like me who had felt my presence and sent her to test me."

"That's a hell of a test," I said.

"What if you had died?" George asked.

"Then I wouldn't have been an ifrit." Bahir smiled. "Eventually I met some of my clansmen. They had the visions as well and they were frightened. I was trying to find some answers. I found only legends cobbled together from fragments of visions and dreams. A long time ago a powerful ifrit ruled a kingdom of djinn. We don't know his name. One of my clansmen called him Shakush, the Hammer, because his dreams gave him a pounding headache as if his skull were being struck by a hammer. Shakush had many warriors and princes under his command. One day a holy man who trespassed in his territory was brought to him. The ifrit king mocked the holy man and ordered him beheaded. As the holy man's head rolled off his shoulders onto the floor, his mouth opened and he cursed the ifrit to madness."

So far this was a paint-by-numbers folkloric cautionary story. Don't be mean to random strangers and those in need.

"Eventually the ifrit king went mad, but his magic was too potent and even the combined might of his warriors couldn't overcome it. They failed to kill him. Sometimes, when the power of your enemy is too great, the only thing you can do is contain it. Shakush's warriors confined his essence to an amulet. Nobody knows what they did with it, but when it surfaced in my dreams, it was an earring on the earlobe of an old woman. The period of technology had weakened the seal on it and magic woke the mad ifrit. At first he was weak, his power a mere whisper. It took him years to corrupt the owners of the earring, but with every victim he grew a little stronger.

"One of my clansmen had the gift of prophecy. He could reach further into his dreams than I could. He told me that Shakush was driven by vengeance. Three ifrit warriors had performed the containment ritual and now Shakush was hunting their descendants, killing them one by one. After he was done, he would turn on the rest of the clan that had betrayed him. That meant that eventually he would make his way to me. I have seen my ancestor's face in my dreams. He was the one who fitted the lid onto the amulet."

If the ifrits were as vindictive as my father claimed, there would be no escape and no place to hide. Shakush would find him.

"Did your people offer to help you?" Curran asked.

"They were not warriors. Within our society there are castes. Only those with greater magic and a violent nature enter battle. My clansmen are artists, teachers, and tradesmen. One is a lawyer, another is a pediatric nurse. The woman who stabbed me is an elementary school teacher. They had drawn straws to see who would perform the test and she pulled a short one. She was terrified out of her wits, but Shakush scared her more. In a fight with Shakush, they would simply become victims. He would devour their magic. They were so happy when they found me. They thought I would protect them from the mad creature Shakush had become."

That must've been so terrible. To think that you had finally found the answers and help you needed, only to realize everyone was counting on you to save them. "What did you do?"

Bahir leaned back. "I had to protect myself. I had to protect my son, so I began training. I tried dojos and martial arts clubs, but it wasn't the right kind of training. So I asked my clansmen and they finally found a man who would teach me. He was a killer, and the things I learned from him turned my stomach."

"But they felt right," Nick said.

Bahir nodded. "Yes. There were no points and no submission holds."

"And your wife?" George asked.

"I kept most of it from her. I didn't want her to have to carry the weight of knowing that an unseen terrible creature was searching for her husband and her son. It was my burden. My clansmen couldn't help me fight, but they helped in other ways. One of them was a smith. He made my weapons. The rest did research. We dug through folklore and historical accounts, what little there were. Finally through a combination of many hours of study and prophetic dreams, we came on the design for a box."

He nodded at the box on the table.

"It should contain the ifrit, sealing him in once again."

"Should?" Mahon asked.

"Should is as certain as we can be. A box of this design was used once by a holy man to contain an enraged desert marid. If it can hold a sandstorm, it should hold Shakush."

"And your wife?" George asked. "I'm just trying to understand why you were never in Eduardo's life."

"It wasn't by choice. The breaking point came when a husband of one of the teachers at the college where I taught at the time brought a gun into the building. He was a disturbed man. She had left him and he was trying to hunt her down. I took his life. It happened very quickly. I saw the gun. He fired at her. I reacted."

His voice sounded flat. "It was almost as if the dagger had taken me over and driven itself into his body. I could've disarmed him. I knew how. But I didn't."

Being trained as an efficient killer wasn't enough. You also had to learn to control your stress and your fear, becoming so used to violence that you could detach yourself from the trauma of it and assess the level of violence necessary to respond. When the fight-or-flight response kicked in, Mother Nature shut off our brains. It was a biological survival mechanism. By the time our minds processed the full impact of a predator's presence, we would already be running for the nearest tree.

Bahir wasn't a natural predator. Given a moment to think, he probably wouldn't have killed the man, but in the pressure cooker of the moment, his body simply reacted and his training took over.

"I had committed a great sin," Bahir said.

"Whoever kills a soul unless for a soul or for corruption in the land—it is as if he had slain mankind entirely," Luther said quietly.

"Yes." Bahir nodded.

The Qur'an had many different verses, some pointing to war, some pointing to peace, but the fifth chapter of it was clear on the subject of murder. Human life was precious.

"I went to the man who taught me and asked him why this had happened. He said I was too old. I started too late. I realized that my son had to be a better fighter than me. Eduardo was six at the time, so I took him to be trained. When Rima found out, she was furious with me. She wanted an explanation, so I told her everything. I had planned out how to tell her, and it sounded reasonable in my head, but when it came to the actual explanation, everything went wrong. It was a jumbled mess. I must've sounded like a man deep in the throes of a psychotic break, raving about murder, holy men, and vengeful ifrits. I had begun to build the box by then, so I brought it out. It was plain steel then."

Nitish had said the inside of it was bone. "What is under the steel?" I asked.

"My father's skull."

Okay, then.

"The lid is made of my mother's bones." Shame twisted his face. "I desecrated their graves to make it. They both carried ifrit blood. I tested their bones for it and the magic in them will help contain him."

Yeah, if I were his wife and he had unloaded all of this on me at once, I would be less than thrilled.

"Rima was horrified. She asked me to check myself into a hospital. I refused. She asked me to stop exposing our son to violence. I told her that violence would find him one way or another. At least we could prepare him. She thought I was mentally ill."

He sighed. "My wife is a gentle soft-spoken woman, but when it concerns our son, she is fierce. The next day I went to work and when I came home, she was gone. I found her two weeks later. She had traveled to Oklahoma and joined a werebuffalo community. I tried to reason with her. I stayed as long as I could, but it became clear to me that she wouldn't change her mind."

"Werebison are herd creatures," Curran said. "And they have a chip on their shoulder. Once she joined them, they would protect her against all predators."

Bahir nodded. "Yes. It became clear that I would have to murder all of them to get to her or Eduardo. I loved my wife and son, but I couldn't bring myself to commit more violence and even if I had, what would it resolve? I left and went about my life, training and hoping that growing up among shapeshifters, my son would learn enough to protect himself when the time came. Meanwhile my wife remarried. Her husband adopted my son. She sent me Eduardo's report cards, and he was listed only as Eduardo Ortego.

It gave me hope that he would be difficult to find. It was a false hope, but I held on to it."

"What is his full name?" George asked.

"Eduardo Bassam Amir-Moez. He was named after his grandfathers." Bahir sighed. "The visions had died down, and for almost a decade I had barely seen any dreams. Then, a year ago, they started again, more vivid than before. Shakush was growing in power with each new victim and coming closer. He had followed the footsteps of my family.

"Over the years, as I watched the atrocities he committed, I understood that this is bigger than me or my son. Allah doesn't charge a soul with more than a person can bear. I'm meant to do this. This is the purpose of my life. If Shakush continues unchecked, he will become a plague on this world, and I won't let it happen. But the smith who had helped me died, so I had to turn to Nitish to have the box finished. I was preparing myself for the final battle. And then I saw my son and I realized that it all had come full circle. I tried to talk to him, but he wouldn't listen to me, so I watched him, hoping to be there when Shakush struck. I tried to give him a weapon that would offer at least some slight advantage. I missed the attack."

He had dragged this weight forward for decades alone. It was a miracle it hadn't broken him.

"Why didn't you come to the Order?" Nick asked, his face dark.

"What would I tell you? That I had visions of distant people murdered? That I was part ifrit? Your Order isn't known for its kindness toward anyone they deem an aberration."

"The Order is people," Nick said. "People change."

"Perhaps," Bahir said.

"What about the draconoid corpse?" Julie asked from the couch.

"It was one of Shakush's creatures. I had a fear that my sword would pass through it just like the dagger had passed through me when my people tested me for the first time. I wanted to make sure that my blade worked so I could use it on Shakush next."

"Talk to me about the box," Luther said. "It is clearly some sort of trans-dimensional containment unit."

"What does that mean?" Mahon asked.

"It is an object that exists as one thing in our reality and something else in a different realm. It leads to a place that is attached to our plane of existence but is also outside it."

"Like the mists of the Celtic gods," I said.

"Yes. That means that someone has to activate a portal to that other place, hold it open, and then close it once the djinn is deposited into the box." Luther turned to Bahir.

Bahir nodded. "There is a ritual. I memorized it. The box must rest on the ground—it won't work on the second floor, for example—and I must draw a complex circle and write sacred verses around it. Then I will open the portal with my blood and hold it open. Once the earring is placed into the box, if everything is done correctly, I will become a conduit and banish it. The problem is getting the earring into the box. Someone must murder the human host and physically take the earring and carry it to me. The box cannot be moved once it's positioned."

"That will be really difficult," Luther said.

Thank you, Captain Obvious. Shakush would do everything in his power to keep from being put into the box. Even if we brought the entire chapter of the Order and managed to pry the earring from the current host, whoever touched it would become Shakush's target. He could go through the knights one by one. Ugh.

"We will help," Mahon said into the sudden silence.

George startled. "Dad?"

He put his arm around her shoulders. "I don't care how powerful he is. Nobody touches my future son-in-law."

"As long as you stay away from the earring," Curran said.

Mahon looked at him.

"He's worried about the wishes you would make," I told him. "Wish one, Curran is the Beast Lord. Wish two, George is his Consort. Wish three, you turn into an even bigger bear."

George stared at me, horrified.

"You think so little of me?" Mahon said. "That really hurts."

He sounded genuinely upset. Oh no. I had hurt my stepfather-in-law's feelings.

"We still don't know where Shakush is," Nick said. "Can you sense him?"

Bahir shook his head.

"I know someone who can," I said. I would probably go straight to hell for this, but there was no choice. We had to save Eduardo and the city.

"You can't use Mitchell," Luther said. "First, it's unethical. Second, it's cruel. Third, he was my colleague and it's a matter of basic human decency. He's a ghoul, for crying out loud."

"What if he were no longer a ghoul?" I asked.

Luther opened his mouth and paused. "Are you thinking of setting him on fire again?"

"Was that what it looked like?"

"Yes. I was concerned, actually."

"Then yes. Something like that."

"I have a moral obligation to safeguard him," Luther said. "The answer is no."

"Why don't we ask Mitchell what he wants to do?" I said. "If he says no, I'll walk away. If he volunteers, you'll help me."

"Help you do what exactly?" Nick asked.

Explaining it was too long and complicated. "You will see. Bahir?"

"Yes?"

"Why haven't you turned into a ghoul?"

Bahir blinked. "Was I supposed to?"

Ghouls were djinn without enough magic to assume their true forms. He must've had enough magic.

"Can you transform into an ifrit?"

Bahir smiled. "Not all the way."

That explained it. He already had enough magic, so he bypassed the ghoul stage.

"Okay." Curran leaned forward, an unmistakable note of command in his voice. Suddenly all of the attention focused on him. "We need to limit this. The more people, the more potential possession targets for the djinn. It will be me, Kate, Bahir, Mahon, George." He glanced at Mahon. "Anybody else?"

"I'll talk to the family," Mahon said.

"Me!" Julie volunteered.

"No," Curran and I said at the same time.

"But . . ."

"You just got a united parental no," Luther said. "Stay down, you've lost the fight."

"I will go." Derek stepped out of the shadows in the hallway.

Curran thought about it.

Derek waited.

"Okay," Curran said finally. "Who else?"

"I will come," Luther said. "With the caveat that if the djinn possesses me, one of you will kill me. My magic reserve is too great."

Curran looked at Nick.

"Six knights," Nick said. "Including me."

"That should be enough," Curran said.

Mahon and Nick rose at the same time, heading for the phone. I went upstairs to get dressed.

≈ CHAPTER ≈
21

CURRAN PULLED INTO the parking lot in front of the Biohazard building, following Luther's truck. Derek stirred in the backseat. He had been so quiet and still, I almost forgot he was there.

There was a moment on the drive when I wondered if it was ever not going to be like this. But then I decided I was crazy. It would always be like this, riding to certain death every few months, trying to protect people we would never meet. Some people painted. Some people baked. We did this, whatever the hell it was. I just didn't want to die. I didn't want Curran to die. I wanted to save Eduardo.

I wanted there to be a stretch of normal, if not for a few months, then at least for a few weeks.

The magic ran thick tonight. Warm wind bathed me as I stepped out of the car. A change was in the air.

A dark shadow slid across the stars above and a jet-black winged horse flew through the air, circling the yard. Arabian horses were never my favorites. They were loyal to a fault and would run themselves to death for the right rider, but they were a bit high-strung for my taste. But this horse was perfect, from the velvet coat and silky mane to the tapered hooves of her elegant legs. Vast wings, black as midnight, spread from her shoulders. She glided on the air currents, a graceful creature of legend come to life. Even Mahon watched, halfway out of his car.

I caught a glimpse of Curran out of the corner of my eye as he moved to stand next to me. We watched the horse gently land on the pavement, Bahir on her back.

"Do you ever wish it were just normal?" I asked him quietly.

"Yes. But then we would never see things like this."

Bahir dismounted, light on his feet.

"Where did you find her?" I asked.

Bahir petted the horse's muzzle. "I didn't. Amal found me."

He clicked his tongue at her. Amal shook herself. Her wings vanished.

Atlanta was getting stranger and stranger by the day.

"Come on," Luther called. We followed him into the building, up the stairs, to the far end of a long hallway, where big double doors stood wide open. A large room spread before us, devoid of furniture. The floor was covered with chalkboard paint. Bronze braziers stood by the walls filled with coals ready to be lit. That had to be the incantation room.

In the middle of the room, in a protective circle drawn on the floor with chalk, Mitchell lay in a small heap. The glyphs around the ward glowed weakly—the spell packed one hell of a wallop. Shreds of fabric littered the floor around the ghoul. A woman sat in a chair by the wall, reading a book.

"Blood," Curran said.

I glanced at Luther.

"We tried putting him into a straitjacket so he wouldn't hurt himself." Luther sighed. "He keeps trying to crack his skull against the floor."

"What happens during tech?" Nick asked.

"Bars come out of the floor," Luther said. "They're down now to keep him from throwing himself against the metal."

I approached the circle. "Mitchell."

Mitchell gave no indication he heard or smelled me.

"He won't respond," Luther said. "I tried."

"I tried screaming a while ago," the woman said. "He's gone somewhere deep inside his head."

I glanced at the lines of the circle. It was designed to keep magic in, not out. Hmm. I had never done it before, but it worked for my father.

I pulled my magic to me. It came eager and ready like an obedient pet.

I gathered it all around me, packing it tight, and let it fuel my voice, reaching to Mitchell with my power.

"*Mitchell.*"

Luther startled. "Jesus, Daniels."

The ghoul uncoiled, raising his deformed head, and rolled to his feet. I walked along the boundary of the circle. The ghoul turned slowly, moving to face me. Up close I could see smears of blood on the paint inside the circle.

"You . . ." the ghoul whispered.

"Can you sense the ifrit? Is he calling you now?"

"Yessss."

"Do you know what you are?" I asked.

"Yessss . . ." He ducked his head, but his gaze bore into me. "I am flame. I am smokeless fire. This"—he stretched his arms to me—"is my prison. Kill me."

I knelt on one knee. He leaned in as close as the boundary of the circle would allow. A mere three inches separated us.

"I can make you whole," I whispered. "But there is a price."

"I'll pay."

"Stop," Nick said. "She'll promise you the world and then she will make you her slave. She can't help it. It's in her blood."

"Wait, what is this talk of whole-making?" Luther waved his arms. "What's going on?"

Mitchell's gaze never wavered. "I would rather be a slave than be this."

"If I make you whole, you must help me fight the ifrit," I told him. "Can you find him once you are whole?"

"Yes."

"Once finished, you will make your home here, in Luther's custody. You will serve the Biohazard Division for five years." That ought to give them enough time to figure out what to do with him.

"Yes."

"Swear on the fire that burns in you."

The ghoul opened his mouth. "I swear."

I rose, pulled the book out of my backpack, and thrust it at Luther. "I'll need these supplies."

He scanned the pages. "What is this?"

"We're going to evolve Mitchell to his proper state."

"Oh, okay. Wait, what?"

THE COALS HAD been lit. I finished drawing the alchemical sign for the ether and was about done with the symbols. Mitchell sat within the two triangles. Just outside the two triangles, a half-gallon beaker of clear liquid, trimethyl borate, waited on a table next to matches and a small vial of my blood. I had drawn it before we left the house.

A gaggle of Luther's colleagues gathered in the room. I had walked him through the djinn ground-state theory and he had explained it to them. The reactions were mixed to say the least. Voices floated to me.

"You do realize that if this works, we've found a cure for ghoulism."

"Yes, but the cure is worse than the disease. We can't run around the countryside turning ghouls into djinn."

"Technically they are already djinn."

"That's beside the point."

"We have no idea what they are capable of."

"What's in the vial?"

"Are you saying we shouldn't do it?" Luther asked.

"No," a woman said. "I'm saying that it's illegal, dangerous, and possibly unethical, but we should definitely do it."

"Yes, what Margo said."

"This is a once-in-a-lifetime opportunity."

"Just as an experiment."

Mages.

"How do you feel about her doing this?" That had to be Mahon. That low-pitched growl could only come from him.

"We let each other be who we are," Curran said. "I don't have to like all of the things she has to do. I love her."

I love you, too. Just keep this in mind after you see what I am going to do.

I drew the final circle around the glyphs. Wards came in all varieties and this one wasn't a containment; rather it functioned like a mirror, focusing any magic entering the ward on the creature within it.

Mitchell looked up at me. "Hurry."

I picked up the beaker of the trimethyl borate and poured it over him, saturating the triangle on the floor.

"She does know it's flammable, right?" someone asked.

I picked up the vial of my blood and pulled out the cork.

"Drink this when I say."

He stretched his clawed hands to me.

"There is still time to step back," I told him.

Mitchell took the vial with his claws.

I struck a match. "Now."

He gulped the blood. I let the match fall into the ward. Emerald-green flames surged up. Mitchell spun around thrashing, his skin blistering, screaming. I focused my magic on him and felt the magic amplify it. My blood burned through him, sliding down his throat, deep into the pit of his stomach, and awakened a weak spark of fire. I reached for it, as it bathed in my blood, and whispered a power word.

"*Amehe.*" Obey.

The shock of it tore at my mind. Agony ripped through me. The world turned hazy. I fought it, trying to keep hold on the flame inside Mitchell's body. If I let my grip slip, it would be all over.

Behind me Curran snarled. *Yes, I used a power word. Sue me.*

The haze melted. I staggered, but Doolittle's repairs to my brain must've held, because I was still me.

Mitchell was still screaming. His skin sloughed off, his raw flesh hissing in the fire.

I pulled and the flame responded, bending to my will. I fanned it, funneling my magic into it. Mitchell collapsed into a ball.

"He's dying!" someone snapped behind me.

Grow. Like blowing on a fledgling fire, trying to help it grow hotter.

"This was really ill-advised . . ."

Grow, I cajoled, pouring magic into it. *Grow.*

"Shush!" Patrice said.

The green flames went out, sucked into Mitchell's body.

Grow!

The tiny flame exploded, turning into a white-hot blaze. Mitchell surged to his feet. Bright orange fire erupted from his mouth and eyes and washed over him, consuming his flesh. I let go. His body convulsed, jerking like a marionette on a string. The fire spun into a whirlwind and within it a new body was taking shape, large, quadrupedal, and muscled.

The flames vanished, absorbed into the new skin. A strange furry beast stood before me on four clawed feet, his head a full foot higher than mine. Bright red and dappled with black rosettes, his body was almost canine, lean and powerful like that of a Doberman. A long thick horse mane of jet-black hair ran along his spine. A long leonine tail coiled around his legs. Twin horns crowned his head, curving forward on the sides of his lean face, ready to gore. His features were unlike anything I had ever seen. His long narrow jaws, studded with sharp perfect fangs, hinted at a wolf and an alligator at the same time, while his eyes, large and bright orange with dark oval pupils, made me think of a predatory cat.

The thing that used to be Mitchell shook his head, sending his mane flying. He raised his head, opened his mouth, and cried out. His voice wasn't a roar or a snarl, it was melodious and high, like the shriek of a bird flying high through the clouds.

"Holy crap," someone said behind me.

Mitchell leaned forward, his eyes even with mine. His deadly jaws unhinged, showing his fangs and the black tongue inside his mouth.

Don't flinch, don't flinch. "Hello, Mitchell."

"The name no longer fits."

"Do you want a different one?"

"Yes. Name me, human."

Make it good. "I name you Adib, after the Wolf Star in the Constellation of Draco."

"I accept my name. I owe you a debt."

"Yes."

He lunged at me. It was so fast, I was in midair before I realized he'd tossed me onto his back. I landed astride and grabbed onto his mane.

Curran surged forward.

"I'm okay," I said.

"I pay my debts." The ifrit hound raised his massive head. "I can hear the madman's voice. Follow me."

He dashed out the door, scattering the mages. I clenched his mane and tried not to fall off.

TRAVELING BY MYSTICAL ifrit hound sounded cool in theory and entirely plausible, since he was the size of a smallish horse. But horses were trained to carry humans, while ifrit hounds were not. It took every muscle in my body to stay on his back. He ran through the streets, leaping over obstructions, dodging occasional cars, and panicking horses.

Three minutes into our race Curran drew even with us, a huge gray beast that was neither lion nor human, designed specifically for running. That was Curran's special power—he molded his body at will to whatever purpose suited him. He'd chased me down more than once in this shape. A few moments later Derek caught up with us. He was still in his human form. Above a shadow swooped across the stars and pulled ahead. The ifrit was fast, but beating a winged horse required a whole other kind of fast. A blue spark flared, illuminating the horse and rider. Bahir must've carried a feylantern. He flew above us like a beacon. Hopefully Mahon, Luther, and the knights would see him.

Magic scoured me. We had crossed the invisible boundary into Unicorn Lane. Of course. Why would it be anywhere else? Unicorn Lane cut through the center of the city, as if some enormous invisible enemy drew a dagger and stabbed deep into the very heart of downtown Atlanta, and now magic geysered out from the wound. Normal rules didn't apply here. This was a place of predators and prey where plants attacked you, moss was poisonous, and glowing eyes tracked your every move.

The magic churned and boiled around me as we darted among the dark ruins of once-mighty skyscrapers. Adib turned left, leaped over the remnants of a gutted building, and shot out of Unicorn Lane running northwest along the crumbling Colier Road. Well, that was unexpected.

Colier Road, a simple two-lane street, once ran through residential neighborhoods, but as Unicorn Lane grew, it swallowed the road's southern end, and Colier became a street that led nowhere. During magic waves, creatures hiding in Unicorn Lane ventured out in search of meat and blood, and the road nicely funneled them directly to their prey asleep in beautiful colonial houses. Anyone with a crumb of brains moved, and over the years, the residential neighborhoods once lining Colier became deserted. Abandoned houses tracked our progress with dark windows.

The ifrit kept running. A large ruin loomed on the left. An old sign flashed by, bent and grimy. PIEDMONT HOSPITAL. That's right. The original hospital complex stood so close to Unicorn Lane that part of it had collapsed in the Shift. Not realizing the full impact of Unicorn Lane's existence, the city had rebuilt it a few miles down the road, but then, as the residential neighborhoods withered, so did the hospital, and if they had built it with that algae, the first flare would've finished it.

The ifrit hound turned, following the road. Years ago this place must've been beautifully landscaped, but now the trees and brush were in full revolt, filling the artificially curved lawns. A stone sign blinked by with some arrows on it, and Adib punched through the wall of green into the empty parking lot. The old hospital crouched in the gloom. At least three stories of it were still standing, and the lamps supporting feylanterns still glowed weakly, trying to combat the darkness of the parking lot. Adib halted in front of the emergency room entrance under a concrete roof. The ride was over. Thank you, Universe.

"We wait for the others," I said, and slid off his back. My thighs were killing me.

We were alone. Curran and Derek must've fallen back.

Adib turned around, raised his head, and inhaled deeply. "I will scout ahead."

"Wait . . ."

The ifrit hound dashed through the broken door of the hospital and vanished into the gloom. Damn it.

I sat on the ground. My body ached as if someone had worked me over with a sack of bricks.

Derek leaped through the greenery and ran to me.

"Where is Curran?" I asked.

"He had to double back. The vehicles and horses couldn't get through the Unicorn, and the bears are slow."

Yeah, I bet Mahon was just loving this race.

"He's helping to lift . . ." Derek paused. "Something is coming."

I reached for my sword.

The sound of hoofbeats echoed through the empty parking lot. A creature walked into our view on the left and halted under a lamppost. It stood six feet tall, the lines of its lean, almost fragile body reminiscent of a gazelle, but its neck and powerful chest was all horse. Pale sandy fur sheathed its flanks, striped with darker cinnamon-brown. A single foot-long horn protruded from its forehead, narrow and sharp like the blade of a saber. Long dark stains stretched across its face from its eyes, as if it had been crying. Crap.

The creature resumed its slow gait, heading for us, the lines of its body mesmerizing.

"Is that a unicorn?" Derek asked.

The creature passed under another lamp. A dark red stain marked its horn. Crap, crap, crap.

"No, it's not." I rose from the ground. "That's a shadhavar. A Persian unicorn."

"I take it they're not nice."

"No."

Derek stood up.

The trees and bushes rustled. More shadhavar emerged from the brush. A small foal on our right shouldered his way past his mother. He was carrying a severed human arm, still in the sleeve, in his teeth. One, two, three, seven, twelve . . . Too many.

"Are we fighting?" Derek asked.

"No, we're going to be sensible and wait for backup." We had much bigger fish to fry. Running into a herd of carnivorous unicorns would be very brave and ridiculously stupid. Why risk getting a horn through your side and being taken out of the fight when there were reinforcements around the corner?

A large shadhavar pawed the ground with his hoof.

Derek glanced at the concrete roof above our heads. "I'll boost you."

"Go."

He grabbed me by the waist and hurled me up. I caught the edge of the roof and pulled myself up onto it. The shadhavar charged.

Derek leaped up, bounced off the building, and dropped by my side.

The shadhavar reared, baring long triangular teeth at us, yellow against their blood-red gums. That was a sight enough to give you nightmares.

"Yes, yes, keep smiling." No worries. Our backup was coming.

The winged horse circled above us.

I glanced up. "When we're fighting, keep an eye on him for me, please."

"Sure," Derek said. "Why?"

"Some people are natural killers. Curran is one. I am, as well. He isn't. Bahir is what happens when you force murder on a decent, kind human being. He is fierce and he'll kill if he has to, because he thinks it's his duty, but he doesn't have enough experience to make calculated decisions. He may try to sacrifice himself for our greater good."

"Pot, kettle," Derek said.

"I sacrificed myself after I've weighed all of our options and realized there is no other choice. He may not see all of the options. He has taken a life, and the guilt is gnawing at him. He may see his sacrifice as atonement. I want him to survive this, if we can make it happen. He and Eduardo deserve to have a conversation."

The winged horse swooped low and Bahir jumped onto the roof. Amal beat her incredible wings, soared above us, and landed on the crumbling wall of the building.

"Do you need assistance?" Bahir asked.

"We'll wait for the vehicles to get here," I told him.

"Oh. In that case I will wait with you."

He sat by me.

"Do you know my son well?"

"I know that he is honest and brave. He doesn't hesitate to put himself between his friends and danger. He is devoted to George and he worked very long hours hoping to build a family with her. I'm proud to call him a friend."

Bahir remained silent.

"Did you speak with George?" I asked.

"Yes. She said she saw him burning. Shakush is torturing my son."

"We saw him burning during one of the ifrit's attacks. I don't know if it was real or another illusion."

"Do you think my son is still alive?" he asked.

He was looking for reassurance. Sadly I had none.

"I saw him in a vision," I said. "He was in a cage starving. He wasn't in the best shape, but I think he's alive because the ifrit is waiting for you."

"He's waiting to kill my son in front of me," Bahir said.

"Yes."

Bahir sighed. "If you come into possession of the earring, you need to know what to expect. The ifrit will seduce you. The moment you touch his prison, he burrows into your soul, tears it open, and feeds on your greatest fear. If you are afraid of growing old, he will offer you youth. If you think yourself ugly, he will promise you beauty. He will move mountains and resurrect the dead, and if he lacks the power to do it, he will trick your mind into thinking he has done it. With every wish, you will surrender a part of your soul to him and he will lie and betray you until he possesses you completely."

"So how do we fight that?" Derek asked.

"You must reject the djinn."

"Easier said than done," I said.

"Yes. But there are forces within our soul that are greater than he. Loyalty. Duty. Love. Honor. If you are not sure, it isn't too late to turn back."

I smiled. "I'll stay, but thank you for the pep talk."

"You have a life."

"So do you and your son. Eduardo is my friend. I refuse to let him die in a cage."

"Yes, but few people would risk certain death for a friend."

"I'm doing it out of selfish reasons," I told him. "If we fail to stop the ifrit, he'll come after my family next. We frustrated him a few times and he's an arrogant sonovabitch who hates losing."

Bahir didn't look entirely convinced.

A distant roar of enchanted water engines announced that the cavalry was coming.

"It's what they do," Derek said. "Don't ask her why. Just take the help. You won't get better."

Thank you, boy wonder.

"If we survive this," Bahir said, "and you need something, anything at all, call on me."

"You may come to regret that offer."

"Anything at all," Bahir said.

The first vehicle tore through the greenery, a large black SUV with a metal grate shielding the radiator. I caught a glimpse of Martha, George's mother, behind the wheel. She was a plump middle-aged African American woman with a wealth of curly hair. I had only spoken with her a few times. She usually knitted during Pack Council meetings, and if our gazes happened to cross, she smiled. She wasn't smiling right now. She saw us on the roof, saw the gathering of shadhavar, and floored it. The SUV plowed into the herd. Some managed to dash aside, but at least three crashed to the ground. Martha threw the vehicle into reverse and rolled over the thrashing bodies.

Holy crap.

Three more vehicles followed the first, bulldozing the herd down. Martha popped her door open and stepped out. A shadhavar tried to ram her. She grabbed its horn and slapped it upside the head. The shadavar moaned and collapsed, its feet jerking. On the other side George exited the vehicle, grabbed the nearest shadhavar by the head, twisted it off its feet, and stomped. Dear God.

The vehicles disgorged shapeshifters. It looked like George's entire extended family had shown up.

"If it moves, kill it," Martha called out. "I don't want to hear anything but us breathing in this parking lot!"

I held my arm out to Derek. "Pinch me."

He reached over.

"Ow."

"She's the alpha of Clan Heavy," he said. "Martha is really nice but only until someone tries to screw with her family."

BY THE TIME Curran and Mahon arrived, together with six knights of the Order, and Luther, Patrice, and another Biohazard mage whose name I hadn't caught, the parking lot was filled with shadhavar bodies. Clan Heavy sustained no casualties.

"You missed the slaughter," I reported.

Curran grimaced. "You missed me carrying horses over the rubble."

Curran and horses didn't get along. He thought they were unpredictable and untrustworthy, and they thought he was a werelion.

I waited until Mahon was out of earshot. "Why didn't you tell me Martha was a terminator in disguise?"

He smiled. "She was Aunt B's best friend. I thought you'd figure it out sooner or later. Where is your ride?"

"He went into the hospital to scout."

"Then we should follow."

It took about thirty seconds to gather everyone. We went through the doors single file: Derek first, tracking Adib's scent; Curran and me; then Bahir, leading Amal gently; the knights; the mages, protected from all sides because they squished easily; and finally Clan Heavy. George walked between her parents. She and Martha wore identical pinched expressions. Mahon was clearly in the doghouse.

We passed through the deserted hallway of the ER, then through the doorway, its doors lying on the floor. A light glowed ahead, in the gap of a crumbling wall. Derek moved toward it. We followed.

A vast garden unrolled before us. Lush flowers bloomed among the greenery. Ponds offered crystal-clear water, reflecting the delicate petals of pink, white, and lavender lotuses. Palms rustled overhead, over curving paths of golden sand.

I stepped through the gap. In the distance, reigning over the splendor, a palace rose. It wasn't the glowing white perfection and slim minarets of the Taj Mahal, with its arched balconies or its golden cupolas. Instead, a forest of colossal columns stood among the greenery, their length painted a brilliant red. Each column terminated in a carved textured pedestal of vivid, almost turquoise, blue, upon which a golden animal statue snarled at the garden, its head and body supporting the sharp rectangular blue roof, decorated with a textured parapet of golden spikes. This was an ancient palace, conceived in the time when dyes were prized, height was awe-inspiring, and elegance and subtlety were faults rather than virtues. It meant to communicate true power—the power to make countless human beings toil all of their lives as slaves to raise those columns to their dizzying height. It hit your senses like a hammer. I hated it.

How much power must it have taken to create this out of nothing?

Next to me, Curran squared his shoulders. The palace was a challenge thrown at unseen opponents. *Come and take it if you dare.* Curran wrinkled his lip, his eyes gold. He dared.

I elbowed Curran. "Hey, when I said blue would be nice for the downstairs, I didn't mean that kind of blue."

"Maybe it's his ace in a hole," he said, his face dark. "Thirty seconds in that palace and we'll go blind."

"It has to be at least three miles wide," Nick said next to me. "How the hell is he folding it into this building?

"The madman lies." Adib emerged from the bushes and stopped midway in the pond.

"The flowers have no scent," Derek said. "I smell dust and a few other things, but none of this."

I crouched by the pond and scooped some water. I could see it in my hand, but I felt nothing. There was no substance.

"The knight-archivarius must've wished for this place," Luther said. "But the djinn didn't have enough power, so he gave her an illusion."

Bahir reached into the scabbard on his waist and unsheathed a blade. It was a beautiful sword, almost straight, single-edged, with a portion of the blade near the tip, about ten inches long, curved for a vicious strike. Bahir cut his arm. Blood ran down his blade and burst into flame. He raised the flaming sword like a torch. His skin gained a darker golden hue. His eyes turned red like two glowing embers. The garden parted before him, melting. A path opened, about a foot across, the ground not some golden sand, but the typical dirt and rocks found in Atlanta.

"Lead the way," Curran told him.

We followed Bahir toward the palace.

THE JOURNEY TO the palace should've taken only fifteen minutes, but it took twice as long. We went over the plan again. Curran had come up with the strategy, and his plans usually worked. Getting everyone to stick to it was another matter entirely. I had asked Nick if he'd brought any more of the Galahad warheads, to which he asked me just how many of the ten-thousand-dollar warheads I thought he was authorized for. I told him that brevity was a virtue and "no" would've been just fine as a response, and then Luther had to give us his "save the city and stop bickering" speech.

Gradually dirt became sand, flowers gained aroma, and moisture saturated the air. About ten feet from the red palace steps, the illusion evolved into reality. I stopped to draw some blood. I could've probably done it earlier, but I didn't want to take chances with its potency. We passed between the colossal columns into a shadowed hall, our steps loud on the polished stone. A throne stood at the end of the hall, a massive carved chair of stone, painted with garish abandon. A woman of incredible beauty sat on the throne. Her dark hair, arranged in artful spiral waves, fell on her diaphanous gown of pale gold and blue. Gold chains wove through her hair, a necklace of blood-red rubies rested around her neck, and a single large earring, its simplicity jarring and out of place, decorated her left ear. A black panther sat by her throne, and the woman stroked the beast's head with her long fingernails. Oh boy. I had walked into an old Sinbad movie. Too bad the monsters wouldn't be Claymation.

Men stood behind the throne, brandishing swords. Some were dark skinned, some lighter, some clothed, others mostly nude, but each was a perfect, handsome male specimen. I did a quick head count. At least forty. She had her own private army of male models.

I reached forward with my magic and met the familiar resistance. That was a hell of a lot of magic and it was wrapped around her like a shield. Using power words directly against her would be out of the question. Attacking her right now was out of the question, too.

"She's shielded," Luther said behind me.

"What he said," I confirmed. "The djinn is pouring every drop of his power into protecting her. We don't have enough firepower to break through it. We have to get her to transform so she'll stop shielding and start attacking."

"That means she'd have to make a wish," Luther pointed out. "If she wishes for the ceiling to crush us, there isn't much we can do about that."

"The ifrit is an old power," I said. "They're not complicated and they respond well to drama. The ifrit will want to break us himself and see us suffer. We need to nudge her toward a fight."

Bahir pulled the hood of his cloak over his face. "Two-thirds of her belongs to the djinn. Leave it to me."

"Not until I talk to her," Nick said. "She is a knight of the Order."

I glanced at Curran. He shrugged. We could wait a couple of extra minutes in our rush to die to make sure Nick's conscience was clear.

"Remember, he will cover her in metal," Curran said. "The faster we hit, the better."

"Can your sword slice through metal?" a female knight asked me.

"We'll find out," I told her. I'd had just about enough of giants. I had a surprise for the djinn and I couldn't wait to show it off.

We reached the throne. The woman gazed at us. Flames rolled over her eyes and died down.

"You should fire your interior decorator," I told her. I couldn't help myself.

The woman gave no indication she heard me. That's the trouble with ancient powers—no sense of humor.

"This is nice," Nick said, stepping forward. "You had your fun, Sam. Time to come home."

"I am home," the woman said, her voice rolling through the cavernous hall.

"This isn't you. This is not what we do," Nick said. "You have a job and a duty to the Order. You swore an oath."

"This is me," she said. "I spent years examining objects of power and resisting their call. Now it's my turn. I've earned this. I am worthy."

She sounded distant, the emotion in her voice muted, as if she'd been sedated. Right. Samantha was gone.

"What happens when the magic ends?" I asked, slipping the backpack off my shoulder. I had brought the last of my undead blood supply for this. Here's hoping it would be enough.

"The magic will never end here," she said. "All of the pleasures are mine in this place. Forever. But you don't belong here. This place is for me alone. Leave and I will spare you."

"Hey, bitch," George stepped forward, her voice sharp. "Where is Eduardo?"

Samantha stared at her, her eyes unblinking.

The skin on Nick's arms burst open. Two green whips shot out of his arms and bounced off Samantha's magic shield. The former knight of the Order opened her mouth. Her teeth didn't belong in a human jaw. She rolled her head back and laughed.

"Laugh all you want." Bahir drew back his hood.

"You!" Samantha hissed. The djinn had to have felt his presence, but seeing him must've pushed the ifrit over the edge.

"I live, creature. I am here. I've come to reclaim my son."

The magic around Samantha surged up, twisting into an invisible tornado. Her face turned dark, her eyes glowing like two embers.

"You have no power to defeat me!" Bahir screamed.

Samantha shrieked, her voice slashing my ears. "I wish for the power to destroy my enemies!"

Wind slammed into me, hurling me backward. I flew, fell, and slid across the floor and rolled to my feet. To my left Derek caught Bahir in midair and set him on the floor.

On the throne, caught in the funnel of a magical tornado, Samantha's body grew. Her legs thickened, her spine reached up, her arms grew massive like tree trunks. Her lips drew back, exposing a forest of teeth; her ears lengthened; her eyes pivoted in her skull, turning into pools of orange fire. The ceiling parted above her, revealing a cage suspended by a thick chain. In the cage Eduardo grabbed the bars and recoiled. He looked like a ghost.

Samantha raised her enormous arms to the sky, her black claws glowing at their tips, and bellowed.

The gaggle of men behind her shivered, morphed, and a pack of leonine creatures snarled in unison, spreading massive leathery wings. Manticores. Shit.

"Clan Heavy," Curran roared. "Take out the manticores."

The werebears went furry. The manticores charged, screaming and gliding above the floor.

"Take your places." Curran's voice cut through the snarls and growls. "Remember the plan."

Plan. Right.

I dashed toward the giantess. A manticore swiped at me from above. I dodged to the side. The claws scraped my scalp and then a thousand-pound polar bear leaped above me, ramming into the manticore. They rolled across the floor, snarling. I kept running.

Samantha's enormous feet loomed before me. A manticore crashed into me. Its claws pinned my right arm to the floor, piercing my bicep. The huge ugly maw gaped over me, trying to swallow my entire head. I stabbed my throwing knife into the side of its neck, freed the blade, and stabbed it again. Hot blood spurted over me.

Suddenly, the manticore vanished, jerked aside. I rolled up and saw Adib bite through the beast's neck with his jaws. Fire dashed down his mane. His claws glowed and bright sparks fell off his furry sides.

I ran for the giantess. On the other side, three knights were moving together, trying to get in position.

I pulled the small vial of my blood out of my pocket as I sprinted. The second giant had healed his injuries. This one would heal even faster, and I probably had only seconds before the ifrit regenerated her body, so this maneuver had to be done fast. I wouldn't get a second chance.

A black viscous liquid coated Samantha's skin, emerging from her pores like sweat. A slightly sweet odor saturated the air. The djinn had covered her in crude oil to keep us from climbing her. The sonovabitch was learning, but not fast enough.

I drew Sarrat. A huge foot rose above me, its sole glowing-hot, the first hint of metal forming in long scales over the skin. I dashed to the side and spun about as she stomped and crushed the vial of my blood onto Sarrat's blade. My magic sparked, reacting to the saber's magic, forming a second edge, crimson and unnaturally sharp.

Above me, Bahir screamed. "Face me!"

Amal swooped down at the giantess's face, like a hawk, and he sliced her cheek with his burning blade. I caught a glimpse of George climbing up the column toward Eduardo's cage.

The giantess swatted at Bahir, trying to grab him with her clawed fingers, forgetting I was even there.

Thank you, Bahir. I charged forward and slashed across the back of the giantess's leg. The crimson edge sliced through the thin fledgling metal and Sarrat cut into the springy mass of tissue just above the heel, severing it. Bye-bye, Achilles tendon.

The giantess bellowed and kicked at me with her now-useless leg. I jumped as far right as I could and instantly knew it wasn't far enough. Curran caught me in midair, the force of his leap taking us to safety. The foot missed us by inches. His feet touched the ground. He twisted and threw me back toward the giantess. We'd practiced this move in our morning sparring, and the conditioning took over. I landed on my feet, sprinted, and sliced the second tendon.

The giant screamed, her roar punching my eardrums. I backed away.

Forty yards away Curran's body boiled, turning leonine, as he tried to build up mass. Next to him Mahon roared, a huge Kodiak.

Samantha fought to stay upright; spun, reeling, as her ankles refused to support her weight; and saw me backing up. Shit. She was facing the wrong way. If they hit her now, they would fail. I had to get her to turn her back to them.

"Is that all you've got, weakling?" I ran around her. She turned toward me, swaying.

The lion and the bear surged forward, breaking into a run.

Samantha's mouth opened, thunder clapped, and a glowing torrent of magic tore toward me. There was no place to go. I threw my arms up. The magic smashed into me.

It didn't hurt.

It felt like an elastic wall had formed between me and the torrent of power. The magic hit it, the impact knocked me back a few feet, but it didn't hurt.

The giantess reeled, clutching at her head, off balance.

Ha! The resistance worked both ways. Payback is a bitch.

The knights closed in on both sides.

Curran and Mahon smashed into the back of the giantess's knees. The impact of their combined weight proved too much for her injured legs. She dropped to her knees. Her palms touched the floor.

Curran's body twisted, flowing into warrior form.

The knights rushed to her. Four of them thrust huge lances into the back of her hands, trying to pin her. Nick's flesh ruptured. Twin whips, green and textured, like the shoots of some magic trees, shot out of him and wrapped about her neck. The knights shot hooked chains into her flesh. Three of them pulled on one side, and Curran pulled on the other, bringing her head lower and lower. The manticores tore at us, and Clan Heavy ripped into them, trying to keep the beasts off our backs.

The giantess raised her shoulders and tucked her chin in, hiding her neck. Nick growled like an animal, straining. His whips snapped and he stumbled back.

"Time!" Luther cried out.

The floor burst and plants spiraled to grab at the giantess's neck and body. Bahir dropped onto her spine and began hacking at the narrow exposed band of her neck with his sword.

"Applying the vector now," Patrice announced. "Three, two, one . . ."

She clamped her hands to the giantess's arm. The giantess shuddered, shaking, as the djinn struggled to regenerate. The giantess's head lowered another foot.

Heat bathed us. Sweat broke on my face. It was hard to breathe. Luther's plants began to wither. Patrice cried out and stumbled back, her palms steaming.

The giantess roared. Metal began to climb up her chest to her neck. Shit.

Curran dropped his chain and lunged under the giantess's chin. His massive arms strained. He snarled and lifted her chin up, stretching her neck. It was my turn. I slipped into the opening. Sarrat kissed her neck and I moved clear. The saber's new blood edge crumbled, its magic exhausted, but the damage was done. Blood poured from both sides of her neck. I had cut both the carotid and the jugular, opening a gap in her neck.

The giantess strained, trying desperately to pull her head down and close her wounds. Curran groaned. His frame shook. His eyes were pure gold.

Two figures fell from above, landing on the giantess's face. George and Eduardo. Eduardo clamped his fists together and brought them down straight onto Samantha's left eye. On the other side a three-legged bear tore into the giantess's right. The last thing she ever saw was the son of the man she hated and the woman who loved him.

Above us, on the giantess's neck, Bahir screamed. Fire sheathed his sword and spread to engulf him. His eyes blazed, bright red, their glow visible even through the flames. Bahir swung the blade into the gap I'd made, and severed the giantess's head from her body. Curran grunted and pushed it aside. It fell into the blood. Her body trembled and sank to the floor.

A bright spark of gold shone in front of me—the earring, tiny in the giantess's ear. I lunged for it, but Nick beat me. He slashed at her earlobe with a short sword. The earring dropped into the pool of blood.

Samantha exhaled in a long gurgling sigh. Her body turned to ash and fell apart. The ash melted into the wind. The manticores vanished; the palace wavered and went out, like the flame of a dying candle. We stood in the empty paved lot, the ruin of the hospital behind us.

"Now!" I yelled at Bahir. "Put the spell down now!"

Bahir grabbed the chalk and drew a circle on the ground, as close as the puddle of blood would allow. His hands shook.

There were at least twenty-five feet between the earring and the circle. Oh hell.

Nick reached for the earring.

"Clear!" Curran roared. "Clear if you want to live!"

People scattered, putting distance between them and the earring. We had to get it to Bahir's box or it would claim another life, and we weren't in any shape to stop another giant.

Nick's fingers touched the gold. He took a step toward the circle. His eyes turned white.

His body snapped into a rigid stance. His hand crept up, shaking from the muscle strain. Muscles in his face jerked. An inch. Another inch. The lure of the djinn was too great. It promised Nick anything and everything, every desire fulfilled, every wish granted, unlimited power, untold wealth, supernatural justice . . . It told him he could have anything he wanted. Nick was about to slide the earring into his ear.

Curran smashed his forearm into the back of Nick's head. The knight crumbled to the ground. The world slowed to a crawl. The earring flew through the air, painfully slow, and Curran's fingers closed about it.

No.

Curran's fur stood on its end. His face turned flat. He took a slow small step toward the circle. His eyes stared into the distance, unseeing, as if he had gone blind.

No, no, no.

"He can't have you," I told him. "You're mine. Fight him. Fight him, Curran."

The muscles on Curran's face shook, reshaping his head. His jaws lengthened. Bigger fangs thrust out of his jaws. He was becoming something monstrous.

Another step. His fur began to smoke.

I was losing him. I could feel him slipping away behind the curtain of the djinn's magic.

I stepped in front of him. "Curran, do you love me?"

He focused on me. Bald patches formed on his hand, the skin bubbling up.

A shape began to form in the air just ahead of us, translucent and weak, but I would recognize its outlines anywhere. The djinn had searched Curran's mind for a powerful emotion and found hate he could use. He was conjuring Hugh d'Ambray, because Curran wanted to kill him. If Curran took the bait, I would lose him forever.

I cut my forearm. My blood ran down my skin, wetting it with liquid heat. "Give me the earring. If you love me, give me the earring."

Curran shook, every muscle on his frame rigid with tension.

"If you ever loved me, you will give it to me. Just open your fingers and let it fall." My blood snapped into a gauntlet, obeying my magic. It should shield me, at least for a few seconds.

Hugh's form was almost solid.

Curran snarled. His fingers opened. The earring fell and I caught it with my gauntleted hand.

Power tore through me, flinging open doors inside my mind. Every secret place, every hidden memory, every guilty thought, it knew them all instantly. It savaged my soul.

I took a step. Far ahead of me flame streamed down from Bahir, lapping at the circle's boundary, binding him and the box into one. He was holding the portal open.

Twenty yards left. Dear God.

Tears streamed down my face.

You can't defeat your father, the voice whispered inside me. *I can help you. I will give you power unlike any you have ever witnessed.*

Agony racked me. Another step. My hair was burning.

I will give you his head. You will never have to worry about him killing anyone again.

A vision swirled in my mind: my father's grave, Julie smiling, Curran kissing me, as we stood in the middle of paradise, happy, free, and safe.

I will free you from these shackles. I will lift you into the sweet air above and let you breathe. I will stop all pain. Take my hand.

Another step. Bahir and his circle were so impossibly far. So very far.

All you have to do is take my hand.

"Do you love me?" Curran asked.

Of course I love you.

"Give me the earring."

No. The pain gripped me, threatening to pull me to my knees. *No. Stay with me. Stay!*

I loved him. I would do anything for him. I had to give him the earring. *STAY!*

I let it fall.

Curran caught the chunk of gold. I collapsed on my knees into the giantess's blood.

Curran took a slow step forward. I dragged myself up, sobbing. He would need me after he took that second step.

It took him thirty seconds to make it. He looked almost dead by the time he had done it and when I asked, he gave the earring to me. I took it, welcoming an eternity of pain.

We walked, two steps at a time. I fell once and had to crawl through the blood, but we were moving. The circle grew closer.

Look into your future. Look into the very depths of your heart. You know what your father wants.

The circle was almost within reach.

A vision thrust into my mind.

He is hiding the future from you. But my power is too great. I can see him. Let me show you what I see . . .

The world disappeared. A hill rolled in front of me, emerald grass under the blue sky. Roland stood on its crest. He was holding a baby.

Magic crashed against me, a familiar yet different magic coming from the child, so strong, it took my breath away.

My son had Curran's gray eyes.

It was the truth. I felt the connection between us stretching through time. I felt the love I had poured into my child. My baby.

My son reached for me . . .

Roland smiled and turned, taking the baby away.

I screamed. He couldn't. It was our child. My life, my soul, everything I hoped for.

This is what he wants. This is what he always wanted. You know it to be true. He will take your son. He will use your child to control you. He will turn him into a monster. You cannot stop it.

"Put the earring into the box, baby," Curran said next to me. "You can do it."

But I can stop it. I will stop it. Don't you love your baby? Don't you want to keep him safe?

I would keep him safe. I would. I don't need you.

Yes, you do. You can't beat him alone.

I don't need you.

"I don't need you. I don't need you. You have no power over me." I heard my own voice and realized I was screaming.

You will die and rot without me. Your family will rot. Everyone you love will be slaughtered. Take my hand and I will give you eternal power.

I opened my fingers.

The earring plunged down, bounced from the rim of the box, and fell into the circle. I had fallen short.

George's hand closed about the gold. The werebear screamed, her face distorted, her eyes terrible. She clenched her teeth. The muscles on her arm were ready to rip. A second arm began to form over her stump.

With a guttural cry, George shoved herself forward and dropped the earring into the box. A burst of fire shot out of the small container. Eduardo loomed above it, the lid in his hand. The fire bathed him, burning his arms.

Eduardo pushed the lid down. The jet of fire held it up, fighting him. Eduardo strained. The lid slid down a hair, then another hair.

"You can do it, son," Bahir called out.

Eduardo strained. Monstrous muscle bulged on his arms. "You have nothing I want!" he roared, and slammed the lid down.

Magic shoved me back. The complicated lines of the circle spun, turning, like layers of an intricate lock coming undone.

A horrible scream tore through the night. I slapped my hands over my ears.

The ground opened inside the circle and the box sank, shooting down like a bullet out of a gun, deep into the darkness. Magic snapped and all was quiet.

EPILOGUE

I SIPPED MY iced tea, holding the glass in my left hand. The right still had no skin under the bandages, despite a week of Doolittle's careful ministrations, but he said in another ten days or so my hand would recover. He'd also said a few other choice words that I didn't know were in his vocabulary. He sat at the other table now watching Eduardo and George slow dancing their way around the lawn. George looked lovely in a pure white dress. Eduardo was still too thin and probably should have been on bed rest still, but trying to outstubborn a werebear and a werebuffalo was a losing proposition.

Eduardo had told me about fifteen times that he was grateful for the rescue. George kept hugging me. She also sent chocolate to our house. They were moving in on the other side of Barabas's house, which meant I would see them often. If either of them told me "thank you" one more time, I would have to run away from home.

I moved my head to toss my braid back before I remembered it wasn't there. The heat from the ifrit had melted all my hair. It was barely touching my shoulders now, and it drove me nuts.

Across the lawn Mahon sat at the table, his hand over his face. I was pretty sure he had teared up and didn't want anyone to know. Bahir sat at the same table, looking slightly out of place. He and Eduardo had spoken. Things weren't quite smoothed over, but George said she remained hopeful.

In the past week, spring had exploded in Atlanta. Everything had turned green, as if nature rejoiced in the ifrit's banishment. Flowers bloomed and the apple blossoms in the tall vases on the white-clothed tables sent a gentle aroma into the warm air. I was so glad George and Eduardo had decided on an open-air wedding instead of trying to pack fifteen hundred people into the Keep's main hall.

A hand slid down my back.

"Hey," Curran said.

"Hey." I leaned against him. He put his arm around me.

"Everyone is getting married," he said.

"Mm-hm."

"We should, too."

In my mind I saw my father on the grassy hill, walking away with our child in his arms. I wrapped my arm around his back, hoping his strength would chase it away. "I thought we agreed we would. You asked, I said yes, we are all good."

"Yes, but it was theoretical. Let's set a date. An actual date."

"Like what?"

"I don't know, how does the sixth of June sound?"

"Ivan Kupala night? The night when everything goes crazy in Slavic pagan folklore?"

"The last day of the Werewolf Summer." Curran grinned at me.

Every first week of June, the Pack celebrated the Werewolf Summer. They ate, they drank, they celebrated being alive, and generally had an all-around good time.

"I mean it. Marry me, Kate."

"No preacher will marry us."

"We don't need a preacher. We'll get Roman to officiate."

"You can't be serious, Your Furriness."

Curran got up off his chair and knelt. Oh my God.

"Marry me."

"What are you doing?" I ground out through clenched teeth. My face was so hot, the wedding cake fifteen feet away had to be melting.

"I'm formally proposing. The first time didn't take."

Kill me, somebody.

"Curran! Get up. People are looking at us."

"Let them look." He smiled at me. "Marry me, Kate."

"Okay. The last night of the Werewolf Summer it is."

He got up, leaned to me, and brushed a kiss on my lips. I kissed him back and heard clapping. The bride and groom had stopped dancing and Eduardo was clapping. Someone else clapped from the left. Andrea. *Screw you, too.*

I smiled and gave them a little wave. "I'm so mad at you right now."

"Don't be mad. Here, I'll bring you more tea."

He laughed, took my glass, and went to the table to refill it.

We would get married. We would have a child. I would love it more than anything I had ever loved in this world, and then my father would take my baby from me.

No. It wasn't happening. I had to find a way to beat him. What the hell was I going to do? How do you kill the unkillable?

Bahir approached the table. "May I sit down?"

"Of course."

He sat on the right. "I wanted to thank you once again."

"No need. How is it going with Eduardo?"

Bahir smiled. "Some fences take time to mend. He is angry with me for leaving him. He's angry with his mother for not telling him any of it. Eduardo was always a sensitive, gentle child."

I tried to reconcile a six-foot-four werebuffalo gouging the giantess's eye with the "sensitive child" and failed. "Mm-hm."

"I understand his stepfather wasn't the most understanding parent. But I'm not losing hope."

Curran had refilled the glasses and was walking back to us. I loved him so much. I loved his eyes, the way he looked at me, the way he walked, the way he made me crazy . . .

Sometimes, when the power of your enemy is too great, the only thing you can do is contain it.

"Bahir," I said quietly. "You told me before the fight that if I ever needed anything, you would help me."

"Yes."

"Does that offer still stand?"

"Of course."

"After the wedding, when things calm down, I would like us to meet. I want you to tell me everything you know about that box."